MW00895687

SIX OF THE BEST

SHORT NOVELS BY MASTERS OF MYSTERY

EDITED BY
ELLERY QUEEN

Carroll & Graf Publishers, Inc.
New York

Grateful acknowledgment is made to the following for their permission to reprint copyrighted material:

The Case Against Carroll by Ellery Queen. Copyright © 1958 by Ellery Queen. Reprinted by permission of Scott Meredith Literary Agency, Inc.
C12: Department of Bank Robberies by Michael Gilbert. Copyright © 1964 by Michael Gilbert. Reprinted by permission of Curtis Brown Ltd.
The Empty Hours by Ed McBain. Copyright © 1960 by Ed McBain. Reprinted by permission of John Farquharson Ltd.
Mme. Maigret's Admirer (retitled *The Stronger Vessel*) by Georges Simenon. Copyright © 1944 by Georges Simenon. Reprinted by permission of the author.
The Clue of the Hungry Horse by Erle Stanley Gardner. Copyright © 1947 by Erle Stanley Gardner. Reprinted by permission of Thayer Hobson and Company.
No Business for an Amateur by John D. MacDonald. Copyright © 1967 by John D. MacDonald. Reprinted by permission of Dorothy P. MacDonald Trust and George Diskant & Associates.

First Carroll & Graf edition 1989

Carroll & Graf Publishers, Inc.
260 Fifth Avenue
New York, NY 10001

Six of the best : short novels of masters of mystery / edited by
   Ellery Queen.
      p.   cm.
     Summary: The case against Carroll/Ellery Queen—C12:
Department of Bank Robberies/Michael Gilbert—The empty hours/
Ed McBain—Mme. Maigret's admirer/Georges Simenon—The clue
of the hungry horse/Erle Stanley Gardner—No business for an
amateur/John D. MacDonald.
    ISBN 0-88184-468-3: $18.95
    1. Detective and mystery stories.   I. Queen, Ellery.   II. Title:
6 of the best.
PN6120.95.D45S59   1989
813'.0872'08—dc19   89-895
                                               CIP

Manufactured in the United States of America

Contents

Ellery Queen
The Case Against Carroll

Carroll felt the heat through his shoes as he got out of the taxi. In the swollen twilight even the Park across Fifth Avenue had a look of suffering. It made him even worry again about how Helena was taking the humidity.

'What?' Carroll said, reaching for his wallet. It was a thirty-sixth birthday present from Helena, and he usually challenged taxi drivers to identify the leather, which was elephant hide. But tonight's hackie was glowering at the slender graystone building with its fineboned black balconies.

'I said,' the driver said, 'that's your house?'

'Yes.' Carroll immediately felt angry. The lie of convenience had its uses, but on days like this it stung. The graystone had been erected in the Seventies by Helena's great-grandfather, and it belonged to her.

'Air-conditioned, no doubt,' the man said, wiping out his ear. 'How would you like to live in one of them de luxe East Side hotboxes on a night like this?'

'No, thank you,' Carroll said, remembering.

'I got four kids down there, not to mention my old lady. What do you think of that?'

Carroll overtipped him.

He used his key on the bronze street door with a sense of sanctuary. The day had been bad all around, especially at Hunt, West & Carroll, Attorneys-at-Law. Miss Mallowan, his secretary, had chosen this day to throw her monthly fainting spell; the new clerk had wasted three hours conscientiously looking up the wrong citations; Meredith Hunt, playing the

7

senior partner with a heavy hand, had been at his foulest; and
Tully West, ordinarily the most urbane of men, had been positively short-tempered at finding himself with only one change of
shirt in the office.

And trickling through the day, acid-like, had been Carroll's
worry about Helena. He had telephoned twice, and she had been
extra-cheery both times. When Helena sounded extra-cheery,
she was covering up something.

Had she found out?

But that wasn't possible.

Unless Tully … But Carroll shook his head, wincing. Tully
West couldn't know. His code coupled snooping with using the
wrong fork and other major crimes.

It's the weather, Carroll decided fatuously; and he stepped into
his wife's house.

Indoors, he felt a little better. The house with its crystal
chandeliers, Italian marble, and shimmering floors was as cameo-
cool as Helena herself – as all the Vanowens must have been,
judging from the Sargents lording it over the walls. He had never
stopped feeling grateful that they were all defunct except Helena.
The Vanowens went back to the patroons, while he was the son
of a track walker for the New York transit system who had been
killed by a subway train while tilting a bottle on the job. Breeding
had been the Vanowens' catchword; they would not have cared
for Helena's choice of husband.

John Carroll deposited his hat and briefcase in the foyer closet
and trudged upstairs, letting his wet palm squeak along the rail.

Helen was in the upstairs sitting-room, reading *Winnie the
Pooh* for the umpteenth time to Breckie and Louanne.

And she was in the wheelchair again.

Carroll watched his wife's face from the archway as she made
the stab of angry helplessness children never tired of. Through
the stab of angry helplessness he felt the old wonder. Her slender
body was bunched, tight in defence, against the agony of her
arthritis-racked legs, but that delicate face under its coif of
auburn was as serene as a nun's. Only he knew what a price she
paid for that serenity.

'Daddy. It's Daddy!'

Two rockets flew at him. Laden down with sleepered arms and legs, Carroll went to his wife and kissed her.

'Now, darling,' Helena said.

'How bad is it?' he growled.

'Not bad. John, you're soaked. Did you have to work so late in this swelter?'

'I suppose that's why you're in the wheelchair.'

'I've had Mrs. Poole keep dinner hot for you.'

'Mommy let us stay up because we were so *good*,' Louanne said. 'Now can we have the choc-o-late, Daddy?'

'We weren't so *very* good,' Breckie said. 'See, see, Louanne, I told you Daddy wouldn't forget!'

'We'll help you take your shower.' Helena strained forward in the wheelchair. 'Breckie angel your bottom's sticking out. John, really. Couldn't you have made it Life Savers today?'

'It's bad, isn't?'

'A little,' Helena admitted, smiling.

A little! Carroll thought as they all went upstairs in the elevator he had had installed two years before, when Helena's condition had become chronic. A little – when even at the best of times she had to drag about like an old woman.

He showered in full view of his admiring family, impotently aware of the health in his long, dark body.

When he pattered back to the bedroom he found a shaker of martinis and, on his bed, fresh linen and his favorite slacks and jacket.

'What's the matter, John?'

'I didn't think it showed,' Carroll said tenderly.

He kissed her on the chocolate smudge left by Breckie's fingers.

Like a character in a bad TV drama, Hunt came with the thunder and the rain.

Carroll was surprised. He was also embarrassed by the abrupt way the children stopped chattering as the lawyer's thickset figure appeared in the dining-room doorway.

'Meredith,' Carroll half rose. 'I thought you were on your way to Chicago.'

'I'm headed for La Guardia now,' Hunt said. 'Legs again, Helena?'

'Yes. Isn't it a bore?' Helena glanced at her housekeeper, who was in the foyer holding Hunt's wet things at arm's length. 'Mr. Hunt will take coffee with us, Mrs. Poole.'

'Yes, ma'am.'

'No, ma'am,' Meredith Hunt said. 'But I thank you. *And* the Carroll small fry. Up kind of late, aren't you?'

Breckie and Louanne edged stealthily toward their mother's chair.

'We like to wait up for our daddy,' Helena smiled, drawing them to her. 'How's Felicia, Meredith? I must call her as soon as this lets up a bit.'

'Don't. My wife is being very Latin American these days.'

Something was terribly wrong. Looking back on the day, John Carroll felt another thrill of alarm.

Helena said extra-cheerily, 'Way past your bedtime, bunny rabbits! Kiss your father and say good night to Mr. Hunt.'

She herded them out with her wheelchair. As she turned the chair into the foyer, she glanced swiftly at her husband. Then she said something crisp to Mrs. Poole, and they all disappeared behind the clang of the elevator door.

Carroll said, 'Life's little surprises. You wanted to talk to me, Meredith?'

'Definitely.' Hunt's large teeth glistened.

'Let's go up to my study.'

'I can talk here.'

Carroll looked at him. 'What's on your mind?'

'You're a crook,' Hunt said.

Carroll sat down. He reached with concentration for the crystal cigarette box on the table.

'When did you find out, Meredith?'

'I knew I was making a mistake the day I let Tully West pull that *noblesse oblige* act for Helena and sweet-talk me into taking you into the firm.' The burly lawyer sauntered about the dining-room, eying the marble fireplace, the paintings, the crystal cabinets, the heirloom silver. 'You can't make a blue ribbon entry out of an alley accident, I always say. The trouble with Tully and Helena, John, is that they're sentimental idiots. They really believe in democracy.'

The flame of the lighter danced very red. Carroll put the cigarette down, unlit.

'I wish you'd let me explain, Meredith.'

'So I've kept an eye on you,' Hunt said, not pausing in his stroll. 'And especially on the Eakins Trust. It's going to give me a lot of satisfaction to show my blueblood partner just how and when his mongrel protégé misappropriated twenty thousand dollars' worth of trust securities.'

'Will you let me explain?'

'Explain away. Horses? The market?' Hunt swung about. A nerve in the heavy flesh beneath his right eye was jumping. 'A woman?'

'Keep your voice down Meredith.'

'A woman. Sure. When a man like you is married to a –'

'Don't!' Carroll said. Then he said, 'Does Tully know?'

'Not yet.'

'It was my brother Harry. He got into a dangerous mess involving some hard character and he had to get out in a hurry. He needed twenty thousand dollars to square himself, and he came to me for it.'

'And you stole it for him.'

'I told him I didn't have it. I don't have it. My take from the firm just about keeps our heads above water. It's my income that runs this house, Meredith. Or did you think I let Helena's money feed me, too? Anyway, Harry threatened to go to Helena for it.'

'And, of course,' Hunt said, showing his teeth again, 'you couldn't let him do that.'

'No,' Carroll said. 'No, Meredith, I couldn't. I don't expect you to understand why. Helena wouldn't hesitate to give me any amount I asked for, but … Well, I had no way of borrowing a wad like that overnight except to go to you or to Tully. Tully was somewhere in northern Canada hunting, and to go to you ...' Carroll paused. When he looked up he said, 'So I took it from the Eakins Trust, proving your point.'

Meredith Hunt nodded with enjoyment.

Carroll pushed himself erect on his fists. 'I've got to ask you to give me time. I'll replace the funds by the first of the year. It won't happen again, Meredith. Harry's in Mexico, and he won't be back. It won't happen again. The first of the year.' He swallowed. 'Please.'

'Monday,' Hurt said.

'What?'

'This is Friday. I'll give you till Monday morning to make up the defalcation. You have sixty hours to keep from arrest, prison, and disbarment. If you replace the money I'll drop the matter to protect the firm. In any event, of course, you're through at the office.'

'Monday.' Carroll laughed. 'Why not tonight? It would be just as merciful.'

'You can get the money from your wife. Or from Tully, if he's stupid enough to give it to you.'

'I won't drag Helena into this!' Carroll heard his voice rising, and he pulled it down with an effort. 'Or Tully – I value his friendship too much. I got myself into this jam, and all I'm asking is the chance to get myself out.'

'That's your problem. I'm being very generous, under the circumstances.' All the lines of Hunt's well-preserved face sagged as his cold eyes flamed with sudden heat. 'Especially since the Eakins Trust isn't the only property you haven't been able to keep your hands off.'

'What's that supposed to mean?'

'Your sex life is your own business as long as you don't poach on mine. Stay away from my wife.'

Carroll's fist caught Hunt's big chin. Hunt staggered. Then he lowered his head and came around the table like a bull. They wrestled against the table, knocking a Sèvres cup to the floor.

'That's a lie,' Carroll whispered. 'I've never laid a finger on Felicia ... on any woman but Helena.'

'I've seen Felicia look at you,' Hunt panted. His head came up, butting. Carroll fell down.

'*John, Meredith.*'

The wheelchair loomed in the doorway. Helena was as pale as her husband.

Carroll got to his feet. 'Go back, Helena. Go upstairs.'

'Meredith. Please leave.'

The big lawyer straightened, fumbling with his expensive silk tie. He was glaring in a sort of victory. Then he went into the foyer, took his hat and topcoat from the chair in which Mrs. Poole had deposited them, and quietly left.

'John, what did he say to you?' Helena was as close to fear as she ever got. 'What happened?'

Carroll began to pick up the fragments of the shattered cup. But his hands were shaking so uncontrollably that he stopped.

'Oh, darling, you promised never to lose your temper again this way –'

Carroll said nothing.

'It's not good for you.' She reached over and pulled his head down to her breast. 'Whatever he said, dearest, it's not worth ...'

He patted her, trying to pull away.

'John, come to bed?'

'No. I've got to cool off.'

'Darling –'

'I'll walk it off.'

'But it's pouring!'

Carroll snatched his hat and topcoat from the foyer closet and plunged out of the house. He sloshed down Fifth Avenue in the rain and fog, almost running.

The next morning John Carroll got out of the taxi before the Hunt house on East 61st Street like a man dreaming. The streets had been washed clean by the downpour of the night before, and the sun was already hot, but he felt dirty and cold. He pressed the Hunt bell with a sense of doom, a vague warning of things he tried not to imagine. He shivered and jabbed at the bell again, irritably this time.

A maid with a broad Italian face finally opened the door. She led him in silence up to Felicia Hunt's rooms on the second floor. Tully West was already there, thoughtfully contemplating the postage-stamp rear garden from Felicia's picture window. West was as tall and fleshless as a Franciscan monk – an easy man with an iron-gray crewcut and unnoticeable clothes.

Carroll nodded to his partner and dropped into one of the capacious Spanish chairs Felicia surrounded herself with. 'Cross-town traffic held me up. Felicia, what's this all about?'

Felicia de los Santos was in her dramatic mood this morning. She had clothed her dark plump beauty in a violently gay gown; she was already at work fingering her talisman, a ruby-and-emerald-crusted locket that had belonged to a Bourbon queen. She was the daughter of a Latin-American diplomat of Castilian blood, she had been educated in Europe after a high-walled childhood, and she was hopelessly torn between the Spanish tradition of the submissive wife and the feminism she had found in the United States. What Felicia de los Santos had seen in Meredith hunt, an American primitive twice her age, Carroll had never fathomed.

'Meredith is missing.' She had a charming accent.

'Missing? Isn't he in Chicago?'

'The Michaelson people say no.' Tully West's witty, rather glacial voice was not amused today. 'They phoned Felicia this morning after trying to reach our office. Meredith never got there.'

'I don't understand that.' Carroll felt his forehead; he had a pounding headache. 'He stopped by last night about half-past nine and said he was on his way to the airport.'

'He wasn't on the plane, John.' Hunt's wife seemed more nervous than alarmed. 'Tully just telephoned La Guardia.'

'All planes were grounded from about eight p.m. yesterday until three in the morning by the fog. Meredith checked in at the field all right, found his flight delayed, and left word at the desk that he'd wait around the airport. But when the fog cleared they couldn't find him.' West sat Felicia Hunt down on her silk divan, gingerly. She appealed to him with her moist black eyes as if for understanding, but he turned to Carroll. 'You say, John, he stopped by last night?'

'For just a few minutes. He didn't mention anything that would explain this.' Carroll shut his eyes.

Felicia Hunt twisted her locket. 'He's left me – deserted me.'

Tully West looked shocked. 'Meredith would as soon leave his wallet. My dear girl!'

The maid said from the doorway, 'Señora. The police.'

Carroll turned sharply.

Three men were in the doorway behind the Indian maid. One was broad and powerful; another was small, gray, and wiry; and the third was tall and young.

The broad man said, 'Mrs. Hunt? Sergeant Velie. This is Inspector Queen.' He did not bother to introduce the tall young man. 'We've got bad news for you.'

'My husband –'

'An officer found him around six thirty this morning over on East 58th, near the Queensboro Bridge, in a parked Thunderbird. He was spread across the wheel with a slug in his brain.'

She got to her feet, clutching the pendant. Then her eyes turned over and she pitched forward.

West and Carroll both caught her before their mouths could close. They hauled her onto the divan and Carroll began to chafe her hands. The maid ran to the bathroom.

'Ever the delicate touch, Velie,' the tall young man remarked from the doorway. 'Couldn't you have hit her over the head?'

Sergeant Velie ignored him. 'I forgot to mention he's dead. Who are you?'

'I'm Tully West, that's John Carroll.' West was very pale. 'We're Hunt's law partners. Mrs. Hunt phoned us this morning when her husband failed to show up in Chicago for a business appointment. He was to have taken the eleven p.m. plane –'

'That's already been checked.' The small gray man was watching the maid wave a bottle of smelling salts under Felicia Hunt's little nose. 'Hunt didn't come back home last night? Phone or anything?'

'Mrs. Hunt says not.'

'Was he supposed to be traveling alone?'

'Yes.'

'Make such trips often?'

'Yes. Hunt was outside man for the firm.'

'Was he in the habit of driving his car to airports?'

'Yes. He'd park it and pick it up on his return.'

'Carrying any valuables last night?'

'Just cash for the trip, as far as I know. And a dispatch case containing some papers and a change of linen.'

Felicia Hunt shuddered and opened her eyes. The maid eased her expertly back on the divan and slipped a pillow under her head. The widow lay there like Goya's Duchess, fingering her locket. Carroll straightened.

'Suicide,' Tully West said, and he cleared his throat. 'It was suicide?'

'Not on your tintype,' Inspector Queen said. 'Hunt was murdered, and when we identify the Colt Woodsman we found in the car, we'll know who murdered him. Until we do, any suggestions?'

Carroll glared around helplessly. Then he clapped his hand over his mouth and ran into the bathroom. They heard him gagging.

'Was Mr. Carroll unusually fond of Mr. Hunt?' asked the tall young man politely.

'No,' Tully West said. 'I mean – oh, damn it all!'

'Detectives will be talking to you people later in the day.' The Inspector nodded at his sergeant, said, 'Come along, Ellery,' to the tall young man, and then he marched out with his old man's stiff-kneed bounce ...

'Come in, please.' Inspector Queen did not look up from the report he was reading.

John Carroll came into the office between Tully West and a detective. The partners' faces were gray.

'Have a seat.'

The detective left. In a rivuleted leather chair at one corner of his father's office, Ellery sprawled over a cigarette. A small fan was going behind the old man, ruffling his white hair. It made the only noise in the room.

'See here,' Tully West said frigidly. 'Mr. Carroll's been interrogated from hell to breakfast by precinct detectives, Homicide Squad men, the Deputy Chief Inspector in charge of Manhattan East, and detectives of the Homicide Bureau. He's submitted without a murmur to fingerprinting. He's spent a whole morning in the Criminal Courts Building being taken apart piece by piece by an Assistant District Attorney who apparently thinks he can parlay this case into a seat in Congress. May I suggest that you people either fish or cut bait?'

The Inspector laid aside the report. He settled back in his swivel chair, regarding the Ivy League lawyer in a friendly way. 'Any special reason, Mr. West, why you insisted on coming along this morning?'

'Why?' West's lips were jammed together. 'Is there an objection to my being here?'

'No.' The old man looked at Carroll. 'Mr. Carroll, I'm throwing away the book on this one. You'll notice there's not even a stenographer present. Maybe if we're frank with each other we can cut corners and save everybody a lot of grief. We've been on this homicide for five days now, and I'm going to tell you what we've come up with.'

'But why me?' John Carroll's voice came out all cracked.

West touched his partner's arm. 'You'll have to forgive Mr. Carroll, Inspector. He's never learned not to look a gift horse in the mouth. Shut up, John, and listen.'

The old man swiveled creakily to look out his dusty window. 'As far as we can reconstruct the crime, Hunt's killer must have followed him to La Guardia last Friday night. A bit past midnight Hunt reclaimed his car at the parking lot and drove off, in spite of the fact that he'd told the airline clerk at ten thirty that he'd wait around for the fog to lift. It's our theory that the killer met him at La Guardia and talked him into taking a ride, maybe on a plea of privacy. That would mean that after reclaiming his car Hunt picked the killer up and they drove off together.

'We have no way of knowing how long they cruised around before crossing the Queensboro Bridge into Manhattan, but at about one forty-five a.m. a patrol car passed the Thunderbird on East 58th, parked where it was later found with Hunt's body in it. The Assistant Medical Examiner says Hunt was killed between two and four a.m. Saturday, so when the patrol car passed at a quarter to two, Hunt and his killer must have been sitting in it, still talking.

'Now.' Inspector Queen swiveled back to eye Carroll. 'Item one: Hunt was shot to death with a bullet from the Colt Woodsman .22 automatic found beside the body. That pistol, Mr. Carroll, is registered in your name.'

Carroll's face went grayer. He made an instinctive movement, but West touched his arm again.

'Item two: motive. There's nothing to indicate it could have had anything to do with Hunt's trip, or any client. Your firm's clients are conservative corporations, and the Chicago people had every reason to want Hunt to stay healthy – he was going to save them a couple of million dollars in a tax-refund suit against the government. Mr. West himself has gone over the contents of Hunt's dispatch case, and he says nothing is missing. Robbery? Hunt's secretary got him three hundred dollars from the bank Friday for his trip, and well over that amount was found in his wallet. Hunt's Movado wrist watch and jade ring were found on him.

'That's the way it stood till Monday morning. Then Hunt himself tipped us off to the motive. He wrote us a letter.'

'Hunt *what?*' Carroll cried.

'By way of Miss Connor, his secretary. She found it in the office mail on Monday morning. Hunt wrote it on airline stationery from La Guardia on Friday night and dropped it into a mailbox there before his killer showed up.

'It was a note to his secretary,' the Inspector went on, 'instructing her that if anything should happen to him over the week-end she was to deliver the enclosure, a sealed envelope, to the police. Miss Connor brought it right in.'

West said, 'Good old Meredith.' He looked disgusted.

'Hunt's letter to us, Mr. Carroll, says that he visited your home on Fifth Avenue before going to the airport Friday evening – tells us why, tells us about your fight … incidentally clearing up the reason for the bruise on his mouth. So, you see, we know all about the twenty grand you lifted from that trust fund, and Hunt's ultimatum to you a few hours before he was knocked off. He even mentioned his suspicions about you and Mrs. Hunt.' The Inspector added mildly, 'That's two pretty good motives, Mr. Carroll. Care to change your statement?'

Carroll's mouth was open. Then he jumped up. 'It's all a horrible misunderstanding,' he stammered. 'There's never been a thing between Felicia Hunt and me –'

'John.' West pulled him down. 'Inspector, Meredith Hunt was stupidly jealous of his wife. He even accused me on occasion of making passes at her. I can't speak about Mrs. Hunt's feelings, but John Carroll is the most devoted married man I know. He's crazy about his wife and children.'

'And the defalcation?'

'John's told me all about that. His no-good brother was in serious trouble and John foolishly borrowed the money from one of the trusts our firm administers to get the brute out of it. I've already replaced it from my personal funds. Any talk of theft or prosecution is ridiculous. If I'd known about Meredith's ultimatum I'd have been tempted to pop him one myself. We all have our weak moments under stress. I've known John Carroll intimately for almost ten years. I can and do vouch for his fundamental honesty.'

Ellery's voice said from his corner, 'And what exactly did Mr. Carroll tell you about this weak moment, Mr. West?'

The lawyer was startled. Then he turned around and said with a smile. 'I don't believe I'll answer that.'

'The gun,' Inspector Queen prompted.

'It's John's, Inspector, of course. He's a Reserve officer, and he likes to keep up his marksmanship. We both do a bit of target shooting now and then at a gun club we belong to down-town, and John keeps the target pistol in his desk at the office. Anyone could have lifted that Woodsman and walked off with it. The fact that John keeps it in the office is known to dozens of people.'

'I see.' The old man's tone specified nothing. 'Now let's get to last Friday night. We'll play it as if you've never been questioned, Mr. Carroll. I suppose you can establish just where you were between two and four a.m. last Saturday?'

Carroll put his head between his hands and laughed.

'Well, can you?'

'I'll try to explain again, Inspector,' Carroll said, straightening up. 'When I lose my temper, as I did with Meredith on Friday night, I get a violent physical reaction. It takes me hours sometimes to calm down. My wife knows this, and after Meredith left for La Guardia she tried to get me to go to bed. I'm sorry now I didn't take her advice! I decided instead to walk it off, and that's just what I did. I must have walked around half the night.'

'Meet anyone you know?'

'I've told you. No.'

'What time was it when you got back home?'

'I don't remember. All I know is, it was still dark.'

'Was it also still foggy?' the voice from the corner said.

Carroll jumped. 'No, it wasn't.'

Ellery said, 'The fog lifted about two a.m., Mr. Carroll.'

'You're sure you can't recall the time even approximately?' Inspector Queen's tone was patience itself. 'I mean the time you got home?'

Carroll began to look stubborn. 'I just didn't notice.'

'Maybe Mrs. Carroll did?'

'My wife was asleep. I didn't wake her.'

'Item three,' the Inspector remarked. 'No alibi. And item four: fingerprints.'

'Fingerprints?' Carroll said feebly.

'John's? Where, Inspector?' Tully West asked in a sharp tone. 'You realize they wouldn't mean anything if you found them on the pistol.'

'We hardly ever find fingerprints on automatics, Mr. West. No, in Hunt's car.'

Through the roaring in his ears John Carroll thought: So that's why they fingerprinted me Monday ... He blinked as he heard the old amusement in his partner's voice.

'Surely you found other prints in the car besides John's and, I assume, Hunt's?'

The old man looked interested. 'Whose, for instance?'

'Well, there must be at least a set traceable to the attendant in the public garage where Hunt parked his car.'

'Well?'

'And, of course,' West said with a smile, 'a few of mine.'

'Yours, Mr. West?'

'Certainly. Hunt drove John and me home from the office in the Thunderbird on Thursday night – the night before the murder. So I'm going to have to insist that you fingerprint me, too.'

Inspector Queen snapped, 'Of course, Mr. West. We'll be glad to oblige,' and glanced over at the leather chair.

'I have a naive question for you, Carroll.' Ellery was studying the smoke-curl of his cigarette. 'Did you kill Meredith Hunt?'

'Hell, no,' John Carroll said. 'I haven't killed anybody since Leyte.'

'I think I'm going to advise you not to say any more, John!' Tully West rose. 'Is that all, Inspector?'

'For now. And Mr. Carroll.'

'Yes?'

'The usual – you're not to leave town. Understand?'

John Carroll nodded slowly. 'I guess I do.'

Through the lobby of Police Headquarters, down the worn steps to the sidewalk, neither partner said anything. But when they were in a taxi speeding uptown, Carroll kicked the jump-seat and muttered, 'Tully, there's something I've got to know.'

'What's that?'

'Do *you* think I murdered Meredith?'

'Not a chance.'

'Do you really mean that?'

West's monkish face crinkled. 'We Wests haven't stuck our

necks out since Great-grandfather West had his head blown off at Chancellorsville.'

Carroll sank back. The older man glanced out the cab window at Fourth Avenue.

'On the other hand, you don't lean your weight on a lily pad when a nice big rock is handy. My knowledge of corporation and tax law – or yours, John – isn't going to do much good if that old coot decides to jump. You may need a topflight criminal lawyer soon. I've been thinking of Sam Rayfield.'

'I see. All right, Tully, whatever you say.' Carroll studied an inflamed carbuncle on their driver's neck. 'Tully, what's the effect of this thing going to be on Helena? And on Breckie, Louanne? My God.'

He turned to the other window, lips trembling ...

A detective from the 17th Precinct made the arrest that afternoon. He and his partner appeared at the Madison Avenue offices of Hunt, West & Carroll just before five o'clock. Carroll recognized them as the men who had questioned him the previous Saturday afternoon; they were apparantly the local detectives 'carrying' the case.

Miss Mallowan fainted out of season. Tully West's secretary dragged her away.

'I'd like to call my wife,' Carroll said.

'Sure, but make it snappy.'

'Listen, sweetheart,' Carroll said into the phone. He was amazed at the steadiness of his voice. 'I'm being arrested. You're not to come running down to the Tombs, do you hear? I want you to stay home and take care of the kids. Understand, Helena?'

'You listen to me.' Helena's voice was as steady as his. 'You're to let Tully handle everything. I'll tell the children you've had to go off on business. And I'll see you as soon as they'll let me. Do *you* understand, darling?'

Carroll licked his lips. 'Yes.'

Tully West came running out as they waited for the elevator. 'I'm getting Rayfield on this right away. And I'll keep an eye on Helena and the kids. You all right, John?'

'Oh, wonderful,' Carroll said wryly.

West gripped his hand and dashed off.

The hard gray-and-green face of the Criminal Courts Building, the night in the cell, the march across the bridge from the prison wing the next morning, his arraignment in one of the chill two-story courtrooms, Helena's strained face as she labored up to kiss him, Tully West's droopy look, the soft impressive voice of Samuel Rayfield, the trap of the judge's gray mouth as he fixed bail at fifty thousand dollars ... to John Carroll, all of it jumbled into an indigestible mass. He was relieved to find himself back in the cell, and he dozed off at once.

Friday morning the pain caught up with him. Everything hurt sharply. When he was taken into the office of the court clerk, he could not bear to look at the two lawyers, or at his wife. He felt as if his clothing had been taken away.

He heard only dimly the colloquy with the clerk. It had something to do with the bail ... Suddenly Carroll realized that it was his wife who was putting up the bail bond, paying the ransom for his freedom out of the Vanowen money.

'Helena, no!'

But he voiced the cry only in his head. The next thing he knew they were marching out.

'Am I free?' Carroll asked foolishly.

'You're free, darling,' Helena whispered.

'But fifty thousand dollars,' he muttered. 'Your money ...'

'Oh, for heaven's sake, John,' West said. 'The bail is returnable on the first day of the trial, when you resubmit to the custody of the court. You know that.'

'John, dear, it's only money.'

'Helena, I didn't do it ...'

'I know, darling.'

Rayfield interposed his genial bulk between them and the lurking photographers and reporters. Somehow he got them through the barrage of flashbulbs.

As the elevator doors closed, Carroll suddenly noticed a tall man lounging in the corridor, a youngish man with bright eyes.

A shock of recognition, rather unpleasant, ran through him. It was that Inspector's son, Ellery Queen. What was he doing here?

The question needled him all the way home.

Then he was safe behind the grayfront on Fifth Avenue. In the Tombs, Carroll had coddled the thought of that safety, wrapping himself in it against the cold steel and antiseptic smell. But they were still with him. When Mrs. Poole took the children tactfully off to the park, Carroll shivered and gave himself up to the martini that West handed him.

'What was it Meredith used to say about your martinis, Tully? Something about having to be a fifth-generation American to know how to mix one properly?'

'Meredith was a middle-class snob.' West raised his glass. 'Here's to him. May he never know what hit him.'

They sipped in silence.

Then Helena set her glass down. 'Tully. Just what does Mr. Rayfield think?'

'The trial won't come up until October.'

'That's not what I asked.'

'Translation,' Carroll murmured. 'What are defendant's chances?'

'Rayfield hasn't said.' West downed the rest of his drink in a gulp, something he never did.

Helena's silky brows drew the slightest bit toward each other. She said suddenly. 'John, you have some enemy you don't know about. Someone who hates you enough to commit murder with your gun. Who is it? Think, darling!'

Carroll shook his head.

'I don't believe it's that at all, Helena,' West said, pouring a refill. 'Taking John's pistol might have been an act of sheer opportunism. Whoever it was might have lifted mine if I'd left it around. Seems to me the question properly is, Who had it in for Meredith?'

Carroll said, 'Ask the police. Ask that lip-smacking little Assistant District Attorney.'

They were all quiet again.

'But it's true,' John Carroll mumbled at last. 'It's true I've got to do something ...'

Tully West's eyes met Helena Carroll's briefly.

'Here, John. Have another martini.'

Carroll spent the weekend in seclusion. The telephone kept ringing, but Helena refused to let him be disturbed.

By Sunday night he had made up his mind. Helena heard him typing away on the portable, but when she tried to go in to him, she found the bedroom door locked.

'John! Are you all right?'

'I'll be out in a minute.'

When he unlocked the door he was tucking an envelope into his inside breast pocket. He looked calmer, as if he had won a battle.

He helped her to the chaise. 'There's something I've never told anyone, Helena, not even you. I gave my word not to.'

'What are you talking about, darling?'

'I've had a big decision to make. Helena, I'm going to come out of this all right. All I ask you to do is stop worrying and trust me. No matter what happens, will you trust me?'

'Oh, John!'

He stooped to kiss her. 'I'll be back in a few minutes.'

He walked over to Madison Avenue and went into a deserted delicatessen store. In the telephone booth he dialed Meredith Hunt's number.

'Serafina? Mr. Carroll. Let me talk to Mrs. Hunt.'

Felicia Hunt's accent vibrated in his ear without its usual charm. 'John, are you mad? Suppose they have my telephone tapped? You know what Meredith wrote to them!'

'I also know he got it all crosseyed,' Carroll said. 'Felicia, I want to see you. Tomorrow I'm going into the office to start helping Tully salvage something from the wreckage, but on my way home I'm stopping in at your place with somebody about six thirty. Will you be there?'

She sounded exasperated. 'I can't go anywhere so soon after the funeral, you know that. Whom are you bringing?'

'No one you know.'
'John, I wish you wouldn't –'
He hung up.

When the maid with the Indian face opened the door Carroll said, 'After you, Gunder,' and the man with him stepped nervously into the Hunt house. He was a chubby citizen with a wet pink scalp and rimless eyeglasses. He carried a small leather case.

'The Señora waits upstairs,' Serafina said sullenly.

'Get Mr. Gunder a magazine or something,' Carroll said. 'This won't take long, Gunder.'

The man seated himself on the edge of a foyer chair. Carroll hurried up the stairs, taking his briefcase with him.

Patricia Hunt was all in black. Even her stockings were black. She gave Carroll a turn; it was rather like walking in on a character drawn by Charles Addams. She wore no make-up and, for the first time since Carroll had known her, no jewelry, not even her pendant. The brilliant fingernails she usually affected were now colorless. Her fingers kept exploring her bosom petulantly.

'Meaning no disrespect to an old Spanish custom,' Carroll said, 'is this mourning-in-depth absolutely necessary, Felicia? You look like a ghost.'

'Thank you,' Felicia said spitefully. 'Always the *caballero*. Where I come from, John, you do certain things in certain ways. Not that I would dare show my face in the street! Reporters ... may they all *rot*. What do you want?'

Carroll set his briefcase down by the escritoire, went to the door, and carefully closed it. She watched him with sudden interest. He glanced about, nodded at the drawn drapes.

'How mysterious,' the widow said in a new tone. 'Are you going to kill me or kiss me?'

Carroll laughed. 'You're a nourishing dish, Felicia, but if I didn't have an appetite for you a year ago I'd hardly be likely to drool now.'

She flung herself on the divan. 'Go away,' she said sulkily. 'I loathe you.'

'Why? Because it took you too long to realize what it would
mean to Señor the Ambassador, your father, if your passes at
me ever got into the newspapers? You didn't loathe me when
you were throwing yourself at me all over town, waylaying me
in restaurants, making Meredith suspect I was fouling his nest.
Have you forgotten those steaming *billets-doux* you kept
sending me, Felicia?'

'And you protected me by saying nothing about them. Very
noble, John. Now get out.'

'Yes, I protected you,' Carroll said slowly, 'but it begins to
look as if I can't protect you any longer. I've told everyone – the
police, the D.A., Helena, Tully, Rayfield – that I walked the
streets in the rain most of the night that Meredith was shot. As
far as they're concerned, right now I have no alibi for the
two-hour stretch between two and four a.m. when they say he
was murdered.'

She was beginning to look apprehensive.

'But now I'm afraid I'm going to have to tell them that
between one o'clock and four-thirty that morning you and I
were alone in this room, Felicia. That the fact is, I've had an alibi
all along – you – and I kept my mouth shut about it because of
how it would look if the story came out.'

She said hoarsely, 'You wouldn't.'

'Not if I can help it.' Carroll shrugged. 'For one thing, I'm
quite aware that nobody, not even Helena, would believe I spent
three and a half hours alone with you that night just trying to
get you to talk Meredith out of ruining my life. Especially if it
also came out, as might very well happen, how you'd run after
me, written me those uninhibited love letters.'

Her white skin turned ghastly.

'They'd jump to the worst possible conclusion about that
night. I don't want that any more than you do, Felicia, although
for a different reason. A woman in Helena's physical condition
never feels very secure about her husband, no matter how
faithful he is to her. A yarn like this ...' Carroll set his jaw. 'I
love Helena, but I have no choice. I'm no storybook hero,
Felicia. I'm facing the possibility of the electric chair. That alibi

is my life insurance policy. I wouldn't be any good to Helena and the children dead.'

'Crucified,' Felicia Hunt said bitterly. 'I'd be crucified! I won't do it.'

'You've got to.'

'I won't! You can't make me!'

Murder glittered from her black eyes. But Carroll did not flinch, and after a moment the glitter flickered and she turned away.

'What do you want me to do?'

'I've typed out a statement. At the moment, all you have to do is sign it. I've brought a man with me to notarize your signature; he's downstairs. He has no idea what kind of document it is. I'll lock it in my safe at the office. Don't look at me that way, Felicia. I've got to protect myself now. You ought to be able to understand that.'

She said venomously, 'Go call your damned notary,' and jumped off the divan.

'You'd better read the statement first.'

Carroll took a long manila envelope from his briefcase. It was unsealed, bound with a red rubber band, opened the envelope, and took from it a folded sheet of typewriter paper. He unfolded it and handed it to her.

She read it carefully, twice. Then she laughed and handed it back.

'Pig.'

Carroll went to the door, paper in hand, and opened it. 'Mr. Gunder? Would you come up now, please?'

The notary appeared, mopping his pink scalp. In the other hand he clutched the leather case. He sneaked a glance at Felicia's figure and immediately looked away.

'This is Mrs. Felicia de los Santos Hunt, widow of the late Meredith Hunt,' Carroll said. 'Do you need proof of her identity?'

'I've seen Mrs. Hunt's picture in the papers.' Gunder had a pink sort of voice, too. He opened his case and spread out on the escritoire an ink pad, several rubber stamps, and a notary's seal.

From his breast pocket he produced a fountain pen as big as a cigar. 'Now,' he said. 'We're all set.'

Carroll laid the statement, folded except for the bottom section, on the escritoire. He kept his hand on the fold. Felicia snatched the pen from the notary and signed her name in a vicious scrawl.

When the notary was finished, Carroll slipped the paper into the manila envelope, put the red rubber band around it, and stowed the envelope in his briefcase. He rezipped the case.

'I'll see you out, Gunder.'

They passed Serafina on the stairs; she was wiping the banister with a damp cloth and did not look around.

In the foyer Carroll gave the little man a ten-dollar bill, relocked the street door behind him, and returned upstairs. Serafina would not give an inch; he had to walk around her.

Her mistress was lying on the divan, also turned away from him. Goya's Duchess, Carroll thought, rear view. He could hear the Indian maid slamming things around in the bathroom.

'Thanks, Felicia. You've saved my life.'

She did not reply.

'I promise I won't use the statement except as a last resort.'

When she continued to ignore him, Carroll picked up his briefcase and left.

Carroll surrendered himself to the Court on the morning of the second Monday in October. In the battlefield of the photographer's flashbulbs, through the crowded corridor, in the courtroom, the only thing he could think of was where the summer had gone. July, August, September seemed never to have existed. Certainly they did not occupy the same space-time as the nightmare he was walking into.

The nightmare shuttled fast, a disconnected sequence of pictures like random frames from a film. The group face of the panel, one compound jury eye and mouth, the shuffling of shoes, mysterious palavers before the bench of the black-robed man suspended in midair – opening statements, questions, answers, gavels, objections ... Suddenly it was Wednesday evening and Carroll was back in his cell.

He felt a childish impulse to laugh aloud, but he choked it off.

He must have dozed, for the next thing he knew Tully West was peering down at him as from a great height, and behind peered a familiar figure. Carroll could not remember the cell door's opening or closing.

'John, you remember Ellery Queen.'

Carroll nodded. 'You gents are doing quite a job on me, Queen.'

'Not me,' Ellery said. 'I'm strictly ground observer corps.'

'Then what do you want?'

'Satisfaction,' Ellery said. 'I'm not getting it.'

Carroll glanced at his partner. 'What's this, Tully?'

'Queen came to me after the session today and expressed interest in your case.' West managed a smile. 'It struck me, John, this might be a nice time to encourage him.'

Carroll rested his head against the cell wall. For days, part of his mind had been projecting itself into the execution chamber at Sing Sing, and another part had counter-attacked with thoughts of Helena and Breckie and Louanne. He took Helena and the children to sleep with him for sheer self-preservation.

'What is it you're not satisfied about?'

'That you shot Hunt.'

'Thanks,' Carroll laughed. 'Too bad you're not on the jury.'

'Yes,' Ellery said. 'But then I don't have the respectful jury mind. I'm not saying you didn't shoot Hunt; I'm just not convinced. Something about this case has bothered me from the start. Something about you, in fact. I wish you'd clear it up, if not for my sake than for yours. It's later than you apparently think.'

Carroll said very carefully, 'How bad is it?'

'As bad as it can be.'

'I've told Queen the whole story, John.' West's urbanity was gone; he even did a little semaphore work with his long arms. 'And I may as well tell you that Rayfield holds out damned little hope. He says today's testimony of the night man at the office building was very damaging.'

'How could it be?' Carroll cried. 'He admitted himself he couldn't positively identify as me whoever it was he let into the building that night. It wasn't me, Tully. It was somebody who deliberately tried to look like me – coat and hat like mine, my stumpy walk from that leg wound on Leyte, easily imitated things like that. And then the guy lets himself into our office and swipes my gun. I should think even a child would see I'm being had!'

'Where would a stranger get a key to your office?' Ellery asked.

'How do I know? How do I know he was even a stranger?'

After a while Carroll became conscious of the silence. He looked up angrily.

'You don't believe me. Actually, neither of you believes me.'

West said, 'It's not that, John,' and began to pace off the cell.

'Look,' Ellery said. 'West tells me you've hinted at certain important information that for some unimaginable reason you've been holding back. If it can do anything to clear you, Carroll, I'd advise you to toss it into the pot now.'

A prisoner shouted somewhere. West stopped in his tracks. Carroll put his head between his hands.

'I did something that Friday night that can clear me, yes.'

'What!' West cried.

'But it's open to all sorts of misinterpretation, chiefly nasty.'

'Nastier than the execution chamber at Sing Sing?'

West said, 'A woman,' with a remote distaste.

'That's right, Tully.' Carroll did not look at Ellery, feeling vaguely offended at his indelicacy. 'And I promised her I wouldn't use this except as a last resort. It wasn't for her sake, God knows. I've kept my mouth shut because of Helena. Helena loves me, but she's a woman, and a sick woman at that. If she shouldn't believe me …'

'Let me get this straight,' Ellery said. 'You were with this other woman during the murder period? You can actually prove an alibi?'

'Yes.'

'And he keeps quiet about it!' West dropped to the steel bunk beside his friend. 'John, how many kinds of idiot are you? Don't you have any faith in Helena at all? What happened? Who's the woman?'

'Felicia.'

West said, 'Oh.'

'Mrs. Hunt?' Ellery said sharply.

'That's right. I wandered around in the rain that night trying to figure out how I was going to stop Meredith from disclosing that twenty thousand dollar lunacy and having me arrested. That's when I thought of Felicia. She'd always been able to get anything out of Meredith that she wanted. I phoned her from a pay station and asked if I couldn't come right over.' Carroll muttered, 'I was pretty panicky, I guess ...' His voice petered out.

'Well, well?' West said.

'She was still up, reading in bed. When I told her what it was about, she said to come over. She let me in herself. The maid was asleep, I suppose – anyway, I didn't see Serafina.'

'And the time?' Ellery demanded.

'It was just about one a.m. when I got there. I left at four thirty.' Carroll laughed. 'Now you know why I've kept quiet about this. Can I expect my wife to believe that I spent three and a half hours in the middle of the night alone with Felicia in her bedroom – and she in a sheer nightgown and peekaboo negligee, by God! – just talking? And not getting anywhere, I might add.'

'Three and a half hours?' Ellery's brows went up.

'Felicia didn't see any reason why she should save my neck. Charming character.' Carroll's shoulders sloped. 'Well, I told you what it would sound like. I'm sure I'd doubt the story myself.'

'How much of the time did you have to fight for your honor?' West murmured. 'If I didn't know John so well, Queen, I'd be skeptical, too. Felicia's had a mad thing for him. But he's always been allergic to her. I suppose, John, she was willing to make a deal?'

'Something like that.'

'One night of amour in return for her influence on dear Meredith in your behalf. Yes, that would be Felicia's little libido at work. But Helena ...' West frowned. 'Quite a situation at that.'

Ellery said, 'It will have to be risked. Carroll, will Mrs. Hunt support your alibi in court?'

'She'd find it pretty tough to deny her own signature. I had her sign a full statement before a notary.'

'Good. Where is the statement?'

'In my safe at the office. It's in a plain manila envelope marked "Confidential" and bound around with a red rubber band.'

'I suggest you give West permission to open your safe, and I'd like to go along as security. Right now.'

Carroll bit his lip. Then, abruptly, he nodded.

'Do you know the combination, West?'

'Unless John's changed it. It's one of those letter-combination safes in which you can make the combination any word you want. John, is the combination word still "Helena"?'

'No. I've changed the damn thing four times this summer. The word now is "rescue".'

'And that,' West said solemnly, 'is sheer poetry. Well, John, if the open-sesame that Queen lugs around in his wallet should work again in this Bastille, we'll be back with you shortly.'

They were as good as West's word. Less than ninety minutes later the guard admitted them once more to Carroll's cell. Ellery had the manila envelope in his hand. He tossed the envelope to the bunk.

'All right, Carroll, let's hear it.'

'You haven't opened it?'

'I'd rather you did that yourself.'

Carroll picked up the envelope. He slipped the red rubber band off and around his wrist and, with an effort, inserted his fingers into the envelope.

West said, 'John. What's the matter?'

'Is this a gag?' Carroll was frantic. His fingers kept clawing around inside the envelope.

'Gag?'

'It's empty! The statement's not here!'

Ellery took the envelope from Carroll's shaking hand, squeezed it open, and peered inside. 'When did you see the contents last?'

'I opened the safe several times this summer to make sure the envelope was still there, but I never thought to examine it. I just took it for granted ...' Carroll sprang from the bunk. 'Nobody could have got into that safe – nobody! Not even my secretary. Nobody knew the combination words!'

'John, John.' West was shaking him.

'But how in God's name ... Unless the safe was broken into! Was it broken into, Queen?'

'No sign of it.'

'Then I don't understand!'

'One thing at a time.' Ellery took Carroll's other arm and they got him back on the bunk. 'The loss isn't necessarily fatal. All you have to do is make sure Mrs. Hunt takes the stand and repeats her statement under oath. She'd have been called to testify, anyway, once the written statement had been placed in evidence. Isn't that right, West?'

'Yes. I'll get hold of Felicia right off.'

Carroll was gnawing his fingernails. 'Maybe she won't agree, Tully. Maybe ...'

'She'll agree.' West was grim. 'Queen, would you come with me? This is one interview I prefer an unbiased witness for. Keep your shirt on, John.'

They were back in Carroll's cell with the first grays of dawn. Carroll, who had dropped off to sleep, sat up stupidly. Then he jerked wide-awake. His partner's monkish flesh had acquired a flabbiness he had never seen before.

Carroll's glance darted to the tall shadow in the corner of the cell.

'What's wrong now?' Carroll chattered. 'What's happened?'

'I'm afraid ... the absolute worst.' Ellery's voice was full of trouble. 'The Hunt house is closed down, Carroll. I'm sorry.

Felicia Hunt seems to have disappeared.'

That was a bad time for John Carroll. Ellery and West had to do some hard and fast talking to keep him from going to pieces altogether. They talked and talked through the brightening gloom and the tinny sounds of the prison coming to life.

'Hopeless. It's hopeless,' Carroll kept muttering.

'No,' Ellery said. 'It only looks hopeless, Carroll. The Fancy Dan who weaves an elaborate shroud for somebody else more often than not winds up occupying it himself. The clever boys trip over their own cleverness. There's a complex pattern here, and it's getting more tangled by the hour. That's good, Carroll. It's not hopeless at all.'

But Carroll only shook his head.

West was circling the cell like a frustrated hawk. 'On the other hand, Queen, let's face the facts. John has lost his alibi – the only thing that could surely save him.'

'Only temporarily.'

'We've got to get that alibi back!'

'We will. Stop running around in circles, West. You're making me nervous. The obvious step is to find that woman.'

West looked helpless. 'But where do I start? Will you help, Queen?'

Ellery grinned. 'I've been hoping you'd ask me that. If Carroll's agreeable, I'd be glad to. Want me to help, Carroll?'

The man on the bunk roused himself. 'Want you? I'd take the devil himself! The question is, What can you do?'

'This and that. Here, have a smoke.' Ellery jabbed a cigarette between Carroll's swollen lips. 'West, you look beat. How about going home and catching some sleep? Oh, and give my father a ring, will you? Tell him about this Felicia Hunt development and ask him for me to hop right on it.'

When West had gone, Ellery seated himself on the bunk. For a moment he watched Carroll smoke. Then he said, 'Carroll.'

'What?'

'Stop feeling sorry for yourself and listen to me. First, let's try to track down that business of the missing alibi statement. Go back to the time when you approached Felicia to sign it. Where did the meeting take place? When? Give me every fact you can remember, and then dig for some you've forgotten.'

He listened closely. When Carroll was finished, Ellery nodded.

'It's about as I figured. After Mrs. Hunt signed the statement and Gunder notarized her signature and went away, you left with the envelope in your briefcase and instead of going home you returned to your office. You never once, you say, let go of the briefcase. In the office you placed the envelope in your safe without checking its contents, locked the safe, and adjusted the dial to a new combination word. And on the three or four subsequent occasions when you checked on the envelope, you claim nobody could have removed the statement from it while you had the safe open, or discovered the new combinations you kept setting.

'When the envelope finally was taken from the safe, the only hands not your own to touch it were mine, last night. And I'll vouch for the fact that the statement couldn't have been stolen from me or lost from the envelope on the way over here.' Ellery tapped the manila envelope still in Carroll's hand. 'So, this was empty when I took it from the safe. Carroll, it's been empty for months. It was empty before you ever put it in the safe.'

Carroll looked at it, dazed.

'Only one conclusion possible.' Ellery lit another cigarette for him, and one for himself. 'The only time the envelope was not actually in your physical possession, or in the safe, or in my hands, was for a couple of minutes in the Hunt house the night Felicia signed the statement. You say that after she signed and Gunder notarized her signature, you slipped the statement into the envelope and the envelope into your briefcase, that you then took Gunder downstairs to pay him off and see him out. During that couple of minutes the briefcase with its contents were out of your sight and control. Therefore that's when the great disappearance took place. And since Mrs. Hunt was the only one in the room with the briefcase ...'

'Felicia?'

'Nobody else. Why should she have taken the statement she had just signed, Carroll? Any idea?'

'She double-crossed me, damn her,' Carroll said in a thick voice. 'And now she's ducked out to avoid having to tell the story under oath.'

'We'll get her to duck right back in if we have to extradite her from Little America.' Ellery rose and squeezed Carroll's shoulder. 'Hang in, Johnny.'

Felicia Hunt's whereabouts remained a mystery for as long as it took Ellery to go from the Tombs to Police Headquarters. His father had just come into the office and he was elbow-deep in reports.

'Yes, West phoned me,' the Inspector said, without looking up. 'If he'd hung on, I'd have been able to tell him in three minutes where Felicia Hunt is. Blast it all, where's that Grierson affidavit!'

Ellery waited patiently.

'Well?' he said at last. 'I'm still hanging.'

'What? Oh!' Inspector Queen leaned back. 'All I did was phone Smallhauser at the D.A.'s office. It seems a couple of days before Carroll's trial started – last Saturday morning – Hunt's widow showed up at the D.A.'s all tricked out in that ghastly mourning she wears, with her doctor in tow. The doctor told Smallhauser Mrs. Hunt was in a dangerously nervous state and couldn't face the ordeal of the trial. He wanted her to get away from the city. Seems she'd bought a cottage up in northern Westchester this summer and a few days up there by herself were just what the M.D. ordered, and was it all right with the D.A.? Well, Smallhauser didn't like it, but he figured that with the cottage having a phone he could always get her back to town in a couple of hours. So he said okay, and she gave her maid a week off and went up there Saturday afternoon. What's the hassle?'

Ellery told him. His father listened suspiciously.

'So that's what West was being so mysterious about,' he exclaimed. 'An alibi! The D.A.'s going to love this.'

'So will Rayfield. He doesn't know about it yet, either.'

The Inspector cocked a sharpening eye. 'What's your stake in this pot?'

'The right,' Ellery said piously. 'And seeing that it prevails.'

His father grunted and reached for the telephone. When he set it down, he had a Mt. Kisco number scribbled on his pad.

'Here, you call her,' he said. 'I'm working the other side of the street. And don't use a city phone for a toll call! You know where to find a booth.'

Ellery was back in front of his father's desk in forty-five minutes.

'What now?' Inspector Queen said. 'I was just on my way to the Bullpen.'

'She doesn't answer.'

'Who doesn't answer?'

'The Hunt lady,' Ellery said. 'Remember the case? I've phoned at five-minute intervals for almost an hour. Either she's gone into an early hibernation, or she's back in Central America charming the hidalgos.'

'Or she just isn't answering her phone. Look, son, I'm up to my lowers this morning. The case is out of my hands, anyway. Keep calling. She'll answer sooner or later.'

Ellery tried all day, slipping in and out of the courtroom every half hour. At a little past three the Assistant District Attorney rested his case, and on the request of the defense Judge Joseph H. Holloway adjourned the trial until the next morning.

Ellery managed to be looking elsewhere when John Carroll was taken from the courtroom. Carroll walked as if his knees were giving way. But as the room cleared, Ellery caught Tully West's eye. West, who was stooping over Helena Carroll in distress, nodded and after a moment came over.

'What about Felicia? She'll testify, won't she?'

Ellery glanced over at the reporters surrounding the portly figure of Rayfield. Some were glancing back, noses in the wind.

'We can't talk here, West. Can you get away?'

'I'll have to take Helena home first.' West was braced, like a man set for a blow. 'Where?'

'My father's office as soon as you can make it.'

'What about Rayfield?'

'Better not say anything to him those newsmen can overhear.

We can get in touch with him tonight.'

It was nearly five o'clock before the tall lawyer hurried into the Inspector's office. He looked haunted.

'Sorry, Helena went to pieces on me. I had to tell her all about John's alibi. Now she's more confused than ever. Damn it, why didn't John trust her in the first place?' West wiped his face. He said slowly. 'And now I suppose you'll tell me Felicia refuses to cooperate.'

'I almost wish that were it.' Ellery was looking haggard himself. 'West, I've been phoning since eight thirty this morning. I tried again only ten minutes ago. She doesn't answer.'

'She isn't there?'

'Maybe.' Inspector Queen was looking annoyed. 'Ellery, why the devil won't you ask the help of the state police? We could have a report on her in an hour.

'No.' Ellery got up. 'West, do you have your car?'

'I cabbed down.'

Ellery glanced at his father. The old man threw up his hands and stamped out.

'I ought to have my head examined! Velie, get me a car.'

They drove out of the city on Saw Mill River Parkway, Sergeant Velie at the wheel and Inspector Queen beside him nursing his grouch. Behind them, from opposite windows, Ellery and West studied the scenery. They were studying it long after darkness fell.

The sergeant turned the unmarked squad car off the Parkway near Mt. Kisco.

'Pull up at that gas station.' They were the first words the Inspector had uttered since leaving the city.

'Stony Ride Road?' the attendant said. 'That's up between here and Bedford Hills. Dirt road that goes way off to hell and gone. Who you looking for?'

'The Hunt place.'

'Hunt? Never heard.'

Ellery stuck his head out. 'How about Santos?'

'Santos. Yeah, dame of that name bought the old Meeker place this summer. You follow along here about a mile and a half ...'

'Using her maiden name,' West said as they drove away. 'Meredith would have loved that.'

The Queens said nothing.

Stony Ride Road climbed and twisted and swooped back, jolting their teeth. The darkness was impressive. They saw only two houses in three miles. A mile beyond the second, they found Felicia Hunt's cottage, Sergeant Velie very nearly drove past it. Its windows were as black as the night itself.

Velie swung the car between two mossy pillars into a crushed-stone driveway.

'No, Velie, stop here and shine your brights dead on the house.' The Inspector sounded troubled.

'She's gone,' West growled. 'She's gone or she never came here at all! What am I going to tell John?'

Ellery borrowed the sergeant's flash and got out. The Inspector put his small hand on Tully West's arm.

'No, Mr. West, we'll wait here.' Trouble was in his look, too.

It was a verdigrised fieldstone cottage with rusty wood trim and a darkly shingled roof, cuddled against wild woods. Ellery played his flash on the door. They saw him extend his foot and toe the door, and they saw it swing back.

He went into the house, flash first. A moment later the hall lit up.

He was in the house exactly two minutes.

At the sight of his face Inspector Queen and Sergeant Velie jumped from the car and ran past him and into the cottage.

Ellery said, 'You can tell John to forget his alibi, West. She's in there – dead.'

Felicia Hunt was lying on the bedroom floor face down, which was unfortunate. The back of her head had been crushed, and the bloody shards of the heavy stoneware vase that had crushed it strewed the floor around her. In the debris were some stiff chrysanthemums, looking like big dead insects. One of them had fallen on her open right palm.

West swallowed and retreated rapidly to the hall.

She had been dressed in a rainbow-striped frock of some iridescent material when death caught her. Jewels glittered on her hands and arms and neck. There were pomponned scuffs on her feet, her legs were bare, and the dead lips and cheeks and eyes showed no trace of make-up.

'She's been dead at least four days, maybe five,' Inspector Queen said. 'What do you make it, Velie?'

'Nearer four,' the big sergeant said. 'Last Sunday some time, I'd say, Inspector.' He glanced with longing at the tightly closed windows.

'Better not, Velie.'

The two men rose. They had touched nothing but the body, and that with profound care.

Ellery stood watching them morosely.

'Find anything, son?'

'No. That rain the other night wiped out any tire tracks or footprints that might have been left. Some spoiling food in the refrigerator, and her car is in the garage behind the house. No sign of robbery.' Ellery added suddenly, 'Doesn't something about her strike you as queer?'

'Yeah,' Sergeant Velie said. 'That posy in her hand ought to be a lily.'

'Spare us, Velie! What, Ellery?'

'The way she's dressed.'

They stared down at her. Tully West came back to the doorway, still swallowing.

The sergeant said, 'Looks like she was expecting somebody, the way she's all dolled up.'

'That's just what it doesn't look like,' Inspector Queen snapped. 'A woman as formally brought up as this one, who's expecting somebody, puts on shoes and stockings, Velie – doesn't go around barelegged and wearing bedroom slippers. She hadn't even made up her face or polished her nails. She was expecting nobody. What about the way she's dressed, Ellery?'

'Why isn't she still in mourning?'

'Huh?'

'She drives up here alone Saturday after wearing nothing but unrelieved black in town, and within twenty-four hours or less she's in a color-happy dress, back wearing her favorite jewelry, and having a ball for herself. It tells a great deal about Felicia de los Santos Hunt.'

'It doesn't tell me a thing,' his father retorted. 'What I want to know is why she was knocked off. It wasn't robbery. And there's nothing to indicate rape, although it's true a would-be rapist might have panicked –'

'Isn't it obvious that this is part and parcel of Hunt's murder and the frame-up of John Carroll?' West broke in with bitterness. 'Rape! Felicia was murdered to keep her from giving John the alibi that would get him off the hook.'

The Inspector nibbled his mustache.

'What does it take to convince you people that somebody is after Carroll's hide!'

'That sounds like sense, Dad.'

'Maybe.'

'At the least, the Hunt woman's murder is bound to give the case against Carroll a different look – Dad, before Velie phones the state police.'

'Well?'

'Let's you and Velie and I really give this place a going over.'

'What for, Ellery?'

'For that alibi statement Felicia signed and then took back when Carroll wasn't looking. It's a long shot, but ... who knows?'

Their session with the state police took the rest of the night. It was sunrise before they got back to the city.

West asked to be dropped off at Beekman Place.

'Sam Rayfield won't thank me for waking him up, but then I haven't had any sleep at all. Who's going to tell John?'

'I will,' Ellery said.

West turned away with a grateful wave.

'So far so bad,' the Inspector said as they sped downtown. 'Now all I have to do is talk the D.A.'s office into joining

Rayfield in a plea to Judge Holloway, and why *I* should have to do it is beyond me!'

'You going home, Inspector?'

'Sure I'm going home, Velie! I can take Smallhauser's abuse over my own phone as well as at Headquarters. And maybe get some sleep, too. How about you, son?'

'The Tombs,' Ellery said.

He parted with Sergeant Velie at the Headquarters garage and walked over to the Criminal courts Building. His head was muddy, and he wanted to cleanse it. He tried not to think of John Carroll.

Carroll woke up instantly at the sound of the cell door.

'Queen! How did you make out with Felicia?'

Ellery said, 'We didn't.'

'She won't testify?'

'She can't testify. John, she's dead.'

It was brutal, but he knew no kinder formula. Carroll was half sitting up, leaning on an elbow, and he remained that way. His eyes kept blinking in a monotonous rhythm.

'Dead ...'

'Murdered.' Carroll blinked the bedroom floor of her cottage with her head smashed in. She'd been dead for days.'

'Murdered.' Carroll blinked and blinked. 'But who –?'

'There's not a clue. So far, anyway.' Ellery lit a cigarette and held it out. Carroll took it. But then he dropped it and covered his face with both hands. 'I'm sorry, John,' Ellery said.

Carroll's hands came down. He had his lower lip in his teeth.

'I'm no coward, Queen. I faced death a hundred times in the Pacific and didn't chicken out. But a man likes to die for some purpose ... I'm scared.'

Ellery looked away.

'There's got to be some way out of this!' Carroll dropped off the bunk and ran in his bare feet to the bars of the cell, to grasp them with both hands. But then he whirled and sprang at Ellery, seizing him by the arms. 'That statement – that's my out, Queen! Maybe she didn't destroy it. Maybe she took it up there with her. If you can find it for me –'

'I've looked,' Ellery said gently. 'And my father looked, and Sergeant Velie, too. We covered the cottage inside and out. It took us over two hours. We didn't call the local police until we were satisfied it wasn't there.'

'But it's got to be there! My life depends on it! Don't you see?' He shook Ellery.

'Yes, John.'

'You missed it. Maybe she put it in an obvious place, like in that story of Poe's. Did you look in her purse? Her luggage?'

'Yes, John.'

'Her suits – coats – the linings –?'

'Yes, John.'

'Her car –?'

'And her car.'

'Then maybe it was on her,' Carroll said feverishly. 'On her person. Did you …? No, I suppose you wouldn't.'

'We would and we did.' Ellery's arms ached. He wished Carroll would let go.

'How about that big ruby-and-emerald locket she was so hipped on? The alibi statement was only a single sheet of paper. She might have wadded it up and hidden it in the locket. Did you look there while you were searching the body?'

'Yes, John. All we found in the locket were two photos, Spanish-looking elderly people. Her parents, I suppose.'

Carroll released him. Ellery rubbed his arms.

'How about books?' Carroll mumbled. 'Felicia was always reading some trashy novel or other. She might have slipped it between two pages –'

'There were eleven books in the house, seven magazines. I went through them myself.'

In the cold cell Carroll wiped the perspiration from his cheeks.

'Desk with a false compartment? … Cellar? … Is there an attic? … Did you search the garage?'

He went on and on. Ellery waited for him to run down.

When Carroll was finally quiet, Ellery called the guard. His last glimpse of the young lawyer was of a spreadeagled figure,

motionless on the bunk, eyes shut. All Ellery could think of was
a corpse.

Judge Joseph H. Holloway shook his head. He was a
gray-skinned, frozen-eyed old-timer of the criminal courts,
known to practising members of the New York bar as Old
Steelguts.

'I didn't come down to my chambers an hour early on a
Monday morning, Counselor Rayfield, for the pleasure of
listening to your mellifluous voice. That pleasure palled on me a
long time ago. I granted an adjournment Friday morning
because of the Hunt woman's murder, but do you have any
evidence to warrant a further postponement? So far I've heard
nothing but a lot of booshwah.'

Assistant District Attorney Smallhauser nodded admiringly.
Judge Holloway's fondness for the slang of his youth –
indulged in only *in camera* of course – was trifled with at the
peril of the trifler. 'Booshwah is *le mot juste* for it, Your Honor.
I apologize for being a party to this frivolous waste of your
time.'

Samuel Rayfield favored the murderous little Assistant D.A.
with a head-shrinking glance and clamped his teeth more firmly
about his cold cigar. 'Come off it, Joe,' he said to Judge
Holloway. 'This is a man's life we're playing with. We're not
privileged to kick him to death simply because he acted like a
damn fool in holding back his alibi. All I want this adjournment
for is time to look for that alibi statement the Hunt woman
signed when she was alive enough to write.'

Judge Holloway's dentures gleamed towards Smallhauser.

'The alibi statement your client *says* the Hunt woman
signed,' the little D.A. said with his prim smile.

The Judge's dentures promptly turned to Rayfield.

'I've got the notary, Gunder, to attest to the fact that she
signed it,' the portly lawyer snapped.

'That she signed some paper, yes. But you people admit
yourselves that Carroll concealed the text of the paper from
Gunder. For all Gunder knows he might have been notarizing

the woman's signature to the lease of a new dog house.' The little D.A. turned his smile on the Judge. 'I'm bound to say, Your Honor, this whole thing smells more and more to me like a stall.'

'Come around some time when you've put on long pants and I'll show you what a real stall smells like, Smallhauser!' the famous lawyer said. 'Joe, I'm not stalling. There's a chance she didn't destroy the statement. Not much of one, I admit, but I wouldn't sleep nights if I thought I hadn't exhausted every avenue of investigation in Carroll's behalf.'

'You wouldn't lose half of a strangled snore,' the Judge said with enjoyment. 'Look, Sam, it's all conjecture, and you know it. You can't even show that Mrs. Hunt stole that alleged statement of hers from Carroll in the first place.'

'Ellery Queen showed —'

'I know what Ellery Queen showed. He showed his usual talent for making something out of nothing. Ellery's idea of proof!' The old jurist snorted. 'And even if the Hunt woman did steal an alibi statement from Carroll, what did she steal it for if not to burn it or flush it down a toilet? And even if she held on to it, where is it? The Queens didn't find it in her Westchester cottage. You yourself ransacked her New York house over the week-end. You got a court order to examine her safe deposit box. You questioned her maid and the people in Carroll's office and God knows who else — all without result. Be reasonable, Sam! That alibi statement either never existed or, if it did, it doesn't exist any more. I can't predicate a postponement on the defendant's unsupported allegation of alibi. You know I can't.'

'Of course, if you'd like to put Carroll on the stand,' Smallhauser said with a grin, 'so I can cross-examine him —'

Rayfield ignored him. 'All right, Joe. But you can't deny that Hunt's wife has also been murdered. That's a fact, and in evidence of it we can produce a corpse. And I don't believe in coincidences. When a man's murder is followed by his wife's murder, I say the two are connected. The connection in this case is obvious. The murder of Felicia Hunt was committed in order to blow up Carroll's alibi for the murder of Meredith Hunt and to cement Carroll's conviction. How can his trial proceed with this area unexplored? I tell you, Joe, this man is being framed by somebody who's committed two murders in order to pull the frame off! Give us time to explore.'

'I remember once sitting here listening to Ellery Queen,' Judge Holloway said glumly. 'You're beginning to sound like his echo. Sam, evidence is what trials are ruled by, and evidence is what you ain't got. Motion denied. My courtroom, gentlemen, ten o'clock on the nose.'

Ellery got the answer that Thursday afternoon in the half-empty courtroom while the jury was out deliberating John Carroll's fate.

It came to him after an agonizing apraisal of the facts as he saw them. He had gone over them countless times before. This time – in the lightning flash he had begun to think would never strike again – he saw it.

By good luck, at the time it came, he was alone. Carroll had been taken back to the Tombs, and his wife and the two lawyers had gone with him so that he would not have to sweat the waiting out alone.

A sickish feeling invaded Ellery's stomach. He got up and went out and found the nearest men's room.

When he returned to the courtroom, Tully West was waiting for him.

'Helena wants to talk to you.' West's face was green, too.

'No.'

'I beg your pardon?'

Ellery shook his head clear. 'I mean – yes, of course.'

West misunderstood. 'I don't blame you. I wish I were anywhere else myself. Rayfield was smart – he bowed out for "coffee".'

Carroll was being held in a detention room under guard. Ellery was surprised at his calm, even gentle, look. It was Helena Carroll's eyes that were wild. He was trying to console her.

'Honey, honey, it's going to come out all right. They won't convict an innocent man.'

'Why are they taking so *long*? They've been out five hours!'

'That's a good sign, Helena,' West said. 'The longer they take, the better John's chances are.'

She saw Ellery then, and she struggled to her feet and was at him so swiftly that he almost stepped back.

'I thought you were supposed to be so marvelous at these things! You haven't done anything for John – anything.'

Carroll tried to draw her back, but she shook him off. Her pain-etched face was livid.

'I don't care, John! You should have hired a real detective while there was still time. I wanted you to – I *begged* you and Tully not to rely on somebody so close to the police!'

'Helena, really.' West was embarrassed.

Ellery said stonily, 'No, Mrs. Carroll is quite right. I wish I had never got mixed up in it.'

She was staring at him intently. 'That almost sounds as if ...'

'As if what, Helena?' West was trying to humor her, get her away.

'As if he knows. *Tully, he does.* Look at his face!' She clawed at Ellery. 'You know, and you won't say anything! You talk, do you hear? Tell me! *Who's behind this?*'

West was flabbergasted. With surprise John Carroll studied Ellery's face for a moment, then he went to the barred window and stood there rigidly.

'Who?' His wife was weeping now. '*Who?*'

But Ellery was as rigid as Carroll. 'I'm sorry, Mrs. Carroll. I can't save your husband. It's too late.'

'Too late,' she said hysterically. 'How can you say it's too late when –'

'Helena.' West took the little woman by the arms and forcibly sat her down. Then he turned to Ellery, his lean face dark. 'What's this all about, Queen? You sound as if you're covering up for someone. Are you?'

Ellery glanced past the angry lawyer to the motionless man at the window.

'I'll leave it up to John,' he said. 'Shall I answer him, John?'

For a moment it seemed as if Carroll had not heard. But then he turned, and there was something about him – a dignity, a finality – that quieted Tully West and Helen Carroll and sent their glances seeking each other.

Carroll replied clearly, '*No.*'

Looking out over the prison yard from the Warden's office, Ellery thought he had never seen a lovelier spring night sky, or a sadder one. A man should die on a stormy night, with all Nature protesting. This, he thought, this is cruel and unusual punishment.

He sought the Warden's clock.

Carroll had fourteen minutes of life left.

The Warden's door opened and closed behind him. Ellery did not turn around. He thought he knew who it was. He had been half expecting his father for an hour.

'Ellery, I looked for you at the Death House.'

'I was down there before, Dad. Had a long talk with Carroll. I thought you'd be here long ago.'

'I wasn't intending to come at all. It isn't my business. I did my part of it. Or maybe that's why I'm here. After a lifetime of this sort of thing, I'm still not hardened to it ... Ellery.'

'Yes, Dad.'

'It's Helena Carroll. She's hounded and haunted me. She's with West. I drove them up. Mrs. Carroll thinks I have some drag with you. Do I?'

Ellery said from the window, 'In practically everything, Dad. But not in this.'

'I don't understand you,' the Inspector said heavily. 'If you have information that would save Carroll, how can you keep buttoned up now? – here? All right, you saw something we didn't. Is it my job you're worried about, because I helped put Carroll on this spot? If you know something that proves his innocence, the hell with me.'

'I'm not thinking of you.'

'Then you can only be thinking of Carroll. He's protecting somebody, he's willing to go to the Chair for it, and you're helping him do it. Ellery, you can't do that.' The old man clutched his arm. 'There's still a few minutes. The Warden's got an open line to the Governor's office.'

But Ellery shook his head.

Inspector Queen stared at his son's set profile for a moment. Then he went over to a chair and sat down, and father and son waited.

At 11:04 the lights suddenly dimmed.

Both men stiffened.

The office brightened.

At 11:07 it happened again.

And again at 11:12.

After that there was no change. Ellery turned away from the window, fumbling for his cigarettes.

'Do you have a light, Dad?'

The old man struck a match for him. Ellery nodded and sat down beside him.

'Who's going to tell her?' his father said suddenly.

'You are,' Ellery said. 'I can't.'

Inspector Queen rose. 'Live and learn,' he said.

'Dad –'

The opening of the door interrupted them. Ellery got to his feet. The Warden's face was as haggard as theirs. He was wiping it with a damp handkerchief.

'I never get used to it,' he said, 'never ... He went very peacefully. Not trouble at all.'

Ellery said, 'Yes, he would.'

'He gave me a message for you, by the way.'

'Thanking him, I suppose,' Inspector Queen said bitterly.

'Why, yes, Inspector,' the Warden said. 'He said to tell your son how grateful he was. What on earth did he mean?'

'Don't ask *him*,' the Inspector said. 'My son's constituted himself a one-man subcommittee of the Almighty. Where you going to wait for me, Ellery?' he demanded as they left the Warden's office. 'I mean while I do the dirty work?'

Ellery said stiffly, 'Take Helena Carroll and Tully West back to the city first.'

'Just tell me one thing. what was Carroll "grateful" to you for? Who'd you help him cover up?'

Ellery shook his head. 'I'll see you at home afterward.'

'Well?' the old man said. He had got into his frayed bathrobe and slippers, and he was nursing a cup of stale coffee with his puffy hands. He looked exhausted. 'And it had better be good.'

'Oh, it's good,' Ellery said. 'If good is the word.' He had not undressed, had not even removed his topcoat. He sat there as he had come in from the long drive to wait for his father. He stared at the blank Queen wall. 'It was a slip of the tongue. I remembered it. It wouldn't have made any difference if the slip had never been made, or if I'd forgotten it altogether. Any difference to Carroll, I mean. He was sunk from the start. I couldn't save him, Dad. He'd had it.'

'What slip?' the old man demanded. 'Of whose tongue? Or was I deaf as well as blind?'

'I was the only one who heard it. It had to go with Felicia Hunt. Her husband dies and she goes into Spanish mourning, total and unadorned. But when she gets off by herself in that hillside cottage, back on go the gay clothes, her favorite jewelry. By herself, mind you – alone. Safe from all eyes, even her maid's.'

Ellery stared harder at the blank wall. 'When we got back to town after finding her body, I went directly to the Tombs to tell Carroll about the murder in Westchester of the only human being who could give him an alibi. Carroll was frantic. His mind went back to the alibi statement she had signed and then taken from his briefcase, unknown to him at the time. It was all he could think of, naturally. If that piece of paper existed, if she had hidden it instead of destroying it, he could still be saved. He kept pounding at me. Maybe she'd hidden it in her luggage, her car, a secret drawer. He went on and on. And one of the places he mentioned as a possible hiding place of the statement was the locket of the ruby-and-emerald pendant Felicia Hunt was so fond of. "Did you look there?" he asked me. "*While you were searching the body?*" '

Ellery flung aside a cigarette he had never lit. 'That question of his was what I finally remembered.'

'He knew she was wearing the pendant ...'

'Exactly, when no one could have known except ourselves when we found her – and the one who had murdered her there five days earlier.'

He sank deeper into his coat. 'It was a blow, but there it was – John Carroll had murdered Felicia Hunt. He'd had the opportunity, of course. You and Velie agreed that the latest she could have been murdered was the preceding Sunday. And on that Sunday Carroll was still free on bail. It wasn't until the next morning, Monday, that he had to resubmit to the custody of the court for the commencement of his trial.'

'But it doesn't add up,' Inspector Queen spluttered. 'The Hunt woman's testimony would get him an acquittal. Why should Carroll have knocked off the only witness who could give him his alibi?'

'Just what I asked myself. And the only answer that made sense was: Carroll must have had reason to believe that when Felicia took the stand in court, she was going to tell the truth.'

'Truth? The truth about what?'

'About Carroll's alibi being false.'

'*False?*'

'Yes. And from his standpoint, of course, that would compel him to kill her. To protect the alibi.'

'But without her he had no alibi, true *or* false!'

'Correct,' Ellery said softly, '*but when Carroll drove up to Westchester he didn't know that.* At that time he thought he had her signed statement locked in his office safe. He didn't learn until days after he had killed her – when West and I opened the safe and found the envelope empty – that he no longer had possession of the alibi statement, hadn't had possession for months, in fact – that, as I pointed out to him, Felicia Hunt must have taken it from his briefcase while he was downstairs showing the notary out. No wonder he almost collapsed.'

'I'll be damned,' the Inspector said. 'I'll be double-damned.'

Ellery shrugged. 'If Carroll's alibi for Meredith Hunt's murder was a phony, then the case against him stood as charged. The alibi was the only thing that gave him the appearance of innocence. If in fact he had no alibi, everything pointed to his guilt of Hunt's murder, as the jury rightfully decided.

'Carroll filled in the details for me earlier tonight in the Death House.' Ellery's glance went back to the wall. 'He said that when he left his house that rainy night after Hunt's ultimatum, to walk off his anger, the fog gave him a slight lease on hope. Maybe Hunt's plane was grounded and Hunt was still within reach. He phoned La Guardia and found that all flights had been delayed for a few hours. On the chance that Hunt was hanging around the airport, Carroll stopped in at his office and got his target pistol. He had some vague idea, he said, of threatening Hunt into a change of heart.

'He took a cab to La Guardia, found Hunt waiting for the fog to clear, and persuaded him to get his car from the parking lot so that they could talk in privacy. Eventually Hunt meandered back to Manhattan and parked on East 58th Street. The talk in the car became a violent quarrel. Carroll's hair-trigger temper went off, and he shot Hunt. He left Hunt in the Thunderbird and stumbled back home in the rain.

'The next morning, when we called on Mrs. Hunt to announce her husband's killing and found Carroll and West there, and you mentioned that the killer had left his gun in Hunt's car. Carroll was sick. Remember he ran into the bathroom? He wasn't acting that time. For the first time he realized that, in his fury and panic, he'd completely forgotten about the gun.

'As a lawyer,' Ellery went on, 'he knew what a powerful circumstantial case loomed against him, and that the only thing that could save him was an equally powerful alibi. He saw only one possible way to get it. He had never destroyed the love letters Felicia Hunt had written him during her infatuation. And he knew her dread of scandal. So he fabricated a statement out of the whole cloth about having spent the murder period in her bedroom "pleading" with her to intercede with her husband, and he took the statement to her. He didn't have to spell out his threat. Felicia understood clearly enough the implication of his proposal ... that if she didn't give him the phony alibi he needed, he would publish her love letters and ruin her with her strait-laced Latin-American family and compatriots. She signed.'

'But why didn't Carroll produce the alibi right away, Ellery? What was his point in holding it back?'

'The legal mind again. If he produced it during the investigation, even if it served to clear him, the case would still be open on the books and later he might find himself back in it up to his ears. But if he stood trial for Hunt's murder and *then* produced the fake alibi and was acquitted – he was safe from the law forever by the rule of double jeopardy. He couldn't be tried again for Hunt's killing after that even if the alibi should at some future date be exposed as a fake.

'He knew from the beginning,' Ellery continued, 'that Felicia Hunt was the weak spot in his plan. She was neurotic and he was terribly afraid she might wilt under pressure when he needed her most. As the trial approached, Carroll told me, he got more and more nervous about her. So the day before it was scheduled to start, he decided to talk to her again. Learning that she'd gone into retreat up in Westchester, he found an excuse to get away from his family and drove up to the cottage. His worst fears were realized. She told him that she had changed her mind. Scandal or no scandal, she wasn't going to testify falsely under oath and lay herself open to perjury. What she didn't tell him – it might possibly have saved her life if she had – was that she'd stolen and destroyed the alibi statement he had forced her to sign months before.

'Carroll grabbed the nearest heavy object and hit her over the head with it. Now at least, he consoled himself, she wouldn't be able to repudiate her signed statement, which he thought was in his office safe.'

'And you've kept all this to yourself,' his father muttered. 'Why, Ellery? You certainly didn't owe Carroll anything.'

Ellery turned from the wall. He looked desperately tired.

'No, I didn't owe Carroll anything ... a man with a completely cockeyed moral sense ... too proud to live on his wife's money, yet capable of stealing twenty thousand dollars ... a faithful husband who nevertheless kept the love letters of a woman he despised for their possible future value to him ... a man with a strange streak of honesty who was capable of playing a scene like an accomplished actor ... a loving father who let himself murder two people.

'No, I didn't owe him anything,' Ellery said, 'but he wasn't the only one involved. And no one knew that better than Carroll. The afternoon that the answer came to me, while we were waiting for the jury to come in, I told Mrs. Carroll I couldn't save her husband, that it was too late. Carroll was the only one present who knew what I meant. He knew I meant it was too late for *him*, that I couldn't save him because I knew he was guilty. And when I put it up to him, he gave me to understand that I wasn't to give him away. It wasn't for his own sake – he knew the verdict the jury was going to bring in. He knew he was already a dead man.

'And so I respected his last request. I couldn't save him, but I could save his family's memories of him. This way Helena Carroll and little Breck and Louanne will always think John Carroll died the victim of a miscarriage of justice.' Ellery shucked his topcoat and headed for his bedroom. 'How could I deny them that comfort?'

Michael Gilbert

C12: Department of Bank Robberies

The drill screamed as it bit into the tough metal. The operator, a small man with a sad monkey-face, hummed to himself as he worked. It was the last eight holes which he was boring, four on either side of the hinge of the strongroom door.

When he had finished the drilling, and had checked, with a thermometer, that the surrounding metal had returned to a safe temperature, he filled each of the holes with Polar Ammon gelatine dynamite, tamping the putty-like stuff delicately home with the blunt end of a pencil; then he used the sharp end to bore a hole in the middle deep enough to take the tube of the copper electric detonator with its plastic-covered lead of tinned iron.

When all the detonators were in, he collected the eight ends, bared them, twisted them together, and covered the joint with insulating tape. Then he collected a pile of old army blankets and, helped now by a second man, draped them from wires which had already been fixed across the door.

Both men then retreated to the guard door at the entrance of the strongroom lobby. Two of the bars had been cut out. They squeezed through the gaps, dragging the plastic-covered lead behind them.

In the farthest corner of the outer lobby stood an ordinary six-volt car battery. The first man separated the lead wires and twisted one of them round the negative terminals.

Both men squatted down, backs against the wall, heads bent forward.

Then the second wire, carefully held in a rubber-gloved hand, was laid on the positive terminal. The shock wave of the explosion pinned them against the wall.

The third man, standing in the doorway of a shop outside, heard the crump of the explosion and swore softly to himself. The next ten minutes were going to be the most difficult.

A newsagent, sleeping four houses away on the opposite side of the street, sat up in bed, and said, 'Cor, what was that? Have they declared war?' His wife said, 'Wassup?' 'Sounded like a bomb.' 'So what?' said his wife. 'It hasn't hit us.' She dragged him down into bed again.

Eight minutes. Nine minutes. Ten minutes. Eleven minutes. *What the hell are they playing at?* Twelve minutes.

The door of the shop opened and two men appeared. Both had heavy satchels slung over their shoulders. One carried the drill, another had the electric cutter which had been used to saw through the bars.

The third man relieved them of drill and cutter and set off at a brisk pace up the street to where the car was parked. Not a word had been spoken from first to last.

Police Constable Owens, of the Gravesend Police, saw the car nosing into the street. He thought it odd that it should have no lights on, and held up a hand to stop it.

The car accelerated. Owens jumped, slipped, and fell into the gutter. He picked himself up in time to see the car corner and disappear.

Police Constable Owens limped to the nearest police box.

A pigeon took off from Boadicea's helmet and went into a power dive. It was aimed at the head of a young man with a brown face and black hair, who had just crossed Westminster Bridge. Detective Inspector Patrick Petrella raised his arm. The pigeon executed a sideslip and volplaned off up into a tree. Petrella regarded the pigeon without malice.

It was a beautiful day. It was spring. He was starting a new job.

The message which had reached him at Gabriel Street Police Station had not been explicit, but he guessed that his spell of duty in South London was over. It had spanned three years; and he had enjoyed most of it, but three years in one place was enough.

He pushed his hat a little farther back on his head, and swung in under the Archway and up the three shallow steps into the main building of New Scotland Yard.

The private secretary, a serious young man in horn-rimmed glasses, inspected him as he came into the anteroom, and then said, 'The A.C.'s ready for you. Will you go in?'

Petrella found himself straightening his shoulders as he marched by the inner door into the presence of Sir Wilfred Romer, Assistant-Commissioner in charge of the Criminal Investigation Branch of the Metropolitan Police, and – in Petrella's humble opinion – the greatest thief catcher since Wensley.

'Sit down,' said Romer. 'You know Superintendent Baldwin, I think.'

Petrella nodded to Superintendent Baldwin, big, red-faced, conscientiously ferocious, known to everyone from the newest recruit upward as Baldy.

Romer said, 'I'm forming a new Department. It'll be known as C12. And, broadly speaking' – here his face split in a wintry smile – 'you're the Department.'

Petrella managed to smile back.

'You'll have two or three people to help you, but the smaller you keep it, the happier I'll be. First, because we haven't got many spare hands, and secondly, because smallness means secrecy. Your first job will be the collection and analysis of information.'

As Romer spoke, an alphabetical index of subjects, from Arson to Zoology on which the remarkable man might be seeking information, flipped through Petrella's aroused imagination.

'On bank robberies,' concluded Romer.

'Yes, sir,' said Petrella. 'Bank robbery.'

'Not bank robbery in general. It's a particular series of bank robberies that's getting under our skin. Never mind the details now. You'll get those from Baldwin. What I wanted to tell you was this. There's one thing we're quite certain of: there's an organizer. I want him put away. That'll be your second job.'

Back in his own office Baldwin filled in a few details.

'The bumph's in these folders,' he said. 'It'll take you a day or two to wade through it all. It goes back about seven years. We didn't know that there was any link-up, not at first. The actual jobs are done by different outfits. All pro stuff. Chick Selling and his crowd have been involved. And Walter Hudd. And the Band brothers. We're fairly certain it was them who did the Central Bank at Gravesend last month. You probably read about it.'

Petrella nodded. He had heard enough about high-class safebreakers to know that they left their signatures on their jobs as surely as great artists in other walks of life. He said, 'What makes you so certain there's a link-up?'

'Three things.' Baldwin ticked them off on the fingers of his big red hand. 'First, they're getting absolutely accurate information. They've never taken a bank that wasn't stuffed with notes. And that isn't as common as you might think. You could open a lot of strongrooms and find nothing in them but Georgian silver and deed boxes.

'Second, the technique's the same. They always work from another building. Sometimes as much as three or four houses away – that means slicing through a lot of brickwork. They've got proper tools for that too, and they use them properly. Someone's taught 'em.

'And last, but not least, someone's supplying them with equipment. It's good stuff – so good it can't even be bought in this country for a legitimate job. When Halter Hudd's boys cracked the Sheffield District Bank they had to cut and run and they left behind a high-speed film-cooled steel cutter that the London Salvage Corps have been asking for ever since they heard about it. It comes from Germany.'

Later, installed in a small room on the top story of the Annex into which four desks had somehow been inserted, Petrella repeated much of this to his two aides. The first was Detective

Sergeant Edwards, a solemn young man with the appearance and diction of a chartered accountant, who was reputed to be extremely efficient in the organization of paper work. The second – as Petrella was delighted to note – was none other than his old protégé, Detective Wilmot, from Highside.

'Who's the fourth?' said Petrella.

'We're getting a female clerical assistant,' said Wilmot. 'I asked at the typing pool who it was going to be but no one seemed to know. I don't mind betting though, as we're the youngest department, we shall get the oldest and ugliest secretary. Someone like Mrs. Proctor, who's got buck teeth and something her best friends have got tired of telling her about. What do we do next?'

Petrella said, 'No one really knows. We shall have to make most of it up as we go along. We've got to have the best possible liaison with the C.R.O. and the Information Room on the old jobs, and any new jobs that come along. Then we'll have to circularize all provincial police forces, asking for information on suspicious circumstances –'

'Such as?' asked Edwards.

'First thing, we might see if we can get the banks to improve the reward system. At present, you only collect the cash if your information leads to someone being arrested. That's not good enough. What happens at the moment is, someone hears a bang in the night. Might be something, might not. They go back to sleep again. If there was a reward – it needn't be a big one – say, fifty pounds for the first man getting on the blower to the police station, we might get some action.

'Next, we'll have to circularize local forces – for information about thefts of explosives, losses of strongroom keys, unexplained caches of notes, suspicious behaviour near banks, bank employees with expensive tastes –'

'Bank managers with expensive mistresses.'

'That'll be enough from you, Wilmot. Do you think you can draft us a circular?'

'Can do,' said Edwards.

'The three of us will have to be on the priority warning list

through the Information Room, and the police station nearest
our home. We may be called out any hour of the day or night.'

'I'll have to warn all my girl friends,' said Wilmot.

That afternoon Petrella was sitting alone at his desk staring at
the tips of his shoes when the door opened, a girl looked in, and
said, 'Are you C12?'

'That's right,' said Petrella.

'You certainly took some finding. Nobody seemed to have
ever heard of you.'

'We're a very important Department. But very hush-hush.'

'They haven't given you much of a room. My name's Orfrey,
by the way.'

'I can't help feeling,' said Petrella, 'that, as we shall be
working together for an indefinite period in a space measuring
not more than twelve feet by ten, I shall find myself addressing
you, sooner or later, by your Christian name.'

Miss Orfrey smiled. Petrella noticed that, when she smiled,
she smiled with the whole of her face, crinkling up her eyes,
parting her lips, and showing small, even white teeth.

'That name's Jane,' she said ...

About a week later Jane Orfrey said to Wilmot, 'Is he always
as serious as this?'

'He's got a lot on his mind,' said Wilmot.

'He might smile sometimes.'

'It's make or break, really,' said Wilmot. 'If we sort out this
lot, he gets the credit. If we don't, he gets a great big black
mark.'

'It doesn't seem to be worrying you.'

'Paper work doesn't mean a lot to me. I'm what you might call
a man of action. What about coming to the pictures tonight?'

'Thank you,' said Jane. 'I'm going to take some of this paper
home.'

'It's a serious matter, sir,' said Sergeant Edwards.

'What is?' said Petrella, coming up from the depths of his
thoughts on the technical construction of strongroom doors.

'Our allowances.'

'What about them?'

'Now that we're working at Scotland yard and on a special job, we ought to get a Special Service increment *and* a Central London increment. But the regulations say that where you're entitled to both, you can have the whole of whichever allowance you select, and fifty per cent of the other one. I've been working it out –'

'And I thought you were doing something useful,' said Petrella.

Sergeant Edwards looked aggrieved ...

Two o'clock on a Monday morning, twelve inches away from Petrella's ear, the telephone screamed. He jerked upright, hit his head against the back of the bed, swore, and snatched the receiver off the instrument.

'Job at Slough,' said a courteous and offensively wide-awake voice. 'They've pulled in the men involved: Ronald, Kenneth, and Leslie Band. There'll be a car round for you in three minutes.'

Petrella was still trying to button his shirt when he heard the car draw up. He finished his dressing sitting beside the driver as they sped along the empty roads toward Slough. The driver didn't seem to be pressing, but Petrella noticed the speedometer needle steady on the seventy mark. At that moment a motorcycle passed them, and he just had time to recognize Wilmot.

Inspector Lansell, of the Buckinghamshire C.I.D., was waiting for them in his office.

'It was the North Midland Bank,' he said. 'They cut their way through from the cellar of an empty shop next door. Must have started some time on Saturday afternoon. Took all Saturday night and Sunday over the job. Blew the main strongroom door at half past one this morning. A chap living across the street heard it, and telephoned us. We had a patrol car a few streets away, and we got them as they came out.'

'Good work,' said Petrella. 'I'll have a word with them now, if I may.'

'They're all yours,' said Lansell courteously.

The Band brothers were small, quiet, brown-faced men, all with good records of regular service in the Royal Engineers. By six o'clock Petrella had got what he could out of them. It wasn't a lot. They had all been in the hands of the police before, and they answered, blocked, or evaded the routine questions.

Petrella had hardly expected more, and was not depressed. He was particularly interested in two pieces of their equipment: a high-speed electric drill with an adjustable tungsten-tipped angle bit which had been used to drill a series of holes down either side of the hinge of the strongroom door; and an oxyacetylene, white flame cutter, coupled with a small pumping device which stepped up the pressure and temperature of the flame.

Both were in ex-works condition. The cutter had initials and a number stamped on the base. It looked like shipyard equipment. There was a department in the Board of Trade which would probably be able to identify it for him. If it had been imported under license, it could be traced back to its maker.

Petrella had another reason for feeling pleased. The banks, some of which had jibbed at his automatic alarm-reward system, would probably support it now that it had shown results.

He said to Inspector Lansell, 'Any idea where my Sergeant is?'

'Haven't seen him,' said Lansell. 'I'll ask.'

But no one in the station had seen him. Petrella travelled back to London on a train, crowded with coughing and sneezing commuters. He remembered the ice patches on the road and a nagging feeling of uneasiness travelled with him.

In the course of that morning he rang Information three times. No accidents to police officers had been reported.

At two o'clock Wilmot arrived, unshaven but unrepentant.

'I've got a feeling,' he said – before Petrella could open his mouth – 'that maybe we're onto something. It was a turn up for the book. I stopped just short of the High Street to ask the way to the station, and I saw these two in an all-night café over the way having a cuppa; and I said, Oh, oh, what are *they* doing?'

'Take a deep breath,' said Petrella, 'and start again. You saw who?'

'Morris Franks and his brother Sammy.'

'That pair,' said Petrella, with distaste. 'What do you imagine they were doing in Slough at three o'clock in the morning?'

'Just exactly what I said to myself. I said, Here's the Band of Brothers robbing a bank – and here's two of the nastiest bits of work that ever come out of Whitechapel sitting in a café, two streets away from the scene of the crime, drinking tea. This'll stand looking into. So I parked my bike – I reckoned you could get on for a bit without me –'

'Thank you.'

'– and I hung around ... for hours and hours. They must've got through twelve cups of tea, each. Just before seven o'clock they come out and took a train back to Paddington. I went with 'em. At Paddington they got on the Metropolitan, got off at Kings Cross, and walked towards the Angel. There were quite a few people about by that time. I don't think they spotted me.'

Petrella was prepared to believe that. Wilmot's urchin figure would have melted as effectively into the background of Kings Cross as any animal into its native jungle.

'They fetched up at a big builder's yard in Arblay Street. Jerry Light and Company. They walked straight in.'

'Do you think they work there?'

'It looked like it. But that wasn't all. I hung round for a bit. Half a dozen others went in. I recognized one of them. It was Stoker. Remember him?'

'Albert Stoker,' said Petrella. 'Yes. I remember him. He tried to kick my teeth in when I was up at Highside. He was working with Boot Howton and the Camden Town boys.'

'If they're all like that,' said Wilmot, 'they're First Division stuff.'

'Mr. Jerry Light would bear looking into,' agreed Petrella.

That afternoon Petrella paid a visit to Arblay Street. Jerry Light's establishment occupied most of the north side. It was the sort of place that only London could have produced. What was originally an open space between two buildings had been filled, in the passage of time, with a clutter of smaller buildings,

miscellaneous huts, sheds, and leanto's, on top of, or propped
up against, each other. Such space as remained was stacked with
bricks, tiles, window frames, chimney pots, kitchen sinks,
lavatory bowls, doors, pipes, and cisterns. An outside flight of
steps lifted itself above the cluster to a door at first-story level
which was labelled, MR. J. LIGHT.

As he watched, this door opened and a man came out. He was
a very large man, with a cropped head, red face, and closely
clipped moustache. A thick neck rose from magnificent
shoulders and chest. It was a Sergeant-Major's figure – the sort
of figure which time, and inertia, would play tricks on,
reversing the chest and the stomach as inevitably as sand
reverses itself in an hour-glass. But it had not done so yet. Mr.
Jerry Light was, he judged, not more than 45 and his eyes were
still sharp as he stood surveying his cluttered kingdom.

Petrella walked away.

Back at Scotland Yard he said to Edwards, 'See if Records has
anything on a Mr. Jerry Light. He runs a builder's yard at
Islington. Wilmot, I think it'd be a good idea if you went along
and asked for a job.

'Suppose Stoker recognizes me? I had a bit of trouble with
him myself at Highside, remember?'

'I'm counting on Stoker recognizing you. Then if you're still
given the job, it'll prove that Light's honest. If you don't get it,
the chances are the outfit's crooked.'

'Suppose they drop a chimney on me!'

'Then we shall *know* they're dishonest,' said Petrella. He had
little fear for Wilmot. He was extremely well equipped to look
after himself ...

Edwards was the first to report.

He said, 'Gerald Abraham Light. He *has* got a record. In 1951
he was sentenced to twelve months' imprisonment at the Exeter
autumn assizes for waylaying and assaulting the manager of the
Exeter branch of the District Bank.'

'Robbery?'

'Not robbing, sir. Assaulting. They knocked two of his teeth
out, kicked in his ribs, and broke an arm.'

'They?'

'There was another man. Alwyn Corder. He got twelve months too.'

'Why did they do it?'

'No motive was suggested at all. Mr. Justice Arbuthnot, in his summing-up, called it, "a particularly cowardly and senseless assault." '

Petrella's mind wasn't on Mr. Justice Arbuthnot. He had experienced a very faint, almost undetectable tremor of excitement – like that of a patient angler near whose bait a fish had swum, not seizing it but troubling it by his passage.

'Alwyn Corder,' he said. 'It's not a common name. I could bear to know what he's doing today.'

'If he's had any other convictions, he should be easy to trace,' said Edwards. 'Incidentally, Light hasn't. That's the only time he's ever stepped out of line.'

'It's the only time he's ever been caught,' said Petrella.

It was seven o'clock that evening before Wilmot returned. C12 kept irregular hours. Sergeant Edwards was filing some papers. Jane Orfrey was filing her nails. Petrella was watching Jane Orfrey.

'Hired and fired,' said Wilmot.

'To start with, it all went like love's old sweet song. Mr. Light said I was just the sort of young man he was looking for. Clean, healthy, and not afraid of work. He explained how he ran his outfit too. He works for big building contractors. Say one of them's doing a clearance job at Southend and wants extra help. Light sends a gang down. However many men he wants. Light takes a ten per cent cut of their wages. They reckon it's worthwhile, because he keeps 'em in regular work.'

'What went wrong?'

'What went wrong was, just as I was about to sign on, in comes Stoker.'

'What happened?'

'It was a bit of an awkward moment, actually. Stoker went bright pink, and said he'd like a word outside with Mr. Light. So they stepped outside, shut the door, and I heard 'em yawning. Then Mr. Light came back and said, very polite, that he hadn't got a vacancy right now, but he'd let me know if he had one. So I scarpered – keeping my chin on my shoulder, in case anyone tried to start anything.'

'Lucky they didn't.'

'I'll say it was lucky,' said Wilmot. 'Because if they had started anything, they might have spoiled this.'

He took a handkerchief out of his side pocket and unwrapped it carefully. Inside was a lump of cobbler's wax. Impressed in the wax was the outline of a key.

'The key was on the inside of the door,' said Wilmot. 'I got it out while they were talking. Nice impression, isn't it? I know a little man who'll make it for us while we wait.'

Petrella said, 'Are you suggesting that we break into this office?'

'That's right.'

'And if we're caught we shall both be sacked.'

'That's why I'm not planning to get caught, personally,' said Wilmot.

It was half an hour after midnight when they backed the little van into the passageway behind Light's yard. A veil of drizzling rain had cut down visibility to a few yards.

'Perfect night for crime,' said Wilmot. 'You hold the ladder. I'll go first. I think I saw some broken bottle on the top of this wall.'

Petrella gave him a minute's start, then followed. Negotiated with care, the ragged *cheveux-de-frise* presented little obstacle. Petrella let himself down on the other side, and Wilmot's hand grabbed his foot and steered it onto an upended cistern.

Five minutes later they were in Jerry Light's office, carefully fastening the blanket Wilmot had brought with him over the only window. Petrella then turned on his lantern torch and stood it on the floor.

'Better get cracking,' he said. 'It looks like a lot of work.'

One closet contained box files full of bills, invoices, and trade correspondence. Another was devoted to builders' catalogues, price lists, and samples mixed with old telephone and street directories, technical publications, and an astonishing collection of paperback novels. The desk was full of mixed correspondence and bills. The safe in the corner was locked.

Three hours of hard work convinced Petrella that Light had a perfectly genuine business.

'There's only one thing here I don't quite understand,' he said. 'Why should he bother to keep a seven-year-old diary in the top drawer of his desk? Anything you kept close at hand like that you'd expect to be important, wouldn't you?'

'Probably forgot to throw it away.'

'But why keep a seven-year-old one, and throw away the other six?'

Wilmot came across to have a look.

'There's something else odd about it too,' said Petrella. 'Do you see?'

Wilmot focused his torch on the open book and studied it.

'Doesn't seem to mean a lot,' he said. 'There's something written on each page. Sort of shorthand. Perhaps it's business appointments.'

'That's what I thought at first. But would he have business appointments on Sunday too?'

'Doesn't seem likely,' agreed Wilmot. 'What are you going to do?'

'We can't take it away. If it's important, he's bound to miss it. We'll have to photograph it.' He produced from his coat pocket a small black box. 'We'll prop it up on the desk. Shine your torch on it, and turn each page when I say.'

It took them an hour to finish the job, replace the book, and tidy up.

'If there's anything important,' said Petrella, 'it's in the safe. I'm afraid that's beyond us.'

'You never know,' said Wilmot. 'I found this key in that closet. It's just the sort of place people do hide their safe keys. See if it fits.'

Petrella took the key, inserted it in the lock, and exerted

pressure. There was a tiny sensation of prickling in his fingers, and the key turned.

'Nice work,' said Wilmot. 'Let's see what he keeps in the old strongbox. Hello! What is it? Something wrong?'

Petrella had relocked the safe. Now he walked across and replaced the key in the closet. He did this without haste, but without loss of time.

'We're getting out of here,' he said. 'That safe's wired to an alarm. I set it off when I turned the key.'

He picked up the torch from the floor and made a careful tour of the room. There wasn't a great deal to do. But it took time.

'All right,' Petrella said at last. 'When I turn out the torch, get the blanket down.'

'Nick of time,' said Wilmot.

They could both hear the car coming ...

As they locked the office door behind them and went down the steps into the yard, headlights swivelled round the corner throwing the main gate into relief. Brakes screamed; a car door slammed; a voice started giving orders.

Wilmot lay across the wall, leaned down, and pulled Petrella up beside him. There was no time for finesse. Petrella heard the cloth of his trousers rip on the broken glass as he swung his legs across, felt a stinging pain in his thigh, and the warm rush of blood down his leg.

Then he was following Wilmot down the ladder. As he reached the ground, Wilmot's hand grabbed his arm.

Footsteps were echoing along the pavement.

Wilmot put his mouth close to Petrella's ear. 'They've sent someone round the back,' he said. 'I'll have to fix him.'

Petrella nodded. The blood was running into his shoe.

Wilmot crouched, pressed against the wall. The dim form of a man appeared at the mouth of the passage and came on, unsuspecting. Wilmot straightened up, and hit him, once, from below, at the exact point where trousers and shirt joined.

The man said something which sounded like 'Aaargh,' and folded forward onto his knees. As Wilmot and Petrella picked their way past him, he was still fighting for breath.

'What *are* these?' said Jane Orfrey.

'They're ten-magnification enlargements of microfilm shots of the pages in a seven-year-old desk diary.'

'But what do they mean?'

'If I knew that,' said Petrella, 'I'd known whether I risked my professional career last night for something or for nothing. I want you to go through every entry. I expect it's a code – the homemade sort that's so damned difficult to decipher – where U.J. can mean Uncle Jimmy, Ursula Jeans, *and* the Union Jack. You'll need a lot of patience with it.' Jane said, 'We got something useful this morning. Do you remember Mallindales? The instalment buying house. It was in answer to one of our circulars about marked and series notes.'

There were two things, thought Petrella, about Jane Orfrey. The first was that she said *we* quite naturally, identifying herself as a member of the outfit. The other was that she had carried out every job she had been given without once saying, 'I'm only here to type letters.' He wondered, not for the first time, how they had been lucky enough to get her.

'You're not listening to a word I'm saying.'

'I'm sorry,' said Petrella. 'We've had a lot of answers in to that particular inquiry.'

'Mallindales told us they had a special stamp which they used on all their banknotes. Remember? The point about it was that it didn't appear to mark the notes at all. But if you held one of them flat, and looked across it in an oblique light, you'd see the letters MD.'

'I remember now,' said Petrella. 'They'd paid in a couple of hundred marked notes the day before the Maritime Bank at Liverpool was broken open. They thought we might locate some of them, because the thieves wouldn't realize they were marked.'

'We *have* located one. It turned up yesterday, in the possession of a character called Looney Bell. He's a small-time thief, who was picked up by the Highside police for illicit door-to-door collection.'

'And this was part of the money he'd collected?'

'That's right. The only person – he says – who gave him a banknote was the local parson.'

Petrella considered the matter. A clergyman who gave away pound notes to strangers who came to the door sounded like an unusual character.

'He might be worth looking into.'

'Wilmot's looking into him now.'

'He's cracked,' reported Wilmot, when he came back after tea. 'He tried to give *me* a pound. He said I looked like a very nice young man.'

'Who is he?'

'The Reverend Mortleman, Vicar of St. John at Patmos, Crouch End. When I'd convinced him that I was a police officer and not a Good Cause, he spun me a yarn about a party who gave him money to give to the deserving poor. Some old girl with more money than sense, who knew Mortleman when he was an assistant clergyman at St. Barnabas, Pont Street, I gather. He wouldn't tell me her name.'

'That sounds plausible,' said Petrella. 'A lot of rich people go to St. Barnabas. One of them might be sending him money for his local charities.'

'I could probably find out who it was if I made a few inquiries.' Petrella considered the matter. He had to be careful not to disperse the efforts of his small force by chasing red herrings. 'Let it stop there for the moment,' he said. 'I'll get the local boys to watch out. If they find any more of these MD notes circulating in those parts, we'll reconsider.'

The next MD note arrived from quite a different source. A waiter at the Homburg-Carleton, going home in the early hours of the morning, started by accusing a taxi driver of overcharging him, then assaulted him, and finished up in custody. The station sergeant, checking his belongings before he was put into a cell, found three pound notes in his wallet, all marked with the Mallindales stamp, and brought them round personally to New Scotland Yard.

Petrella said, 'Three of them together! That looks more like it.

Where did he say he got them from?'

'He said they were his share of that evening's take.'

'Then they must have come from someone dining at the Homburg. Good work, Sergeant. We'll follow it up.'

Jane Orfrey spent the afternoon with the restaurant manager, and came back with a list of three public dinners, five private dinners, and the names of the 84 people who had actually booked tables that night.

'It's impossible to identify their guests,' she said. 'And there were one or two people who came in without booking.'

'It's not so bad,' said Petrella. 'Agreed, we can't do anything about the people who didn't book. But there weren't a lot of those. And why bother about the guests? Guests charge it to their bills. As for the big dinners, it's only the organizers of those who matter. A bit more work and we can boil this down to quite a short list.'

'Suppose we boil it down to twelve names,' said the girl. 'What do we do then? Go and ask them all if they know any bank robbers?'

Petrella looked at her curiously. 'You need a break,' he said. 'You've been overworking.'

Jane said stiffly, 'It's the most interesting job I've ever done. I don't want to fall down on it, that's all.'

'When we heard we were going to get a secretary,' said Petrella, 'I remember Wilmot said' – at this point, he remembered what Wilmot *had* said, and improvised rapidly – ' "As we're the youngest Department, we're bound to get the worst secretary." I think we had a bit of luck there. I think we got the best.'

'It's nice of you to say so.'

'It must have been a slip-up in the typing pool. They'd earmarked someone like Mrs. Proctor for us, and they pulled the wrong card out of the filing cabinet.'

'I don't think the typing pool had much say in the matter,' said Jane. 'I was posted here direct by Uncle Wilfred.'

'Uncle Wilfred?'

'The Assistant Commissioner. He's my mother's elder brother.'

'Good heavens,' said Petrella, thinking back quickly over some of Wilmot's strictures on the top brass. 'You might have told us sooner.'

'You're the only person I have told,' said Jane.

Petrella, looking at his watch, was surprised to see that it was nearly half past seven. He was on the point of saying 'Let's go out and get something to eat,' when it occurred to him that Jane might think he was asking her out because she was the Assistant Commisioner's niece.

He swallowed the words, and said an abrupt, 'Good night.'

After he had gone, Jane sat for a whole minute staring at the closed door. Then she said out loud, 'Silly cuckoo. You oughtn't to have told him. Now he's clammed up again.'

When Petrella arrived at Scotland Yard on Monday morning, he could almost feel the thunder in the air. He went straight to Chief Superintendent Baldwin's office.

'You got my note?' said Baldwin.

'I didn't get any note,' said Petrella, 'but I heard the early morning news. It's not too good, is it?'

'It's damned bad,' said Baldwin. 'Two jobs on the same night. The Manchester one was the biggest haul yet. What was really unfortunate was that the bank knew they were vulnerable – it was one of the payoff days for the Town Centre Reconstruction – and they'd asked the police to keep a special watch.'

Petrella said, 'How did they get in?'

'It was clever. One thing the police were on the lookout for was empty premises, near the bank. There weren't any. Just a block of offices, all let. The people who pulled this job must have planned it six months ago. That was when they took this office, two away from the bank. They cut through the wall, crossed the intervening office after it closed on Saturday, cut through the second wall, broke into the bank itself, and opened the strongroom some time on Sunday night. No one heard them. It isn't a residential area.'

'What now?'

'Now,' said Baldwin grimly, 'the local force, prodded by the banks, are asking us to help, and when they say help, they mean something more than research and coordination.'

'What did they have in mind?'

'Two or three mobile teams of special officers, working on the lines of the murder squad.'

Petrella felt cold.

'That'll be quite an organization,' he said. 'I suppose we should be swallowed up in it.'

Seeing his face, Baldwin laughed and said, 'It may never happen. But it means we've got to get results, quick. How far have you got?'

It was a question Petrella found embarrassing to answer. It seemed pompous to say, 'We're still analyzing information. You can't expect results until the analysis is complete.' So he said, 'We've one definite line. It may lead somewhere.' He explained about Jerry Light.

'Do you think he runs the whole show?'

'I don't think so, no. My guess is that he runs the heavy mob. This organization has its own Flying Squad. When a job's being done, one or two of them will be on hand to get back the equipment, and collect the organizer's share of the loot.'

'If that's so,' said Baldwin, 'there must be a link between Light and the head man.'

'We're working on that angle,' said Petrella. He thought it wiser not to say too much about the diary, or the circumstances in which it had come into their possession. 'Another way would be to trace the equipment, from the factory. It would mean going over to West Germany.'

'That could be fixed,' said Baldwin. 'We'd need a few days to make the arrangements. You'd go yourself. Do you talk any German?'

'Enough to get on with,' said Petrella, in German.

When he got back to his room, he was tackled by Sergeant Edwards, with a worried face.

'You'd hardly think,' he said, 'that a man with an uncommon name like Alwyn Corder could disappear off the face of the earth, would you?'

So much had happened recently that it took Petrella a
moment to think who Alwyn Corder was. Then he said, 'You
mean the other man, the one who helped Light assault that bank
manager, at Exeter?'

'Yes. Corder was one of the joint managing directors in a
demolition firm. Light worked for the same firm.'

'Managing director? Are you sure?'

'Quite sure. It's all in the company office records. The other
director was a Douglas Marchant. Marchant and Corder started
the firm just after the war. It went broke in 1952. I've searched
every record we possess – not only the Directories, but Electors
Registers, Motor Car Licence lists, Passport Office lists –'

'Perhaps he's dead.'

'The Register of Deaths at Somerset House was the first place
I searched.'

'Well,' said Petrella. 'Perhaps –' and got no further, because
Wilmot came in like an express train.

'Guess what?' he said. 'A third banknote's turned up, *and
we've got a cross reference.*'

Three heads went up, like three nestlings offered food.

'A jobbing printer in New Cross. Luckily he used the note for
a subscription to the local police charity. When they saw the
mark, they took it back to him, and he said it was part of a
payment he'd had that morning for a job he'd done printing the
souvenir menus for a charity dinner' – Wilmot paused with
considerable artistry – 'at the Homburg-Carleton.'

'Good work,' said Petrella softly. 'Which charity?'

'It's a Society which sends kids to the seaside.'

Petrella turned up his list. 'That's right,' he said. 'The
S.S.H.U.C. They were having a show that night. Can't be a
coincidence.'

'Who was the organizer?' said Jane.

'Mrs. Constantia Velden, O.B.E.'

'I'm sure I know the name. Doesn't she do a lot of these
things? She's almost a professional organizer.'

'Out of my line.'

'It's in mine,' said Jane. 'I did a London season.'

She departed.

There was a lot of checking and cross-checking to be done, and it was after six before she came back. Sergeant Edwards and Wilmot had gone home. Petrella saw, from the pink patches in her cheeks and the sparkle in her eye, that something had happened.

'I've located your woman organizer,' she said. 'She lives in a very nice house in St. Johns Wood, with a cook, a chauffeur and three dalmations. Oozing with money and good works.'

'What else?'

'How do you know there's something else?'

'Because you're almost bursting to tell me.'

'I've a good mind not to,' said Jane. 'Well, all right. As a matter of fact, it didn't take very long to find out about Mrs. Velden. And it was a nice day. So I went up on to Crouch End and saw the Reverend Mortleman.'

'The devil you did! What did you say?'

'I said I was Mrs. Velden's secretary, and she was a bit anxious, because he hadn't acknowledged the last lot of money she'd sent him.'

Petrella stared at her.

'He was most upset. Said he was sure he had acknowledged it. He insisted on me coming in, so that he could find a carbon copy of his letter to Mrs. Velden. He did find it too. So I apologized. Then we had tea together.'

When Petrella had recovered his breath he said, 'You were taking a bit of a chance, weren't you? Suppose he'd known Mrs. Velden's secretary by sight.'

'He couldn't have known her new one.'

'Her new one?'

'She's been advertising in *The Times*. That's what gave me the idea. Couldn't I answer the advertisement?'

Before Petrella could string together some of the many ways of saying no to this outrageous proposal she hurried on.

'I don't suppose Mrs. Velden's a master criminal. She certainly doesn't sound like one. But all this money is coming *through* her. She must have some connection with the organizers. If I was working for her, and kept my eyes open, I could probably spot –'

Petrella found his voice at last. 'You're not even a policewoman,' he said. 'You're a typist.'

It wasn't, perhaps, the best way of putting it. Jane turned dark red, and said, 'Of all the stupid, stuffy, ungrateful things to say –'

'I'm sorry ...'

'Don't you *want* to solve this? Don't you *want* to find out who's running it?'

'Now you're being silly.'

'At least I'm not being pompous.'

Petrella said, 'I'm sorry if I sound pompous, but what you don't seem to realize is that I can't possibly let you take an active part in this, without getting into frightful trouble with the Establishment.' He added hastily, 'It's very late and we're both a bit tired, I expect. Come and have something to eat.'

'Thank you,' said Jane, 'but as a typist, I know my place.' She made a dignified exit.

Petrella swore, and took a running kick at the metal wastepaper basket. It rose in a neat parabola and broke a window.

Next morning Petrella made a point of getting to the office early. He found Jane alone there, typing furiously. He selected the most propitiatory of half a dozen opening gambits which he had worked out during a sleepless night.

Before he could start, Jane said, 'I'm sorry I was stupid last night. Obviously you couldn't do it.'

This took the wind out of Petrella's sail so effectively that he could only stare at her.

'As a matter of fact,' he said at last, 'I had a word with the A.C. – with your uncle, that is – and he said that, compared with some of the things you'd tried to talk him into letting you do, this sounded comparatively harmless.'

'Bully for Uncle Wilfred.'

'But he laid down certain conditions. First, you're to report,

by telephone, to this office every night between five and seven.
Use a call box, not a private telephone. Second, if ever you're
going out anywhere, you're to let us know where you're going.'

'It all seems a bit unnecessary to me,' said Jane. 'But I'll do it
if you insist.'

'All that remains now is for you to get the job.'

'I rather think I've got it. I went round to see Mrs. Velden last
night. It turned out that she knew a friend of a friend of my
mother's. We got on like a house on fire.' Seeing the look in
Petrella's eye, she added hastily, 'Of course, if you'd said no, I
wouldn't have taken the job. I thought there was no harm in
seeing if I could get it. And I'll remember to telephone you every
night.'

'It won't be me for the next few nights,' said Petrella gently.
'I'm off to Germany.'

The Baron von der Hulde und Oberath propelled a cedarwood
cabinet of cigars across his desk toward Petrella, helped himself
to one, lit both of them with a long match, and picked up the
photograph again.

'Certainly this is one of our drills,' he said.

'How long has it been in production?'

'Five years. A little more.'

'And in that time how many have you exported to England?'

'I should have to consult my records. Perhaps a hundred.'
Petrella's heart sank.

'It is a highly efficient drill,' said the Baron. 'I sent half a
dozen the other day to one of your Safe Deposits.'

'Safe Deposits?'

'A good Safe Deposit only possesses one key for each of its
safes. If the depositor loses it, the safe has to be broken open.
The screws of the hinges have to be drilled out – but it takes an
exceptionally good drill to do it. Any ordinary one would break,
or melt. A number of cooling devices had been tried before.
None successfully. Then we invented this method, It is so very
simple. As the drill gets hotter, it sweats. Just like the human
body. It exudes its own lubricant. We call it "film cooling." '

'I see,' said Petrella. 'And no one else but you makes these drills?'

'We have the world patent.'

'Then you could compile, from your records, a list of people in England whom you have supplied?'

'I could no doubt do so, but it might take a couple of days.'

'It'll be worth waiting for.'

'When the list is ready I will telephone your hotel. The Goldenes Kreuz, isn't it? Take another cigar with you, please. You can smoke it this evening.'

First, he stood himself a large, and rather heavy, meal at the Barberina. Then he moved on to one of the many beer cellars in the Augusta Platz and ordered a stein of what described itself as the world-famous Münchner Löwenbräu, which tasted no better and no worse than any lager beer he had drunk in an English pub.

On the wall opposite was an advertisement, depicting a man with a monocle smoking a cigar. It looked like a stylized version of the Baron von der Hulde und Oberath. As this thought occurred to him, another one crossed his mind, and he put down his beer slowly.

The Baron had said, 'I will telephone your hotel – the Goldenes Kreuz.' How did he know which hotel to telephone? Petrella had certainly not told him.

He went back, very carefully, over the events of the morning. He had driven straight from the airport to the headquarters of the city police, to check in with Inspector Laufer, a contact arranged for him by Baldy. The Inspector had given him the names of the possible manufacturers of drills, of which the Baron had been the largest and the most likely.

Might the Inspector have telephoned the Baron, to tell him Petrella was coming, and might he have mentioned the name of his hotel?

No. That was impossible. For the simple reason that Petrella had not, at that time, chosen a hotel. He had gone to the Goldenes Kreuz after leaving the police station.

It was at this point that his thoughts became linked with a

suspicion which had never been quite out of his mind since he had left the hotel.

He was being followed.

It was impossible to say how he knew, but now that he gave his mind to it, he was quite certain. In London the discovery would not have worried him. Here, in a foreign country, in a strange city, it was less agreeable.

His first idea was to telephone Inspector Laufer, but he dismissed it as soon as he thought of it. There was no explanation he could make which would not sound ludicrous. Dortmund might not be beautiful, but it was a well-organized modern city, with an efficient police force, and well-lit streets. All he had to do was to walk back to his hotel, go up to his room, bolt the door on the inside, and go to bed.

He paid his bill, recovered his coat and hat, and climbed the steps which led up to the street.

A storm of rain had cleared the air and emptied the streets. He stepped out briskly. No one seemed to be taking the least interest in him. Halfway down the Augusta Platz he had to turn right, into the smaller street which would, in turn, bring him to the Station Square.

It was at this moment that he heard the car start off behind him. Something in the note of the engine sounded a warning. He jerked his head round, and saw the car coming, straight at him.

Without stopping to think, he jerked himself to one side, spotted a narrow side street ahead, and ran down it. It was when he heard the car going into reverse that he realized his mistake. He should have stuck to the main street.

The side street stretched ahead of him, badly lit, absolutely empty, sloping steeply downhill. Behind him, the headlamps of the car flicked on, pinning him.

He reckoned he had a good twenty yards' start. On his left stretched the unbroken wall of a large building; no entrance, not even a recess. The right-hand side was blocked by a high iron railing.

He put on speed. There was a T junction at the bottom, and

what looked like a rather better-lighted road. He swung round the corner. The car, which had been catching up, cornered behind him.

Petrella sidestepped. His plan was to turn in his tracks, and run in the opposite direction before the car could turn. He had reckoned without the driver. As he side-stepped, the car swerved too. The wing caught him in the small of the back, scooped him up, and tossed him against the fence which bordered the road.

The car screamed to a halt, and went into reverse.

Petrella was lying at the inner edge of the pavement, close to the fence. There was a stabbing pain in his chest, and he seemed to have lost the use of his legs.

He could see the driver now, with his head out of the side window. He had a heavy, white, bad-tempered face.

As he watched, the driver manoeuvered the near-side wheels of his car carefully up onto the pavement, judged the distance to where Petrella lay, and started to reverse.

When he's been over me once, thought Petrella, he'll come back again just to make sure. Petrella's legs were like sacks of sand, but he still had the use of his arms. Pressing on the pavement, he rolled himself over, and then over again until he was pressed hard against the bottom of the wooden fence.

It was no use. The car was on him now. The near-side wheels were going over him.

Petrella heaved wildly, felt the skirting board at the foot of the fence bend, and heaved again. There was a dull crack. A complete length of board gave way, and Petrella went rolling, over and over, down a grassy bank to come to rest with a thud at the bottom.

He was on gravel. His groping hand found a wire, and he hauled himself up on his knees. The fall had done something for his legs, which were now hurting as much as his chest; but they seemed to be answering signals again. He crawled forward, pulling himself by the wire.

The fence rocked and splintered as his pursuers, too bulky to squeeze through the space underneath, battered it down.

Petrella crawled faster.

Behind him he heard the fence go down with a crack.

There was a circular opening on the left. It looked like a drain. He crawled into it, until a bend in the pipe forced him to stop. Footsteps thundered past. Men were shouting. There was a rumbling, thudding noise, which shook the ground; a hiss of steam, and the clanking of iron on iron.

For the first time he realized that he was on a railway line. The wire he had been following must have been a signal wire. What he was in now was some sort of rainwater conduit. There was plenty of water coming down it too.

More voices, angry voices. Official voices. A dog barking.

Petrella pushed himself backward until he was out in the open again. Some way up the line an argument was going on. Orders were being shouted in loud, angry German.

Petrella propped himself against the bank, and started massaging the life back into his sodden legs. A dog slipped out of the darkness, and stood watching him.

'Good boy,' said Petrella hopefully. The dog gave a sharp bark, like a Sergeant-Major calling the parade to attention.

Two men appeared. They were in the green uniform of the railway police. As soon as they saw him, both of them started to shout.

When they seemed to have finished, Petrella said in impeccable German, 'Conduct me, at once, if you please, to Inspector Laufer, of the Municipal Police.'

Even the dog seemed impressed by this.

Constantia Velden was a compulsive talker. She didn't really need a secretary, Jane Orfrey decided. What she needed was a captive audience. And Jane, for two whole days, had been it.

There were advantages, of course. Within an hour, and without any actual effort on her part, she had learned almost all there was to know about Constantia; about her late husband, who had been an administrative officer in the Air Force, and had died of hepatitic jaundice in 1955; about her brother, Douglas, a Wing Commander, D.S.O., D.F.C., now the managing director of a firm manufacturing window frames, with a London office in Lennox Street; about Constantia's charitable enterprises; about the time Constantia had shaken hands with the Queen; about life; about money.

Money seemed to come into most of Mrs. Velden's calculations. Reading between the lines, Jane deduced that she had inherited a reasonable competence from her late husband, and that she was helped out, where necessary, by her brother. He advised her on her investments and looked after her tax. He had also brought Alex into the picture, and probably paid his salary as well.

Alex was the only other resident at the Loudon Road house, and was chauffeur, butler, gardener, and footman combined. A husky, brown-haired, freckled boy, who looked no more than sixteen and was in his early twenties. He did everything that was beyond the strength or capacity of Mrs. Velden and her cohort of daily women. What spare time Alex had, he spent polishing his employer's car and tuning up his own motorcycle.

He was out with her now. A lunch date with brother Douglas, she gathered. Jane munched her way through a solitary meal, and wondered, for the twentieth time, what possible connection her talkative, middle-aged employer could have with an organization which had made bank robbery a fine art. Her faith told her that the connection was there. After 48 hours, her reason was beginning to doubt it.

It was three o'clock before the car reappeared in Loudon Road and Alex jumped out and held the door open for Mrs. Velden. Jane caught a glimpse of her, and of the man who followed her out. So Douglas had accompanied his sister home. Interesting.

Then the drawing-room door opened, and he came in, holding it open for his sister and closing it behind her.

He was a man of about six foot, with the round shoulders and barrel chest of a boxer; thick black hair, graying round the edges; a face dominated by a long straight nose which turned out, suddenly, at the end, over a bush of gray moustache. Like a downpipe, she thought, emptying into a clump of weeds. A disillusioned pair of eyes peered out from under thick black eyebrows.

'Wing Commander Marchant, Jane Orfrey.'

'Plain Douglas Marchant, if you don't mind,' said the man. 'You're my sister's new secretary. Has she driven you mad yet?'

'Really, Douglas …'

'If she hasn't, she will. She goes through secretaries at the rate of two a week. She's a Gorgon. She doesn't realize that the days of indentured labour are over. There are more jobs than secretaries. Girls please themselves. Isn't that right?'

'More or less,' said Jane.

'As soon as you present yourself to an agency they offer you a dozen jobs, and say, Take your pick.'

'It isn't quite as easy as that.'

'What agency do you use, by the way?'

It came out so swiftly that Jane gaped for a moment, and said, 'As a matter of fact, I got this job through an advertisement.'

'But you must have an agency,' said Douglas gently. 'You'll never get properly paid if you don't.'

'Really, Douglas,' said Constantia. 'Are you trying to lure her away?'

'I don't see why not. I don't mind betting you underpay her.'

'Perhaps she doesn't want to work in an office.'

'I think it would be terribly dull,' said Jane.

'You wouldn't be dull in my office,' said Douglas. 'Eighteen pounds a week, and luncheon vouchers.'

Jane felt it was time she asserted herself. 'If I had to work in an office,' she said, 'I'd choose a professional office, I think. Not a commercial one.'

'There, if I may say so, you display your ignorance,' said Douglas. 'Professional men overwork their staff and underpay them. They operate on too small a scale to do anything else. We're just the opposite. We've got factories all over England. There's hardly a building goes up that hasn't got our windows in it.'

'You may be right,' said Jane. 'But personally I find businessmen so boring. They think and talk of nothing but money.'

'What businessmen have you worked for?' inquired Douglas politely.

Damn, thought Jane. I walked into that one. Better watch out. He's a lot cleverer than he looks.

'Two or three,' she said. And to Constantia, 'Should I see if we can raise a cup of tea?'

'Not for me,' said Douglas. 'I've got to be off. A bit of money grubbing to do. I'll get Alex to drive me back into town, if you don't mind.'

Jane telephoned Sergeant Wilmot at six o'clock that evening, from a call box on Hampstead Heath. 'This is urgent,' she said. 'See what you can find out about Douglas Marchant. Ex-R.A.F. Runs a business which makes windows. Not widows – windows. It's got a head office in Lennox Street, and factories all over the place.'

'Wasn't he the other director in the firm Light worked for, just after the war?'

'That's right. And he's Mrs. Velden's brother. He gives her money. Any banknotes she's been passing could easily have come from him.'

'I suppose they could have.'

She could hear the doubt in Wilmot's voice, and said urgently, 'We're looking for a man who *could* run a show like this. Well, I'm telling you, Douglas Marchant fills the bill. I can't explain it all over the telephone. But he's big enough and bad enough –'

'A big bad wolf,' said Wilmot. 'Okay, I'll take your word for it. We'll certainly have him checked up.'

'Any news from Germany?'

'Not a word,' said Wilmot.

As Jane came out of the telephone booth she heard a motorcycle start up and move off. When she got back the house was in darkness, and she let herself in with her own key, and went into the drawing room.

She felt restless and uneasy, and had no difficulty in putting her finger on the cause of it. The powerful and unpleasant personality of Douglas Marchant seemed to linger in the room, like the smell of a cigar long after its owner had departed. She realized that it was the first time she had been alone in the house.

Leaving the light on in the drawing room, she went along to what Constantia called her business room at the end of the hall. Her objective was Constantia's desk. She found that all the drawers in it were locked, so was the filing cabinet, and so were the closets under the bookcases which lined one wall. The books in the shelves were mostly political and military history, and this surprised her, until it occurred to her that they probably represented the departed Mr. Velden's taste rather than Constantia's.

She took down one of the six volumes of Lloyd George's *War Memoirs*, blew the dust off the top, and opened it.

From an ornate bookplate the name jumped out at her – ALWYN CORDER.

Jane stared at it in blank disbelief. Then she started taking down books at random. The bookplate was in most of them. For a moment she was unable to think straight. She knew that she had stumbled on something desperately important.

A slight sound at the door made her swing around. Alex was smiling at her. 'Looking for something to read?' he said.

Sergeant Edwards said to Wilmot, 'It's a big company. Douglas Marchant is the chairman. Leaves most of the work to his staff, and comes up twice a week from the country to justify his director's fees.'

'Anything known?'

'As far as Records know, the company and Marchant are both as clean as two proverbial whistles. What have we got on them?'

'What we've got,' said Wilmot, 'is a woman's instinct. Jane doesn't like his smell. She thinks he's a bad one.'

'It doesn't seem a lot to go on,' said Edwards doubtfully. 'When's Petrella coming back?'

'Baldy hasn't heard a chirrup out of him for twenty-four

hours,' said Wilmot. 'If you ask me, he's found himself a Rhinemaiden.'

It was after midnight when the bedside telephone rang. The redheaded girl, who had been sharing Douglas Marchant's flat, and bed, for the past month, groaned and said, 'Don't take any notice, Doug. It's probably a wrong number.'

'Hand it over,' said Douglas, who was lying on his back beside her. He balanced the instrument on his stomach and unhooked the receiver. As soon as he heard the voice at the other end he cupped a hand over the receiver and said, 'Out you get, honey. It's business.'

'This is a nice time to do business.'

'Get up and get us both a cup of tea.'

Not until the girl had grumbled her way into a dressing gown and out of the room did Douglas remove his hand from the receiver and say, 'Sorry, Alex, there was someone here. It's all right now. Go ahead.'

His pyjama top was unbuttoned, showing a chest fuzzed with graying black hair. One of his thick hands held the telephone. The other was fumbling on the bedside table for a cigarette. His face was expressionless.

At the end he said, 'Let's see if I've got this straight. Each of the three evenings she's been there, she's been out about the same time and made a call from a public phone booth. And this evening you found her in the library, snooping through a lot of books which had the old bookplates still in them. Damn, damn, *and damn.*'

There was a long silence as if each was waiting for the other to speak.

Then Douglas said, 'If she's what we think she is, and if she's got a regular reporting time, she won't pass any of this on until six o'clock tomorrow night. We ought to do something about it before then, I think.'

Alex said, 'Yes, I think we ought.'

'I can't attend to it myself. I'm flying over to Germany tomorrow afternoon. There's been some trouble at the factory.

Could you think of an excuse to take her out in the car?'

Alex said, 'Suppose I said I had left some papers at the office which had to be taken to the airport – and you had a message for your sister – something like that.'

'It's worth trying,' said Douglas.

'When I get her in the car – what then?'

'My dear Alex, I must leave all the arrangements to you. A moonlight picnic, perhaps.'

As he rang off, the red-haired girl came back with two cups of tea. Douglas drank his slowly. He didn't seem to want to talk. The redheaded girl thought that Douglas, though a generous spender, was a tiny bit odd, and had been becoming odder just lately.

Now the look in his eyes frightened her. At the age of 25 she was something of an expert on men, and she made up her mind, there and then, to clear out while Douglas was in Germany – and not to come back.

When, late the following afternoon, Alex told Jane that he had to collect some papers and take them to the airport, and that she should go too so that he could give her a message for his sister, her first reaction was to say no. Then she reflected that no harm could really be planned on the crowded roads between Central London and London Airport.

'I'll have to ask Mrs. Velden,' she said.

'I've asked her. She says the trip'll do you good.'

'When do we start?'

'Right now.'

'I'll have to get a coat,' said Jane.

She ran up to her room and stood listening. The house was quiet. She tiptoed across the corridor and into Mrs. Velden's bedroom. As she had hoped, there was a bedside telephone extension. She grabbed the receiver, and dialled the special number which she knew by heart.

'Hello,' said Wilmot's voice. 'What's up?'

'No time to explain,' said Jane. 'Alex is taking me, in Mrs. Velden's car, to London Airport. We're calling at the Lennox Street office first. Can you put a tail on?'

'Can do,' said Wilmot. 'But why –'

He found himself talking to a dead telephone. Jane had gone.

It was half past five by the time they reached Lennox Street. While Alex was inside, Jane looked cautiously round to see if Wilmot had been as good as his word. She could see a small green van, apparently delivering parcels at the far end of the road, but nothing else.

By six o'clock, with dusk coming up, they were across Kew Bridge, and had joined the tail end of the home-going traffic on the Twickenham Road.

'Quicker this way,' said Alex, 'until they've finished messing about with the flyover on the Great West Road. Trouble is, everyone else knows it too. Let's try a short cut.'

He swung expertly across the traffic and turned into a long road of neat houses, with neat gardens and neat cars in neat garages. At the far end of the road the street lamps petered out and they came to a halt in an area of empty lots and high fences.

'It's a dead end,' said Jane.

'Not the last time I came here, it wasn't,' said Alex. 'Let's have a squint at the map. It's in the pocket.'

As he leaned over her, she felt the needle go into her arm. For a moment she thought it was an accident – that a loose pin in Alex's coat might have stuck into her. Then she realized what had happened, and started to fight, but Alex was lying half on top of her, his thick leather driving glove feeling for her mouth.

A minute later the boy sat back in his seat, and relaxed cautiously. He had given her a full shot of pelandramine. She'd be out for an hour, and dopey for another hour after that. So there was no hurry.

He looked at himself in the driving mirror; and was pleased with the unexcited face that looked back. He stripped off the driving gloves and felt his own pulse, timing it with his wrist watch. 84. Twelve faster than it should be, but not bad. He took out a comb and ran it through his hair.

Then he examined the girl. Her mouth was open and she was breathing noisily. Her cheeks were flushed. Anyone looking at her would think that she'd been drinking too much, and had passed out. Just the ticket.

He felt in the right-hand doorpocket and took out a small bottle of gin. A few drops round her mouth and chin. A little on her dress. Enough for people to smell it, if he was stopped.

He opened the door. There was no one in sight. He threw the gin bottle and the empty hypodermic syringe over the fence, got back, turned the car, and drove off slowly the way he had come.

The mist was thicker. At the Slough roundabout he took the Staines road, driving carefully now. He crossed Staines Bridge, following the Egham road. At Egham the road forked. The main road, with its string of garages, its traffic and its orange neon lighting, went away to the left. The right fork, a much smaller road, followed the river toward Windsor. In summer this road too would be crowded with traffic heading for the open spaces of Runnymede Meadow. Now, on a damp February night, it was empty.

Half a mile along, Alex turned out his headlights and drove very carefully off the road and onto the rough grass. There was some danger of getting the car bogged down, but his town-and-country studded tires would grip most surfaces. There was a worse danger. Somewhere ahead was the Thames, its bank unprotected by any fence.

Alex stopped the car, got out, and walked forward, counting his paces. It was fifty yards to the bank. He came back, climbed in, and drove the car forward cautiously in low gear.

When he stopped again, he was only five yards from the edge. At this point, where the bank curved, it had been reinforced with concrete bags against the sweep of the winter floods. A yard below his feet, the river ran, cold, gray, and sleek.

Alex walked back to the car. Jane had slumped over sideways, so that when he opened the door she nearly fell out. He got his hands under her body and lifted her onto the wet grass.

Alone, islanded by the mist, touching the girl's body, moving it, arranging it, gave him a sense of power, near to exultation. He crouched beside her for a full minute to let the singing noise in his ears die down and the lights stop flashing in front of his eyes. Then he got up slowly, went round to the back of the car, opened the boot compartment and took out two fourteen-pound weights and a coil of odd-looking plaited cord.

With the cord he tied Jane's wrists together in front of her, passing the ends through the handles of the weights and knotting them.

When he stood up, he saw three pairs of yellow eyes looking at him through the mist. He thought, for a moment, that it was his imagination playing tricks again. The he heard the engines, growling to themselves, as the cars bumped across the grass in low gear, closing in.

He bent quickly, hoisted the girl onto his shoulders, and walked to the bank.

A man's voice shouted urgently, and an orange spotlight flicked on.

Alex humped his powerful shoulders, threw the girl ahead of him into the water, and jumped after her. While he was still in mid-air, a second body flashed past him.

Jane came up out of a tangle of nightmare, of darkness and cold, of lights and noises, into the reality of a hospital bed. The sun was slanting through the uncurtained window, and Sergeant Wilmot was perched on a chair beside her.

'Good morning,' he said. 'Are you ready to talk?'

'I'm all right,' said Jane. 'I'll get dressed, if you can find my clothes.'

'The doctor says he'll let you out in a day or two, if you're good. Let's have the story.'

She told him what she could remember, and Sergeant Wilmot wrote it down in his round, schoolboy hand.

'I felt the needle go in my arm,' she said. 'I don't really know what happened after that.'

'Alex took you in the car to Runnymede, and pitched you into the river. Having first tied a couple of weights onto you. I wonder how many of his girl friends he's got rid of that way before?' He pulled a length of cord out of his pocket. 'Simple, but you've got to hand it to him. It's clever. It's made of paper.

Twenty or thirty separate strands of it, plaited tight together. Strong enough – but it'd melt after you'd been a day or two in the water.'

Jane shuddered uncontrollably, and Sergeant Wilmot said, 'I never had much tact,' and put the cord away.

'Who pulled me out?'

'I did,' said Wilmot. 'It's the sort of thing you sometimes get a medal for. We were behind you all the way. If it hadn't been for the fog and the mess up on Staines Bridge we'd have been close enough to stop you going in the water.'

'What's happened to Alex?'

'He's in the hospital at the Scrubs. In a private room. And that's where he's going to stay until Patrick gets back.'

'Haven't we heard anything yet?'

'He's been off the air for nearly forty-eight hours. He'll turn up. Don't worry.'

'Who said I was worrying?'

'You looked worried. Just for a moment.'

Jane laughed and said, 'If I'm going to be kept here, you can do something for me. Get me those photo-copies of the diary pages, and a classified directory of London. I've had a hunch and I want to work it out.'

When Wilmot had gone, she stretched luxuriously, and then settled down into the warm bed. She liked the way Wilmot called Petrella, Patrick; and she wondered if she'd ever be able to do it herself. A minute later, she was asleep …

At eleven o'clock on the following morning the door of her room opened. Jane, who was deep in a street directory, her bed covered with slips of paper, said, 'Put in a down on the table, could you, nurse –' looked up, and saw that it was Petrella.

'Hello,' she said.

'As soon as my back's turned,' said Petrella, 'you have to go and do a damn silly thing like that.'

'Listen who's talking,' said Jane. 'What have *you* been up to? And what's wrong with your leg?'

'Someone tried to run me over. I rolled down a bank onto a railway.'

'Well, I fell into a river. That's not much worse.'

They both laughed. Petrella sat down on the end of the bed, and said, 'You know why they had to shut your mouth, don't you?'

'Something about those books. I couldn't work it out.'

'Listen, and I'll tell you. In 1951 two men were sentenced at the Exeter assizes for assaulting a bank manager. One was our friend Jerry Light of Islington. The other was one of the managing directors of the demolition firm he worked for. A man called Alwyn Corder, who disappeared so completely that even Sergeant Edwards couldn't trace him. Because the simple explanation eluded us all. When Corder came out of prison, *he changed his name to Velden.* All legal and above-board, by deed poll, registered in the High Court. I checked it this morning. And in that name he married Constantia Marchant, Douglas Marchant's sister. It was a business alliance. Douglas was his fellow director in the demolition firm.'

'I see,' said Jane. 'Yes, I see.' A lot of tiny pieces were falling into place, and a certain pattern was appearing.

'There's a lot that isn't clear yet,' said Petrella. 'But the outline's there. Douglas Marchant, and Alwyn Corder, his brother-in-law, now known as Kenneth Velden, and their old foreman, Jerry Light, are the three people who started this racket, and ran it. That's for sure. Then Velden died. The other two couldn't simply hang on to his share. They paid it over to his widow.'

'Then Douglas *is* head of the whole affair?'

'It's got to be proved.'

'And it would help to prove it if you could show that he was still keeping in touch with Jerry Light?'

Petrella grinned, and said, 'Cough it up.'

'Cough *what* up?'

'Whatever it is you've discovered.'

'All right. It's this diary you found in Light's desk. The entries are meeting places – they're pubs. *Rsg Sn* is the Rising Sun. *Wdmn* is the Woodman, and so on. The letter and numbers after the pub are the postal district, and the last number's the time of day. That's what first made me think they must be pubs, because the times are all between eleven and two, or six and ten.'

Petrella got up, and stood for a long moment staring down at her.

Then he said, 'That's very good indeed,' limped across to the door, and went quietly out, shutting the door behind him.

'Douglas Marchant,' said Petrella to Baldwin, 'makes windows. The windows go into new buildings all over England. In nearly all big building projects the subcontractors get paid on the same day in the month. Therefore, there must be a lot of money in the main contractors' bank the day before. That's how the intelligence system works. When the bank has been chosen, a gang of specialist safebreakers do the actual work. Jerry Light gives them their instructions, and their kit. And his men collect the appropriate rake-off after the job's over. That's what the Franks brothers were waiting for, in Slough, that morning.'

'How are we going to prove all this?'

'If we could get one of Jerry Light's boys to sing, he *might* give us Light. *If* we hooked Light, he *might* give us Marchant.'

'You don't sound very hopeful.'

'They're going to be a tough bunch to drive that sort of wedge into. They've been working together too long, and they know each other too well.'

'Have you any better ideas?'

'Yes,' said Petrella slowly. 'I have an idea, but it's so irregular that we're going to need all the backing the A.C. can give us. First, I want Jerry Light's phone tapped.'

Baldwin made a face. 'You know what they think about that, don't you? Anything else?'

'That's just a start,' said Petrella. 'The next really is a bit hot. Now, listen –'

At London Airport the loudspeaker in the Arrival Lounge said, 'We have a message for Mr. Douglas Marchant, believed to be traveling from Dortmund. Would Mr. Marchant report to the reception desk?'

Douglas hesitated for a long moment.

If things really had started to happen, might it not be wisest to turn straight round and take the next airplane back to Germany?

He rejected the idea as soon as it occurred to him. It was by abandoning careful, prearranged plans and acting on the impulse of blind panic that people gave themselves away and got caught. He marched firmly up to the reception desk and smiled at the girl behind it.

He produced his passport. 'I understand you have a message for me.'

'Mr. Douglas Marchant? Would you telephone this number? You can use the telephone in the office, if you wish.'

'Thank you,' said Douglas. He dialled the number, which he recognized as his sister. Constantia's.

'Douglas. Thank heavens you're back. I didn't know where to get hold of you, so I had to leave a message at the airport.'

'What's happened?'

'Alex and Jane Orfrey have both disappeared. And they've taken the car with them.'

'When did this happen?'

'Two nights ago. I've been so worried.'

'You've told the police?'

'Of course. But they've done nothing. They even suggested' – Douglas heard his sister choke – 'that they might have eloped together.'

'I suppose it's possible.'

'Don't be absurd. Alex was a chauffeur – a mechanic –'

'And Jane was your secretary.'

'That's different. She was a girl of good family.'

Douglas was about to say something flippant, when he realized that his sister was upset; and being upset, might do something stupid.

'I'll make some inquiries,' he said. 'I'll ring you back as soon as I have any news for you.'

As soon as he had rung off, he dialled another number. The girl who answered the telephone said, 'Who's that? Mr. Wilberforce. I'll see if Mr. Simmons is in.' And a few seconds later, 'No, I'm sorry. He's just gone out. Can I get him to ring you back?'

'Don't bother,' said Douglas. 'When he does come back, would you give him a message? Tell him that I got the letter he sent me on the third of March.'

'Right char,' said the girl.

As soon as she had rung off, she walked through to the inner office and said. 'That was Mr. Wilberforce, Mr. Simmons. You did say you weren't in if he telephoned.'

'That's what I said,' agreed Mr. Simmons, a short, sharp-looking man in thick bifocals. 'And that's when I meant. Did he leave a message?'

'He just said that he got the letter you sent on the third of March.'

'You're sure he said the third of March?'

'I'm not deaf yet,' said the girl.

'All right,' said Mr. Simmons. 'Plug a line through to this telephone, and you can go to lunch.'

''Tisn't lunchtime.'

'Then go and buy yourself a new hat.'

Mr. Simmons listened until he heard the outer door shut, drew the telephone toward himself, and dialled an Islington number.

Jerry Light, who answered the telephone, said, 'You're sure it was the third of March he said? All right. Thanks very much,' and rang off. He opened the drawer of his desk, extracted the diary that lay there, and opened it at the first week in March.

Then he looked at his watch. It was just after twelve. He crammed a hat on his head, went down the outside staircase into the yard, said, 'Watch things, Sammy. I'm going out,' to the shaggy young man who was sawing a length of timber, and set off at a brisk pace. He seemed to be walking haphazardly, choosing small empty streets. But his course was steadily northeast.

One o'clock was striking when he went through the door of a small public house in the neighbourhood of Hackney Downs, said, 'Wotcher, Len,' to the landlord, and walked through the serving area into the private room behind.

Douglas Marchant was sitting in front of the fire, nursing a glass of whiskey. He indicated another glass, ready poured, which stood on the table.

Light said, 'Ta,' took a drink and added, 'I take it you saw the news.'

'That's why I came back from Germany. All that the papers said was that Alex got out of the hospital at the Scrubs yesterday morning and clean away. No details. It mightn't be true.'

'It's true all right,' said Light. 'He telephoned me this morning.'

Marchant's lip went up. 'At your place?'

'No. He had sense enough not to do that. He got me through Shady Simmons.'

'Did he tell you how he got picked up?'

'He thinks it was just bad luck. A police patrol car spotted him tipping the girl into the river.'

'I don't believe in bad luck like that,' said Marchant. 'Do you?'

'Not really,' said Light. 'I think they're moving in on us.'

'What did Alex want?'

'A place to hide out in. He spent last night on the Embankment. And for you to get him out of the country.'

'Or what?'

'So far, he's kept his mouth shut. If he did decide to talk, he could tell them a hell of a lot they want to know.'

Marchant drank a little more whiskey. 'We'll have to do something about him,' he said. 'The only place he'd be safe would be in East Germany.'

'I can think of somewhere that'd be a damned sight safer,' said Jerry.

A red coal dropped from the fire. The clock on the mantelshelf ticked. In the bar, Douglas could hear the landlord saying, 'Nice sort of day for March.' He had said it to every customer who came in.

Douglas finished his drink and got up. He said, 'I think you're right. We're going to pack up this lark soon. We don't want any loose ends. I've got to go and hold my sister's hand – she's having hysterics. We'll go out the back way.'

As the two men emerged from the alleyway, a girl approached them. She had a collector's tray of little red and white flowers. 'For the Cottage Hospital,' she said. She was a nice-looking girl. Douglas felt in his pocket, found half a crown, dropped it in her tin, and said, 'Keep the flower. You can sell it again.'

The girl said, 'Thank you, sir.' Douglas noticed that she had an outsize flower with a black center pinned onto the shoulder of her dress.

At nine o'clock that night Jerry Light left his flat in Albany Street and walked to the garage where he parked his car. The attendant said, 'She ought to be all right now.'

In the act of getting into the car, Light paused, 'What do you mean, now?'

'Now the distributor head's been fixed.'

'I didn't tell you to do that.'

'It wasn't us. The man came round from the makers with it. He fixed it himself.'

'Oh,' said Light. 'Yes. Of course. I'd forgotten about that. He fixed it, did he? Come to think of it, I won't be needing the car just now. I've changed my mind.'

He left the garage, hailed a taxi, and was driven through Regent's Park to Clarence Gate. Here he dismissed the taxi. Five minutes' quick walk brought him to a row of garages in a cul-de-sac behind Baker Street station.

Light was tolerably sure that no one knew about his second car. It was a new M.G. Magnette, with a capacious boot compartment in which he had stored two bulging suitcases and a carry-all. He had rented the garage in another name, had installed the car in it three months before, and had not visited it since.

The only trouble was that it was now raining so hard that it was difficult to keep observation as he walked. He didn't think anyone was following him, but was not quite sure.

He backed the car out and drove slowly into the park, which he proceeded to circle twice. Headlights showed, blurred by the rain, in his mirror. Cars overtook him. Cars passed him. At the end of the second circuit he was reasonably happy, turned out of the park at Gloucester Gate, and headed north.

'He's making it damned difficult for us,' said Wilmot into his car wireless. 'I wish he'd used his first car. I'd got that fixed nicely. All we'd have had to do then would be sit back and track him on the radio repeater. Over.'

'Count your blessings,' said Petrella into his wireless. 'If it wasn't raining so damned hard, he'd probably have spotted us long ago. Over and out.'

Jerry Light drove steadily up Highgate Hill, across the North Circular Road, and on toward Barnet. His plan was very simple. He was not a believer in elaboration. His instructions to Alex had been to come by Underground to High Barnet and then to walk out onto the main North Road and along it for a quarter of a mile, past the golf course, timing himself to get to the point where the road forked by eleven o'clock. Alex was to come alone, and make damned sure he wasn't followed.

Light looked at his watch. He was in nice time. Five minutes to eleven, and that was High Barnet station on the right. The rain was coming down like steel rods. Alex must be getting very wet.

Light followed the main road past the Elstree fork. There was very little traffic. A couple of London-bound cars came toward him over the long swell of the hill. There was nothing behind him as far as he could see.

His headlights picked out Alex standing by the roadside.

Light crawled to a stop beside him. Leaning across, he turned down the far side window. He used his left hand to do this. His right hand was resting on the floor of the car.

'That you, Jerry?' said Alex. 'I'm damned wet.'

'It's me,' said Light. He brought up his right hand, and shot Alex twice through the chest at point-blank range.

Alex jerked back onto his heels, went down to his knees, and fell forward, his face in the water which was cascading down the gutter.

Resting his forearm on the ledge of the window, Light took careful aim, and shot again.

The repeated detonations had deafened him, and he could hear nothing. The first thing he noticed was that headlights, backed by a powerful spotlight, had come on behind him. He slammed the car into gear, almost lifting it off the ground as he drove it forward.

A siren sounded.

The car behind him was almost on top of him. Light saw, out of the corner of his eye, a minor road to the left, swerved sharply, and went into a skid.

On a dry surface it would have come off, but the wet macadam was like ice. Instead of correcting at the end of the skid, the car swung wildly out of control, went through the fence, wires twanging like harp strings, turned, once, right over, and smacked into the concrete base of a pylon, dislocating two of the overheard lines and plunging half of High Barnet into darkness and confusion.

So Petrella came for a second time into the presence of Assistant Commissioner Romer, and came with the heavy consciousness of failure.

'I reckoned,' he said, 'that if we let Alex go, they'd be in a cleft stick. Either they left him in the lurch, in which case he'd split. Or they helped him, and we caught them red-handed. Now Alex is dead, and we're further off than ever from proving any connection between the crooks who do the work, and the man at the top, who draws the big profits.'

'Douglas Marchant?'

'Yes, sir. I've no doubt in my own mind that he's the man who founded the organization, and who runs it.'

'It's not just what's in your mind,' said Romer. 'There's a good deal of concrete evidence too. That was a nice photograph our girl collector with the flowers got of him, talking to Light, outside the pub.'

'He could explain that, sir. He's in windows. Light's a builder. It could have been an ordinary business chat.'

'Light's a criminal,' said Romer, 'a man who committed a cold-blooded murder a few hours after meeting Marchant secretly at an out-of-the-way public house. I don't doubt that he could explain the coincidence. Most things can be explained, if you try hard enough. Here's another one. Two days ago, Marchant went across to Germany. He visited your old friend, the Baron von der Hulde und Oberath. They had a long talk. The German police have got a man in the packing department. He saw Marchant coming and going, and is prepared to identify him. Last night there was a fire at the factory.'

'A fire!'

'Nothing serious. It broke out in the dispatch department, and destroyed all records of dispatches during the last five years.'

'I see,' said Petrella.

'It's particularly intriguing because our man remembers, four or five days ago, helping to pack and dispatch a drill – to a place called Fyledean Court, near Lavenham, in Wiltshire.'

'Did you say a *drill*, sir?'

'Curb your excitement. It wasn't a drill for drilling holes in metal plates. It was a drill for planting seed potatoes. Curious, all the same, that the dispatch records should have been destroyed immediately afterwards.'

'It's going to be even more difficult to prove anything now.'

'There's one rule I always follow,' said Romer. 'When you get a smack in the eye, don't sit down. Get up and counterattack at once. I spoke to the Chief Constable of Wiltshire before you came in. He's promised to cooperate with you in every way.'

'Cooperate in what, sir?'

'You're going down with the search warrant which I've secured for you, and you're going to turn Fyledean Court upside down.'

'But –' said Petrella.

'But what, Inspector?'

'If I *don't* find anything. isn't there going to be the most awful row?'

'I'm prepared to accept that risk,' said Romer coldly. 'He shouldn't have tried to have my niece drowned. I'm rather fond of her.'

Petrella drove, while Wilmot read the map.

'We'll go down to Christchurch first,' he said.

'I thought we were going to Lavenham.'

'We're going to call on Mr. Wynne.'

'Who's Mr. Wynne, when he's at home?'

'Mr. Wynne,' said Petrella, 'was, until he retired, the manager of the Exeter branch of the District Bank.'

'The old boy Light and Corder assaulted.'

'That's right,' said Petrella. 'That's where this story began. I want to hear about it, before we tackle Douglas.'

It was a lovely day. The early March sun was bright, but not yet very warm. Spring was round the corner, waiting for its cue.

Wilmot abandoned the map and said, 'To hell with it! You know what? You ought to do something about Jane.'

'Which Jane?' said Petrella, but the car had swerved a full foot to the right before he corrected it.

'Is there more than one?' said Wilmot innocently. 'I mean Jane Orfrey, the girl detective, the pride of the Women Police. The one I pulled out of the river a week ago.'

'What do you suggest I ought to do about her?'

'You could always marry her. If the worst came to the worst, I mean.'

Petrella drove in silence for nearly a quarter of a mile, and Wilmot, who knew him better than most people, began to kick himself for having presumed.

At last Petrella said, 'I've never proposed to a girl. I wouldn't know how to start.'

'Don't worry,' said Wilmot, relieved. 'It's all a matter of technique. You get in front of her, and work your feet up till you're pretty close. Then you distract her attention – and grab her with both hands. Under the arms, high up, is a favourite –'

'You make it sound like unarmed combat.'

'It is a bit like that. Mind you, you'll find Jane's got a pretty high standard, now she's been kissed by a real expert.'

'What expert?'

'Me,' said Wilmot. 'When I pulled her out of the water, I had to use the kiss-of-life technique. Smashing. It'll probably go better still when she's conscious –'

'Certainly I remember Marchant and Corder,' said Mr. Wynne. 'It's such a beautiful morning. Let's step out into the garden. I have good cause to remember,' he went on. 'One of my ribs never really mended. I get a sharp twinge there if I stoop suddenly.'

He was one of those men who look old when they are young, and young when they are old. The lines on his face were the deep lines of age, but his eyes had the brightness, his skin the pinkness, of youth. He's looked exactly like that, Petrella decided, for half a century; like a tough old tree.

'I read all about the assault those two men made on you,' Petrella said, 'but what interested me most was the suggestion that your refusal to grant this company credit was based on some sort of personal feeling.'

'Personal feeling?' Mr. Wynne drew his lips in sharply, then puffed them out again like a goldfish after an ant's egg. 'They must have imagined that. Bank managers aren't allowed much personal discretion. All substantial overdrafts are referred to Area.'

'But in this case it was suggested that you refused to recommend credit because of some sort of quarrel.'

'If there was a quarrel,' said Mr. Wynne, 'it was very one-sided.' He stared up at an airplane, from Hurn on the cross-Channel run, which was gaining height in a leisurely circle against the pale blue-green sky. 'I can remember the managing director – his name was Marchant, and he'd been in the Air Force – coming to see me in my office one morning. I hadn't quite made up my mind what I was going to recommend.

He wanted a very large credit, but he had reasonable security, and the company had quite a good financial record. When I said that I should need time to think about it, he got very angry.' A slight smile played across the corners of Mr. Wynne's mouth. 'Very angry indeed. He said that I'd promised him the credit and that I must let him have it.'

'And had you?'

'Of course not,' said Mr. Wynne. 'Are you fond of tomatoes?'

They had drifted to the bottom of the garden. Along the fence which separated the garden from the recreation ground was quite a pretentious greenhouse. The far side was covered with wire netting.

'I have trouble with the children throwing things,' explained Mr. Wynne. 'Children seem to be brought up without discipline today. I have forced some early Cardinal Joys – they're pentagams, of course. Would you like to try one?'

'No, thanks,' said Petrella. 'You were telling me about Marchant making a scene in your office.'

'Yes. He lost his temper, and threatened me. I wasn't impressed.'

'When you say he threatened you – do you mean physically?'

'I thought at one moment that he was going to strike me. He went very red, jumped to his feet, and came round to my side of the desk.' Mr. Wynne blinked.

'And what did you do?'

'I told him to control himself. After a while he did so, and went away.'

'And after that you decided not to recommend him for credit.'

'If you mean that I nursed a grudge against him, you're quite mistaken. I shouldn't allow my personal feelings to enter into a matter like that. It did, of course, occur to me that a man who had so little control over himself might not be the safest person to conduct a business. That big fellow there is an Ecbalium Agreste, or squirting cucumber –'

*

'Pickled gherkins,' said Wilmot to Petrella, as they drove northward to keep a mid-day rendezvous with the Chief Constable. 'Are all bank managers like that?'

'They tend to clothe themselves in the armour of their own rectitude,' said Petrella. 'But I should think Mr. Wynne is an extreme specimen.'

'No wonder Marchant blew his top. Old Wynne would have saved the banks a few shocks in the last seven years if he'd been a bit more tactful with him, wouldn't he?'

It was nearly four o'clock when they first caught sight of Fyledean Court. They had taken the Tilshead road, across the wastelands which form the central hump of Salisbury Plain. Then they had dropped down off the escarpment, leaving behind them the barren acres of the Firing Range, back to the civilization of the Lavenham Valley. It was like coming out of war into peace.

Fyldedean Court lay at the head of a long, curving, shallow valley. A private approach road ran north from the Lavenham-Devizes road through unfenced fields of stubble, sloping up to a windbreak of black and leafless trees.

At the turn of the road Petrella stopped the car.

'You walk from here,' he said to Wilmot. 'Keep out of sight over the crest, and work your way in from behind. Pick up anything you can, while I keep 'em busy in front.'

He gave Wilmot five minutes' start, then drove slowly down the road to the Court, and rang the bell. A gray-haired woman answered the door, inquired his name in a broad Wiltshire accent, and showed him into a room which might have been a gunroom or a library according to its owner's tastes. There were a lot of bookshelves, but very few books; a clutter of catalogues, boxes of cartridges, bottles of linseed oil, and tins of saddlesoap.

He sat there for nearly ten minutes, listening to the life of the house and farm going on around him. A heavy truck drove up, discharged some load, and drove off again. Then Douglas Marchant came in.

'My housekeeper tells me that you're a policeman,' he said.

'Well –' began Petrella cautiously.

'Does that mean I can't offer you a drink?'

'There's no rule about it, but actually I won't have one just now.'

'You don't mind if I do,' said Marchant, and opened the large closet beside the fireplace. There were box files on the lower shelves, and a decanter and some bottles and glasses higher up.

Marchant helped himself to whiskey, put in a long splash of soda, and said, 'Well now.'

Both men were standing.

Petrella said. 'I'm a Detective Inspector attached to New Scotland yard. We've been investigating a number of bank robberies, which seemed to us to be connected – possibly organized by the same people.'

'They're smart operators,' said Marchant. 'I've read about them in the papers.'

'And I have a warrant to search your house.'

Exactly the correct reactions, Petrella observed. Incredulity, followed by anger, followed by an affection of ridicule. But then, he had had ten minutes to think it all out.

'If it isn't a joke,' said Marchant, 'and you really do suspect me of being connected with these – these bank robberies – would you spare a few minutes telling me why? If this house is full of – er – stolen goods – they'll still be here in ten minutes' time. Incidentally, I suppose that's one of your men I spotted, leaning over the gate at the back.'

Petrella said. 'Did you know a man named Light?'

'Jerry Light? Certainly. He was my Squadron Sergeant-Major during the war, and came in with me when I started a demolition and scrap metal business after the war.'

'Have you seen him since?'

'I see him whenever we happen to work on the same contracts. He supplies labour. I supply windows.'

'When did you see him last?'

'Two days ago – in London.'

'Why did you meet him in an out-of-the-way public house, and not at his office?'

'I do much more of my work in public houses than in offices.'

'I don't suppose you met Baron von der Hulde in a public house?'

Marchant looked surprised. 'You keep dodging about,' he complained. 'I thought we were talking about poor old Jerry.'

'*Poor* old Jerry,' said Petrella softly.

'You must know – he was killed – a motor smash. The night before last.'

'I knew,' said Petrella. 'I was wondering how you did. It hasn't been in the newspapers.'

'One of his employees told a business friend of mine. These things get round very quickly in the trade.'

'I'm sure they do,' said Petrella. 'Does everybody in the building trade also know that if Light hadn't been killed, he would have been charged with murder?'

Marchant stood up, his face went red and he said, 'If that's a joke, it's in poor taste. I've told you. Light was my friend.'

'So was the man he shot. Alex Shaw.'

'Alex –'

'Or am I wrong? Wasn't it you who found Alex the job as chauffeur to your sister, Constantia?'

'Certainly. But –'

'Into whose hands, incidentally, quite a few stolen banknotes seem to have found their way.'

'You're confusing me,' said Marchant. 'And you're going too fast. Are you telling me that Alex was a bank robber?'

'Alex was a very rare bird,' said Petrella. One half of his mind was occupied with what he was saying. The other half was noticing that Marchant was still standing up, and had put down his empty whiskey glass on the table. 'He was a professional killer. Not just a muscle man, like Franks and Stoker and the other simple hooligans Light employed to run your dirty business.'

'*My* business?'

'Yes. *Your* business. And that's really the oddest twist in the whole affair. Because, as far as I can see, you made bank robbery your business from motives of personal spite. You once had a good, legitimate business, and a bank killed it, so you decided to get your own back on all banks.'

Marchant walked over to the closet, which still stood half open, took out the decanter, poured himself out a second whiskey, and then said politely, 'Please go on.'

'There's not a lot more to it. You were well placed, of course. As a demolition expert you knew all there was to be known about cutting through brickwork and steel. Light, I imagine, was your contact with the professional criminal element. You supplied the equipment, mostly from Germany, organized the whole show, and took' – Petrella's eyes wandered round the room for a moment – 'I would guess, a very handsome share of the profits.'

Marchant said, 'Is that your curtain line? I'm sorry. Really I am. I haven't met anything more fascinating since I stopped reading comics. Now – get on with your search, apologize, and be off with you.'

The door opened, and Wilmot looked in.

'Sorry to interrupt,' he said. 'But I thought you ought to have this at once,' and he thrust a piece of paper into Petrella's hand.

Petrella read it and said, 'Thank you, Sergeant. Don't go away.' And to Marchant, 'That potato drill *that's just been delivered*. When you declared it at the Customs, did you tell them about the other piece of machinery?'

'What other piece?'

'Sergeant Wilmot hasn't had time to make a close examination, but he says that there appears to be a second piece of machinery screwed to the framework, inside the larger piece, and painted to resemble it. It looks like a high-speed metal drill. Curious requirement for a farmer.'

'I know nothing about it.'

'It would be an excellent way of bringing stuff into the country. You'd need some cooperation from the German manufacturer, of course.'

'On a level,' said Marchant, 'with your other fairy stories.' But he was sweating.

He's getting ready to jump, thought Petrella. But which way?

There are two of us here, now. I'm nearer the window. Wilmot's between him and the door.

'If you'd care to look at the declaration I made to the Customs –' He opened the closet door and the whole of the back of the closet hinged inward. Marchant went through it, and slammed the door behind him.

Petrella jumped at the same moment, but he was a fraction of a second too late. The closet door was shut, and immovable.

'Out into the passage,' he said.

Wilmot grabbed the handle, and pulled, but the door held fast. The mechanism at the back of the closet must have bolted the passage door as well.

'Damn it,' said Petrella. 'He had that lined up, didn't he?' As he spoke, he was looking round for a weapon. There was a poker in the grate, but it was too small to be much use. He opened another closet and found a twelve-bore gun in it. He made sure that it was unloaded, then grabbed it by the barrel and swung the butt at the window.

It was a narrow, leaded casement, and it took five minutes to beat an opening through it. Wilmot went first, and dragged Petrella after him. As they reached the farmyard they heard the airplane, and saw it taxi-ing out of the Dutch barn two hundred yards away.

'It's a Piper Aztec,' said Wilmot. 'Lovely little job. I spotted her as I came in. Take off and land on a tennis court.'

'We ought to have thought of that,' said Petrella. 'With his record – an airplane was the obvious thing.'

They could only stand and watch. The silver toy swung round, nose into the wind; a sudden burst of power, and it was away.

'We'll try the telephone, but I don't mind betting it's disconnected. The whole thing was laid out like a military operation. He went twice to that closet. Twice, *in front of my eyes*, to put me off my guard.'

The plane swung back almost overheard.

'Once he gets to Germany we can whistle for him. Come on.'

Wilmot didn't seem to hear him. He was still staring after the dwindling plane. 'He won't get to Germany,' he said. 'I emptied his main tank. There'll be enough in the starter tank and Autovac to get him as far as the coast.'

Petrella cut out the clipping from the *New Forest Advertiser*, and pasted it carefully into the scrapbook.

UNEXPLAINED FATALITY

The Piper Aztec two-seater aircraft, registration G/XREZ, which crashed on Tuesday evening at Christchurch has now been identified. The pilot, who died in the crash, was Wing Commander Marchant, D.S.O., D.F.C., of Fyledean Court, who has been farming in the Devizes locality for some years. Wing Commander Marchant was a popular figure locally and a generous contributor to all Service charities.

The cause of the accident has not yet been ascertained, but eyewitness accounts speak of the engine having cut out, which would suggest a mechanical defect or fuel stoppage. The pilot was evidently trying to land the aircraft on the local recreation ground. Tragically, he failed in the attempt by a few yards only, and crashed in the back garden of a Christchurch resident, Mr. Alfred Wynne, a retired bank official. Mr. Wynne's extensive tomato and cucumber house was entirely demolished.

This appeared the same day Petrella announced his engagement to Jane Orfrey.

Ed McBain

The Empty Hours

They thought she was colored at first.

The patrolman who investigated the complaint didn't expect to find a dead woman. This was the first time he'd seen a corpse, and he was somewhat shaken by the ludicrously relaxed grotesqueness of the girl lying on her back on the rug, and his hand trembled a little as he made out his report. But when he came to the blank line calling for an identification of RACE, he unhesitatingly wrote 'Negro.'

The call had been taken at Headquarters by a patrolman in the Central Complaint Bureau. He sat at a desk with a pad of printed forms before him, and he copied down the information, shrugged because this seemed like a routine squeal, rolled the form and slipped it into a metal carrier, and then shot it by pneumatic tube to the radio room. A dispatcher there read the complaint form, shrugged because this seemed like a routine squeal, studied the precinct map on the wall opposite his desk, and then dispatched car eleven of the 87th Precinct to the scene.

The girl was dead.

She may have been a pretty girl, but she was hideous in death, distorted by the expanding gases inside her skin case. She was wearing a sweater and skirt, and she was barefoot, and her skirt had pulled back when she fell on the rug. Her head was twisted at a curious angle, the short black hair cradled by the rug, her eyes open and brown in a bloated face.

The patrolman felt a sudden impulse to pull the girl's skirt down over her knees. He knew, suddenly, she would have

111

wanted this. Death had caught her in this indecent posture, robbing her of female instinct. There were things this girl would never do again, so many things, all of which must have seemed enormously important to the girl herself. But the single universal thing was an infinitesimal detail, magnified now by death: she would never again perform the simple feminism and somehow beautiful act of pulling her skirt down over her knees.

The patrolman sighed and finished his report. The image of the dead girl remained in his mind all the way down to the squad car.

It was hot in the squadroom on that night in early August. The men working the graveyard shift had reported for duty at 6:00 p.m., and they would go home until eight the following morning. They were all detectives and perhaps privileged members of the police force, but there were many policemen – Detective Meyer Meyer among them – who maintained that a uniformed cop's life made a hell of a lot more sense than a detective's.

'Sure, it does,' Meyer insisted now, sitting at his desk in his shirt sleeves. 'A patrolman's schedule provides regularity and security. It gives a man a home life.'

'This squadroom is your home, Meyer,' Carella said. 'Admit it.'

'Sure,' Meyer answered, grinning. 'I can't wait to come to work each day.' He passed a hand over his bald pate. 'You know what I like especially about this place? The interior decoration. The décor. It's very restful.'

'Oh, you don't like your fellow workers, huh?' Carella said. He slid off the desk and winked at Cotton Hawes, who was standing at one of the filing cabinets. Then he walked toward the water cooler at the other end of the room, just inside the slatted railing that divided squadroom from corridor. He moved with a nonchalant ease that was deceptive. Steve Carella had never been one of those weight-lifting goons, and the image he presented was hardly one of bulging muscular power. But there was a quiet strength about the man and the way he moved, a confidence in the way he casually accepted the capabilities and limitations of his body. He stopped at the water cooler, filled a paper cup, and turned to look at Meyer again.

'No, I like my colleagues,' Meyer said. 'In fact, Steve, if I had my choice in all the world of who to work with, I would choose you honorable, decent guys. Sure.' Meyer nodded, building steam. 'In fact, I'm thinking of having some medals cast, so I can hand them out to you guys. Boy, am I lucky to have this job! I may come to work without pay from now on. I may just refuse my salary, this job is so enriching. I want to thank you guys. You make me recognize the real values in life.'

'He makes a nice speech,' Hawes said.

'He should run the line-up. It would break the monotony. How come you don't run the line-up, Meyer?'

'Steve, I been offered the job,' Meyer said seriously. 'I told them I'm needed right here at the Eighty-seventh, the garden spot of all the precincts. Why, they offered me chief of detectives, and when I said no, they offered me commissioner, but I was loyal to the squad.'

'Let's give *him* a medal,' Hawes said, and the telephone rang.

Meyer lifted the receiver. 'Eighty-seventh Squad, Detective Meyer. What? Yeah, just a second.' He pulled a pad into place and began writing. 'Yeah, I got it. Right. Right. Okay.' He hung up. Carella had walked to his desk. 'A little colored girl,' Meyer said.

'Yeah?'

'In a furnished room on South Eleventh.'

'Yeah?'

'Dead,' Meyer said.

The city doesn't seem to be itself in the very early hours of the morning.

She is a woman, of course, and time will never change that. She awakes as a woman, tentatively touching the day in a yawning, smiling stretch, her lips free of color, her hair tousled, warm from sleep, her body richer, an innocent girlish quality about her as sunlight stains the eastern sky and covers her with early heat.

She dresses in furnished rooms in crumby rundown slums, and she dresses in Hall Avenue penthouses, and in the countless apartments that crowd the buildings of Isola and Riverhead and Calm's Point, in the private houses that line the streets of Bethtown and Majesta, and she emerges a different woman, sleek and businesslike, attractive but not sexy, a look of utter competence about her, manicured and polished, but with no time for nonsense; there is a long working day ahead of her.

At five o'clock a metamorphosis takes place. She does not change her costume, this city, this woman, she wears the same frock or the same suit, the same high-heeled pumps or the same suburban loafers, but something breaks through that immaculate shell, a mood, a tone, an undercurrent. She is a different woman who sits in the bars and cocktail lounges, who relaxes on the patios or on the terraces shelving the skyscrapers, a different woman with a somewhat lazily inviting grin, a somewhat tired expression, an impenetrable knowledge on her face and in her eyes: she lifts her glass, she laughs gently, the evening sits expectantly on the skyline, the sky is awash with the purple of the day's end.

She turns female in the night.

She drops her femininity and turns female. The polish is gone, the mechanized competence; she becomes a little scatterbrained and a little cuddly; she crosses her legs recklessly and allows her lipstick to be kissed clear off her mouth, and she responds to the male hands on her body, and she turns soft and inviting and miraculously primitive. The night is a female time, and the city is nothing but a woman.

And in the empty hours she sleeps, and she does not seem to be herself.

In the morning she will awake again and touch the silent air in a yawn, spreading her arms, the contented smile on her naked mouth. Her hair will be mussed, we will know her, we have seen her this way often.

But now she sleeps. She sleeps silently, this city. Oh, an eye open in the buildings of the night here and there, winking on, off again, silence. She rests. In her sleep we do not recognize her. Her sleep is not like death, for we can hear and sense the murmur of life beneath the warm bedclothes. But she is a strange woman whom we have known intimately, loved passionately, and now she curls into an unresponsive ball beneath the sheet, and our hand is on her rich hip. We can feel life there, but we do not know her.

She is faceless and featureless in the dark. She could be any city, any woman, anywhere. We touch her uncertainly. She has pulled the black nightgown of early morning around her, and we do not know her. She is a stranger, and her eyes are closed ...

The landlady was frightened by the presence of policemen, even though she had summoned them. The taller one, the one who called himself Detective Hawes, was a redheaded giant with a white streak in his hair, a horror if she'd ever seen one. The landlady stood in the apartment where the girl lay dead on the rug, and she talked to the detectives in whispers, not because she was in the presence of death, but only because it was three o'clock in the morning.

The landlady was wearing a bathrobe over her gown. There was an intimacy to the scene, the same intimacy that hangs alike over an impending fishing trip or a completed tragedy. Three A.M. is a time for slumber, and those who are awake while the city sleeps share a common bond that makes them friendly aliens.

'What's the girl's name?' Carella asked. It was three o'clock in the morning, and he had not shaved since 5 P.M. the day before, but his chin looked smooth. His eyes slanted slightly downward, combining with his clean-shaven face to give him a curiously oriental appearance. The landlady liked him. He was a nice boy, she thought. In her lexicon the men of the world were either 'nice boys' or 'louses.' She wasn't sure about Cotton Hawes yet, but she imagined he was a parasitic insect.

'Claudia Davis,' she answered, directing the answer to Carella whom she liked, and totally ignoring Hawes who had no right to be so big a man with a frightening white streak in his hair.

'Do you know how old she was?' Carella asked.

'Twenty-eight or twenty-nine, I think.'

'Had she been living here long?'

'Since June,' the landlady said.

'That short a time, huh?'

'And *this* has to happen,' the landlady said. 'She seemed like such a nice girl. Who do you suppose did it?'

'I don't know,' Carella said.

'Or do you think it was suicide? I don't smell no gas, do you?'

'No,' Carella said. 'Do you know where she lived before this, Mrs. Mauder?'

'No, I don't.'

'You didn't ask for references?'

'It's only a furnished room,' Mrs. Mauder said, shrugging. 'She paid me a month's rent in advance.'

'How much was that, Mrs. Mauder?'

'Sixty dollars. She paid it in cash. I never take checks from strangers.'

'But you have no idea whether she's from this city, or out of town, or whatever. Am I right?'

'Yes, that's right.'

'Davis,' Hawes said, shaking his head. 'That'll be a tough name to track down, Steve. Must be a thousand of them in the phone book.'

'Why is your hair white?' the landlady asked.

'Huh?'

'That streak.'

'Oh.' Hawes unconsciously touched his left temple. 'I got knifed once,' he said, dismissing the question abruptly. 'Mrs. Mauder, was the girl living alone?'

'I don't know. I mind my own business.'

'Well, surely you would have seen ...'

'I think she was living alone. I don't pry, and I don't spy. She gave me a month's rent in advance.'

Hawes sighed. He could feel the woman's hostility. He decided to leave the questioning to Carella. 'I'll take a look through the drawers and closets,' he said, and moved off without waiting for Carella's answer.

'It's awfully hot in here,' Carella said.

'The patrolman said we shouldn't touch anything until you got here,' Mrs. Mauder said. 'That's why I didn't open the windows or nothing.'

'That was very thoughtful of you,' Carella said, smiling. 'But I think we can open the window now, don't you?'

'If you like. It does smell in here. Is – is that her? Smelling?'

'Yes,' Carella answered. He pulled open the window. 'There. That's a little better.'

'Doesn't help much,' the landlady said. 'The weather's been terrible – just terrible. Body can't sleep at all.' She looked down at the dead girl. 'She looks just awful, don't she?'

'Yes. Mrs. Mauder, would you know where she worked, or if she had a job?'

'No, I'm sorry.'

'Anyone ever come by asking for her? Friends? Relatives?'

'No, I'm sorry. I never saw any.'

'Can you tell me anything about her habits? When she left the house in the morning? When she returned at night?'

'I'm sorry. I never noticed.'

'Well, what made you think something was wrong in here?'

'The milk. Outside the door. I was out with some friends tonight, you see, and when I came back a man on the third floor called down to say his neighbor was playing the radio very loud and would I tell him to shut up, please. So I went upstairs and asked him to turn down the radio, and then I passed Miss Davis' apartment and saw the milk standing outside the door, and I thought this was kind of funny in such hot weather, but I figured it was *her* milk, you know, and I don't like to pry. So I came down and went to bed, but I couldn't stop thinking about that milk standing outside in the hallway. So I put on a robe and came upstairs and knocked on the door, and she didn't answer. So I called out to her, and she still didn't answer. So I figured something must be wrong. I don't know why. I just figured ... I don't know. If she was in here, why didn't she answer?'

'How'd you know she was here?'

'I didn't.'

'Was the door locked?'

'Yes.'

'You tried it?'

'Yes. It was locked.'

'I see,' Carella said.

'Couple of cars just pulled up downstairs,' Hawes said, walking over. 'Probably the lab. And Homicide South.'

'They know the squeal is ours,' Carella said. 'Why do they bother?'

'Make it look good,' Hawes said. 'Homicide's got the title on the door, so they figure they ought to go out and earn their salaries.'

'Did you find anything?'

'A brand-new set of luggage in the closet, six pieces. The drawers and closets are full of clothes. Most of them look new. Lots of resort stuff, Steve. Found some brand-new books, too.'

'What else?'

'Some mail on the dresser.'

'Anything we can use?'

Hawes shrugged. 'A statement from the girl's bank. Bunch of canceled checks. Might help us.'

'Maybe,' Carella said. 'Let's see what the lab comes up with.'

The laboratory report came the next day, together with a necropsy report. In combination, the reports were fairly valuable. The first thing the detectives learned was that the girl was a white Caucasian of approximately thirty years of age.

Yes, white.

The news came as something of a surprise to the cops because the girl lying on the rug had certainly looked like a Negress. After all, her skin was black. Not tan, not coffee-colored, not brown, but black – that intensely black coloration found on primitive tribes who spend a good deal of their time in the sun. The conclusion seemed to be a logical one, but death is a great equalizer not without a whimsical humor all its own, and the funniest kind of joke is a sight gag. Death changes white to black, and when that grisly old man comes marching in there's no question of who's going to school with whom. There's no longer any question of pigmentation, friend. That girl on the floor looked black, but she was white, and whatever else she was she was also stone-cold dead, and that's the worst you can do to anybody.

The report explained that the girl's body was in a state of advanced putrefaction, and it went into such esoteric terms as 'general distention of the body cavities, tissues, and blood vessels with gas,' and 'black discoloration of the skin, mucous membranes, and irides caused by hemolysis and action of hydrogen sulfide on the blood pigment,' all of which broke down to the simple fact that it was a damn hot week in August and the girl had been lying on a rug which retained heat and speeded the post-mortem putrefacation. From what they could tell, and in weather like this it was mostly a guess, the girl had been dead and decomposing for at least forty-eight hours, which set the time of her demise as August first or thereabouts.

One of the reports went on to say that the clothes she'd been wearing had been purchased in one of the city's larger department stores. All her clothes – those she wore and those found in her apartment – were rather expensive, but someone at the lab thought it necessary to note that all her panties were trimmed with Belgian lace and retailed for $25 a pair. Someone else at the lab mentioned that a thorough examination of her garments and body revealed no traces of blood, semen, or oil stains.

The coroner fixed the cause of death as strangulation.

It is amazing how much an apartment can sometimes yield to science. It is equally amazing, and more than a little disappointing, to get nothing from the scene of a murder when you are desperately seeking a clue. The furnished room in which Claudia Davis had been strangled to death was full of juicy surfaces conceivably carrying hundreds of latent fingerprints. The closets and drawers contained piles of clothing that might have carried traces of anything from gunpowder to face powder.

But the lab boys went around lifting their prints and sifting their dust and vacuuming with a Söderman-Heuberger filter, and they went down to the morgue and studied the girl's skin and came up with a total of nothing. Zero. Oh, not quite zero. They got a lot of prints belonging to Claudia Davis, and a lot of dust collected from all over the city and clinging to her shoes and her furniture.

They also found some documents belonging to the dead girl – a birth certificate, a diploma of graduation from a high school in Santa Monica, and an expired library card. And, oh, yes, a key. The key didn't seem to fit any of the locks in the room. They sent all the junk over to the 87th, and Sam Grossman called Carella personally later that day to apologize for the lack of results.

The squadroom was hot and noisy when Carella took the call from the lab. The conversation was a curiously one-sided affair. Carella, who had dumped the contents of the laboratory envelope onto his desk, merely grunted or nodded every now and then. He thanked Grossman at last, hung up, and stared at the window facing the street and Grover Park.

'Get anything?' Meyer asked.

'Yeah. Grossman thinks the killer was wearing gloves.'

'That's nice,' Meyer said.

'Also, I think I know what this key is for.' He lifted it from the desk.

'Yeah? What?'

'Well, did you see these canceled checks?'

'No.'

'Take a look,' Carella said.

He opened the brown bank envelope addressed to Claudia Davis, spread the canceled checks on his desk top, and then unfolded the yellow bank statement. Meyer studied the display silently.

'Cotton found the envelope in her room,' Carella said. 'The statement covers the month of July. Those are all the checks she wrote, or at least everything that cleared the bank by the thirty-first.'

'Lots of checks here,' Meyer said. 'Twenty-five, to be exact. What do you think?'

'I know what *I* think,' Carella said.

'What's that?'

'I look at those checks, I can see a life. It's like reading somebody's diary. Everything she did last month is right here, Meyer. All the department stores she went to, look, a florist, her hairdresser, a candy shop, even her shoemaker, and look at this. A check made out to a funeral home. Now who died, Meyer, huh? And look here. She was living at Mrs. Mauder's place, but here's a check made out to a swank apartment building on the South Side, in Stewart City. And some of these checks are just made out to names, *people*. This case is crying for some people.'

'You want me to get the phone book?'

'No, wait a minute. Look at this bank statement. She opened the account on July fifth with a thousand bucks. All of a sudden, bam, she deposits a thousand bucks in the Seaboard Bank of America.'

'What's so odd about that?'

'Nothing, maybe. But Cotton called the other banks in the city, and Claudia Davis has a very healthy account at the Highland Trust on Cromwell Avenue. And I mean *very* healthy.'

'How healthy?'

'Close to sixty grand.'

'What!'

'You heard me. And the Highland Trust lists no withdrawals for the month of July. So where'd she get the money to put into the Seaboard account?'

'Was that the only deposit?'

'Take a look.'

Meyer picked up the statement.

'The initial deposit was on July fifth,' Carella said. 'A thousand bucks. She made another thousand-dollar deposit on July twelfth. And another on the nineteenth. And another on the twenty-seventh.'

Meyer raised his eyebrows. 'Four grand. That's a lot of loot.'

'And all deposited in less than a month's time.'

'Not to mention the sixty grand in the other bank. Where do you suppose she got it, Steve?'

'I don't know. It just doesn't make sense. She wears underpants trimmed with Belgian lace, but she lives in a crumby room-and-a-half with bath. How the hell do you figure that? Two bank accounts, twenty-five bucks to cover her backside, and all she pays is sixty bucks a month for a flophouse.'

'Maybe she's hot, Steve.'

'No.' Carella shook his head. 'I ran a make with C.B.I. She hasn't got a record, and she's not wanted for anything. I haven't heard from the Feds yet, but I imagine it'll be the same story.'

'What about that key? You said –'

'Oh, yeah. That's pretty simple, thank God. Look at this.'

He reached into the pile of checks and sorted out a yellow slip, larger than the checks. He handed it to Meyer. The slip read:

THE SEABOARD BANK OF AMERICA
Isola Branch   P 1698

<u>July 5</u>

We are charging your account as per items below. Please see that the amount is deducted on your books so that our accounts may agree.

FOR	Safe deposit rental #375		5	00
	U.S. Tax			50
	AMOUNT OF CHARGE		5	50

CHARGE	Claudia Davis	ENTERED BY
	1263 South Eleventh	*BPL*
	Isola	

'She rented a safe-deposit box the name day she opened the new checking account, huh?' Meyer said.

'Right.'

'What's in it?'

'That's a good question.'

'Look, do you want to save some time, Steve?'

'Sure.'

'Let's get the court order *before* we go to the bank.'

The manager of the Seaboard Bank of America was a bald-headed man in his early fifties. Working on the theory that similar physical types are *simpatico*, Carella allowed Meyer to do most of the questioning.

It was not easy to elicit answers from Mr. Anderson, the manager of the bank, because he was by nature a reticent man. But Detective Meyer Meyer was the most patient man in the city, if not the entire world. His patience was an acquired trait, rather than an inherited one. Oh, he had inherited a few things from his father, a jovial man named Max Meyer, but patience was not one of them. If anything Max Meyer had been a very impatient if not downright short-tempered sort of fellow. When his wife, for example, came to him with the news that she was expecting a baby, Max nearly hit the ceiling. He enjoyed little jokes immensely, was perhaps the biggest practical joker in all Riverhead, but this particular prank of nature failed to amuse him. He had thought his wife was long past the age when bearing children was even a remote possibility. He never thought of himself as approaching dotage, but he was after all getting on in years, and a change-of-life baby was hardly what the doctor had ordered. He allowed the impending birth to simmer inside him, planning his revenge all the while, plotting the practical joke to end all practical jokes.

When the baby was born, he named it Meyer, a delightful handle which when coupled with the family name provided the infant with a double-barrelled monicker: Meyer Meyer.

Now, that's pretty funny. Admit it. You can split your sides laughing over that one, unless you happen to be a pretty sensitive kid who also happens to be an Orthodox Jew, and who happens to live in a predominately Gentile neighborhood. The kids in the neighborhood thought Meyer Meyer had been invented solely for their own pleasure. If they needed further provocation for beating him up, and they didn't need any, his name provided excellent motivational fuel. 'Meyer Meyer, Jew on fire!' they would shout, and then they would chase him down the street and beat hell out of him.

Meyer learned patience. It is not very often that one kid, or even one grown man, can successfully defend himself against a gang. But sometimes you can talk yourself out of a beating. Sometimes, if you're patient, if you just wait long enough, you can catch one of them alone and stand up to him face to face, man to man, and know the exultation of a fair fight without the frustration of overwhelming odds.

Listen, Max Meyer's joke was a harmless one. You can't deny an old man his pleasure. But Mr. Anderson, the manager of the bank, was fifty-four years old and totally bald. Meyer Meyer, the detective second grade who sat opposite him and asked questions, was also totally bald. Maybe a lifetime of devoted patience doesn't leave any scars. Maybe not. But Meyer Meyer was only thirty-seven years old.

Patiently he said, 'Didn't you find these large deposits rather odd, Mr. Anderson?'

'No,' Anderson said. 'A thousand dollars is not a lot of money.'

'Mr. Anderson,' Meyer said patiently, 'you are aware, of course, that banks in this city are required to report to the police any unusually large sums of money deposited at one time. You are aware of that, are you not?'

'Yes, I am.'

'Miss Davis deposited four thousand dollars in three weeks' time. Didn't that seem unusual to you?'

'No. The deposits were spaced. A thousand dollars is not a lot of money, and not an unusually large deposit.'

'To me,' Meyer said, 'a thousand dollars is a lot of money. You can buy a lot of beer with a thousand dollars.'

'I don't drink beer,' Anderson said flatly.

'Neither do I,' Meyer answered.

'Besides, we *do* call the police whenever we get a very large deposit, unless the depositor is one of our regular customers. I did not feel these deposits warranted such a call.'

'Thank you, Mr. Anderson,' Meyer said. 'We have a court order here. We'd like to open the box Miss Davis rented.'

'May I see the order, please?' Anderson said. Meyer showed it to him. Anderson sighed and said, 'Very well. Do you have Miss Davis' key?'

Carella reached into his pocket. 'Would this be it?' he said. He put a key on the desk. It was the key that had come to him from the lab together with the documents they'd found in the apartment.

'Yes, that's it,' Mr. Anderson said. 'There are two different keys to every box, you see. The bank keeps one, and the renter keeps the other. The box cannot be opened without both keys. Will you come with me, please?'

He collected the bank key to safety-deposit box number 375 and led the detectives to the rear of the bank. The room seemed to be lined with shining metal. The boxes, row upon row, reminded Carella of the morgue and the refrigerated shelves that slid in and out of the wall on squeaking rollers.

Anderson pushed the bank key into a slot and turned it, and then he put Claudia Davis' key into a second slot and turned that. He pulled the long, thin box out of the wall and handed it to Meyer who carried it to the counter on the opposite wall and lifted the catch.

'Okay?' he said to Carella.

'Go ahead.'

Meyer raised the lid of the box.

There was $16,000 in the box. There was also a slip of notepaper. The $16,000 was neatly divided into four stacks of bills. Three of the stacks held $5,000 each. The fourth stack held only $1,000. Carella picked up the slip of paper. Someone, presumably Claudia Davis, had made some annotations on it in pencil.

```
7/5    20,000
7/5    -1,000
       ───────
       19,000
7/12   -1,000
       ───────
       18,000
7/19   -1,000
       ───────
       17,000
7/27   -1,000
       ───────
       16,000
```

'Make any sense to you, Mr. Anderson?'

'No. I'm afraid not.'

'She came into this bank on July fifth with twenty thousand dollars in cash, Mr. Anderson. She put a thousand of that into a checking account and the remainder into this box. The dates on this slip of paper show exactly when she took cash from the box and transferred it to the checking account. She knew the rules, Mr. Anderson. She knew that twenty grand deposited in one lump would bring a call to the police. This way was a lot safer.'

'We'd better get a list of these serial numbers,' Meyer said.

'Would you have one of your people do that for us, Mr. Anderson?'

Anderson seemed ready to protest. Instead, he looked at Carella, sighed, and said, 'Of course.'

The serial numbers didn't help them at all. They compared them against their own lists, and the out-of-town lists, and the F.B.I. lists, but none of those bills was hot.

Only August was.

Stewart City hangs in the hair of Isola like a jeweled tiara. Not really a city, not even a town, merely a collection of swank apartment buildings overlooking the River Dix, the community had been named after British royalty and remained one of the most exclusive neighborhoods in town. If you could boast of a Stewart City address, you could also boast of a high income, a country place on Sands Spit, and a Mercedes Benz in the garage under the apartment building. You could give your address with a measure of snobbery and pride – you were, after all, one of the élite.

The dead girl named Claudia Davis had made out a check to Management Enterprises, Inc., at 13 Stewart Place South, to the tune of $750. The check had been dated July ninth, four days after she'd opened the Seaboard account.

A cool breeze was blowing in off the river as Carella and Hawes pulled up. Late-afternoon sunlight dappled the polluted water of the Dix. The bridges connecting Calm's Point with Isola hung against a sky awaiting the assault of dusk.

'Want to pull down the sun visor?' Carella said.

Hawes reached up and turned down the visor. Clipped to the visor so that it showed through the windshield of the car was a hand-lettered card that read POLICEMAN ON DUTY CALL – 87TH PRECINCT. The car, a 1956 Chevrolet, was Carella's own.

'I've got to make a sign for my car,' Hawes said. 'Some wise guy tagged it last week.'

'What did you do?'

'I went to court and pleaded not guilty. On my day off.'

'Did you get out of it?'

'Sure. I was answering a squeal. It's bad enough I had to use my own car, but for Pete's sake, to get a ticket!'

'I prefer my own car,' Carella said. 'Those three cars belonging to the squad are ready for the junk heap.'

'*Two*,' Hawes corrected. 'One of them's been in the police garage for a month now.'

'Meyer went down to see about it the other day.'

'What'd they say? Was it ready?'

'No, the mechanic told him there were four patrol cars ahead of the sedan, and they took precedence. Now how about that?'

'Sure, it figures. I've still got a chit in for the gas I used, you know that?'

'Forget it. I've never got back a cent I laid out for gas.'

'What'd Meyer do about the car?'

'He slipped the mechanic five bucks. Maybe that'll speed him up.'

'You know what the city ought to do?' Hawes said. 'They ought to buy some of those used taxicabs. Pick them up for two or three hundred bucks, paint them over, and give them out to the squads. Some of them are still in pretty good condition.'

'Well, it's an idea,' Carella said dubiously, and they entered the building. They found Mrs. Miller, the manager, in an office at the rear of the ornate entrance lobby. She was a woman in her early forties with a well-preserved figure and a very husky voice. She wore her hair piled on the top of her head, a pencil stuck rakishly into the reddish-brown heap. She looked at the photostated check and said, 'Oh, yes, of course.'

'You knew Miss Davis?'

'Yes, she lived here for a long time.'

'How long?'

'Five years.'

'When did she move out?'

'At the end of June.' Mrs. Miller crossed her splendid legs and smiled graciously. The legs were remarkable for a woman of her age, and the smile was almost radiant. She moved with an expert femininity, a calculated conscious fluidity of flesh that suggested availability and yet was totally respectable. She seemed to have devoted a lifetime to learning the ways and wiles of the female and now practiced them with facility and charm. She was pleasant to be with, this woman, pleasant to watch and to hear, and to think of touching. Carella and Hawes, charmed to their shoes, found themselves relaxing in her presence.

'This check,' Carella said, tapping the photostat. 'What was it for?'

'June rent. I received it on the tenth of July. Claudia always paid her rent by the tenth of the month. She was a very good tenant.'

'The apartment cost seven hundred and fifty dollars a month?'

'Yes.'

'Isn't that high for an apartment?'

'Not in Stewart City,' Mrs. Miller said gently. 'And this was a river-front apartment.'

'I see. I take it Miss Davis had a good job.'

'No, no, she doesn't have a job at all.'

'Then how could she afford –?'

'Well, she's rather well off, you know.'

'Where does she get the money, Mrs. Miller?'

'Well ...' Mrs. Miller shrugged. 'I really think you should ask *her*, don't you? I mean, if this is something concerning Claudia, shouldn't you ...?'

'Mrs. Miller,' Carella said, 'Claudia Davis is dead.'

'What?'

'She's ...'

'What? No. No.' She shook her head. 'Claudia? But the check ... I ... the check came only last month.' She shook her head again. 'No.'

'She's dead, Mrs. Miller,' Carella said gently. 'She was strangled.'

The charm faltered for just an instant. Revulsion knifed the eyes of Mrs. Miller, the eyelids flickered, it seemed for an instant that the pupils would turn shining and wet, that the carefully lipsticked mouth would crumble. And then something inside took over, something that demanded control, something that reminded her that a charming woman does not weep and cause her fashionable eye make-up to run.

'I'm sorry,' she said, almost in a whisper. 'I am really, really sorry. She was a nice person.'

'Can you tell us what you know about her, Mrs. Miller?'

'Yes. Yes, of course,' She shook her head again, unwilling to accept the idea. 'That's terrible. That's terrible. Why, she was only a baby.'

'We figured her for thirty, Mrs. Miller. Are we wrong?'

'She seemed younger, but perhaps that was because ... well, she was a rather shy person. Even when she first came here, there was an air of – well, lostness about her. Of course, that was right after her parents died, so –'

'Where did she come from, Mrs. Miller?'

'From California. Santa Monica.

Carella nodded. 'You were starting to tell us – you said she was rather well off. Could you ...?'

'Well, the stock, you know.'

'What stock?'

'Her parents had set up a securities trust account for her. When they died, Claudia began receiving the income from the stock. She was an only child, you know.'

'And she lived on stock dividends alone?'

'They amounted to quite a bit. Which she saved, I might add. She was a very systematic person, not at all frivolous. When she received a dividend check, she would endorse it and take it straight to the bank. Claudia was a very sensible girl.'

'Which bank, Mrs. Miller?'

'The Highland Trust. Right down the street. On Cromwell Avenue.'

'I see,' Carella said. 'Was she dating many men? Would you know?'

'I don't think so. She kept pretty much to herself. Even after Josie came.'

Carella leaned forward. 'Josie? Who's Josie?'

'Josie Thompson. Josephine, actually. Her cousin.'

'And where did *she* come from?'

'California. They both came from California.'

'And how can we get in touch with this Josie Thompson?'

'Well, she ... Don't you know? Haven't you ...?' Mrs. Miller faltered.

'What, Mrs. Miller?'

'Why, Josie is dead. Josie passed on in June. That's why Claudia moved, I suppose. I suppose she couldn't bear the thought of living in that apartment without Josie. It *is* a little frightening, isn't it?'

'Yes,' Carella said.

DETECTIVE DIVISION SUPPLEMENTARY REPORT	SQUAD	PRECINCT	PRECINCT REPORT	DETECTIVE DIVISION REPORT NUMBER
pdcn 360 rev 25m	87	87	32-101	DD 60 R-42

NAME AND ADDRESS OF PERSON REPORTING	DATE ORIGINAL REPORT
Miller Irene (Mrs. John) 13 Stewart Place S.	8-4-60
SURNAME GIVEN NAME INITIALS NUMBER STREET	

DETAILS

Summary of interview with Irene (Mrs. John) Miller at office of Management Enterprises, Inc., address above, in re homicide Claudia Davis, Mrs. Miller states:

Claudia Davis came to this city in June of 1955, took $750-a-month apartment above address, lived there alone. Rarely seen in company of friends, male or female. Young recluse type living on substantial income of inherited securities. Parents, Mr. and Mrs. Carter Davis, killed on San Diego Freeway in head-on collision with station wagon, April 14, 1955. L.A.P.D. confirms traffic accident, driver of other vehicle convicted for negligent operation.

Mrs. Miller describes girl as medium height and weight, close-cropped brunette hair, brown eyes, no scars or birthmarks she can remember, tallies with what we have on corpse. Further says Claudia Davis was quiet, unobtrusive tenant, paid rent and all service bills punctually, was gentle, sweet, plain, childlike, shy, meticulous in money matters, well liked but unapproachable.

In April or May of 1959, Josie Thompson, cousin of deceased, arrived from Brentwood, California. (Routine check with Criminal Bureau Identification negative, no record. Checking now with L.A.P.D., and F.B.I.) Described as slightly older than Claudia, rather different in looks and personality. 'They were like black and white,' Mrs. Miller says, 'but they hit it off exceptionally well.' Josie moved into the apartment with cousin. Words used to describe relationship between two were 'like the closest sisters,' and 'really in tune,' and 'the best of friends,' etc.

Girls did not date much, were constantly in each other's company, Josie seeming to pick up recluse habits from Claudia. Went on frequent trips together. Spent summer of '59 on Tortoise Island in the bay, returned Labor Day. Went away again at Christmas time to ski Sun Valley, and again in March this year to Kingston, Jamaica, for three

weeks, returning at beginning of April. Source of income was fairly
standard securities–income account. Claudia did not own the stock,
but income on it was hers for as long as she lived. Trust specified that
upon her death the stock and the income be turned over to U.C.L.A.
(father's alma mater). In any case, Claudia was assured of a very, very
substantial lifetime income (see Highland Trust bank account) and was
apparently supporting Josie as well, since Mrs. Miller claims neither
girl worked. Brought up question of possible lesbianism, but Mrs.
Miller, who is knowledgeable and hip, says no, neither girl was a dike.

On June 3, Josie and Claudia left for another weekend trip.
Doorman reports having helped them pack valises into trunk of
Claudia's car, 1960 Cadillac convertible. Claudia did the driving. Girls
did not return on Monday morning as they had indicated they would.
Claudia called on Wednesday, crying on telephone. Told Mrs. Miller
that Josie had had a terrible accident and was dead. Mrs. Miller
remembers asking Claudia if she could help in any way. Claudia said,
quote, No, everything's been taken care of already, unquote.

On June 17, Mrs. Miller received a letter from Claudia (letter
attached – handwriting compares positive with checks Claudia signed)
stating she could not possibly return to apartment, not after what had
happened to her cousin. She reminded Mrs. Miller lease expired on
July 4, told her she would send check for June rent before July 10. Said
moving company would pack and pick up her belongings, delivering
all valuables and documents to her, and storing rest. (See Claudia
Davis' check number 010, 7/14, made payable to Allora Brothers, Inc.,
'in payment for packing moving, and storage.')

Claudia Davis never returned to the apartment. Mrs. Miller had not
seen her and knew nothing of her whereabouts until we informed her
of the homicide.

DATE OF THIS REPORT

August 6

Det 2/gr Carella S.L. 714-56-32 Det/Lt. Peter Byrnes

RANK	SURNAME	INITIALS	SHIELD NUMBER	COMMANDING OFFICER

The drive upstate to Triangle Lake was a particularly scenic
one, and since it was August, and since Sunday was supposed to
be Carella's day off, he thought he might just as well combine a
little business with pleasure. So he put the top of the car down,
and he packed Teddy into the front seat together with a picnic
lunch and a gallon Thermos of iced coffee, and he forgot all
about Claudia Davis on the drive up through the mountains.

Carella found it easy to forget about almost anything when he was with his wife.

Teddy as far as he was concerned – and his astute judgment had been backed up by many a street-corner whistle – was only the most beautiful woman in the world. He could never understand how he, a hairy, corny, ugly, stupid, clumsy cop, had managed to capture anyone as wonderful as Theodora Franklin. But capture her he had, and he sat beside her now in the open car and stole sidelong glances at her as he drove, excited as always by her very presence.

Her black hair, always wild, seemed to capture something of the wind's frenzy as it whipped about the oval of her face. Her brown eyes were partially squinted against the rush of air over the windshield. She wore a white blouse emphatically curved over a full bosom, black tapered slacks form-fitted over generous hips and good legs. She had kicked off her sandals and folded her knees against her breasts, her bare feet pressed against the glove-compartment panel. There was about her, Carella realized, a curious combination of savage and sophisticate. You never knew whether she was going to kiss you or slug you, and the uncertainty kept her eternally desirable and exciting.

Teddy watched her husband as he drove, his big-knuckled hands on the wheel of the car. She watched him not only because it gave her pleasure to watch him, but also because he was speaking. And since she could not hear, since she had been born a deaf mute, it was essential that she look at his mouth when he spoke. He did not discuss the case at all. She knew that one of the Claudia Davis checks had been made out to the Fancher Funeral Home in Triangle Lake and she knew that Carella wanted to talk to the proprietor of the place personally. She further knew that this was very important or he wouldn't be spending his Sunday driving all the way upstate. But he had promised her he'd combine business with pleasure.

This was the pleasure part of the trip, and in deference to his promise and his wife, he refrained from discussing the case, which was really foremost in his mind. He talked, instead, about the scenery, and their plans for the fall, and the way the twins were growing, and how pretty Teddy looked, and how she'd better button that top button of her blouse before they got out of the car, but he never once mentioned Claudia Davis until they were standing in the office of the Fancher Funeral Home and looking into the gloomy eyes of a man who called himself Barton Scoles.

Scoles was tall and thin and he wore a black suit that he had probably worn to his own confirmation back in 1912. He was so much the stereotype of a small-town undertaker that Carella almost burst out laughing when he met him. Somehow, though, the environment was not conducive to hilarity. There was a strange smell hovering over the thick rugs and the papered walls and the hanging chandeliers. It was a while before Carella recognized it as formaldehyde and then made the automatic association and, curious for a man who had stared into the eyes of death so often, felt like retching.

'Miss Davis made out a check to you on July fifteenth,' Carella said. 'Can you tell me what it was for?'

'Sure can,' Scoles said. 'Had to wait a long time for that check. She gave me only a twenty-five dollar deposit. Usually take fifty, you know. I got stuck many a time, believe me.'

'How do you mean?' Carella asked.

'People. You bury their dead, and then sometimes they don't pay you for your work. This business isn't *all* fun, you know. Many's the time I handled the whole funeral and the service and the burial and all, and never did get paid. Makes you lose your faith in human nature.'

'But Miss Davis finally *did* pay you.'

'Oh, sure. But I can tell you I was sweating that one out. I can tell you that. After all, she was a strange gal from the city, has the funeral here, nobody comes to it but her, sitting in the chapel out there and watching the body as if someone's going to steal it away, just her and the departed. I tell you, Mr. Carella – is that your name?'

'Yes, Carella.'

'I tell you, it was kind of spooky. Lay there two days, she did, her cousin. And then Miss Davis asked that we bury the girl right here in the local cemetery, so I done that for her, too – all on the strength of a twenty-five-dollar deposit. That's trust, Mr. Carella, with a capital T.'

'When was this, Mr. Scoles?'

'The girl drowned the first weekend in June,' Scoles said. 'Had no business being out on the lake so early, anyways. The water's still icy cold in June. Don't really warm up none till the latter part July. She fell over the side of the boat – she was out there rowing, you know – and that icy water probably froze her solid, or give her cramps or something, drowned her anyways.' Scoles shook his head. 'Had no business being out on the lake so early.'

'Did you see a death certificate?'

'Yep, Dr. Donneli made it out. Cause of death was drowning, all right, no question about it. We had an inquest, too, you know. The Tuesday after she drowned. They said it was accidental.'

'You said she was out rowing in a boat. Alone?'

'Yep. Her cousin, Miss Davis, was on the shore watching. Jumped in when she fell overboard, tried to reach her, but couldn't make it in time. The water's plenty cold, believe me. Ain't too warm even now, and here it is August already.'

'But it didn't seem to affect Miss Davis, did it?'

'Well, she was probably a strong swimmer. Been my experience most pretty girls are strong girls, too. I'll bet your wife here is a strong girl. She sure is a pretty one.'

Scoles smiled, and Teddy smiled and squeezed Carella's hand.

'About the payment,' Carella said, 'for the funeral and the burial. Do you have any idea why it took Miss Davis so long to send her check?'

'Nope. I wrote her twice. First time was just a friendly little reminder. Second time, I made it a little stronger. Attorney friend of mine in town wrote it on his stationery; that always impresses them. Didn't get an answer either time. Finally, right out of the blue, the check came, payment in full. Beats me. Maybe she was affected by the death. Or maybe she's always slow paying her debts. I'm just happy the check came, that's all. Sometimes the live ones can give you more trouble than them who's dead, believe me.'

They strolled down to the lake together, Carella and his wife, and ate their picnic lunch on its shores. Carella was strangely silent. Teddy dangled her bare feet in the water. The water, as Scoles had promised, was very cold even through it was August. On the way back from the lake Carella said, 'Honey, would you mind if I make one more stop?'

Teddy turned her eyes to him inquisitively.

'I want to see the chief of police here.'

Teddy frowned. The question was in her eyes, and he answered it immediately.

'To find out whether or not there were any witnesses to that drowning. *Besides* Claudia Davis, I mean. From the way Scoles was talking, I get the impression that lake was pretty deserted in June.'

The chief of police was a short man with a potbelly and big feet. He kept his feet propped up on his desk all the while he spoke to Carella. Carella watched him and wondered why everybody in this town seemed to be on vacation from an M-G-M movie. A row of files in a locked rack was behind the chief's desk. A host of WANTED fliers covered a bulletin board to the right of the rack. The chief had a hole in the sole of his left shoe.

'Yep,' he said, 'there was a witness, all right.'

Carella felt a pang of disappointment. 'Who?' he asked.

'Fellow fishing at the lake. Saw the whole thing. Testified before the coroner's jury.'

'What'd he say?'

'Said he was fishing there when Josie Thompson took the boat out. Said Claudia Davis stayed behind, on the shore. Said Miss Thompson fell overboard and went under like a stone. Said Miss Davis jumped in the water and began swimming towards her. Didn't make it in time. That's what he said.'

'What else did he say?'

'Well, he drove Miss Davis back to town in her car. 1960

Caddy convertible, I believe. She could hardly speak. She was sobbing and mumbling and wringing her hands, oh, in a hell of a mess. Why, we had to get the whole story out of that fishing fellow. Wasn't until the next day that Miss Davis could make any kind of sense.'

'When did you hold the inquest?'

'Tuesday. Day before they buried the cousin. Coroner did the dissection on Monday. We got authorization from Miss Davis, Penal Law 2213, next of kin being charged by law with the duty of burial may authorize dissection for the sole purpose of ascertaining the cause of death.'

'And the coroner reported the cause of death as drowning?'

'That's right. Said so right before the jury.'

'Why'd you have an inquest? Did you suspect something more than accidental drowning?'

'Not necessarily. But that fellow who was fishing, well *he* was from the city, too, you know. And for all we knew him and Miss Davis could have been in this together, you know, shoved the cousin over the side of the boat, and then faked up a whole story, you know. They both coulda been lying in their teeth.'

'Were they?'

'Not so we could tell. You never seen anybody so grief-stricken as Miss Davies was when the fishing fellow drove her into town. Girl would have to be a hell of an actress to behave that way. Calmed down the next day, but you shoulda seen her when it happened. And at the inquest it was plain this fishing fellow had never met her before that day at the lake. Convinced the jury he had no prior knowledge of or connection with either of the two girls. Convinced me, too, for that matter.'

'What's his name?' Carella asked. 'This fishing fellow.'

'Courtenoy.'

'What did you say?'

'Courtenoy. Sidney Courtenoy.'

'Thanks,' Carella answered, and he rose suddenly. 'Come on, Teddy. I want to get back to the city.'

Courtenoy lived in a one-family clapboard house in Riverhead.

He was rolling up the door of his garage when Carella and Meyer pulled into his driveway early Monday morning. He turned to look at the car curiously, one hand on the rising garage door. The door stopped, halfway up, halfway down. Carella stepped into the driveway.

'Mr. Courtenoy?' he asked.

'Yes?' He stared at Carella, puzzlement on his face, the puzzlement that is always there when a perfect stranger addresses you by name. Courtenoy was a man in his late forties, wearing a cap and a badly fitted sports jacket and dark flannel slacks. His hair was graying at the temples. He looked tired, very tired, and his weariness had nothing whatever to do with the fact that it was only seven o'clock in the morning. A lunch box was at his feet where he had apparently put it when he began rolling up the garage door. The car in the garage was a 1953 Ford.

'We're police officers,' Carella said. 'Mind if we ask you a few questions?'

'I'd like to see your badge,' Courtenoy said. Carella showed it to him. Courtenoy nodded as if he had performed a precautionary public duty. 'What are your questions?' he said. 'I'm on my way to work. Is this about that damn building permit again?'

'What building permit?'

'For extending the garage. I'm buying my son a little jalopy, don't want to leave it out on the street. Been having a hell of a time getting a building permit. Can you imagine that? All I want to do is add another twelve feet to the garage. You'd think I was trying to build a city park or something. Is that what this is about?'

From inside the house a woman's voice called, 'Who is it, Sid?'

'Nothing, nothing,' Courtenoy said impatiently. 'Nobody. Never mind, Bett.' He looked at Carella. 'My wife. You married?'

'Yes, sir, I'm married,' Carella said.

'Then you know,' Courtenoy said cryptically. 'What are your questions?'

'Ever see this before?' Carella asked. He handed a photostated copy of the check to Courtenoy, who looked at it briefly and handed it back.

'Sure.'

'Want to explain it, Mr. Courtenoy?'

'Explain what?'

'Explain why Claudia Davis sent you a check for a hundred and twenty dollars.'

'As recompense,' Courtenoy said unhesitatingly.

'Oh, recompense, huh?' Meyer said. 'For what, Mr. Courtenoy? For a little cock-and-bull story?'

'Huh? What are you talking about?'

'Recompense for *what*, Mr. Courtenoy?'

'For missing three days' work, what the hell did you think?'

'How's that again?'

'No, what did you *think*?' Courtenoy said angrily, waving his finger at Meyer. 'What did you think it was for? Some kind of payoff or something? Is that what you thought?'

'Mr. Courtenoy –'

'I lost three days' work because of that damn inquest. I had to stay up at Triangle Lake all day Monday and Tuesday and then again on Wednesday waiting for the jury decision. I'm a bricklayer. I get five bucks an hour and I lost three days' work, eight hours a day, and so Miss Davis was good enough to send me a check for a hundred and twenty bucks. Now just what the hell did you think, would you mind telling me?'

'Did you know Miss Davis before that day at Triangle Lake, Mr. Courtenoy?'

'Never saw her before in my life. What is this? Am I on trial here? What is this?'

From inside the house the woman's voice came again, sharply, 'Sidney! Is something wrong? Are you all right?'

'Nothing's wrong. Shut up, will you?'

There was an aggrieved silence from within the clap-board structure. Courtenoy muttered something under his breath and then turned to face the detectives again. 'You finished?' he said.

'Not quite, Mr. Courtenoy. We'd like you to tell us what you saw that day up at Triangle Lake.'

'What the hell for? Go read the minutes of the inquest if you're so damn interested. I've got to get to work.'

'That can wait, Mr. Courtenoy.'

'Like hell it can. This job is away over in –'

'Mr. Courtenoy, we don't want to have to go all the way downtown and come back with a warrant for your arrest.'

'My *arrest*! For what? Listen, what did I –?'

'Sidney? Sidney, shall I call the police?' the woman shouted from inside the house.

'Oh, shut the hell up!' Courtenoy answered. 'Call the police,' he mumbled. 'I'm up to my ears in cops and she wants to call the police. What do you want from me? I'm an honest bricklayer. I saw a girl drown. I told it just the way I saw it. Is that a crime? Why are you bothering me?'

'Just tell it again, Mr. Courtenoy. Just the way you saw it.'

'She was out in the boat,' Courtenoy said, sighing. 'I was fishing. Her cousin was on the shore. She fell over the side.'

'Josie Thompson.'

'Yes, Josie Thompson, whatever the hell her name was.'

'She was alone in the boat?'

'Yes. She was alone in the boat.'

'Go on.'

'The other one – Miss Davis – screamed and ran into the water, and began swimming towards her.' He shook his head. 'She didn't make it in time. That boat was a long way out. When she got there, the lake was still. She dove under and came up, and then dove under again, but it was too late, it was just too late. Then, as she was swimming back, I thought *she* was going to drown, too. She faltered and sank below the surface, and I waited and I thought sure she was gone. Then there was a patch of yellow that broke through the water, and I saw she was all right.'

'Why didn't you jump in to help her, Mr. Courtenoy?'

'I don't know how to swim.'

'All right. What happened next?'

'She came out of the water – Miss Davis. She was exhausted and hysterical. I tried to calm her down, but she kept yelling and crying, not making any sense at all. I dragged her over to the car, and I asked her for the car keys. She didn't seem to know what I was talking about at first. "The keys!" I said, and she just stared at me. "Your car keys!" I yelled. "The keys to the car." Finally she reached in her purse and handed me the keys.'

'Go on.'

'I drove her into town. It was me who told the story to the police. She couldn't talk, all she could do was babble and scream and cry. It was a terrible thing to watch. I'd never before seen a woman so completely off her nut. We couldn't get two straight words out of her until the next day. Then she was all right. Told the police who she was, explained what I'd already told them the day before, and told them the dead girl was her cousin, Josie Thompson. They dragged the lake and got her out of the water. A shame. A real shame. Nice young girl like that.'

'What was the dead girl wearing?'

'Cotton dress. Loafers, I think. Or sandals. Little thin sweater over the dress. A cardigan.'

'Any jewelry?'

'I don't think so. No.'

'Was she carrying a purse?'

'No. Her purse was in the car with Miss Davis.'

'What was Miss Davis wearing?'

'When? The day of the drowning? Or when they pulled her cousin out of the lake?'

'Was she there then?'

'Sure. Identified the body.'

'No, I wanted to know what she was wearing on the day of the accident, Mr. Courtenoy.'

'Oh, a skirt and blouse, I think. Ribbon in her hair. Loafers. I'm not sure.'

'What color blouse? Yellow?'

'No. Blue.'

'You said yellow.'

'No, blue. I didn't say yellow.'

Carella frowned. 'I thought you said yellow earlier.' He shrugged. 'All right, what happened after the inquest?'

'Nothing much. Miss Davis thanked me for being so kind and said she would send me a check for the time I'd missed. I refused at first and then I thought, What the hell, I'm a hard-working man, and money doesn't grow on trees. So I gave her my address. I figured she could afford it. Driving a Caddy, and hiring a fellow to take it back to the city.'

'Why didn't she drive it back herself?'

'I guess she was still shaken up. Listen, that was a terrible experience. Did you ever see anyone die up close?'

'Yes,' Carella said.

From inside the house Courtenoy's wife yelled, 'Sidney, tell those men to get out of our driveway!'

'You heard her,' Courtenoy said, and finished rolling up his garage door.

Nobody likes Monday morning.

It was invented for hangovers. It is really not the beginning of a new week, but only the tail end of the week before. Nobody likes it, and it doesn't have to be rainy or gloomy or blue in order to provoke disaffection. It can be bright and sunny and the beginning of August. It can start with a driveway interview at seven A.M. and grow progressively worse by nine-thirty that same morning.

Monday is Monday and legislature will never change its personality. Monday is Monday, and it stinks.

By nine-thirty that Monday morning Detective Steve Carella was on the edge of total bewilderment and, like any normal person, he blamed it on Monday. He had come back to the squadroom and painstakingly gone over the pile of checks that Claudia Davis had written during the month of July, a total of twenty-five, searching them for some clue to her strangulation, studying them with the scrutiny of a typographer in a print shop.

Several things seemed evident from the checks, but nothing seemed pertinent. He could recall having said, 'I look at those checks, I can see a life. It's like reading somebody's diary,' and he was beginning to believe he had uttered some famous last words in those two succinct sentences. For if this was the diary of Claudia Davis, it was a singularly unprovocative account that would never make the nation's best-seller lists.

Most of the checks had been made out to clothing or department stores. Claudia, true to the species, seemed to have a penchant for shopping and a checkbook that yielded to her spending urge. Calls to the various stores represented revealed that her taste ranged through a wide variety of items. A check of sales slips showed that she had purchased during the month of July alone three baby-doll nightgowns, two half slips, a trenchcoat, a wrist watch, four pairs of tapered slacks in various colors, two pairs of walking shoes, a pair of sunglasses, four Bikini swimsuits, eight wash-and-wear frocks, two skirts, two cashmere sweaters, half a dozen best-selling novels, a large bottle of aspirin, two bottles of Dramamine, six pieces of luggage, and four boxes of cleansing tissue. The most expensive thing she had purchased was an evening gown costing $500.

These purchases accounted for most of the checks she had drawn in July. There were also checks to a hairdresser, a florist, a shoemaker, a candy shop, and three unexplained checks that were drawn to individuals, two men and a woman.

The first was made out to George Badueck.

The second was made out to David Oblinsky.

The third was made out to Martha Fedelson.

Someone on the squad had attacked the telephone directory and come up with addresses for two or three. The third, Oblinsky, had an unlisted number, but a half hour's argument with a supervisor had finally netted an address for him. The completed list was now on Carella's desk together with all the canceled checks. He should have begun tracking down those names, he knew, but something was bugging him.

'Why did Courtenoy lie to me and Meyer?' he asked Cotton Hawes. 'Why did he lie about something as simple as what Claudia Davis was wearing on the day of the drowning?'

'How did he lie?'

'First he said she was wearing yellow, said he saw a patch of yellow break the surface of the lake. Then he changed it to blue. Why did he do that, Cotton?'

'I don't know.'

'And if he lied about that, why couldn't he have been lying

about everything? Why couldn't he and Claudia have done in little Josie together.'

'I don't know,' Hawes said.

'Where'd that twenty thousand bucks come from, Cotton?'

'Maybe it was a stock dividend.'

'Maybe. Then why didn't she simply deposit the check? This was cash, Cotton, *cash*. Now where did it come from? That's a nice piece of change. You don't pick twenty grand out of the gutter.'

'You sure don't.'

'I know where you can get twenty grand, Cotton.'

'Where?'

'From an insurance company. When someone dies.' Carella nodded once, sharply. 'I'm going to make some calls. Dammit, that money had to come from *some* place.'

He hit pay dirt on his sixth call. The man he spoke to was named Jeremiah Dodd and was a representative of the Security Insurance Corporation, Inc. He recognized Josie Thompson's name at once.

'Oh, yes,' he said. 'We settled that claim in July.'

'Who made the claim, Mr. Dodd?'

'The beneficiary, of course. Just a moment. Let me get the folder on this. Will you hold on, please?'

Carella waited impatiently. Over at the insurance company on the other end of the line he could hear muted voices. A girl giggled suddenly, and he wondered who was kissing whom over by the water cooler. At last Dodd came back on the line.

'Here it is,' he said. 'Josephine Thompson. Beneficiary was her cousin, Miss Claudia Davis. Oh, yes, now it's all coming back. Yes, this is the one.'

'What one?'

'Where the girls were mutual beneficiaries.'

'What do you mean?'

'The cousins,' Dodd said. 'There were two life policies. One for Miss Davis and one for Miss Thompson. And they were mutual beneficiaries.'

'You mean Miss Davis was the beneficiary of Miss

Thompson's policy and vice versa?'

'Yes, that's right.'

'How large were the policies?'

'Oh, very small.'

'Well, how *small* then?'

'I believe they were both insured for twelve thousand five hundred. Just a moment; let me check. Yes, that's right.'

'And Miss Davis applied for payment on the policy after her cousin died, huh?'

'Yes. Here it is, right here. Josephine Thompson drowned at Lake Triangle on June fourth. That's right. Claudia Davis sent in the policy and the certificate of death and also a coroner's jury verdict.'

'Did you pay her?'

'Yes. It was a perfectly legitimate claim. We began processing it at once.'

'Did you send anyone up to Lake Triangle to investigate the circumstances of Miss Thompson's death?'

'Yes, but it was merely a routine investigation. A coroner's inquest is good enough for us, Detective Carella.'

'When did you pay Miss Davis?'

'On July first.'

'You sent her a check for twelve thousand five hundred dollars, right?'

'No, sir.'

'Didn't you say ...?'

'The policy insured her for twelve-five, that's correct. But there was a double-indemnity clause, you see, and Josephine Thompson's death was accidental. No, we had to pay the policy's limit, Detective Carella. On July first we sent Claudia Davis a check for twenty-five thousand dollars.'

There are no mysteries in police work.

Nothing fits into a carefully preconceived scheme. The high point of any given case is very often the corpse that opens the case. There is no climactic progression; suspense is for the movies. There are only people and curiously twisted motives, and small unexplained details, and coincidence, and the unexpected, and they combine to form a sequence of events, but there is no real mystery, there never is.

There is only life, and sometimes death, and neither follows a rule book. Policemen hate mystery stories because they recognize in them a control that is lacking in their own very real, sometimes routine, sometimes spectacular, sometimes tedious investigation of a case. It is very nice and very clever and very convenient to have all the pieces fit together neatly. It is very kind to think of detectives as master mathematicians working on an algebraic problem whose constants are death and a victim, whose unknown is a murderer. But many of these mastermind detectives have trouble adding up the deductions on their twice-monthly pay checks. The world is full of wizards, for sure, but hardly any of them work for the city police.

There was one big mathematical discrepancy in the Claudia Davis case.

There seemed to be $5,000 unaccounted for.

Twenty-five grand had been mailed to Claudia Davis on July 1, and she presumably received the check after the Fourth of July holiday, cashed it some place, and then took her money to the Seaboard Bank of America, opened a new checking account, and rented a safety-deposit box. But her total deposit at Seaboard had been $20,000 whereas the checks had been for $25,000, so where was the laggard five? And who had cashed the check for her?

Mr. Dodd of the Security Insurance Corporation, Inc., explained the company's rather complicated accounting system to Carella. A check was kept in the local office for several days after it was cashed in order to close out the policy, after which it was sent to the main office in Chicago where it sometimes stayed for several weeks until the master files were closed out. It was then sent to the company's accounting and auditing firm in San Francisco. It was Dodd's guess that the canceled check had already been sent to the California accountants, and he promised to put a tracer on it at once. Carella asked him to please hurry. Someone had cashed that check for Claudia and, supposedly, someone also had one-fifth of the check's face value.

The very fact that Claudia had not taken the check itself to Seaboard seemed to indicate that she had something to hide. Presumably, she did not want anyone asking questions about insurance company checks, or insurance policies, or double indemnities, or accidental drownings, or especially her cousin Josie. The check was a perfectly good one, and yet she had chosen to cash it *before* opening a new account. Why?

And why, for that matter, had she bothered opening a new account when she had a rather well-stuffed and active account at another bank?

There are only whys in police work, but they do not add up to mystery. They add up to work, and nobody in the world likes work. The bulls of the 87th would have preferred to sit on their backsides and sip gin-and-tonics, but the whys were there, so they put on their hats and their holsters and tried to find some becauses.

Cotton Hawes systematically interrogated each and every tenant in the rooming house where Claudia Davis had been killed. They all had alibis tighter than the closed fist of an Arabian stablekeeper. In his report to the lieutenant, Hawes expressed the belief that none of the tenants was guilty of homicide. As far as he was concerned, they were all clean.

Meyer Meyer attacked the 87th's stool pigeons. There were money-changers galore in the precinct and the city, men who turned hot loot into cold cash — for a price. If someone had cashed a $25,000 check for Claudia and kept $5,000 of it during the process, couldn't that person conceivably be one of the money-changers? Meyer put the precinct stoolies on the ear, asked them to sound around for word of a Security Insurance Corporation check. The stoolies came up with nothing.

Detective Lieutenant Sam Grossman took his laboratory boys to the murder room and went over it again. And again. And again. He reported that the lock on the door was a snap lock, the kind that clicks shut automatically when the door is slammed.

Whoever killed Claudia Davis could have done so without performing any locked-room gymnastics. All he had to do was close the door behind him when he left.

Grossman also reported that Claudia's bed had apparently not been slept in the night of the murder. A pair of shoes had been found at the foot of a large easy chair in the bedroom and a novel was wedged open on the arm of the chair. He suggested that Claudia had fallen asleep while reading, had awakened, and gone into the other room where she had met her murderer and her death. He had no suggestions as to just who that murderer might have been.

Steve Carella was hot and impatient and overloaded. There were other things happening in the precinct, things like burglaries and muggings and knifings and assaults and kids with summertime on their hands hitting other kids with baseball bats because they didn't like the way they pronounced the word 'senor.' There were telephones jangling, and reports to be typed in triplicate, and people filing into the squadroom day and night with complaints against the citizenry of that fair city, and the Claudia Davis case was beginning to be a big fat pain in the keester. Carella wondered what it was like to be a shoemaker. And while he was wondering, he began to chase down the checks made out to George Badueck, David Oblinsky, and Martha Fedelson.

Happily, Bert Kling had nothing whatsoever to do with the Claudia Davis case. He hadn't even discussed it with any of the men on the squad. He was a young detective and a new detective, and the things that happened in that precinct were enough to drive a guy nuts and keep him busy forty-eight hours every day, so he didn't go around sticking his nose into other people's cases. He had enough troubles of his own. One of those troubles was the line-up.

On Wednesday morning Bert Kling's name appeared on the line-up duty chart.

The line-up was held in the gym downtown at Headquarters on High Street. It was held four days a week, Monday to Thursday, and the purpose of the parade was to acquaint the city's detectives with the people who were committing crime, the premise being that crime is a repetitive profession and that a crook will always be a crook, and it's good to know who your adversaries are should you happen to come face to face with them on the street. Timely recognition of a thief had helped crack many a case and had, on some occasions, even saved a detective's life.

So the line-up was a pretty valuable in-group custom. This didn't mean that detectives enjoyed the trip downtown. They drew line-up perhaps once every two weeks and, often as not, line-up duty fell on their day off, and nobody appreciated rubbing elbows with criminals on his day off.

The line-up that Wednesday morning followed the classic pattern of all line-ups. The detectives sat in the gymnasium on folding chairs, and the chief of detectives sat behind a high podium at the back of the gym. The green shades were drawn, and the stage illuminated, and the offenders who'd been arrested the day before were marched before the assembled bulls while the chief read off the charges and handled the interrogation. The pattern was a simple one. The arresting officer, uniformed or plain-clothes, would join the chief at the rear of the gym when his arrest came up. The chief would read off the felon's name, and then the section of the city in which he'd been arrested, and then a number.

He would say, for example, 'Jones, John, Riverhead, three.' The 'three' would simply indicate that this was the third arrest in Riverhead that day. Only felonies and special types of misdemeanours were handled at the line-up, so this narrowed the list of performers on any given day. Following the case number, the chief would read off the offense, and then say either 'Statement' or 'No statement,' telling the assembled cops that the thief either had or had not said anything when they'd put the collar on him.

If there had been a statement, the chief would limit his questions to rather general topics since he didn't want to lead the felon into saying anything that might contradict his usually incriminating initial statement, words that could be used against him in court. If there had been *no* statement, the chief would pull out all the stops. He was generally armed with whatever police records were available on the man who stood under the blinding lights, and it was the smart thief who understood the purpose of the line-up and who knew he was not bound to answer a goddamned thing they asked him. The chief of detectives was something like a deadly earnest Mike Wallace, but the stakes were slightly higher here because this involved something a little more important than a novelist plugging his new book or a senator explaining the stand he had taken on a farm bill. These were truly 'interviews in depth,' and the booby prize was very often a long stretch up the river in a cozy one-windowed room.

The line-up bored the hell out of Kling. It always did. It was like seeing a stage show for the umpteenth time. Every now and then somebody stopped the show with a really good routine. But usually it was the same old song-and-dance. It wasn't any different that Wednesday. By the time the eighth offender had been paraded and subjected to the chief's bludgeoning interrogation, Kling was beginning to doze. The detective sitting next to him nudged him gently in the ribs.

'... Reynolds, Ralph,' the chief was saying, 'Isola, four. Caught burgling an apartment on North Third. No statement. How about it, Ralph?'

'How about what?'

'You do this sort of thing often?'

'What sort of thing?'

'Burglary.'

'I'm no burglar,' Reynolds said.

'I've got his B-sheet here,' the chief said. 'Arrested for burglary in 1948, witness withdrew her testimony, claimed she had mistakenly identified him. Arrested again for burglary in 1952, convicted for Burglary One, sentenced to ten at Castleview, paroled in '58 on good behavior. You're back at the old stand, huh, Ralph?'

'No, not me. I've been straight ever since I got out.'

'Then what were you doing in that apartment during the middle of the night?'

'I was a little drunk. I must have walked into the wrong building.'

'What do you mean?'

'I thought it was my apartment.'

'Where do you live, Ralph?'

'On – uh – well –'

'Come on, Ralph.'

'Well, I live on South Fifth.'

'And the apartment you were in last night is on North Third. You must have been pretty drunk to wander that far off course.'

'Yeah, I guess I was pretty drunk.'

'Woman in that apartment said you hit her when she woke up. Is that true, Ralph?'

'No. No, hey, I never hit her.'

'She says so, Ralph.'

'Well, she's got it all wrong.'

'Well, now, a doctor's report says somebody clipped her on the jaw, Ralph, now how about that?'

'Well, maybe.'

'Yes or no?'

'Well, maybe when she started screaming she got me nervous. I mean, you know, I thought it was my apartment and all.'

'Ralph, you were burgling that apartment. How about telling us the truth?'

'No, I got in there by mistake.'

'How'd you get in ?'

'The door was open.'

'In the middle of the night, huh? The door was open?'

'Yeah.'

'You sure you didn't pick the lock or something, huh?'

'No, no. Why would I do that? I thought it was my apartment.'

'Ralph, what were you doing with burglar's tools?'

'Who? Who, me? Those weren't burglar's tools.'

'Then what were they? You had a glass cutter, and a bunch of jimmies, and some punches, and a drill and bits, and three celluloid strips, and some lockpicking tools, and eight skeleton keys. Those sound like burglar's tools to me, Ralph.'

'No. I'm a carpenter.'

'Yeah, you're a carpenter, all right, Ralph. We searched your apartment, Ralph, and found a couple of things we're curious about. Do you always keep sixteen wrist watches and four typewriters and twelve bracelets and eight rings and two mink stoles and three sets of silverware, Ralph?'

'Yeah. I'm a collector.'

'Of other people's things. We also found four hundred dollars in American currency and five thousand dollars in French francs. Where'd you get that money, Ralph?'

'Which?'

'Whichever you feel like telling us about.'

'Well, the U.S. stuff I – I won at the track. And the other, well a Frenchman owed me some gold, and so he paid me in francs. That's all.'

'We're checking our stolen-goods list right this minute, Ralph.'

'So check!' Reynolds said, suddenly angry. 'What the hell do you want from me? Work for your goddamn living! You want it all on a platter! Like fun! I told you everything I'm gonna ...'

'Get him out of here,' the chief said. 'Next, Blake, Donald, Bethtown, two. Attempted rape. No statement ...'

Bert Kling made himself comfortable on the folding chair and began to doze again.

The check made out to George Badueck was numbered 018. It was a small check, five dollars. It did not seem very important to Carella, but it was one of the unexplained three, and he decided to give it a whirl.

Badueck, as it turned out, was a photographer. His shop was directly across the street from the County Court Building in Isola. A sign in his window advised that he took photographs for chauffeur's licenses, hunting licenses, passports, taxicab permits, pistol permits, and the like. The shop was small and crowded. Badueck fitted into the shop like a beetle in an ant trap. He was a huge man with thick, unruly hair and the smell of developing fluid on him.

'Who remembers?' he said. 'I get millions of people in here every day of the week. They pay me in cash, they pay me with checks, they're ugly, they're pretty, they're skinny, they're fat, they all look the same on the pictures I take. Lousy. They all look like I'm photographing them for you guys. You never see any of these official-type pictures? Man, they look like mug shots, all of them. So who remembers this – what's her name? Claudia Davis, yeah. Another face, that's all. Another mug shot. Why? Is the check bad or something?'

'No, it's a good check.'

'So what's the fuss?'

'No fuss,' Carella said. 'Thanks a lot.'

He sighed and went out into the August heat. The County Court Building across the street was white and Gothic in the sunshine. He wiped a handkerchief across his forehead and thought, Another face, that's all.

Sighing, he crossed the street and entered the building. It was cool in the high-vaulted corridors. He consulted the directory and went up to the Bureau of Motor Vehicles first. He asked the clerk there if anyone named Claudia Davis had applied for a license requiring a photograph.

'We only require pictures on chauffeurs' licenses,' the clerk said.

'Well, would you check?' Carella asked.

'Sure. Might take a few minutes, though. Would you have a seat?'

Carella sat. It was very cool. It felt like October. He looked at his watch. It was almost time for lunch, and he was getting hungry. The clerk came back and motioned him over.

'We've got a Claudia Davis listed,' he said. 'but she's already got a license, and she didn't apply for a new one.'

'What kind of license?'

'Operator's.'

'When does it expire?'

'Next September.'

'And she hasn't applied for anything needing a photo?'

'Nope. Sorry.'

'That's all right. Thanks,' Carella said.

He went out into the corridor again. He hardly thought it likely that Claudia Davis had applied for a permit to own or operate a taxicab, so he skipped the Hack Bureau and went upstairs to Pistol Permits. The woman he spoke to there was very kind and very efficient. She checked her files and told hiim that no one named Claudia Davis had ever applied for either a carry or a premises pistol permit.

Carella thanked her and went into the hall again. He was very hungry. His stomach was beginning to growl. He debated having lunch and then returning and decided, Hell, I'd better get it done now.

The man behind the counter in the Passport Bureau was old and thin and he wore a green eyeshade. Carella asked his question, and the old man went to his files and creakingly returned to the window where Carella waited.

'That's right,' he said.

'What's right?'

'She did. Claudia Davis. She applied for a passport.'

'When?'

The old man checked the slip of paper in his trembling hands. 'July twentieth,' he said.

'Did you give it to her?'

'We accepted her application, sure. Isn't us who issues the passports. We've got to send the application on to Washington.'

'But you did accept it?'

'Sure, why not? Had all the necessary stuff. Why shouldn't we accept it?'

'What was the necessary stuff?'

'Two photos, proof of citizenship, filled-out application, and cash.'

'What did she show as proof of citizenship?'

'Her birth certificate.'

'Where was she born?'

'California.'

'She paid you in cash?'

'That's right.'

'Not a check?'

'Nope. She started to write a check, but the blamed pen was on the blink. We use ballpoints, you know, and it gave out after she filled in the application. So she paid me in cash. It's not all that much money, you know.'

'I see. Thank you,' Carella said.

'Not at all,' the old man replied, and he creaked back to his files to replace the record on Claudia Davis.

The check was numbered 007, and it was dated July twelfth, and it was made out to a woman named Martha Fedelson.

Miss Fedelson adjusted her pince-nez and looked at the check. Then she moved some papers aside on the small desk in the cluttered office, and put the check down, and leaned closer to it, and studied it again.

'Yes,' she said, 'that check was made out to me. Claudia Davis wrote it right in this office.' Miss Fedelson smiled. 'If you can call it an office. Desk space and a telephone. But then, I'm just starting, you know.'

'How long have you been a travel agent, Miss Fedelson?'

'Six months now. It's very exciting work.'

'Had you ever booked a trip for Miss Davis before?'

'No. This was the first time.'

'Did someone refer her to you?'

'No. She picked my name out of the phone book.'

'And asked you to arrange this trip for her, is that righ?'

'Yes.'

'And this check? What's it for?'

'Her airline tickets, and deposits at several hotels.'

'Hotels *where*?'

'In Paris and Dijon. And then another in Lausanne, Switzerland.'

'She was going to Europe?'

'Yes. From Lausanne she was heading down to the Italian

Riviera. I was working on that for her, too. Getting transportation and the hotels, you know.'

'When did she plan to leave?'

'September first.'

'Well, that explains the luggage and the clothes,' Carella said aloud.

'I'm sorry?' Miss Fedelson said, and she smiled and raised her eyebrows.

'Nothing, nothing,' Carella said. 'What was your impression of Miss Davis?'

'Oh, that's hard to say. She was only here once, you understand.' Miss Fedelson thought for a moment, and then said, 'I suppose she *could* have been a pretty girl if she tried, but she wasn't trying. Her hair was short and dark, and she seemed rather – well, withdrawn, I guess. She didn't take her sunglasses off all the while she was here. I suppose you would call her shy. Or frightened. I don't know.' She smiled again. 'Have I helped any?'

'Well, now we know she was going abroad,' Carella said.

'September is a good time to go,' Miss Fedelson answered. 'In September the tourists have all gone home.' There was a wistful sound to her voice.

Carella thanked her for her time and left the small office with its travel folders on the cluttered desk top.

He was running out of checks and running out of ideas. Everything seemed to point toward a girl in flight, a girl in hiding, but what was there to hide, what was there to hide from? Josie Thompson had been in that boat alone. The coroner's jury had labeled it accidental drowning. The insurance company hadn't contested Claudia's claim, and they'd given her a legitimate check that she could have cashed anywhere in the world. And yet there *was* hiding, and there *was* flight – and Carella couldn't understand why. He shook his head.

He took the list of remaining checks from his pocket. The girl's shoemaker, the girl's hairdresser, a florist, a candy shop. None of them really important. And the remaining check made out to an individual, the check numbered 006 and dated July eleventh, and written to a man named David Oblinsky in the amount of $45.75.

Carella had his lunch at two-thirty and then went downtown. He found Oblinsky in a diner near the bus terminal. Oblinsky was sitting on one of the counter stools, and he was drinking a cup of coffee. He asked Carella to join him, and Carella did.

'You traced me through that check, huh?' he said. 'The phone company gave you my number and my address, huh? I'm unlisted, you know. They ain't supposed to give out my number.'

'Well, they made a special concession because it was police business.'

'Yeah, well, suppose the cops called and asked for Marlon Brando's number? You think they'd give it out? Like hell they would. I don't like that. No, sir, I don't like it one damn bit.'

'What do you do, Mr. Oblinsky? Is there a reason for this unlisted number?'

'I drive a cab is what I do. Sure there's a reason. It's classy to have an unlisted number. Didn't you know that?'

Carella smiled. 'No, I didn't.'

'Sure, it is.'

'Why did Claudia Davis give you this check?' Carella asked.

'Well, I work for a cab company here in this city, you see. But usually on weekends or on my day off I use my own car and I take people on long trips, you know what I mean? Like to the country, or the mountains, or the beach, wherever they want to go. I don't care. I'll take them wherever they want to go.'

'I see.'

'Sure. So in June sometime, the beginning of June it was, I get a call from this guy I know up at Triangle Lake, he tells me there's a rich broad there who needs somebody to drive her Caddy back to the city for her. He said it was worth thirty bucks if I was willing to take the train up and the heap back. I told him, no sir. I wanted forty-five or it was no deal. I knew I had him over a barrel, you understand? He'd already told me he checked with the local hicks and none of them felt like making the ride. So he said he would talk it over with her and get back to me. Well, he called again – you know, it burns me up about the phone company. They ain't supposed to give out my number like that. Suppose it was Doris Day? You think they'd give out her number? I'm gonna raise a stink about this, believe me.'

'What happened when he called you back?'

'Well, he said she was willing to pay forty-five, but like could I wait until July sometime when she would send me a check because she was a little short right at the moment. So I figured what the hell, am I going to get stiffed by a dame who's driving a 1960 Caddy? I figured I could trust her until July. But I also told him, if that was the case, then I also wanted her to pay the tolls on the way back, which I don't ordinarily ask my customers to do. That's what the seventy-five cents was for. The tolls.'

'So you took the train up there and then drove Miss Davis and the Cadillac back to the city, is that right?'

'Yeah.'

'I suppose she was pretty distraught on the trip home.'

'Huh?'

'You know. Not too coherent.'

'Huh?'

'Broken up. Crying. Hysterical,' Carella said.

'No. No, she was okay.'

'Well, what I mean is –' Carella hesitated. 'I assumed she wasn't capable of driving the car back herself.'

'Yeah, that's right. That's why she hired me.'

'Well, then –'

'But not because she was broken up or anything.'

'Then why?' Carella frowned. 'Was there lot of luggage? Did she need your help with that?'

'Yeah, sure. Both hers and her cousin's. Her cousin drowned, you know.'

'Yes I know that.'

'But anybody coulda helped her with the luggage,' Oblinsky said. 'No, that wasn't why she hired me. She really *needed* me, mister.'

'Why?'

'Why? Because she don't know how to drive, that's why.'

Carella stared at him. 'You're wrong,' he said.

'Oh, no,' Oblinsky said. 'She can't drive, believe me. While I was putting the luggage in the trunk, I asked her to start the car, and she didn't even know how to do that. Hey, you think I ought to raise a fuss with the phone company?'

'I don't know,' Carella said, rising suddenly. All at once the check made out to Claudia Davis' hairdresser seemed terribly important to him. He had almost run out of checks, but all at once he had an idea.

The hairdresser's salon was on South Twenty-third, just off Jefferson Avenue. A green canopy covered the sidewalk outside the salon. The words ARTURO MANFREDI, INC., were lettered discreetly in white on the canopy. A glass plaque in the window repeated the name of the establishment and added, for the benefit of those who did not read either *Vogue* or *Harper's Bazaar*, that there were two branches of the shop, one here in Isola and another in 'Naussau, the Bahamas.' Beneath that, in smaller words 'Internationally Renowned.'

Carella and Hawes went into the shop at four-thirty in the afternoon. Two meticulously coifed and manicured women were sitting in the small reception room, their expensively sleek legs crossed, apparently awaiting either their chauffeurs, their husbands, or their lovers. They both looked up expectantly when the detectives entered, expressed mild disappointment by only slightly raising newly plucked eyebrows, and went back to reading their fashion magazines.

Carella and Hawes walked to the desk. The girl behind the desk was a blonde with a brilliant shellacked look and a finishing-school voice.

'Yes?' she said. 'May I help you?'

She lost a tiny trace of her poise when Carella flashed his buzzer. She read the raised lettering on the shield, glanced at the photo on the plastic-encased I.D. card, quickly regained her polished calm, and said coolly and unemotionally, 'Yes, what can I do for you?'

'We wonder if you can tell us anything about the girl who wrote this check?' Carella said. He reached into his jacket pocket, took out a photostat of the check, and put it on the desk before the blonde. The blonde looked at it casually.

'What is the name?' she asked. 'I can't make it out.'

'Claudia Davis.'

'D-A-V-I-S?'

'Yes.'

'I don't recognize the name,' the blonde said. 'She's not one of our regular customers.'

'But she did make out a check to your salon,' Carella said. 'She wrote this on July seventh. Would you please check your records and find out why she was here and who took care of her?'

'I'm sorry,' the blonde said.

'What?'

'I'm sorry, but we close at five o'clock, and this is the busiest time of the day for us. I'm sure you can understand that. If you'd care to come back a little later –'

'No, we wouldn't care to come back a little later,' Carella said. 'Because if we came back a little later, it would be with a search warrant and possibly a warrant for the seizure of your books, and sometimes that can cause a little commotion among the gossip columnists, and that kind of commotion might add to your international renown a little bit. We've had a long day, miss, and this is important, so how about it?'

'Of course. We're always delighted to cooperate with the police,' the blonde said frigidly. 'Especially when they're so well mannered.'

'Yes, we're all of that,' Carella answered.

'July seventh, did you say?'

'July seventh.'

The blonde left the desk and went into the back of the salon. A brunette came out front and said, 'Has Miss Marie left for the evening?'

'Who's Miss Marie?' Hawes asked.

'The blonde girl.'

'No. She's getting something for us.'

'That white streak is very attractive,' the brunette said. 'I'm Miss Olga.'

'How do you do.'

'Fine, thank you,' Miss Olga said. 'When she comes back, would you tell her there's something wrong with one of the dryers on the third floor?'

'Yes, I will,' Hawes said.

Miss Olga smiled, waved, and vanished into the rear of the salon again. Miss Marie reappeared a few moments later. She looked at Carella and said, 'A Miss Claudia Davis was here on July seventh. Mr. Sam worked on her. Would you like to talk to him?'

'Yes, we would.'

'Then follow me, please,' she said curtly.

They followed her into the back of the salon past women who sat with crossed legs, wearing smocks, their heads in hair dryers.

'Oh, by the way,' Hawes said, 'Miss Olga said to tell you there's something wrong with one of the third-floor dryers.'

'Thank you,' Miss Marie said.

Hawes felt particularly clumsy in this world of women's machines. There was an air of delicate efficiency about the place, and Hawes – six feet two inches tall in his bare soles, weighing a hundred and ninety pounds – was certain he would knock over a bottle of nail polish or a pail of hair rinse. As they entered the second-floor salon, as he looked down that long line of humming space helmets at women with crossed legs and what looked like barbers' aprons covering their nylon slips, he became aware of a new phenomenon. The women were slowly turning their heads inside the dryers to look at the white streak over his left temple.

He suddenly felt like a horse's rear end. For whereas the streak was the legitimate result of a knifing – they had shaved his red hair to get at the wound, and it had grown back this way – he realized all at once that many of these women had shelled out somebody's hard-earned dollars to simulate identical white streaks in their own hair, and he no longer felt like a cop making a business call. Instead, he felt like a customer who had come to have his goddamned streak touched up a little.

'This is Mr. Sam,' Miss Marie said, and Hawes turned to see Carella shaking hands with a rather elongated man. The man wasn't particularly tall, he was simply elongated. He gave the impression of being seen from the side seats in a movie theater, stretched out of true proportion, curiously two-dimensional. He wore a white smock, and there were three narrow combs in the breast pocket. He carried a pair of scissors in one thin, sensitive-looking hand.

'How do you do?' he said to Carella, and he executed a half bow, European in origin, American in execution. He turned to Hawes, took his hand, shook it, and again said, 'How do you do?'

'They're from the police,' Miss Marie said briskly, releasing Mr. Sam from any obligation to be polite, and then left the men alone.

'A woman named Claudia Davis was here on July seventh,' Carella said. 'Apparently she had her hair done by you. Would you be kind enough to tell us what you remember about her?'

'Miss Davis, Miss Davis,' Mr. Sam said, touching his high forehead in an attempt at visual shorthand, trying to convey the concept of thought without having to do the accompanying brainwork. 'Let me see, Miss Davis, Miss Davis.'

'Yes.'

'Yes, Miss Davis. A very pretty blonde.'

'No,' Carella said. He shook his head. 'A brunette. You're thinking of the wrong person.'

'No, I'm thinking of the right person,' Mr. Sam said. He tapped his temple with one extended forefinger, another piece of visual abbreviation. 'I remember Claudia Davis. A blonde.'

'A brunette,' Carella insisted, and he kept watching Mr. Sam.

'When she left. But when she came, a blonde.'

'What?' Hawes said.

'She was a blonde, a very pretty, natural blonde. It is rare. Natural blondness, I mean. I couldn't understand why she wanted to change the color.'

'You dyed her hair?' Hawes asked.

'That is correct.'

'Did she say *why* she wanted to be a brunette?'

'No, sir. I argued with her. I said, "You have *beau*-tiful hair, I can do *mar*-velous things with this hair of yours. You are a *blonde*, my dear, there are drab women who come in here every day of the week and *beg* to be turned into blondes." No. She would not listen. I dyed it for her. Made her a brunette.'

Mr. Sam seemed to become offended by the idea all over again. He looked at the detectives as if they had been responsible for the stubbornness of Claudia Davis.

'What else did you do for her, Mr. Sam?' Carella asked.

'The dye, a cut, and a set. And I believe one of the girls gave her a facial and a manicure.'

'What do you mean by a cut? Was her hair long when she came here?'

'Yes, beautiful long blonde hair. She wanted it cut. I cut it.' Mr. Sam shook his head. 'A pity. She looked terrible. I don't usually say this about someone I worked on, but she walked out of here looking terrible. You would hardly recognize her as the same pretty blonde who came in not three hours before.'

'Thank you, Mr. Sam. We know you're busy.'

In the street outside Hawes said, 'You knew before we went in there, didn't you, Mr. Steve?'

'I suspected, Mr. Cotton. Come on, let's get back to the squad.'

They kicked it around like a bunch of advertising executives. They sat in Lieutenant Byrnes' office and tried to find out how the cookie crumbled and which way the Tootsie rolled. They were just throwing out a life preserver to see if anyone grabbed at it, that's all. What they were doing, you see, was running up the flag to see if anyone saluted, that's all.

The lieutenant's office was a four-window office because he was top man in this particular combine. It was a very elegant office. It had an electric fan all its own, and a big wide desk. It got cross ventilation from the street. It was really very pleasant. Well, to tell the truth, it was a pretty ratty office in which to be holding a top-level meeting, but it was the best the precinct had to offer. And after a while you got used to the chipping paint and the soiled walls and the bad lighting and the stench of urine from the men's room down the hall. Peter Byrnes didn't work for B.B.D. & O. He worked for the city. Somehow, there was a difference.

'I just put in a call to Irene Miller,' Carella said. 'I asked her to describe Claudia Davis to me, and she went through it all over again. Short dark hair, shy, plain. Then I asked her to describe the cousin, Josie Thompson.' Carella nodded glumly. 'Guess what?'

'A pretty girl,' Hawes said. 'A pretty girl with long blonde hair.'

'Sure. Why, Mrs. Miller practically spelled it out the first time we talked to her. It's all there in the report. She said they were like black and white in looks and personality. Black and white, sure. A brunette and a goddamn blonde!'

'That explains the yellow,' Hawes said.

'What yellow?'

'Courtenoy. He said he saw a patch of yellow breaking the surface. He wasn't talking about her clothes, Steve. He was talking about her *hair.*'

'It explains a lot of things,' Carella said. 'It explains why shy Claudia Davis was preparing for her European trip by purchasing baby-doll nightgowns and Bikini bathing suits. And it explains why the undertaker up there referred to Claudia as a pretty girl. And it explains why our necropsy report said she was thirty when everybody talked about her as if she were much younger.'

'The girl who drowned wasn't Josie, huh?' Meyer said. 'You figure she was Claudia.'

'Damn right I figure she was Claudia.'

'And you figure Josie cut her hair afterward, and dyed it, and took her cousin's name, and tried to pass as her cousin until she could get out of the country, huh?' Meyer said.

'Why?' Byrnes said. He was a compact man with a compact bullet head and a chunky economical body. He did not like to waste time or words.

'Because the trust income was in Claudia's name. Because Josie didn't have a dime of her own.'

'She could have collected on her cousin's insurance policy,' Meyer said.

'Sure, but that would have been the end of it. The trust called for those stocks to be turned over to U.C.L.A. if Claudia died. A college, for Pete's sake! How do you suppose Josie felt about that? Look, I'm not trying to hang a homicide on her. I just think she took advantage of a damn good situation. Claudia was in that boat alone. When she fell over the side, Josie really tried to rescue her, no question about it. But she missed, and Claudia drowned. Okay. Josie went all to pieces, couldn't talk straight, crying, sobbing, real hysterical woman, we've seen them before. But came the dawn. And with the dawn Josie began thinking. They were away from the city, strangers in a strange town.

'Claudia had drowned but no one *knew* that she was Claudia. No one but Josie. She had no identification on her, remember? Her purse was in the car. Okay. If Josie identified her cousin correctly, she'd collect twenty-five grand on the insurance policy, and then all that stock would be turned over to the college, and that would be the end of the gravy train. But suppose, just suppose Josie told the police the girl in the lake was Josie Thompson? Suppose she said, "I, Claudia Davis, tell you that girl who drowned is my cousin, Josie Thompson"?'

Hawes nodded. 'Then she'd still collect on an insurance policy, and also fall heir to those fat security dividends coming in.'

'Right. What does it take to cash a dividend check? A bank account, that's all. A bank account with an established signature. So all she had to do was open one, sign her name as Claudia Davis, and then endorse every dividend check that came in exactly the same way.'

'Which explains the new account,' Meyer said. 'She couldn't use Claudia's old account because the bank undoubtedly knew both Claudia *and* her signature. So Josie had to forfeit the sixty grand at Highland Trust and start from scratch.'

'And while she was building a new identity and a new fortune,' Hawes said, 'just to make sure Claudia's few friends forgot all about her, Josie was running off to Europe. She may have planned to stay there for years.'

'It all ties in,' Carella said. 'Claudia had a driver's license. She was the one who drove the car away from Stewart City. But Josie had to hire a chauffeur to take her back.'

'And would Claudia, who was so meticulous about money matters, have kept so many people waiting for payment?' Hawes said. 'No, sir. That was Josie. And Josie was broke. Josie was waiting for that insurance policy to pay off so she could settle those debts and get the hell out of the country.'

'Well, I admit it adds up,' Meyer said.

Peter Byrnes never wasted words. 'Who cashed that twenty-five-thousand-dollar check for Josie?' he said.

There was silence in the room.

'Who's got the missing five grand?' he said.

There was another silence.

'Who *killed* Josie?' he said.

Jeremiah Dodd of the Security Insurance Corporation, Inc., did not call until two days later. He asked to speak to Detective Carella, and when he got him on the phone, he said, 'Mr. Carella, I've just heard from San Francisco on that check.'

'What check?' Carella asked. He had been interrogating a witness to a knifing in a grocery store on Culver Avenue. The Claudia Davis or rather the Josie Thompson Case was not quite yet in the Open File, but it was ready to be dumped there, and was the farthest thing from Carella's mind at the moment.

'The check paid to Claudia Davis,' Dodd said.

'Oh, yes. Who cashed it?'

'Well, there are two endorsements on the back. One was made by Claudia Davis, of course. The other was made by an outfit called Leslie Summers, Inc. It's a regular company stamp marked "For Deposit Only" and signed by one of the officers.'

'Have you any idea what sort of a company that is?' Carella asked.

'Yes,' Dodd said. 'They handle foreign exchange.'

'Thank you,' Carella said, and hung up the phone.

He went there with Bert Kling later that afternoon. He went with Kling completely by chance and only because Kling was heading downtown to buy his mother a birthday gift and offered Carella a ride. When they parked the car, Kling asked, 'How long will this take, Steve?'

'Few minutes, I guess.'

'Want to meet me back here?'

'Well, I'll be at 720 Hall, Leslie Summers, Inc. If you're through before me, come on over.'

'Okay, I'll see you,' Kling said.

They parted on Hall Avenue without shaking hands. Carella found the street-level office of Leslie Summers, Inc., and walked in. A counter ran the length of the room, and there were several girls behind it. One of the girls was speaking to a customer in French and another was talking Italian to a man who wanted lire in exchange for dollars. A board behind the desk quoted the current exchange rate for countries all over the world.

Carella got in line and waited. When he reached the counter, the girl who'd been speaking French said, 'Yes, sir?'

'I'm a detective,' Carella said. He opened his wallet to where his shield was pinned to the leather. 'You cashed a check for Miss Claudia Davis sometime in July. An insurance-company check for twenty-five thousand dollars. Would you happen to remember it?'

'No, sir, I don't think I handled it.'

'Would you check around and see who did, please?'

The girl held a brief consultation with the other girls, and then walked to a desk behind which sat a corpulent, balding man with a razor-thin mustache. They talked with each other for a full five minutes. The man kept waving his hands. The girl kept trying to explain about the insurance-company check. The bell over the front door sounded. Bert Kling came in, looked around, saw Carella, and joined him at the counter.

'All done?' Carella asked.

'Yeah, I bought her a charm for her bracelet. How about you?'

'They're holding a summit meeting,' Carella said.

The fat man waddled over to the counter. 'What is the trouble?' he asked Carella.

'No trouble. Did you cash a check for twenty-five thousand dollars?'

'Yes. Is the check no good?'

'It's a good check.'

'It looked like a good check. It was an insurance-company check. The young lady waited while we called the company. They said it was bona fide and we should accept it. Was it a bad check?'

'No, no, it was fine.'

'She had identification. It all seemed very proper.'

'What did she show you?'

'A driver's license or a passport is what we usually require. But she had neither. We accepted her birth certificate. After all, we *did* call the company. Is the check no good?'

'It's fine. But the check was for twenty-five thousand, and we're trying to find out what happened to five thousand of –'

'Oh, yes. The francs.'

'What?'

'She bought five thousand dollars' worth of French francs,' the fat man said. 'She was going abroad?'

'Yes, she was going abroad,' Carella said. He sighed heavily. 'Well, that's that, I guess.'

'It all seemed very proper,' the fat man insisted.

'Oh, it was. Thank you. Come on, Bert.'

They walked down Hall Avenue in silence.

'Beats me,' Carella said.

'What's that, Steve?'

'This case.' He sighed again. 'Oh, what the hell!'

'Yeah, let's get some coffee. What was all this business about all those francs?'

'She bought five thousand dollars' worth of francs,' Carella said.

'The French are getting a big play lately, huh?' Kling said smiling. 'Here's a place. This look okay?'

'Yeah, fine,' Carella pulled open the door of the luncheonette.
'What do you mean, Bert?'

'With the francs.'

'What about them?'

'The exchange rate must be very good.'

'I don't get you.'

'You know. All those francs kicking around.'

'Bert, what the hell are you talking about?'

'Weren't you with me? Last Wednesday?'

'With you where?'

'The line-up. I thought you were with me.'

'No, I wasn't,' Carella said tiredly.

'Oh, well, that's why.'

'That's why what? Bert, for the love of –'

'That's why you don't remember him.'

'Who?'

'The punk they brought in on that burglary pickup. They
found five grand in French francs in his apartment.'

Carella felt as if he'd just been hit by a truck.

It had been crazy from the beginning. Some of them are like
that. The girl had looked black, but she was really white. They
thought she was Claudia Davis, but she was Josie Thompson.
And they had been looking for a murderer when all there
happened to be was a burglar.

They brought him up from his cell where he was awaiting
trial for Burglary One. He came up in an elevator with a police
escort. The police van had dropped him off at the side door of
the Criminal Courts Building, and he had entered the corridor
under guard and been marched down through the connecting
tunnel and into the building that houses the district attorney's
office, and then taken into the elevator. The door of the elevator
opened into a tiny room upstairs. The other door of the room
was locked from the outside and a sign on it read NO
ADMITTANCE.

The patrolman who'd brought Ralph Reynolds up to the
interrogation room stood with his back against the elevator door

all the while the detectives talked to him, and his right hand was on the butt of his Police Special.

'I never heard of her,' Reynolds said.

'Claudia Davis,' Carella said. 'Or Josie Thompson. Take your choice of names. Either one will do.'

'I don't know either one of them. What the hell *is* this? You got me on a burglary rap, now you try to pull in everything was ever done in this city?'

'Who said anything was done, Reynolds?'

'If nothing was done, why'd you drag me up here?'

'They found five thousand bucks in French francs in your pad, Reynolds. Where'd you get it?'

'Who wants to know?'

'Don't get snotty, Reynolds! Where'd you get that money?'

'A guy owed it to me. He paid me in francs. He was a French guy – so he'd pay in francs.'

'What's his name?'

'I can't remember.'

'You'd better start trying.'

'Pierre something.'

'Pierre what?' Meyer said.

'Pierre La Salle, something like that. I didn't know him too good.'

'But you lent him five grand, huh?'

'Yeah.'

'What were you doing on the night of August first?'

'Why? What happened on August first?'

'You tell us.'

'I don't know what I was doing.'

'Were you working?'

'I'm unemployed.'

'You know what we mean!'

'No. What do you mean?'

'Were you breaking into apartments?'

'No.'

'Speak up! Yes or no?'

'I said no.'

'He's lying, Steve,' Meyer said.

'Sure he is.'

'Yeah, sure I am. Look, cop, you got nothing on me but Burglary One, if that. And that you got to prove in court. So stop trying to hang anything else on me. You ain't got a chance.'

'Not unless those prints check out,' Carella said quickly.

'What prints?'

'The prints we found on the dead girl's throat,' Carella lied.

'I was wearing –!'

The small room was as still as death.

Reynolds sighed heavily. He looked at the floor.

'You want to tell us?'

'No,' he said. 'Go to hell.'

He finally told them. After twelve hours of repeated questioning he finally broke down. He hadn't meant to kill her, he said. He didn't even know anybody was in the apartment. He had looked in the bedroom, and the bed was empty. He hadn't seen her asleep in one of the chairs, fully dressed.

He had found the French money in a big jar on one of the shelves over the sink. He had taken the money and then accidentally dropped the jar, and she woke up and came into the room and saw him and began screaming. So he grabbed her by the throat. He only meant to shut her up. But she kept struggling. She was very strong. He kept holding on to her, but only to shut her up.

But she kept struggling so he had to hold on. She kept struggling as if – as if he'd really been trying to kill her, as if she didn't want to lose her life. But that was manslaughter, wasn't it? He wasn't trying to kill her. That wasn't homicide, was it?

'I didn't mean to kill her!' he shouted as they took him into the elevator. 'She began screaming! I'm not a killer! Look at me! Do I look like a killer?' And then, as the elevator began dropping to the basement, he shouted, 'I'm a burglar!' as if proud of his profession, as if stating that he was something more than a common thief, as if he was a trained workman, a skilled artisan.

'I'm not a killer! I'm a burglar!' he screamed. 'I'm not a killer!

I'm not a killer! I'm not a killer!' And his voice echoed down the elevator shaft as the car dropped to the basement and the waiting van.

They sat in the small room for several moments after he was gone.

'Hot in here,' Meyer said.

'Yeah.' Carella nodded.

'What's the matter?'

'Nothing.'

'Maybe he's right,' Meyer said. 'Maybe he's only a burglar.'

'He stopped being that the minute he stole a life, Meyer.'

'Josie Thompson stole a life, too.'

'No,' Carella said. He shook his head. 'She only borrowed one. There's a difference, Meyer.'

The room went silent.

'You feel like some coffee?' Meyer asked.

'Sure.'

They took the elevator down and then walked out into the brilliant August sunshine. The streets were teeming with life. They walked into the human swarm, but they were silent.

At last Carella said, 'I guess I think she shouldn't be dead. I guess I think that someone who tried so hard to make a life shouldn't have had it taken away from her.'

Meyer put his hand on Carella's shoulder. 'Listen,' he said earnestly. 'It's a job. It's only a job.'

'Sure,' Carella said. 'It's only a job.'

Georges Simenon

Mme. Maigret's Admirer

In the Maigret household, as in most families, there had arisen
certain traditions which had come, in time, to take on much
significance. For instance, after they had been living in the Place
des Vosges for years and years, the Inspector had acquired the
habit, in summer, of beginning to loosen the knot of his dark tie
as he started up the stairway from the court – a process which
lasted exactly the length of time it took him to reach the first
floor.

The apartment house, like all those on the Place, had once
been a sumptuous mansion; the first flight of the staircase rose
majestically with wrought-iron railings and imitation marble
walls. But the second flight became narrow and steep; and thus
Maigret, who was growing rather short of wind, could mount to
his own floor with his collar open.

By the time he had gone down a dimly lit corridor and
inserted his key in his own door (the third on the left), he would
have his coat over his arm. Unfailingly he would call out, 'Here
I am!' – sniff around, deduce from the aromas what there was
for lunch, then enter the dining room, where the large window
would be open upon the dazzling spectacle of the Place where
four fountains sang.

This June there was a slight addition to the ritual.

The weather was particularly hot. The P.J. – as Maigret's
colleagues always shortened their formal title of *Police
Judiciaire*, or Judiciary Police – thought of nothing but their
vacations. Occasionally gentlemen could be seen in shirt-sleeves
on the smartest boulevards; and beer poured in torrents at every
sidewalk café.

'Have you seen your admirer?' Maigret would ask his wife as he settled himself by the window and mopped his brow.

No one could have thought, at this moment, that he had just come from hours of work in that anti-criminal laboratory which is the Judiciary Police – hours of poring over the darkest and most disheartening involutions of the human soul. When he was off duty, the least trifle could amuse him, especially when it involved teasing the ever naive Mme. Maigret. For two weeks now, his standing joke had been to ask her for news of her admirer.

'Has he taken his two little prowls around the place? Is he still just as mysterious, just as distinguished? When I think that you have a weakness for distinguished men ... and married me!'

Mme. Maigret would be coming and going from kitchen to table. She had no use for a maid; a cleaning woman for the heavy work was enough. She would play up the game with faint irritation: 'I never said he was distinguished!'

'Ah, but you've described him: pearl-gray hat, little pointed mustaches (probably dyed), cane with a carved irony head ...'

'Go on! Laugh! Some day you'll admit I'm right. This isn't just a man like anybody else. There's something serious behind the way he's acting ...'

From the window one would notice automatically the comings and goings on the Place – somewhat deserted in the morning but filled in the afternoon with the mothers and servants of the neighborhood, sitting on the benches and watching the children at play.

The square, girded with grillwork, is one of the most typical in Paris. The houses stand about it in precise identity, with their arcades and their steep slate roofs. And the four fountains sing ...

At first Mme. Maigret had scarcely noticed the stranger, and that by accident. It was hard not to notice him; both in appearance and in attitude he seemed twenty or thirty years dated – an elderly gallant such as one now sees only in the cartoons of humorous magazines. It was early one morning, when all the windows around the Place were open, and you could watch the servants going about their housework.

'He looks as if he were hunting for something,' Mme. Maigret thought to herself.

That afternoon she had gone to visit her sister. The next morning, at precisely the same hour, she rediscovered her stranger. With even stride he strolled around the Place, once, twice, then vanished in the direction of the Boulevard.

'Fellow with a weakness for cute little maids – likes to watch them shake out the rugs,' said Maigret, when his wife, relating this and that of the day's events, brought up her elderly gallant.

But that very afternoon she was not a little startled to see him, at three o'clock, sitting on a bench directly facing her house – motionless, both hands clasped on the ivory head of his cane. At four, he was still there. Not until five did he rise and go off down the Rue des Tournelles, without having exchanged a word with anyone, without so much as having glanced at a newspaper.

'Don't you think there's something funny about that, Maigret?' For Mme. Maigret had always called her husband by his family name.

'I told you once: he was happy just watching the pretty little maids around him.'

The next day Mme. Maigret brought it up again: 'I kept a sharp eye on him; he sat there two hours on the same bench without a move ...'

'Come now! Maybe it was to watch you! From that bench anybody can see into our apartment, and this gentleman is in love with you and –'

'Don't be silly!'

'Besides, he uses a cane and you've always loved men with canes. I'll bet he wears a monocle ...'

'And why, pray?'

'You've always had a weakness for men with monocles.'

They chaffed each other gently, securely savoring the inner peace of twenty years of marriage.

'But listen! I looked all around him, very carefully. To be sure, there was one maid, sitting right opposite him. She's a girl I'd already noticed at the fruit store, first of all because she's so pretty, then because she seems very distinguished ...'

'That's it!' Maigret cried triumphantly. 'Your distinguished servant sits opposite your distinguished gentleman. You may have noticed that women are apt to sit down without too much heed to the perspectives which they may uncover; so your admirer has spent the day leering at –'

'That's all you ever think of!'

'Since I haven't yet seen your mystery-man –'

'Can I help it if he never shows up when you're home?'

And Maigret, whose life intersected so many tragedies, plunged himself into these simple pleasantries and never forgot to demand the latest news of the individual who had become, in their private language, Mme. Maigret's admirer.

'Go on; laugh if you want to. But just the same there's something about him, I don't know what, but it fascinates me and makes me just a little afraid ... I don't know how to say it. When once you look at him, you can't take your eyes off him. For hours on end he just sits there and doesn't move a muscle. He doesn't even shift his eyes behind his glasses.'

'You can see behind his glasses ... from here?'

Mme. Maigret almost blushed, as though caught red-handed. 'I went over to look at him closer. Especially I wanted to see if you were right about ... perspectives. Well, the blonde maid always has two children with her and she couldn't be more proper and you can't see a thing.'

'She stays there all afternoon, too?'

'She comes around three, usually before *he* does. She always has her crocheting with her. They leave at almost the very same moment. For whole hours she works at her crocheting without so much as raising her head excepting to call the children if they wander too far away.'

'And you really don't think, darling, that the Paris squares are full of hundreds of maids knitting or crocheting for hours on end while they mind their employers' children?'

'Well, maybe ...'

'And just as many retired old men who have no interest in life but to warm themselves in the sun while contemplating an agreeable young figure?'

'But this one isn't old!'

'You told me yourself that his mustache was dyed and he must be wearing a wig.'

'Yes, but that doesn't make him old.'

'About my age, then?'

'Sometimes he acts older and sometimes younger ...'

And Maigret grumbled with assumed jealousy, 'One of these days I'll have to go over there in person and settle accounts with this admirer of yours!'

Neither of them took any of this seriously. In the same way they had for some time taken a great and playful interest in a loving pair who met every night under the arcades. The Maigrets had followed intently each quarrel, each reconciliation, until the girl, who worked at the creamery, had one night met another young man at precisely the same spot.

'You know, Maigret ...'

'What?'

'I've been thinking ... I've been wondering if that man is there to spy on somebody ...'

The days went by and the sun grew hotter and hotter. Now, in the evening, the Place was filled with an ever denser crowd of working people from the nearby streets who came seeking a little fresh air by the four fountains.

'What looks funny to me is that he never sits down in the mornings. And why does he always walk around the Place twice, as if he were waiting for a signal?'

'What's your pretty blonde doing all this time in the morning?'

'I can't see her then. She works in a house down on the right and from here you can't see what goes on there. I meet her when I'm marketing, but she doesn't talk to a soul except to tell what she wants to buy. She doesn't even argue about the price, so she gets cheated at least twenty per cent. She always looks as though she were thinking about something else.'

'Fine! The next time I need a really delicate investigation handled, I'll put you on it instead of my men.'

'Make fun of me! Go on! But someday you'll see ...'

It was eight o'clock. Maigret had finished dinner – amazingly early, since he was usually kept late at the Quai-des-Orfèvres. He was in shirtsleeves, his pipe in his mouth, his elbows resting on the window while he vaguely contemplated the rosy sky, soon to be invaded by darkness, and the Place des Vosges, filled with a crowd exhausted by the precocious summer.

Behind him he heard the noises which meant that Mme. Maigret was finishing the dishes and would soon join him with her sewing.

Evenings like this were rare – evenings with no dirty mess to clear up, no murderer to discover, no thief to shadow, evenings when a man's thoughts could roam at peace. Maigret's pipe had never tasted so good. Then suddenly, without turning, he called out, 'Henriette?'

'Do you want something?'

'Come here …'

With the stem of his pipe he guided her eye to the bench directly facing them. At one end of the bench a bum was napping. At the other end …

'That's the one!' Mme. Maigret asserted. 'Of all things!'

It seemed to her almost indecent that her afternoon admirer should have so violated his schedule as to appear on the bench at such an hour.

'He looks as though he's fallen asleep,' Maigret murmured, as he relit his pipe. 'If there weren't two flights of stairs to climb, I'd go have a look at your admirer, just to see what he's really like.'

Mme. Maigret went back to the kitchen. Maigret followed the argument of three small boys, who wound up rolling in the dust while more boys circled them on roller skates.

Maigret had not moved by the time his second pipe was finished. Neither had the stranger. The bum had lurched off toward the wharfs of the Seine. Mme. Maigret had taken her place by the window, cloth and scissors and dress pattern in her lap – the housewife incapable of sitting still for an hour with nothing to do.

'Is he still there?'

'Yes.'

'Aren't they going to close the gates?'

'In a few minutes. The watchman's beginning to herd people toward the exits.'

The watchman seemed not to notice the stranger. The man on the bench still did not move and three of the gates were already locked. The watchman was about to turn the key in the fourth when Maigret, without a word, seized his coat and started downstairs.

From the window Mme. Maigret saw him arguing with the man in green, who took his duties seriously. At last the man admitted the Inspector, who walked straight toward the stranger with the glasses.

Mme. Maigret had risen. She felt that something was happening and she gestured to her husband, a gesture that meant, 'Is this it?' She couldn't have said clearly what *it* was, but for days and days she had been apprehensive that *something* was about to happen. Maigret nodded to her, stationed the watchman by the gate, and climbed back to their apartment.

'My collar, my tie …'

'He's dead?'

'About as dead as anyone can be. For at least two hours or I'm losing my touch.'

'Do you think he had an attack?'

Silence from Maigret. Tying a tie was always something of a problem for him.

'What are you going to do?'

'What should I be doing? Start the investigation going. Notify Headquarters, the medical office, the whole works …'

A velvet darkness had fallen on the Place. The song of the fountains seemed louder. As always, the fourth one had a tone a trifle sharper than the others.

A few moments later, Maigret entered the tobacco shop in the Rue du Pas-de-la-Mule, made a series of phone calls, and found a policeman to station at the gate instead of the watchman.

Mme. Maigret had no wish to go downstairs. She knew that her husband loathed the thought of her intervening in his cases. She understood, too, that for once he was at ease; no one had noticed the corpse with the glasses, nor the comings and goings of the Inspector.

Besides, the Place was almost deserted. The people from the flower shop downstairs were sitting in front of their door, and the dealer in automobile accessories, in his long gray smock, had come over to chat with them.

They were astonished to see a car stop before the gate and proceed into the square. They drew nearer when they saw a second car with a solemn gentleman who must belong to Police Headquarters. At last, when the ambulance arrived, the group of curious onlookers had grown to almost fifty people, not one of whom suspected the reason for this strange assembly, since the shrubbery concealed the focal scene.

Mme. Maigret had not lit the lamps; she rarely did when she was alone. She kept looking around the Place, watching the windows open, but she saw no sign of the pretty blonde maid.

The ambulance left first, headed for the Medico-Legal Institute. Then a car with certain people; then Maigret, chatting on the sidewalk with some men before he crossed the street and re-entered his home.

'You aren't lighting up,' he grumbled.

She turned the switch.

'Close the window. It's cooled off.'

This was no longer the detached Maigret of a short while ago, but Maigret of the P.J., Maigret whose attacks of bad temper made young Inspectors tremble.

'Stop that sewing! You get on my nerves! Can't you sit still a minute?'

She stopped. He paced up and down the little room, his hands behind his back, favoring his wife with an occasional curious glance.

'Why did you tell me he seemed sometimes young, sometimes old?'

'I don't know ... just an impression. Why? How old is he?'

'He can't be more than thirty.'

'What are you saying?'

'I'm saying that this pal of yours isn't remotely what he seemed to be. I'm saying that under his wig there was young blond hair, that his dyed mustache was a phony, that he was wearing a sort of corset which gave him that stiffness of an elderly gallant.'

'But –'

'No buts about it. I'm still wondering just what sort of miracle made you sniff out this case.'

He seemed to hold her responsible for what had happened, for his ruined evening, for all the hard work ahead.

'You know what's happened? Your admirer's been murdered, there on that bench.'

'It isn't possible! Right in front of everybody?'

'In front of everybody, and undoubtedly at the exact moment when there were the most witnesses.'

'Do you think the maid –'

'I've sent the bullet down to an expert. He could phone me any minute.'

'But how could anybody fire a revolver in –'

Maigret shrugged his shoulders and waited for the phone call. It came promptly.

'Hello! ... Yes, I thought so, too ... But I needed you to confirm it.'

Mme. Maigret was all impatience; but her husband deliberately took his time, grumbling to himself as though it were no concern of hers. 'Compressed air rifle ... special model ... very rare ...'

'I don't understand ...'

'That means the fellow was killed from a distance – by somebody, for instance, ambushed in one of the windows on the Place. He could take his time to aim, but he must have been a first-class shot. He hit the heart exactly; death was instantaneous.'

Like that, there in the sunlight, while the crowd ...

Mme. Maigret suddenly began to cry, from sheer nervous

exhaustion. She apologized awkwardly, 'I'm sorry. It was too much for me. It does seem to me as though I have something to do with this. I know it's silly, but ...'

'When you've pulled yourself together, I'll take your deposition as a witness.'

'Me? A witness?'

'Hang it, you're the only person so far who can give us any useful information, thanks to the curiosity that drove you to ...' And Maigret went on, still as if talking to himself, to give her a few of the facts:

'The man hadn't a single paper on him. Pockets practically empty, aside from a few hundred-franc bills, some change, a very small key, and a nail file. We'll try to identify him anyway.'

'Only thirty!' Mme. Maigret repeated.

It was astonishing. And now she could understand the almost sinister fascination she had sensed in this youth congealed, like a wax image, into the postures of an old man.

'Are you ready to testify?'

'I'm listening.'

'I ask you to note that I am questioning you in my official capacity and that I shall be obliged tomorrow to draw up a formal deposition as a result of this interview.'

Mme. Maigret smiled. It was a pale smile; she found this shift to an official relationship oddly impressive.

'Did you notice this man today?'

'I didn't see him this morning; I went marketing at the Halles. In the afternoon he was at his usual place.'

'And the blonde maid?'

'She was there, too, as usual.'

'You never caught them speaking to each other.'

'They'd have had to talk very loud; they were about eight meters apart.'

'And they'd sit there, motionless, all afternoon?'

'Except when the woman was crocheting.'

'Always crocheting? For a whole two weeks?'

'Yes.'

'You didn't notice what type of crochet work she was doing?'

'No. If it had been knitting, that's something I know about, but —'

'When did the woman leave this afternoon?'

'I don't know. I was fixing the custard. Probably around five, as usual.'

'Around five ... which is just when the doctor fixes the time of death. But there's a leeway of minutes one way or the other. Did the woman leave before five or after five, before the murder or after the murder? And why the devil did you have to pick today of all days to make a custard? If you're going to take up spying on people, you should carry it through to the finish!'

'Do you think that woman ...?'

'I don't think anything! All I know is that I've nothing to base my investigation on but your reports ... which are something short of detailed. Do you happen to know so much as where your blonde maid works?'

'She always goes home to 17 *bis*.'

'And who lives at 17 *bis*?'

'I don't know ... People with a big American car and a chauffeur who looks like a foreigner.'

'That's all you've noticed, is it? You'd make a fine policeman, I must say! A big American car and a chauffeur who —' He was play-acting, as he so often did when an investigation led nowhere; now his anger dissolved into a smile. 'You know, old girl, if you hadn't taken an interest in your admirer's carryings-on, I'd be in a beautiful jam right now? I'm not saying that the situation is perfect, or that the investigation will solve itself like *that*; but at least we've got something to start with, however slight ...'

'The beautiful blonde?'

'The beautiful blonde. And that reminds me —' He hurried to the phone and ordered an Inspector stationed in front of 17 *bis* with instructions, if a beautiful blonde emerged, not to lose sight of her at any cost.

'And now to bed. There'll be time enough tomorrow morning.'

He was half asleep when the timid voice of his wife ventured, 'You don't think maybe it might be a good idea to —'

'No, no, and no!' He half sat up in bed. 'Just because you very nearly displayed a minor talent is no reason to start in giving me advice! Besides, it's time to sleep.'

And time for the moon to silver the slate roofs of the Place des Vosges, time for the four fountains to continue their recital of chamber music, with the fourth seeming always a little hurried, a little out of tune.

When Maigret, face daubed with shaving soap, suspenders hanging down, cast his first glance out over the Place des Vosges, an impressive group had already gathered about the bench where the corpse had been discovered.

The owner of the flower shop, better informed than the rest since she had been present (even if at a distance) when the police arrived, was giving voluble explanations. Her categorical gestures emphasized the certainty of her opinions.

Everyone in the neighborhood was there. Passersby, who a moment before had been hurrying to be on time at shop or office, had suddenly found leisure to stop at the scene of the crime.

'Do you know that woman over there?' The Inspector used the handle of his razor to indicate a young woman who stood out from those around her. The fresh elegance of her English-cut costume seemed more suited to a morning stroll on the Bois de Boulogne than to the Place des Vosges.

'I have never seen her. At least I don't think so ...'

It might mean nothing. The apartments on the first floors of the Place des Vosges may contain the upper middle class and even the lesser levels of the world of Society. Still Maigret stared at the woman irritably; women of her class rarely set out afoot at eight in the morning, unless it's to walk the dog.

'Now, look: this morning you're going to do some extensive marketing. You're to go into every shop. Listen to everything they say, and above all try to find out anything you can about the blonde maid and her employers.'

'And for once you can't make fun of me for gossiping!' Mme. Maigret smiled. 'When will you be back?'

'Do I know?'

For he knew the investigation had gone ahead while he slept, and he hoped to find at the Quai-des-Orfèvres some solid basis for his own inquiries.

At eleven o'clock the previous evening, for instance, the famous medico-legal expert, Dr. Hébrard, was in full evening dress, attending a first night at the Comédie-Française, when he received a message. He waited until the last act, and then paused at a box to congratulate an actress with whom his relations were non-professional. A quarter of an hour later, at the Medico-Legal Institute (which is the new name for the morgue), one of his assistants handed him his white working smock while an attendant withdrew from one of the endless niches in the wall the frozen corpse of the unknown man from the bench in the Place des Vosges.

At the same time, in the Palace of Justice, where the files contain details on all the criminals of France and most of the criminals of the world, two men in gray smocks patiently compared fingerprints.

Not far from them, up a spiral staircase, the specialists of the police laboratory began their meticulous work on certain objects: one dark suit (old-fashioned), two shoes (buttoned), one cane (rattan with carved ivory handle), one wig, one pair of glasses, and one tuft of blond hair cut from the dead man's head.

When Maigret had greeted his colleagues, held a brief talk with his chief, and entered his office (which still smelled of cold pipe smoke despite the open window), three reports were waiting for him, neatly arranged on his desk.

First, Dr Hébrard's report:

Death almost instantaneous. Bullet fired from distance of at least 20 meters, possibly 100. Weapon of small caliber but great penetrative force.

Probable age: 28.

Complete absence of occupational deformations; probably that man had never worked at manual labor. On the other hand, evidence of extensive pursuit of sports, especially rowing and boxing.

Perfect health. Remarkable physique. Scar on left shoulder indicates bullet wound, probably deflected by shoulder-blade, some three years ago.

Finally, a certain thickening of the ends of the fingers indicates unknown had carried on fairly extensive work on typewriter.

Maigret read slowly, smoking his pipe in little puffs and breaking off now and then to watch the Seine flowing in the morning dazzle of the sun. From time to time he would jot down a word or two, which only he could understand, in the notebook renowned alike for its cheapness and for its accumulation, over the years, of a hieroglyphic mass of notes, written around and even over each other.

The laboratory report was no more sensational:

The clothes had been worn by others before their present owner; everything indicated he had bought them, untraceably, from a pawnshop or second-hand dealer.

Same origin for the cane and the buttoned shoes.

The wig was of reasonably good quality but nondescript – a model available at any wig-maker's.

Examination of the dust in the garments revealed a sizable quantity of very fine flour – not pure, but mixed with traces of bran.

Glasses: unground glass, with no effect on the sight.

From the files, nothing; no trace of the victim's fingerprints on record.

Maigret sat dreamily for a few minutes, his elbows on his desk. The case looked neither good nor bad – perhaps at the moment rather on the bad side, since Chance, usually reasonably cooperative, had contributed not the slightest assistance.

At last he rose, clapped on his hat, and approached the usher stationed in the corridor. 'If anybody asks for me, I'll be back in about an hour.'

He was too near the Place des Vosges to take a taxi. He strolled back along the Seine. In the fruit shop on the Rue des Tournelles he noticed Mme. Maigret in spirited conversation with three or four of the neighborhood gossips. He turned his head to hide a smile, and continued on his way.

When Maigret first entered the police force, one of his chiefs, absorbed in the then new methods of scientific detection, used to keep telling him, 'Look here, young man! Go easy on the imagination. A policeman works with facts, not ideas!' Which had not kept Maigret from using his imagination, and cutting out a nice little career for himself with it.

Just so now, as he reached the Place des Vosges, he was concerned less with the technical details of the morning's reports than with what he would call the *feel* of the crime.

He tried to imagine the victim, not as the corpse he had seen, but as a living boy of twenty-eight – blond, heavy-set, well built, undoubtedly elegant, putting on every morning his elderly-gallant outfit, his costume bought off some flea-ridden pushcart – and yet always wearing the best linen under it.

Then taking two turns around the Place and going off along the Rue des Tournelles.

Where did he go? What did he do until three in the afternoon? Did he retain his role of the hero of some nineteenth-century comedy by Labiche, or did he have a nearby room where he changed?

How was it possible for him then to sit motionless for three hours on a bench, without opening his mouth, without making a single gesture, staring at one point in space?

How long had this been going on?

And where did he go at night? What was his private life? Whom did he see? Whom did he talk to? To whom did he surrender the secret of his personality? Why the flour and the traces of bran in his clothes? The bran indicated a mill rather than a bakery. What would he be doing in a mill?

Maigret's thoughts carried him past 17 *bis*. He retraced his steps, entered the gate and addressed the concierge.

She showed no reaction to his police badge. 'Well? What do you want?'

'I wanted to know which of your tenants employs a maid – rather pretty, blonde, elegant ...'

'Mlle. Rita?' she interrupted.

'Might well be. Every afternoon she takes two children out in the Place –'

'Her employers' children. Monsieur and Mme. Krofta – they've lived on the first floor for fifteen years and more. They were even here before me. M. Krofta is in the import and export business; I think his office is in the Rue du 4-Septembre ...'

'Is he at home?'

'He just went out, but I think Madame is upstairs.'

'And Rita?'

'I don't know. I haven't seen her this morning; I was busy doing the stairs ...'

A few moments later, Maigret rang at the first floor apartment. He could hear a noise far off inside, but nobody answered. He rang again. At last the door opened. He saw a fairly young woman, trying to cover her body with a scant dressing gown.

'Yes?'

'I'd like to speak to M. or Mme. Krofta. I'm an Inspector from the Judiciary Police.'

She opened the door reluctantly, holding the gown tightly closed in front of her. Maigret entered a magnificent apartment, with vast, high-ceilinged rooms, tasteful furnishings, and expensive ornaments.

'Do forgive me for receiving you like this, but I'm alone with the children. How did you happen to get here so quickly? It can't be fifteen minutes since my husband left.'

She was a foreigner, to judge from a light accent and a thoroughly Central European charm. Maigret had already recognized in her the well-tailored woman whom he had noticed that morning, listening to the gossips in the midst of the Place des Vosges.

'You were expecting me?' he murmured in a tone intended to disguise his astonishment.

'You or somebody. But I hadn't any idea the police would be so quick. I suppose my husband is coming back?'

'I don't know.'

'You didn't see him?'

'No.'

'But then how …?'

There was quite evidently a misunderstanding, from which Maigret could hardly help learning something useful. He had no intention of clearing it up.

The young woman, possibly to gain a moment to think things over, stammered, 'Do you mind for just a minute? The children are in the bathroom and I can't help wondering if they're up to something.'

She went off with supple steps. She was truly beautiful, in body as well as face.

He could hear her exchanging whispers with the children in the bathroom. Then she came back, a faint smile of welcome on her lips.

'Please excuse me; I never even asked you to sit down. I do wish my husband were here. He's the one who really knows the value of the jewels; after all, he bought them.'

Jewels? And why this faint discomfort, this impatience for the husband's return? She seemed almost afraid to speak, anxious to keep the conversation such that she could say nothing compromising.

Maigret had no desire to be helpful. He gazed at her with as neutral an expression as possible, putting on what he called his 'fat-and-friendly' face.

'You keep reading in the papers about robberies but, it's funny, you never think it can happen to you. Why, even last night I didn't have any idea … It was only this morning …'

'When did you get home?' Maigret put in.

She gave a start. 'How did you know I went out?'

'Because I saw you.'

'You were here in the neighborhood already?'

'I'm here all year around. I'm one of your neighbors.'

This bothered her. She was obviously wondering what might be hidden behind words that were so simple, yet so mysterious.

'Why, I went out, as I often do, for a breath of air before I settled down to getting the children dressed. That's why you found me in such a state. When I come home, I always slip on something for around the house and ...' She could not suppress a sigh of relief as she heard footsteps pause outside the door and a key turn in the lock. 'My husband ...' she murmured, and called out, 'Boris! Come in here.'

Well, Well! thought Maigret, so the husband's a looker, too. Older than she is, forty-five at a guess, distinguished, well groomed, Hungarian or Czech.

'The Inspector got here just ahead of you. I was telling him you'd be right back.'

Boris Krofta examined Maigret with a polite attention which seemed to mask a trace of defiance. 'I beg your pardon,' he murmured. No accent here; perfect French, even a trifle too perfect. 'But ... I do not fully understand ...'

'Inspector Maigret, Judiciary Police.'

'How odd. And you wished to speak to *me*?'

'To the employer of one Rita who takes two children out in the Place des Vosges every afternoon.'

'Yes ... But ... you cannot mean that you have already found her, that you have recovered the jewels? I know that I must seem somewhat peculiar to you; but the coincidence is so curious that I keep trying to explain to myself ... You must realize that I have just returned from the local police station where I lodged a complaint against this very Rita. I come home, I find you here, and you tell me ...'

There was a nervous tension in his gestures. His wife, who had obviously no intention of leaving the two men alone, examined the Inspector with curious eyes.

'On what grounds did you lodge a complaint?'

'The jewel robbery. The girl disappeared yesterday, without giving us notice. I thought she had run off with a lover; I intended to insert an advertisement for another maid in the papers this morning. Last night we did not leave the house. This morning, while my wife was out, the idea suddenly struck me of looking in the jewel box. It was then that I understood Rita's abrupt departure; the box was empty.'

'What time was it when you made this discovery?'

'Barely nine. I was in my dressing gown. As soon as I could dress, I hurried to the station.'

'Meanwhile your wife returned?'

'Yes, while I was dressing ... What I still do not understand is that you should arrive here this morning –'

'Pure coincidence!' Maigret murmured innocently.

'Nevertheless, I should like a few details. Did you know, this morning, that the jewels had been stolen?'

An evasive gesture from Maigret meant nothing either way, but served to augment Boris's nervousness.

'At least do me the favor of telling me the reason for your visit. I do not believe that it is a custom of the French police to invade people's homes, seat themselves comfortably, and –'

'And listen to what people tell them?' Maigret ended his sentence. 'You must admit it isn't my fault. Since I got here, you've done nothing but talk about a jewel robbery which doesn't interest me in the least, since I came here because of a far more serious crime –'

'More serious?' the young woman exclaimed.

'You don't know that a crime was committed yesterday afternoon in the Place des Vosges?'

He watched her think it over, remember that Maigret had said he was a neighbor, reject the possibility of saying no, and end with a smiling murmur, 'I do think I vaguely heard something of the sort in the square this morning. Some of the old ladies were gossiping ...'

'I fail to see,' the husband interrupted, 'what concern –'

'– this case is of yours? So far I don't know myself, but I've a notion we'll find out sooner or later. What time did Rita disappear yesterday afternoon?'

'A little after five,' Boris Krofta answered without a shadow of hesitation. He turned to his wife. 'That's right isn't it, Olga?'

'Exactly. She brought the children back at five. She went up to her room and I never heard her come down. Around six I went up; I was beginning to wonder why she hadn't started dinner. By then her room was empty.'

'Would you please show me to her room?'

'My husband will take you up. I don't like to go out in the halls like this.'

Maigret could already have found his way around the house; its plan was almost identical with that of his own. After the second floor, the staircase grew even narrower and darker before it reached the rooms under the roof. Krofta opened the third.

'This is it. I left the key in the lock.'

'Your wife just said she was the one who came up here.'

'Of course. But afterwards I came up, too ...'

The open door revealed what could have been any maid's room, with its iron bed, wardrobe, and washstand, save for the splendid view of the Place des Vosges from the window set in the roof.

Beside the wardrobe there was a wicker suitcase in the current style. Inside the wardrobe were dresses and underclothes.

'Your maid went off without her baggage?'

'I imagine she may have preferred to take the jewels. Their value is approximately two hundred thousand francs ...'

Maigret's fat fingers felt of a little green hat, then picked up another trimmed with a yellow ribbon.

'Can you tell me how many hats your maid had?'

'I have no idea. Possibly my wife can tell you, but I doubt it.'

'How long was she with you?'

'Six months.'

'You found her through an ad?'

'Through an employment agency, which recommended her warmly. And I must say that her work was impeccable.'

'You haven't any other servants?'

'My wife insists on looking after the children herself, so that one maid is all we need. Besides, we live on the Côte d'Azur for much of the year; we have a gardener there and his wife helps with the housework.'

Maigret was mopping his brow. His handkerchief fell to the floor and he bent over to pick it up. 'That's funny ...' he muttered as he stood up. He looked Krofta over from head to foot, opened his mouth, then shut it.

'You were about to say ...?' Krofta asked politely.

'I wanted to ask you a question. But it's so indiscreet that you might think it was out of place ...'

'Pray do.'

'You insist? I wanted to ask you, just at random you understand, if ... Well, the maid was very pretty: did you ever happen to have any relations with her other than those of employer and servant? Purely routine question, of course; you don't have to answer it.'

Oddly enough, Krofta paused to think, suddenly more concerned than he had been. He took his time about answering, looked about him slowly, and finally sighed, 'Will my answer be a matter of record?'

'There's every chance that it'll never come up.'

'In that case, I prefer to confess to you that what you suggest did indeed take place.'

'In your apartment?'

'No. That would be complicated – the children, you know ...'

'You had dates outside?'

'Never! I would come up here now and then, and ...'

'I can take it from there,' Maigret smiled. 'And I'm greatly satisfied by your answer. You see, I'd noticed that there was a button missing on the sleeve of your coat. Just now I found that button on the floor at the foot of the bed.'

He held out the button. Krofta seized it with astonishing eagerness.

'When was the last time that it happened?' Maigret asked.

'Three or four days ago ... let me think ... yes, four.'

'And Rita was willing?'

'Oh, yes – of course!'

'She was in love with you?'

'She gave that impression.'

'You didn't know of any rival?'

'My dear Inspector! The question did not arise. If Rita had had a lover, I should never have considered him a rival. I adore my wife and my children; in fact, I cannot understand how I let myself ...'

And Maigret went on down the stairs, sighing to himself, As for you, my fine friend, I wonder if there was one minute when you weren't lying?

He stopped at the concierge's loge and sat down facing her.

She was shelling peas. 'Well, did you see them? They're certainly upset about this jewel business.'

'Were you in your loge yesterday at five?'

'Sure I was. And my son was right where you are, doing his homework.'

'Did you see Rita bring the children home?'

'Just like I see you this minute.'

'And you saw her come down a few minutes later?'

'That's what M. Krofta was asking me just now. I told him I didn't see a thing. He says it isn't possible. I must've left my loge, I wasn't paying attention – after all, so many people come and go. Just the same it seems to me I would've noticed her, because it wasn't the right time for her to be going out.'

'Have you ever run into M. Krofta on the staircase to the third floor?'

'Go on – what would he be doing up here? Oh, I see ... You think he'd be sniffing around the maid? You just don't know Mlle. Rita. Now they're saying she's a thief. Well, maybe she is. But when it comes to letting your employer fool around with you ...'

Maigret resignedly lit his pipe and moved off.

'Well Inspectoress Maigret?' he joked affectionately as he settled down by the window. His shirt-sleeves were two brilliant splotches in the sun.

'Well, for lunch you're going to have to be satisfied with a chop and an artichoke. I even bought them ready-cooked to save time. The way these gossips go on ...'

'What are they saying? Come on; let's hear the results of your investigation.'

'First of all, Rita *wasn't* a maid!'

'How do you know?'

'All the people in the shops noticed she didn't know how to figure in sous, which means she hadn't ever done any marketing before. Then you know how it is, they'll give a servant a rebate of one sou on every franc so she'll bring all the family trade to that store. Well, the first time the butcher offered her that, she just stared at him amazed. She did take it after that, but I'm sure it was just so she wouldn't look unusual.'

'Fine! So we have a young girl of good family acting the part of a servant at the Kroftas'.'

'I think she was a student. In the stores in this neighborhood you hear them talking all kinds of languages – Italian, Hungarian, Polish. It seems she used to listen as though she understood, and if anybody made a joke she'd smile.'

'And how about her admirer in the Place?'

'People had noticed him, but not so much as I did. Oh, yes – one more thing: the Gastambides' maid spends a lot of her afternoons on the Place, and she says that Rita didn't know how to crochet and the only thing you could use that piece she was making for would be a dish-rag.'

Maigret's small eyes smiled at his wife's intent efforts to gather her memories and express them methodically.

'And that isn't all. Before her, the Kroftas had a maid from their own country and they dismissed her because she was in the family way.'

'By Krofta?'

'Oh, no! He's too much in love with his wife. They say he's so jealous that they hardly have any company at all.'

Thus all these bits of gossip, true or false, sincere or malicious, served moment by moment to alter the portraits of the characters – or perhaps to complete them.

'Since you've done such a good job,' Maigret murmured, as he lit a fresh pipe, 'I'm going to give you a tip: the shot that killed our bewigged and bespectacled unknown was fired from Rita's garret room. It won't be hard to prove when we get around to a reconstruction. I checked the angle of aim from there; it agrees absolutely with the position of the body and the trajectory of the bullet.'

'Do you think that she ...?'

'I don't know ...'

He sighed and put on his collar and tie; she helped him with his coat. Half an hour later, he sank into his armchair at Headquarters and mopped his face; it was even hotter than the day before, and a storm was brewing.

An hour later, all three of Maigret's pipes were hot, the ashtray was overflowing, and the blotter was covered with words and fragments of phrases crazily intertwined. As for the Inspector, he was yawning, obviously half asleep, trying to fix his eyes on what he had jotted down in the course of his daydream.

If Krofta had caused Rita's disappearance, the jewel theft was a sound device for averting suspicion.

That was attractive, but it proved nothing; the maid might very well have stolen her mistress's jewels.

Krofta had hesitated before saying that he had been his maid's lover.

That could mean that it was true and he was sick of it; it could also mean that it was false, that he had seen Maigret picked up the button or thought the Inspector's question concealed some sort of trap.

According to Krofta, the button had been there for four days; but the floor looked recently swept.

And why had Mme. Krofta gone for a walk so early this morning? Why had she hesitated to admit having heard of the crime, since Maigret had seen her stay so long with the gossips?

Why had Krofta asked the concierge if she'd seen Rita go out?

Private investigation on his own? Or wasn't it more likely that he knew the police would ask the question, and hoped to plant a suggestion in the woman's mind?

Suddenly Maigret rose. This whole collection of details and remarks now no longer merely irritated him, but began to oppress him painfully. Wherever he turned, it was impossible not to end with the question: where is Rita?

In flight, if she had murdered or stolen. But if she had neither murdered nor stolen, then ...

A moment later he was in the chief's office, demanding brusquely, 'Can you get me a blank search warrant?'

'Things aren't going so well?' the director of the P.J. smiled. Better than anyone else, he knew Maigret's moods. 'All right, but you'll be discreet about it, won't you, Maigret?'

While the chief attended to the warrant, Maigret was called to the phone.

'I just thought of something!' Mme. Maigret's voice was excited and worried. 'I don't know if I ought to say it over the phone ...'

'Tell me anyway.'

'Supposing that it isn't the one you thought who fired the shot ...'

'I understand. Go on.'

'Supposing, for example, if was her employer ... you follow me? ... I've been wondering if maybe she mightn't be still in the house? Maybe held prisoner? Maybe – dead?'

It was touching to behold Mme. Maigret hot on the trail for the first time in her life. But what the Commissioner did not admit was that she had arrived at very nearly the same point he had reached himself.

'Is that all?' he asked ironically.

'Are you making fun of me? Don't you really think –'

'In short, you think that if we institute a search of 17 –'

'Just think, supposing she's still alive!'

'We'll see ... And meanwhile, try to make dinner a little more substantial than lunch!'

Mme. Lécuyer, concierge of 17 *bis*, was assuredly a splendid woman who did her best to bring up her children properly; but she had the serious defect of getting easily rattled.

'You know how it is,' she confessed, 'with all these people questioning me ever since early morning, I don't know whether I'm coming or going ...'

'Calm yourself, Mme. Lécuyer.' Maigret had installed himself by the window, near the boy who, as on the previous evening, was doing his homework.

'I've never done any harm to anybody and –'

'Nobody's accusing you of doing anybody any harm. All we're asking you is to try to remember ... How many tenants have you?'

'Twenty-two. I should tell you the second and third floors are split up into little apartments, one and two rooms.'

'None of these tenants had any relations with the Kroftas?'

'How would they? The Kroftas are rich people – they have their car and their chauffeur.'

'By the way, do you know where they keep their car?'

'Over by the Boulevard Henri IV. The chauffeur hardly ever comes here.'

'Did he come yesterday afternoon?'

'I don't know any more ... I think so.'

'With the car?'

'No. The car hasn't been here yesterday or today. Of course, the Kroftas haven't really what you'd call gone out ...'

'Let's see: was the chauffeur in the house yesterday around five?'

'No. He left at four thirty. I remember because my boy had just got home from school.'

'That's right,' the boy agreed, raising his head from his book.

'Now one more question: were any big boxes taken out of here after five? For instance, was there a moving van parked around here?'

'No, I'm certain of it.'

'Nobody brought out any furniture, or packing-cases, or cumbersome packages?'

'What do you want me to say?' she groaned. 'How do I even know how big a package you'd call cumbersome?'

'A package capable of containing, for instance, a human corpse.'

'The saints preserve us! Is *that* what you're thinking of? You think somebody's gone and murdered somebody in my house?'

'Go over your memory hour by hour.'

'No! I didn't see anything like that.'

'No truck, no wagon, not even a handcart came in here?'

'I just told you!'

'There's no empty room in the house? All your vacancies are filled?'

'Every blessed one. There was one single room on the third, but that's been rented for two months.'

At this moment the boy raised his head. Without taking his pen-holder from his mouth, he said, 'And the piano, mama?'

'What do you think that has to do with it? That wasn't a box going out; that was a box coming in – and having a frightful time with the staircase.'

'They delivered a piano?'

'Yesterday at six thirty.'

'What company?'

'I don't know. There wasn't any name on the truck. It didn't come in here in the court. It was a big packing-case and three men worked at it for a good hour.'

'They took the case away?'

'No. M. Lucien came down with the men to treat them to a drink at the corner bar.'

'Who's M. Lucien?'

'The man who rents that little room I was talking about. He's been up there two months – very quiet and well behaved. They say he composes music.'

'He's acquainted with the Kroftas?'

'I don't think he's ever laid eyes on them.'

'He was in his room yesterday at five?'

'He came in around four thirty – about when the chauffeur left.'

'Did he tell you then that he was expecting a piano?'

'No, he just asked me if there was any mail for him.'

'Did he get much?'

'Very little.'

'Thank you, Madame Lécuyer. Just stay calm, now.'

Maigret went out and gave his instructions to the two Inspectors who were patrolling the Place des Vosges. Then he re-entered the building, hastily passing the loge for fear the concierge's berattlement might finally prove contagious.

Maigret did not stop at the first floor, nor at the second. On the third, he leaned over and made out the scratches which the piano had left on the floor. They seemed to end at the fourth door. He knocked, and heard muffled steps, like those of an old lady in bed-slippers, then a cautious murmur of, 'Who is it?'

'M. Lucien, please?'

'Next door.'

But at the same moment another voice stammered several words. The door opened a crack, and a fat old woman tried to make out Maigret's face in the dim light. 'He isn't here right now, M. Lucien isn't. Can I take a message for him?'

Automatically Maigret leaned forward to make out the second person who was in the room.

In the half light he could catch only a cluttered glimpse of old furniture, old clothes, and frightful ornaments. Through the crack of the door came that odor peculiar to the rooms of old people.

Near the sewing machine a woman sat, stiffly, like a formal caller. Inspector Maigret experienced the greatest surprise of his career as he recognized his own wife!

'I happened to hear that Mlle. Augustine did a little dressmaking,' Mme. Maigret hastened to say. 'I came to see her about that and we got to talking ... Do you know, she has the room right next to that maid who stole the jewels!'

Maigret shrugged his shoulders, wondering what his wife was leading up to.

'The funniest thing is that her other neighbor had a piano delivered yesterday – an enormous packing-case ...'

This time Maigret frowned, furious that his wife had, God knows how, reached the same results that he had. 'Since M. Lucien isn't in, I'd better go down,' he announced.

He didn't lose a minute. The Inspectors from the Place des Vosges were posted on the staircase, not far from the Kroftas' door. A locksmith was sent for, and likewise the Commissioner from the district station.

In short order, M. Lucien's door was forced. In the room was nothing but a cheap piano, a chair, a bed, a wardrobe, and, against the wall, the packing-case in which the piano had been brought.

'Open that case!' Maigret ordered. The bets were down now, and he was frankly scared. He dared not touch it himself, for fear of finding it empty. He pretended to fill his pipe calmly, and he tried not to tremble when his man called out, 'Inspector! A woman!'

'I know.'

'She's alive!'

And he repeated, 'I know.' If there was a woman in the case, it had to be the notorious Rita; and he was morally certain she was alive, and tightly bound and gagged. 'Try to bring her to. Call a doctor.'

In the hall he passed Mlle. Augustine and his wife. Mme. Maigret's smile was unique in the annals of their household – a smile to suggest the disquieting possibility that she might exchange the role of docile spouse for that of detective.

As the Inspector reached the first floor, the door of the Kroftas' apartment opened. Krofta himself was there, hyperexcited but still holding himself well in hand.

'Isn't M. Maigret here?' he demanded of the Inspectors.

'Here I am, M. Krofta.'

'Somebody wants you on the telephone. From the Ministry of the Interior.'

This was not quite correct. It was the chief of the P.J. 'That you, Maigret? I thought I could reach you there. While you've been up to God knows what in that house, the person whose phone you're using has put the wind up at his Embassy, and they've taken it up with the Foreign Office!'

'I get it,' Maigret groaned.

'Maigret, would you believe it? A *spy* case! The directive is to keep everything quiet, no statement to the press. For a long time Krofta's been his country's agent in France. He's the *clearing-house* for the reports from secret agents.'

Krofta had remained in a corner of the room, pale but smiling. Now as Maigret hung up, he suggested, 'May I offer you any refreshment, my dear Inspector?'

'No, thank you.'

'It appears that you have found my servant?'

And the Commissioner hammered out each syllable: 'I found her in time – yes, M. Krofta! Good day!'

'As for me,' Mme. Maigret said as she put the finishing touches to her chocolate crème, 'as soon as they told me the maid didn't know how to crochet ...'

'Inspectoress,' her husband nodded approvingly.

'They really could convey important information that way, for hours every day? I don't know if I understand it all, but this girl, this Rita, was really spending all her time spying on her employers?'

Maigret hated to explain a case, but under these circumstances it seemed too cruel to leave Mme. Maigret in the dark. 'She was spying on spies,' he grunted. 'That's why, just when I can lay my hands on the whole gang, they tell me, "Not a move! Silence and discretion"!'

'A fine case, just the same – with flashes of genius. Look at the situation: on one side the Kroftas, with all the reports for their government passing through their hands.

'On the other side, a woman and a man – Rita and the "old" gentleman of the bench, your strange admirer. Who were they working for? That's no concern of mine now. That's up to the Deuxième Bureau; spies are their meat. Probably they were agents of another power, possibly of a different faction in their own country.

'In any event, they needed the daily centralized reports at Krofta's, and Rita got hold of them without much trouble. But how to pass them on? Spies are distrustful. The least suspicious move would ruin her.

'Hence the idea of the old gallant and the bench. And the brilliant idea of the crocheting. Rita's hands were far more skillful than they seemed: *their jerky movements produced, not standard crochet patterns, but whole messages in Morse code!*

'Across from Rita her accomplice commits the whole business to memory. It's an example of the incredible patience of some secret agents. Whatever he learns, he has to remember word for word for hours until he spends the night typing it out in his rooms at Corbeill, near the mills.

'I wonder how Krofta caught onto their signals – two regular turns around the place, meaning all's well, and so on.'

Mme. Maigret listened without daring to express the slightest opinion, she was so afraid that Maigret might stop.

'Now you know as much as I do. The Kroftas had to get rid of the man first, then take care of Rita – but not kill her; they needed to know who she was working for and how much she'd been able to transmit.

'For some time Krofta had kept a bodyguard installed in the house – M. Lucien, a first-rate shot. Krofta telephones, Lucien arrives, loses no time in going to the girl's room and using his compressed air rifle to strike down the indicated target.

'Nobody sees anything, nobody hears anything – excepting Rita. She still has to bring the children back and play out the comedy, or she knows that the distant marksman will bring her down, too.

'She knows what will happen to her. They try to force her secrets out of her. She resists ... so far. They threaten her with death, and order the piano for M. Lucien so that the case can be used to carry out the body.

'Krofta's already arranging his defense. He makes his complaint, announces the maid's disappearance, invents the theft of the jewels ...'

There was silence. Evening was settling over the Place. The sky was turning blue, and the four fountains were tuning their silvery sound to the liquid silver of the moon.

'And then you took over!' Mme. Maigret said suddenly.

He looked at her dubiously. She went on, 'It's so annoying, the way they kept you from pushing it through just at the best moment.'

Then he burst out in unconvincing rage, 'You know what's

even more annoying? Finding you there in Mlle. Augustine's room! You, getting ahead of me! Though after all the case meant more to you,' he smiled. 'He was your admirer.'

Erle Stanley Gardner

The Clue of the Hungry Horse

It was 7:55 when Lew Turlock answered the phone and was advised that long distance was calling Miss Betty Turlock. Would he please put her on the phone?

'She isn't here.'

The voice of the operator had that synthetic sweetness which showed Lew Turlock he was talking directly with the city. The Rockville operator would have spoken more naturally. Sometimes the local girls tried to imitate the voices of the big-city operators, but it never quite clicked, probably because they overdid it.

'When will she be in?' came drifting dulcetly over the party line.

Lew called over his shoulder to his wife, 'Betty wasn't coming home tonight, was she, Millie?'

'She's spending the night with Rose Marie Mallard,' his wife called. 'Who wants her?'

'Long distance,' Turlock said to his wife and then into the phone, 'She won't be here tonight.'

'Is there another number where we can reach her?'

'Nope,' Turlock said, 'no other number. The folks out where she's staying don't have a telephone.'

He hung up and went back to a perusal of the *Rockville Gazette*.

'Now who in the world do you suppose would be calling Betty from the city?' Mrs. Turlock asked.

Her husband merely grunted.

'Seems as though you could have found out who it was,' she

said. 'Betty wouldn't sleep a wink if she knew someone was trying to get her from the city.'

Lew started to say something, then lowered his paper and cocked his head, listening.

'What is it?' his wife asked.

'Those horses over at Calhoun's,' Turlock said, 'they're acting mighty queer. A lot of snorting and stamping.'

'Well,' Mrs. Turlock said tartly, 'let Sid Rowan worry about that. We've got enough to do without worrying about the neighbors' horses. Sid's getting lazier every day. Anyhow, I don't see how you can hear them. I can't hear a thing.'

Turlock said shortly, 'Just guess my ears are tuned to horse noises. That mare of Lorraine Calhoun's is a package of dynamite. Sounds like she's kicking the side of her stall.'

With the boom in land values Lew's next-door neighbor had sold out six months ago to Carl Carver Calhoun, a wealthy broker. It had been difficult for Turlock to adjust himself to this new situation. In the first place, Calhoun was only there on week-ends. He had hired Sid Rowan and his wife to look after the place, paying a salary that Turlock was firmly convinced was exactly twice as much as any couple were worth, four times as much as Rowan was worth.

Under the new owner the adjoining property had undergone a steady transformation. The cattle and work horses had been sold, and high-spirited riding horses had taken their place. A couple of diary cows had been retained and a half dozen head of beef cattle, but the rest had been sold. A tennis court had been built and a swimming pool was now in process of construction.

Calhoun was cordial enough. In fact, he went out of his way to be friendly. But, as Turlock had pointed out to his wife, you just couldn't make a real neighbor out of a millionaire. 'Go over to borrow a cup of rice,' he had pointed out, 'and when you went to pay it back, like as not they'd smile and say, "Oh, that's all right." '

The telephone rang again.

This time the voice of the long-distance telephone operator

announced that her party would speak with anyone who answered the phone. A second later, a girl's voice, touched with impatience, asked, 'Who is this talking, please?'

'Lew Turlock.'

'Oh, you're Betty's father, aren't you?'

'Yes.'

'Look, would you do something for me?'

'What is it?'

'You don't know me. I'm Irma Jessup, a friend of Lorraine Calhoun and also of your daughter. Now listen, it's very important that I talk with Betty. I have to reach her no matter where she is.'

'There isn't a phone out where she's staying.'

'I understand. But is it far from where you are?'

'Six or seven miles.'

'Look, could you get word to her? Or perhaps some neighbor who has a phone would call her? Couldn't you get word to her *some* way?'

'Well, I suppose I could,' Turlock said reluctantly, 'if it's downright important.'

'Well, it is. Just tell her to call Irma Jessup at Trinidad 6273. And she'll be using a neighbor's telephone, won't she?'

'Yes.'

'Then tell her to reverse the charges so there won't be any trouble about that. Tell her I'll be waiting right here at the telephone.'

'You want to give me that number again?'

The voice was impatient with the delay and Lew Turlock's stupidity. 'It's a pay station, Trinidad 6273. Tell her that Irma Jessup wants her to call at once. I'll be waiting by the telephone. She may call me collect. Now is that plain?'

Turlock sighed. 'That's plain,' he said. 'Goodbye.'

'What is it?' Mrs. Turlock called from the living room as Turlock hung up the phone.

'Oh, some friend of the Calhouns – girl by the name of Irma Jessup – says she has to get Betty right away. It's terribly important. I suppose it's an invitation to a theater party or something. Don't know why I didn't make her tell me what it was all about.'

'You aren't going out there?'

'I think Jim Thornton will run over and get her for me. It's only a quarter of a mile from his place over there ... Say, what do you suppose is the matter with those horses? Guess I'd better go take a look. Don't see any lights over there. I s'pose Sid Rowan and his wife have gone to the movies again.'

'Oh, quit worrying about the horses,' Mrs. Turlock said. 'You can't do your work and Sid's too.'

'You know Jim Thornton's number?' Turlock called to his wife.

'Six seven four – ring three.'

'Okay.'

Turlock picked up the telephone. When he had Jim Thornton on the line, he said, 'Jim, this is Lew Turlock. I hate to bother you, but Betty's staying over with Rose Marie Mallard tonight. Long distance is trying to get her and says it's real important. Now, do you suppose you could ...'

'Sure thing,' Thornton said. 'I'll get 'em over here right away.'

'It ain't too much trouble?'

'Shucks, no. I have a signal with them. I put up an old automobile spotlight on the side of the house. It's pointed right toward their windows and whenever someone wants one of them on the phone, I turn on that spotlight. It may take a few minutes for them to see it, but usually someone comes right over. Usually it's Rose Marie. I'll switch on the light right away, Lew. How's everything coming?'

'So-so.'

'Don't want to sell that Jersey milk cow, do you? I know a man who's trying to buy up some good cows, willing to pay a good price.'

'How much?'

Thornton's voice became suddenly cautious, indicating his recognition of the fact that they were talking on a party line. 'Remember my telling you what I got for that bay horse?'

'Uh huh.'

'Well, he's offered five dollars less than that for the right sort of cows.'

'I'll think it over. Probably be seeing you tomorrow.'

'Okay. Be seeing you.'

Turlock hung up. Within a matter of five minutes the phone was ringing again.

'That'll be Betty now,' Mrs. Turlock said.

Lew Turlock put down his paper and walked patiently over to the telephone. When Betty was home, she always answered the telephone. When she was away, her father took over the job. Mrs. Turlock had a slight impediment of hearing which, as she expressed it, 'made the words sound all blurred over the telephone.' But there were those who claimed she could hear all right when it came to listening in on party-line conversations.

Lew Turlock picked up the receiver and said, 'Hello.'

The voice which came rushing at him over the wire showed all of the nervous rapidity of a person who has an explanation to make and is very anxious to be certain it is accepted.

'Oh, Mr. Turlock,' the voice pleaded. 'This is Rose Marie. Betty isn't here right now. She's going to join me a little later. There was something came up. She is coming out almost ... well, almost any time now. If you can leave the message, I'll see that she gets it.'

Lew Turlock gripped the telephone receiver. He started to ask a question and then realized that there were other ears on the party line. This would make a choice morsel of gossip. Magnified, distorted, repeated, it would brand his daughter as a girl who resorted to the familiar expedient of saying she was spending a night with a girl friend who would give her an alibi and then ...

Lew Turlock fought to keep his voice casual. 'Tell her Irma Jessup called up and wants Betty to call back just as soon as she possibly can. She's to put the call through collect. Trinidad 6273. That's all. I'm sorry I bothered you but Irma Jessup said it was terribly important. I told her that I couldn't reach Betty until later on in the evening.'

'Okay. I'll … I'll tell her –' Rose Marie stammered.

'Thanks,' Lew interrupted, keeping his voice casual, and hung up.

It took two or three seconds for him to compose himself sufficiently to walk back to the living room and face his wife. But Mrs. Turlock was engrossed in her book and barely looked up. She took it for granted that Rose Marie had promised to drive back to her home and relay the message to Betty.

Lew stood, debating just what to do next. His mind was a turmoil of thought, but all the time he was fighting to keep his manner and speech completely casual.

Across on the Calhoun place a horse snorted and kicked. The wind was from the east, carrying the sound plainly. Lew Turlock welcomed it as a diversion. 'I'm going across and take a look at those horses,' he said. 'One of them may have a foot caught or something.'

'Sid Rowan certainly doesn't believe in doing any more work than is necessary to get by,' Mrs. Turlock snorted. 'I can't say that I like the idea of having neighbors who go away and leave the place in the hands of someone like Sid Rowan. After all, the Calhouns aren't there over five or six days a monhth. And when they are, there's a continual screeching and shouting.'

'I know,' Lew said, and opened the table drawer to take out a flashlight. 'I'll be back in five or ten minutes.'

As Lew Turlock crossed the kitchen and opened the back door, his wife was saying something about Sid Rowan traipsing off to a movie three or four nights a week and delegating his responsibilities to the neighbors. Having warmed to this subject, she found it more interesting than her book.

Turlock quietly closed the back door, shutting off his wife's tirade.

The boundary line between the Turlock and Calhoun properties ran directly across the crest of a commanding knoll. For this reason the houses were nearer together than would otherwise have been the case, each builder desiring to take advantage of the view and the cool breezes.

Using the beam of his flashlight to guide him, Lew Turlock crossed the narrow strip of lawn, opened the gate in the fence, and approached the Calhoun barn.

It had been raining earlier in the day, but now the clouds had broken up. The stars were gleaming brightly, interrupted only by an occasional blotch of drifting clouds. The air, washed clean of impurities by the rain, felt cool and crisp. The smell of damp earth was a delightful aroma in Turlock's nostrils. It exerted a quieting influence, stilling somewhat the thoughts which raced around and around in his brain like a weary squirrel wheel of worry.

Lew Turlock knew he must make some excuse to get out to George Mallard's place. Somehow, he must get Rose Marie off to one side and quiz her before she had had a chance to get in touch with Betty and fix up some story. That, Turlock decided, was the Calhoun influence. Lorraine Calhoun's smilingly superior manners had started all the girls putting on airs, trying to be sophisticated. Take Rosemary, for instance, who had ceased to be plain 'Rosemary' but must now be called Rose Marie. Her parents had no business letting her get away with that stuff. If he'd been her father ...

Lew, walking doggedly toward the barn, his mind occupied with his own problems, noticed that the beam of his flashlight was reflected back at him from the chrome finish on a convertible car, parked almost in front of the stable door.

He let the light play over the car. It was Lorraine Calhoun's convertible. The top was down, showing the red leather of the interior – a car, Lew thought morosely, that cost more than a Diesel tractor – and used just as a plaything – to speed a rich man's daughter around on her playtime engagements.

A horse snorted and kicked.

Lew Turlock opened the barn door. Somewhere at the back of the barn a horse gave a low nicker in appreciation of the human companionship.

Turlock, accustomed to sensing the moods of animals, detected the tension all up and down the long line of stalls. The horses were nervous, as though a thunderstorm had been approaching.

A horse snorted. Lew could hear the iron ring turn in its hasp as the horse lunged back on the rope. Then there was the sound of nervous hoofs on the wood floor of the stall and another long snort.

Lew found the light switch and clicked on the lights.

With the blaze of illumination the horses instantly became silent.

Lew's eyes, running down the long line of stalls, caught sight of a girl's leg and a high-heeled shoe, the toe pointed slightly upward. Beyond that, he could see part of a hand stretched out, palm upward.

Even in the first moment of soul-numbing excitement, Turlock remembered about the horses. He mustn't alarm them. He spoke to them as he hurried down the line of stalls. 'Whoa, boys, take it easy. Steady.'

She was lying on her side, sprawled out grotesquely, in such a position that the mare had to stand at an angle to avoid trampling the still body.

The cruel, disfiguring wound in the top of her head, with the sinister red pool seeping from it onto the stable floor, told its own story.

Lew gave a strangled cry, 'Betty!'

He knelt by the girl, then noticed her clothes. They were not Betty's clothes.

'Miss Calhoun – Lorraine,' he said.

The figure lay starkly still. Lew touched the arm.

It needed only that one touch of the lifeless flesh to tell Lew Turlock that nothing he could do would be of any use.

He left the body exactly as he had found it, but he carefully stepped over it, untied the mare and led her out.

The nervous mare drew back on the rope as she came to the sprawled figure, then reared and jumped, alighting with a pound of hoofs on the floor beyond.

Lew tied her up and then went to the extension telephone which Calhoun had had installed in his barn within the last two weeks.

*

Sheriff Bill Eldon received the call at his home. He was, at the moment, suffering through one of the frequent visits of his wife's sister, Doris. Time did not dull the sharpness of her mind – or of her tongue.

The Sheriff listened to Lew Turlock's heavy voice stolidly giving him the details.

'You say she was kicked by the mare?'

'That's what it looked like. She must have gone into the stall and the mare caught her right in the middle of the forehead.'

'You didn't move her?'

'Well, I got her out of that stall.'

'You shouldn't have done that, Lew. You should have left the body ...'

'Not the body,' Lew said, 'the mare. She was stomping around and all excited.'

'You didn't move the body?'

'Shucks, no. The mare jumped over it slick as could be. I knew enough not to touch the body. So did the mare.'

'How about the Calhouns? Are they home?' the Sheriff asked.

'No, no one's home. Sid Rowan and his wife must have gone to the show.'

'Okay,' the Sheriff said. 'I'll get the Coroner and come out. I'll call up the theater and tell them to put a message on the screen for Sid Rowan to get out there right away. See that no one touches anything. G'bye.'

Doris Nelson was sitting in the front parlor, straining her ears to listen. She waited only to hear the click of the receiver and then rasped out, 'Who is it? Who's killed? What happened?'

Grinning maliciously, the Sheriff picked up the receiver again. His second call would give him a valid excuse to ignore the questions. He said to the operator, 'Get me James Logan, the Coroner, right away. It's official and important.'

A few moments later the Sheriff had notified the Coroner, called the movie theater, and left instructions to have Sid Rowan called from the show. Then he had slipped out of the side door and got his car out of the driveway – all without answering Doris' rapid-fire staccato of eager questions, in itself no small feat.

Logan, the Coroner, and Lew Turlock both lived well to the south of town. The Turlock ranch was some five miles out, and the Sheriff, taking it for granted that Logan would be there ahead of him, drove at conservative speed along the main street of Rockville, carefully regarding the rights of other cars that were on the road. Although he had switched on his official red spotlight, he refrained from using the siren. After all, there was nothing he could do. The girl was dead.

The Calhouns were prominent people. There would be quite a bit of publicity over the thing. The city newspapers would probably telephone in for complete facts. The Calhoun girl was pretty as a picture. But she was a city girl, and she should have known better than to go prowling around a nervous mare at night.

Once south of town, the Sheriff speeded up the car and rolled briskly along the pavement. As he turned off on the dirt road which led up to the hill where the two houses were situated, he noticed that there were several fresh car tracks just ahead of him and that one of the puddles left in the road was still churned with yellowish muddy water. This meant that the Coroner would be there ahead of him.

The Sheriff liked that. He was always nervous when he had to stand around waiting for the Coroner. He turned up the driveway, which skirted the base of the hill, then climbed up to the knoll, and slid his car to a stop just behind that of the Coroner.

Logan was already in the barn. The Sheriff walked on in.

Logan said, 'I've looked around, Bill. It's evidently accidental. She went into the stall to get something and the mare kicked her. It must have happened right after the horses were fed. The mare got nervous with the body lying there and didn't eat a bite. The chute is still filled with hay. That mare's hot-blooded and nervous. Miss Calhoun probably didn't know enough about horses to understand she had to speak to a horse when she entered the stall. She walked in without saying a word. The mare saw her out of the corner of her eye and let fly.'

'How long's she been dead?' the Sheriff asked.

'We can find out when Sid Rowan comes and tells us what time he fed the horses. Must've happened within five minutes of the time he put down the feed. This probably will be Sid now.'

A car drew up outside. A man and woman got out and entered the stable.

'What's the trouble here?' Sid Rowan said, his voice showing irritation. 'Can't I get away to a movie without ...'

He broke off as the Sheriff stepped forward.

Rowan was in the middle fifties, a stringy, wiry man with steel-gray eyes, long of leg and arm but quick-moving despite an awkward shuffle about his walk. His wife was four or five years younger and inclined to be fleshy and slow-moving.

The Sheriff told them what had happened.

'But she wasn't here,' Rowan said. 'There was no one here. No one was home. The family were coming down tomorrow! You know how it is. They used to come down every week-end, now they come down about two week-ends out of the month, the whole bunch of them – servants, family, friends. Three or four automobile-loads sometimes. Shucks, wait a minute, that's her car parked out there now. She must have come down unexpected.'

'You didn't know she was here?'

'Why, no. I didn't look for her until tomorrow. They're all coming then.'

'You have no idea what time she got here?'

'No.'

'You must have fed the horses and then gone to the movies as soon as you had the hay down.'

'That's right. I went up and put hay in the chutes and then the missus and I beat it for the first show. No sense in sticking around here all the time. You can't make a man work both day and night.'

'You must have fed at about half-past six if you made the first show?'

'I started about half-past six. Guess I finished about twenty minutes of seven and took right off.'

'It was dark in the barn by that time?'

'Sure.'

'And you switched on the lights?'

'Of course.'

'And then turned them off when you left?'

'That's right.'

'Did she have a key to the house?'

'I suppose so. Sure. Calhoun had keys made for all members of the family.'

'Do you live in the house or ...'

'No. There's an apartment over the garage where the wife and I live.'

Logan said, 'Well, we don't know *why* she came to the stable, but it's a cinch she came here, walked in, and the mare kicked her.'

Sid Rowan nodded.

'I'm not so sure,' Sheriff Eldon said.

They looked at him quizzically. 'How else could it have happened, Bill?' the Coroner asked.

Bill Eldon turned to Turlock.

'You heard the horses snorting?' the Sheriff asked.

'That's right. This mare was making quite a commotion. Snorting and stamping and occasionally kicking at the side of the stall. She wanted out.'

'She was tied up with a rope?'

'That's right. A halter and a rope through that iron ring.'

'How long had you been hearing that racket before you came over?'

'Must have been half an hour anyway. Maybe longer.'

'You called me at eight twenty-five,' the Sheriff said. 'I made a note of the time.'

'Well, I called you within five minutes of the time I got over here.'

'Now then, when you got here,' the Sheriff said, 'the stable was dark?'

'That's right.'

'You had a flashlight and located the light switch and turned on the lights?'

'Yes.'

'And the body was lying here on the floor?'

'That's right.'

The Sheriff turned to Logan. 'There you are.'

'I don't get it,' Logan told him.

'Rowan left the place at twenty minutes to seven,' the Sheriff said. 'It was dark by that time. The sun sets right around six o'clock. Inside the barn it was dark as a pocket. You couldn't see your way around without lights. Now then, if this young woman entered the barn, she naturally turned on the lights to see where she was going. Who turned off those lights?'

'Gosh, Bill, you've got something there,' the Coroner said. 'There must have been someone with her.'

'That's right, someone who turned off the lights.'

Logan gave a low whistle.

'*After* this had happened,' the Sheriff went on.

Logan looked at Rowan. 'No chance she got in while you were feeding the horses and then when you went out –'

'Not a chance in the world,' Rowan interrupted half-angrily.

Logan motioned toward the horse's manger. 'The horse hasn't hardly touched a bit of food ... This is Lorraine Calhoun, Rowan?'

'Sure. She must have driven up right after I left. After I came down that ladder from the loft, I remember looking in at the mare. She'd just started to eat.'

The Sheriff avoided the body by hugging the edge of the stall. He walked in to the manger and said, 'The chute's pretty well clogged up with hay. That mare didn't even pull the hay away from the bottom of the chute so the rest of it could come down.'

The Sheriff picked up half a dozen of the dried barley stalks and looked at the quality of hay with a professional eye. 'Lots of grain on this hay,' he said. 'It's pretty good ... Hello, what's *this*?'

His flashlight exploring the far corner of the manger disclosed a small black leather-covered book, blending so perfectly with the shadows in the manger that it took the beam of the flashlight to disclose it.

Bill Eldon picked up the book and turned his body so the light struck the pages. 'Seems to be a diary,' he said. 'Her name's in front – Lorraine Calhoun. Logan, if you don't mind, I think I'll get Quinlan to take some photographs of the position of that body. Let's try not to touch anything until he gets down here.'

The Sheriff moved over directly under the light. Opening the diary, he said, 'Gosh, I hate to pry into this thing. Guess we won't read it, boys.'

He started to put it in his pocket and then said, 'Well, we might take a look at the *last* entry in it. It may tell us something.'

The Sheriff turned to the current date, opened the diary, and read, '*I guess some people think I'm a fool. I'm going to have a showdown with Frank and that mealy-mouthed Betty tomorrow. Well, why wait? Why not catch ...*'

That ended the last entry.

The Sheriff abruptly closed the book and put it in his pocket. He turned to Lew Turlock. 'Where's Betty tonight, Lew?' he asked casually.

Lew Turlock fidgeted uneasily. He glanced over toward his house, and then his eyes met the curious gaze of James Logan, Sid Rowan, and Rowan's wife.

'Sheriff,' he blurted, 'could I speak with you alone – sort of private like?'

Over in the dark corner of the barn Lew Turlock told the Sheriff the story of his daughter's deception.

'Told you she was going out with the Mallard girl, did she?' the Sheriff asked.

Turlock nodded miserably. 'She and Rosemary – or Rose Marie she's calling herself now – were supposed to be working on some stuff they're doing in this benefit play for the Red Cross. She left right after supper.'

'What time?'

'Well, Millie had dinner early so Betty could get away. I guess Betty left the place about – well, about six. She helped her mother with the dishes. But she was all ready to go except for that. Soon as she dried the dishes she jumped in the car and drove away.'

'And Mallard hasn't any telephone?'

'That's right. I called up by getting Jim Thornton to signal him to come over to the home. Betty's a *good* girl. I don't know what it's all about. Probably some kid stuff. But if word gets around that Betty's supposed to be there, but ain't – well, you can look at Sid Rowan's wife, standing over there with her ears stuck out a foot –'

'Come on,' the Sheriff said. 'We're going out to Mallard's place right quick.'

He called back over his shoulder, 'Lew Turlock and I are going out to see if his daughter saw Lorraine tonight. She's visiting friends who haven't any phone. Jim, will you get in touch with George Quinlan and ask him to come down and take some pictures of that body and the stall? Make everyone keep back away from the body!'

The Sheriff opened the door of the county car and Lew Turlock, miserably dejected, climbed in beside the Sheriff. 'Gosh, Bill,' he said, 'you know how easy it is to get talk started around here. Particularly with someone like Sid Rowan's wife. She's all burned up with curiosity right now.'

'I know,' Bill Eldon said sympathetically.

'Matter of fact, I thought there for a minute it was Betty lying dead in the barn. The light's down at the far end, and what with the shadows in the stall and the body lying sort of half face-down – you can imagine how I felt. Hang it, Bill, Betty is all right. I don't know what the explanation is but –'

'Sure, sure,' the Sheriff soothed. 'You're getting yourself all worried, Lew. Betty's all right, but if this Lorraine Calhoun was going to see her tonight, we'd sort of ought to talk with Betty. I haven't ever met any of these Calhouns. Too bad a thing like this had to happen. Guess the country's changing, Lew. Must have been fifty little ranches sold to city people. Some of the folks are going to farm, but most of 'em are just using 'em for sort of week-end residences.'

His manner casual, his voice drawling characteristically, the Sheriff talked on, steering the conversation away from the gnawing worry that was eating away at Turlock's mind.

They passed Jim Thornton's house, rolled on down the dirt road another quarter of a mile, and then turned into Mallard's place.

George Mallard came out to meet them.

The Sheriff did the talking, for which Lew Turlock was duly grateful. And the Sheriff was diplomatic, asking about the crops, discussing the prospects of early rains, and then casually asking whether Rosemary was home.

'Rose *Marie*,' Mallard corrected him with a grin. 'She's gone a little highfalutin' on us. No, she ain't home. Someone telephoned to her about three quarters of an hour ago maybe, and she jumped in the car and went tearing out.'

The Sheriff was elaborately casual. 'Well, that's all right,' he said. 'She's going to be in that Red Cross play next month, isn't she?'

'That's right.'

'She and Betty Turlock.'

'Uh huh.'

'Kind of want to see her about the play,' the Sheriff said. 'Haven't any idea where she went, have you, George?'

'No, I haven't. You know the way youngsters are these days. She came tearing in, grabbed her hat and coat, bounced into the car, and tore out of the driveway. These kids have more on their minds these days than the Governor of the state.'

The Sheriff started the motor on his car. 'Well, I'll be seeing you, George, I'm kinda busy right now. Tell your daughter just as soon as she comes in to call my house. No, wait a minute ... You tell her to jump in the car and come to my office.'

Mallard looked curious. 'What is it? Anything –'

The Sheriff's grin was reassuring. 'This doggone Red Cross play is going to have us all jumping until it comes off, I guess. Bet your daughter looks good in it. Can't tell what will happen one of these days with a good-looking girl like that. She might be on the stage in one of these little local plays and some movie scout might see her, and next thing you know, she'd be in Hollywood.'

'I don't want Rose Marie in Hollywood,' George Mallard said positively.

'I know,' the Sheriff grinned, 'but you just can't tell.'

He turned the car around and was fifty yards from the house when a car speeding along the paved road slowed so rapidly that the tires screamed a protest and turned into the driveway.

'Reckon, this here is Rosemary now,' Bill Eldon said, 'and she's got Betty with her.'

Lew Turlock heaved a sigh of relief.

The Sheriff drove alowly, found a place on the side of the dirt road where he could park, and blinked his lights to signal the oncoming car.

'Maybe you'd better do the first part of the talking,' Eldon said to Turlock.

Lew Turlock nodded. He got out of the car, crossed in front of the headlights, and was waiting by the side of the road when Rose Marie drew abreast.

Illumination from the instrument light in the dashboard showed that a beautiful blonde girl with deep blue eyes and smooth, fine-textured skin was at the wheel, alone in the car.

Lew Turlock stepped forward. 'Hello,' he said somewhat inanely, his eyes going past Rose Marie to the empty seat beside her.

'Oh,' she said. 'It's ... Mr. Turlock ... How do you do, Mr. Turlock. Oh, I'm sorry. I hope you didn't come out here just to –'

'Where is Betty?' Turlock asked.

She shifted her position behind the steering wheel. She frowned for a moment, then smiled, and said, 'Oh, she'll be along. She's right behind me.'

The Sheriff slid out from behind the steering wheel. 'Hello, Rose Marie,' he said. 'Just where is Betty?'

Rose Marie Mallard looked from one man to the other. The

deep blue eyes showed sudden panic. The pathetic attempt at a smile was wiped off her face.

'Where is she?' the Sheriff asked, and then added, 'Right now. I want to see her.'

Rose Marie's words were hardly audible above the purr of the idling motor.

'I don't know,' she said. 'I've been trying to find her.'

The Sheriff's voice hardened. 'Now let's be frank,' he said. 'Suppose you tell me all you know about Betty Turlock.'

'I don't know a thing. She was to be here ... a little later.'

'And spend the night with you?'

'Yes.'

'What time was she supposed to be here?'

'She ... well, later.'

'How much later?'

'I don't know. I don't know as *she* did.'

The Sheriff said, 'There's been an accident over at Calhoun's. We're looking for Betty, and other people are going to be looking for Betty maybe. It's going to be kind of too bad if no one seems to know right where she is. Particularly because Betty's mother's going to say she's over here working on that play.'

'An accident, Sheriff?'

'Lorraine Calhoun's been killed.'

'*Lorraine!* Oh, but Betty *couldn't* have done anything like that!'

'Like what?'

'Why, killing ... You said it was an accident?'

'A horse kicked her, yes.'

Rose Marie's exclamation was an 'Oh!' which indicated great relief.

'Now after you got that telephone call from Lew here,' the Sheriff said, 'you jumped in your car and went out to try and find Betty, didn't you?'

There was a moment's hesitancy, then a reluctant nod.

'Now then,' the Sheriff said, 'let's not get into any *more* trouble, Rose Marie. Where did you go?'

'Out – out along the river road.'

'You were looking for her parked in an automobile?'

'Yes.'

'Whose automobile?'

'Hers – that is, Mr. Turlock's.'

'And who did you expect would be with her?'

'Why ... I was just looking for *her*.'

There was a note of impatience in the Sheriff's voice. 'You tell us the facts,' he said, 'and let us do the thinking. We're all friends of Betty's and we don't any one of us want to see a lot of talk get started. Now, you don't need to try to cover up things from us. You tell us the truth, only tell it to us fast.'

She said, 'She was to meet Frank Garwin tonight.'

'Who's Garwin?' the Sheriff asked.

It was Lew Turlock who answered the question. 'Friend of the Calhouns,' he said.

The Sheriff studied Lew Turlock's face for a moment, then turned back to Rose Marie Mallard. 'You tell us,' he said.

Her voice was thin with fright, but she said readily enough, 'When the Calhouns bought the place and moved in, Lorraine was spending the summer up in Maine with friends. She only got back here about three weeks ago. Frank Garwin is a friend of – well, a friend of the family. He ... they all sort of like him and ... He wanted to be a lawyer and he and Lorraine were going together steady and then – well, he didn't have the money for an education and Lorraine loaned him enough to get himself through college and ...'

'How about the army? Was he ...'

'No, he has a bad heart. He stayed on and studied and – well, he got to seeing something of Betty ... It's a mix-up. I don't know too much about it. All I know is they're miserable.'

'Who's miserable?'

'Both of them.'

'Lorraine?'

Rose Marie lashed out bitterly at that name. 'Not Lorraine,' she said. 'She was playing around in Maine and that's why she didn't want to come back to California when her folks bought

this place. If you ask me, I think she came back to give Frank
Garwin the gate. And then she saw how things were and she
just decided to play dog in the manger. Not that she cares a
thing in the world about Frank, but it's her own pride, her own
selfishness, her own conceit. She couldn't stand the idea of
having some other girl take a boy friend away from her, the
great Lorraine Calhoun – sophisticated, polished, traveled,
patronizing, snobbish little –'

'She's dead,' the Sheriff reminded her.

'I'm sorry. I forgot. I – well, I'm sorry.'

Suddenly a light blazed into brilliance ahead.

'That's Mr. Thornton,' Rose Marie said desperately. 'He does
that whenever someone wants us on the phone. That's probably
Betty now.'

They waited while she turned her car and then followed her
to Thornton's house. But it wasn't Betty Turlock on the phone.
It was long distance again, Irma Jessup calling. It seemed she
had once more called Turlock's residence and Mrs. Turlock,
innocently enough, had told the operator Betty could be reached
through the Thornton residence.

Sheriff Eldon stepped to the telephone. 'Hello,' he said.

The woman's voice at the other end of the line said
impatiently, 'I didn't want to talk with you again, I –'

'Now listen to me a minute,' Eldon said. 'This is the Sheriff
talking. There's been an accident over at the Calhoun place
and –'

He ceased talking as he heard the receiver at the other end of
the line dropped on the hook. The line went abruptly dead.

Bill Eldon sat in the Sheriff's office in the courthouse, a reading
light flooding the battered desk where he had spread out the
diary of Lorraine Calhoun.

The door opened and George Quinlan came breezing in.

'You get those pictures?' the Sheriff asked.

'Pictures of the whole business,' Quinlan asked. 'We've
turned the body over to the doctor. I got C.C. Calhoun himself
on the phone. He should be here any time now. He's all broken

up. He didn't know his daughter was here. She'd gone out for the evening.

Steps ascending the uncarpeted wooden stairs of the courthouse sounded abnormally loud against the background of night-time silence.

'This may be Calhoun now,' Quinlan said.

'Sounds like there are two of them,' the Sheriff said.

The door was pushed open, and a tall distinguished man strode into the room. 'My name's Calhoun,' he said. 'I want to see the Sheriff.'

Calhoun's wavy hair was touched with gray. His regular features, carefully groomed appearance, and well-modulated voice gave him an air of quiet authority. He was wearing a pearl-gray double-breasted suit with a light topcoat of about the same color.

Bill Eldon got up from behind his desk and held out his hand. 'I'm Eldon, the Sheriff,' he said. 'Mighty sorry to have to meet you under circumstances like this, Mr. Calhoun.'

Calhoun surveyed him with large dark eyes and shook hands. Then he stood slightly to one side and indicated another man standing just behind him in the doorway.

'Mr. Parnell,' he said, 'one of my business associates. He's going to take charge of – of details.'

Parnell, square-jawed and coldly direct of eye, was a few years younger than Calhoun. He had put on weight which the careful tailoring of an expensive double-breasted suit could soften, but not entirely hide.

Once more the Sheriff shook hands and introduced Quinlan, the Deputy Sheriff. The four men sat down.

'Suppose you tell us about it,' Calhoun said, after a few preliminaries.

The Sheriff briefly outlined what had happened.

Calhoun shook his head. 'I simply can't believe it.'

The Sheriff's voice showed his sympathy. 'Her trip down here seems to have been sorta unexpected.'

'It must have been. We were all intending to come tomorrow. But then Lorraine had her own car and was free to do as she pleased.'

'Twenty-one?' the Sheriff asked.

'Going on twenty-two.'

The Sheriff said, 'Just as a matter of routine, I'm going to have to ask you to go down and identify the body and ... well, you know how it is. There's a lot of formality to be gone through.'

Parnell broke into the thread of the conversation. 'That's why I'm along. Times like this, things are pretty tough on a father. I'm prepared to make whatever arrangements are necessary.'

Parnell had a rapid-fire diction, frequently accompanied by swift explanatory gestures. He was exactly the type of man to take charge of details for a bereaved friend and make a good job of it.

'Would you like to go see your daughter now?' the Sheriff asked Calhoun.

'Naturally,' Calhoun said shortly and started putting on his gloves.

'Let's get started and get it over with,' Parnell said brusquely. 'It's a disagreeable duty, but after that's over with, Mr. Calhoun can rest.'

'Has the mare been shot?' Calhoun asked.

'Why, no,' the Sheriff said in some surprise.

'Don't you shoot vicious animals?'

'Well, now ...' The Sheriff hesitated and then went on, 'Of course, being as how you were coming down here right away, I wanted to wait and get an authorization from you. After all, the mare –'

'You have my authorization,' Calhoun said. 'I never want to see that mare again. Shoot her at once, please.'

'Well, now, we'd better wait until morning because –'

'I want her shot *tonight*,' Calhoun said with cold, implacable hatred behind each word.

The Sheriff nodded to Quinlan. 'Guess you can keep the office for a while, George. We'll go on down and go through the necessary formalities.'

Calhoun remained wordless during the trip to the undertaking parlor. And when Bill Eldon introduced him to

Logan, the Coroner and town mortician, he merely bowed. Then
Carl Carver Calhoun, his face drawn into hard lines of sorrow,
bent over the still figure lying on the marble slab.

Suddenly he straightened and turned.

'What's the idea?' he asked coldly. 'Where's the other one?'

'The other what?'

'The other body – that of my daughter.'

He read his answer in the expression of consternation on the
faces of those about him.

'You mean to say *this* is the body you found in my barn?' he
asked.

'Isn't that your daughter?' Logan asked.

'Definitely not.'

'Do you know who it is?' Bill Eldon asked.

'I not only don't know who it is, but I certainly don't
appreciate having been advised that my daughter was dead. I
can't, of course, expect urban efficiency here in a rural
community, but after all ...' Calhoun controlled himself with an
effort, moved his shoulders in an expressive gesture, and turned
to his friend, Parnell. 'Let's get out of here,' he said.

'Just a moment,' the Sheriff intervened. 'Let's get this thing
straight. You're *sure* this isn't your daughter?'

'I guess I should know my own daughter, Sheriff.'

The Sheriff turned to Parnell in silent question.

Parnell shook his head. 'That's definitely not Lorraine, if
that's what you want to know, Sheriff.'

'And neither one of you knows who she is?'

'I've never seen her before,' Calhoun said.

'Nor I,' Parnell added.

The Sheriff moved closer to look down at the body of the
young woman.

'How did you happen to make such a ghastly mistake?'
Calhoun asked.

'Well, of course,' the Sheriff explained, 'the way the lights
were there in the stable, the face was pretty much in shadow and
she was lying more or less face down. And that kick in her
forehead and the blood hadn't helped any; but Sid Rowan

identified her as Lorraine Calhoun and so did Lew Turlock.'

Logan added hastily, 'Of course, when you come right down to it, Bill, Lew Turlock just took a quick look and saw there was a body and ran to notify you on the phone. He never did get a really good look at the face. You remember he thought at first it was his daughter, Betty. And then when Sid Rowan came in, I noticed particularly that he just – well, he wanted to keep away from the place. He really didn't take a *good* look. He just went over and gave a quick glance and said it was Lorraine. I s'pose it was the fact that Miss Calhoun's car was parked out in front of the stable that did it.'

The Sheriff said almost musingly, 'That sort of ties in all along the line. *Two* people must have gone into that barn. This young woman and someone else.'

'Meaning my daughter Lorraine?' Calhoun asked.

'Not meaning anyone yet,' the Sheriff said. 'Just a person. You see, Mr. Calhoun, the lights weren't on in the barn, so whoever entered must have turned them on.'

'Go ahead. Let's hear the rest of it,' Calhoun said.

'And another thing,' the Sheriff went on. 'In the manger of the mare's stall we found your daughter's diary with her name in the front of it. And I guess that sort of helped people to believe that the girl was your daughter. You see, things were pretty messy there in the stable – well, I can understand how the mistake happened to be made.'

'I can't,' Calhoun said shortly.

'And,' the Sheriff continued, 'when Lew Turlock found the body, there weren't any lights on in the barn. The horses had been stamping around for a while and Turlock had looked out of his window a couple of times in the half hour before he went over to investigate.'

'I don't see what you're getting at,' Calhoun said.

'It isn't hardly reasonable to suppose that this woman was wandering around there in the stable in the dark,' the Sheriff said. 'She must have turned on the lights when she went in. And she certainly didn't turn them off – after this happened. So I sort of figured someone must have been with her and ...'

Calhoun interrupted, 'Are you trying to insinuate that Lorraine took this girl into the stable and then after an accident of this sort calmly turned around, walked out, turned the lights off, not notified the authorities, not called the doctor, not ... Bah!'

'Now just take it easy,' the Sheriff said. 'I'm talking about *somebody*. I haven't mentioned your daughter's name a'tall. I'm just talking about somebody that went in the stable with this woman.'

'Well, your meaning is plain enough,' Calhoun said. 'Now let's get this straight, Sheriff. I'm relatively a newcomer in this county but I'm certainly not going to be pushed around. I don't like your insinuations. The body of this young woman happens to have been found in my stable. I suppose in view of that fact and my prominence in the city, there will be some newspaper comment about this. But let me warn you of one thing. In the event your bungling methods tend to add to that publicity, or make it sensational, or in the event the name of any one of my family is dragged into this thing, you will regret it as long as you live! As a matter of fact, I presume I have an action against you right now if I care to press it. Your slipshod methods have caused me to believe my daughter was dead. I left an important meeting and drove here at breakneck speed only to find myself the victim of a bucolic inefficiency which would have been ludicrous if it weren't so tragic. I advise you to think that over. Good night, sir.'

Calhoun nodded to Parnell. The two men started from the undertaking parlor.

After a few steps, however, Parnell turned back. 'Let's not have any misunderstanding, boys,' he pleaded. 'I've known Carl Calhoun for only a relatively short time, but it's been my privilege to know him well. Put yourself in his place. A young woman blunders into his stable and gets kicked by a horse. So far you've bungled things pretty much. From here on, let's get it right. The city newspapers will just give this only a couple of paragraphs if you boys use your heads. If you fellows keep messing it up, you'll stir up trouble. Once some newspaper gets

the idea there's any mystery about it, or that Lorraine Calhoun
was mixed up in it – well, you can see what will happen then.
You can't push Calhoun around and he's nuts about his
daughter – so take it easy.'

'Where's Lorraine now?' the Sheriff asked.

Parnell's face lost its conciliatory smile and showed irritation.
'How the hell should *I* know? Be your age – or perhaps you'd
better try not to be. Damn it all, Sheriff, Lorraine Calhoun
would no more have left an injured girl in case there'd been an
accident ...'

Parnell started to say something else, but changed his mind.
Turning away, he hurried after Calhoun.

Logan and the Sheriff exchanged glances.

'Well,' Logan said, as the steps down the hallway receded, 'it
looks as though we got a bear by the tail, Bill.'

The Sheriff nodded.

'Of course, he's got us there on that identification business,'
Logan went on. 'When you come right down to it, I'm the one
that's responsible for that. You found that diary and there was
something in it about Betty Turlock, so then you and Lew went
chasing off to find her. I'm the one that's supposed to make the
identification, I guess; but what with Lew Turlock and Sid
Rowan and her car sitting out in front – well, it's a mistake
anybody could have made.'

'How about Sid's wife? Didn't she take a look?' the Sheriff
asked.

'No, she didn't. After you left, Bill, I kept thinking about
George Quinlan coming down and taking pictures, so naturally
I was anxious to keep things just the way they were. I kept
everyone away from the body. But Mrs. Rowan didn't seem to
want to go near the body. I remember noticing it at the time
because she's rather a nosey busybody and likes to know
everything. They say she's quite a gossip.'

Bill Eldon nodded, then stepped over and looked down at the
silent body on the slab.

'Dirty shame a girl like this has to die,' he said. 'She evidently
was mighty good-looking, had everything to live for. Nice

trim-looking girl. Just a *nice*-looking girl. Good figure. We've got to find out who she is, how she happened to be in that stable, and who went in there with her.'

'You still think someone went in with her, Bill?'

The Sheriff didn't answer for a moment. He was looking at the U-shaped mark left by the horseshoe, almost in the center of the girl's forehead.

'See anything strange about that, Jim?' he asked.

'About what?'

'About that horseshoe mark.'

Logan shook his head.

'That's awful high for a mare to kick,' the Sheriff said. 'And notice that most of the force seems to have been at the upper part of the shoe. Now a horse would have to kick awful high to get a girl on the forehead if she was standing up. And then the force would be on the lower part of the shoe.'

'By George, you've got something there!' Logan exclaimed. 'The girl must have been down on her hands and knees when she was kicked.'

'And another thing,' the Sheriff said. 'You got a tape measure handy, Jim?'

'I can get one.'

'Get it,' the Sheriff said.

Logan started down the long passageway toward the front of the building, but after he had taken half a dozen steps, he suddenly turned and came back to the Sheriff.

'Bill,', he said, 'let's be careful what we do. We're already in a mess. Rush Medford, the District Attorney, doesn't like you. And more than that, he's always catering to people who have money and influence. He's got his eye on a political plum, maybe getting an appointment to one of the upper courts. A man like Calhoun can twist him around his finger.'

Bill Eldon, looking down at the dead girl, said nothing. His eyes were half closed in thoughtful concentration.

'Bill Eldon,' Logan said irritably, 'you listen to me! You ain't as young as you used to be and there's been a lot of talk around about cleaning out the courthouse ring, beginning with you.

And you watch Rush Medford. He's a back-stabber if I ever saw one. Back of all that smooth palaver of his, he's just laying for a chance to throw the hooks into you. Now, we've kind of led with our chins on this one and, the way I see it, the only thing to do is to back up and back up fast. We'll lose a little skin off our noses doing it, but it's better to do that than to lose our heads.'

The Sheriff abruptly turned away from the corpse. 'Jim,' he said, 'I don't ever aim to back up from anything that I think is right. Let's go get the tape measure.'

He walked with Logan to the front office where the Coroner opened a desk drawer, handed the Sheriff a small steel tape graduated to sixteenths of an inch. 'This all right?' he asked.

The Sheriff looked at the tape, nodded, and turned back toward the room in the rear of the establishment.

'Now you look here, Bill,' Logan persisted. 'Calhoun's on the warpath. Calhoun's got influence. And you just can't go bargin' around –'

The Sheriff walked away while Logan was talking. It wasn't, Logan realized, any intentional discourtesy – merely that the Sheriff had his mind completely centered on something else.

Logan started to follow him, then changed his mind, walked back to the desk, and sat down.

Logan himself held an elective office. Being Coroner made all the difference between carrying on his undertaking business at a good profit and just being able to eke out a living.

Logan knew what was going to happen in this case. If Bill Eldon didn't back up and back up fast, Calhoun would be after the Sheriff's scalp – might be anyway. Edward Lyons, publisher of the *Rockville Gazette*, had turned against Bill Eldon within the last two years. The first time Lyons had tried to throw the weight of his paper against the Sheriff, Bill Eldon had outfoxed him and neatly turned the tables. Since that time Lyons had been lying low, waiting for his political wounds to heal. But no one who knew Lyons thought for a moment he was finished. He was merely biding his time.

If Jim Logan stayed with the Sheriff on this thing, it would be a question of sink or swim. The time for Logan to bail out was right now. That was the sensible thing to do. All he had to do was to pick up the telephone and call Ed Lyons at the *Rockville Gazette.*

Logan heard the sound of the Sheriff's steps in the corridor. The Sheriff tossed the steel tape measure on Logan's desk.

'That mark of the horseshoe is four and fifteen-sixteenths inches at the widest part, Jim. I want you to verify that yourself, I'm goin' out.'

'Where?'

'Lookin' for a couple who might be doing a little necking. Any suggestions where they might be?'

'The river road,' Logan said, his manner preoccupied.

'They ain't there.'

'Only other place I know of is the ball park. They go there sometimes.'

'Thanks,' Eldon said. 'I'll try the ball park. Night, Logan.'

'Good night, Bill,' the Coroner said, not looking up.

The Sheriff left him sitting there at the desk, his eyes on the telephone, indecision in his manner.

The wide gate to the auto entrance of the ball park was propped open and the Sheriff drove in to what seemed a deserted enclosure. But as he swung his car in a wide searching circle, so that the headlights illuminated all parts of the field, he suddenly flushed quarry; an automobile which had been standing in dark silence by the bleachers blazed into brilliance and started for the exit.

The Sheriff moved to head it off. The other car gathered speed. The Sheriff switched on his red spotlight.

The car, bathed in blood-red brilliance, took to headlong flight. It tore past the gate posts, screamed into a turn, and started on the road toward town.

The Sheriff gave it the siren.

The other car kept on. The Sheriff poured gas into the motor of the County car and really settled down to dangerous driving. If the car ahead wanted to play rough, Bill Eldon was willing to do his part.

But the driver of the car ahead was only fairly good at that sort of thing, and it took less than half the distance to town for the Sheriff to work alongside and crowd the other car over to the ditch.

'What's the matter?' the Sheriff asked, rolling down the window of his car. 'Can't you folks hear the siren?'

Betty Turlock at the wheel was white-faced with apprehension. She tried to say something but her quivering lips failed.

The Sheriff raised his five-cell flashlight. The searching beam stabbed into the interior of the car. He saw that the back seat was empty and then let the light dwell searchingly on the features of the young man who sat at Betty Turlock's side.

The Sheriff shut off the motor of his car, opened the door, and got out. 'You shouldn't have done that, Betty.'

'I – I thought the officers were making a roundup of petting parties. I didn't want to be caught.'

The Sheriff pushed his hat back on his head. 'You know, Betty, this is a small community and things have a way of getting around. You're supposed to be with Rose Marie Mallard working on that Red Cross business. And if I was you, I'd get out there just as fast as I could. I'll take this young man with me. What's his name?'

'Frank Garwin,' the man said.

'Oh, yes, pleased to meet you, Frank. You don't live here, do you?'

'No.'

'Come down once in a while to visit the Calhouns, don't you?'

'That's right.'

'Friend of Lorraine?'

'Yes.'

'Know a girl named Irma Jessup?'

'Yes.'

'Who is she?'

'A friend of Lorraine's.'

'And of yours?'

'Yes, I've known her for a long time.'

'You know her, Betty?'

'I've never met her. But I've heard Frank speak of her.'

'She's been trying to get you long-distance telephone. Seems like there's been an accident out at Calhoun's. A horse kicked a young woman.'

'Good heavens!' Betty Turlock said.

Garwin said nothing, but the Sheriff noticed he moved his head over toward the open window on Betty's side of the car, and as he did so, his hand rested for a moment on Betty's.

'Was she hurt badly?' Betty asked.

'Killed,' the Sheriff said. 'We're sort of looking around. Your dad's been looking for you and you'd better get out to Mallard's right away. You can come with me, Frank.'

Garwin came around to the Sheriff's car and climbed in beside him.

'Get going,' the Sheriff said to Betty Turlock.

She sent the Turlock car lurching forward in a way that would have been a shock to Lew Turlock if he could have seen the tire-spinning take-off.

Turning to Frank Garwin, the Sheriff said, 'Just sit in here a minute, son. I want to ask you a couple of questions.'

'Yes, sir.'

'You been out there with Betty long?'

'Not very long.'

'Live in the city?'

'Yes.'

'You don't have a car?'

'No.'

'How'd you come to town?'

'On the seven o'clock bus.'

'And had a date with Betty?'

'That's right.'

'She picked you up?'

'Yes, sir.'

'Where?'

'Out at the high school.'

'How'd you get from the bus station to the high school?'

'I walked.'

'Betty's been gone from her house some little time.'

Garwin said, 'I – I was late.'

'What made you late, Frank?'

He merely shook his head.

The Sheriff's voice was kindly. 'When this accident happened out at Calhoun's, I naturally looked around a bit. In the manger I found what seems to be Lorraine Calhoun's diary. Because it's evidence, I've been reading it here and there, sort of hitting the high spots. I guess you're the Frank she mentions in there, aren't you?'

'I suppose so. What did she say about me?'

'I'm asking the questions right now,' the Sheriff said, his voice kindly but authoritative. 'Now Lorraine seemed to think you belonged to her and that Betty had been doing a little cutting in.'

Garwin hesitated.

'Better start talkin',' the Sheriff said.

The authority in the Sheriff's voice brought forth a sudden rush of words.

'I suppose I'm a first-class heel. My folks were cleaned out in the depression. Both of them died within three years of the failure of the bank in which they had their life sayings. I'd been a basketball player in prep school and I overdid things. I have an athlete's heart. They say I can probably get over it if I take care of myself. But I can't do any heavy work for a while. I wanted to go to college. I had always wanted to fit myself for a career, and the way things were, it just seemed impossible.

'Lorraine and I were – well, I guess we were in love. I thought I was, anyway. She offered to finance me through college out of her allowance. I took her up on it. And then afterwards – well, I met Betty and ... gosh, I felt like a heel. I couldn't turn around and give Lorraine a double-cross and – well, I tried to let her see that perhaps we'd changed. But she just couldn't see things that way.'

'So you started seein' Betty on the sly?' the Sheriff asked.

'Certainly not,' Garwin flared up. 'I told Betty that – well, as soon as I realized how things were drifting, I told her I couldn't see her any more.'

'And so you took the bus and came down here for her to meet you?'

'That was her idea. She said that she just couldn't give me up without seeing me once more and talking things over. She – well, it's hard for her to understand.'

'Yes, I can see how she might feel,' the Sheriff said. 'Now, you haven't told me what made you late.'

'I was to meet her at the high school. It was the last time I was ever to see her alone. I felt that if Lorraine wanted me to go ahead with it – and announce our engagement – well, that was the way it had to be. And I wasn't even going to come down any more on week-ends. I couldn't bear to be visiting next door to Betty and see her just as a casual acquaintance. It meant too much to me.

'Well, I got off the bus and went to the high school grounds. Betty drove up shortly afterwards. And then I just couldn't face it. I felt certain that if I saw Betty and held her in my arms once more, I couldn't ever give her up. On the other hand, I couldn't go to Lorraine and tell her that we were finished – not after the things she'd done for me. You don't understand how these things look to Lorraine. She thinks that Betty deliberately cut in and that I'd been heel enough to ... Oh, I just can't tell you the whole mess, Sheriff. It's all mixed up and –'

'I know, son,' the Sheriff said sympathetically. 'So you waited there in the high school grounds and decided you were going to wait right there out of sight until Betty drove away?'

'That's right.'

'And then what happened?'

'Then I – well, I heard her crying when she thought I wasn't going to meet her and ... gosh, I just seemed to have got everything all balled up. I have a knack for doing everything wrong. I couldn't let her think I'd stood her up on that last meeting.'

'As you get older,' the Sheriff said, 'you'll find the best way to play things is straight from the shoulder. Now let's get this all straight. How long were you there?'

'I can't tell you exactly how long it was before I spoke to her. I got in on the seven o'clock bus. I was at the high school by seven fifteen. Betty drove up about ten minutes later. I stood there in the shadows, watching her. She shut off her lights and the motor and waited. After ten or fifteen minutes, she got the idea I wasn't going to show up. I was standing so close to her I could hear her sobbing. After a while I couldn't stand it so I joined her.'

The Sheriff switched on the ignition and started his car. 'We've got Betty's reputation to consider,' he said. 'I'll drive you over to San Rodolpho, son, and you can pick up a bus there that will take you back to the city without anyone knowing you were here. We'll all pretend she was with Rose Marie all the time. If you've fallen out of love with Lorraine, you won't be doing her any favor to marry her while you're loving someone else. However, you work out your own problem. You'll like it better that way.'

When the Sheriff returned to his office in the courthouse, he found George Quinlan talking to an exceedingly difficult young woman who quite evidently had backed the Deputy Sheriff into a corner.

Quinlan's face lit up with relief. 'Here's the Sheriff now.'

She turned to Bill Eldon – a chestnut-haired girl who had the sculptured appearance which comes only to women who have both the time and the egotism to cultivate it.

The Sheriff noticed a strong superficial resemblance to the dead girl. Nor did he need Quinlan's introduction to realize the identity of his caller.

'Miss Lorraine Calhoun,' Quinlan said, and his manner indicated that he was retiring from the field of battle just as definitely as though he had added, 'And you can count me out from here on.'

The young woman was nervously lighting one cigarette from the stub of another.

'Will you *kindly* explain to me what this is all about?'
Lorraine asked the Sheriff.

'Well, now, ma'am,' the Sheriff said, 'you might just as well
sit down. We've got some talking to do. The way it looks to me,
you're going to be the one that explains to *me* what it's all
about.'

There was no antagonism in the Sheriff's voice, merely a
quiet, calm persistence. Lorraine was shrewd enough to note the
dogged power back of that good-natured drawl. Abruptly she
changed her tactics.

Her smile was meant as a dazzling reward for a man who
would come to heel without too much difficulty.

'My diary is private. I want it back.'

'So I gather,' the Sheriff said. 'When did you have it last,
Miss Calhoun?'

'That's not your business.'

The Sheriff said, 'If someone stole that diary, it's my duty to
recover it. If you left it in the manger there in the barn, then
naturally the Coroner will want to know whether the dead girl
was there when you left it and what time it was.'

She thought that over while she regarded him with
thoughtful eyes. Once more she changed her tactics. 'I'm glad
you've explained it to me. I can see now that you're absolutely
right.'

'That's fine. Now when was the last time you had this
particular diary?' the Sheriff asked.

'Around six o'clock, shortly before I left the city.'

'And what did you do?'

She said, 'I made an entry in the diary. Then I put it in the
glove compartment of my automobile.'

'And locked it up?'

'I don't know. The glove compartment was *un*locked when I
returned to my car.'

'I notice there's one page torn out of your diary – the date of
April 17th.'

Her eyes and voice showed surprise. 'A page missing!'

'Yes, torn out.'

'I can't believe it!'

'Where were you on April 17th?'

'Let's see. I was – yes, I was in Kansas City visiting a friend, stopping over on my way to New York.'

'Now you drove down from the city, drove directly to your house, and parked your car in front of the stables?'

'Yes.'

'And the stable was dark?'

'That's right.'

'The horses had been fed?'

'I don't know.'

'But Sid Rowan wasn't there?'

'No. There was no one home. I was upset and I – I took a long walk.'

'Where to?'

'Heavens, I don't know. I just walked for miles along the country road.'

'Your diary indicates that you might be a little jealous of Betty Turlock.'

She threw back her head and laughed throatily. 'Jealous of little Betty Turlock? Don't be silly!'

'But your diary mentions a man who is evidently a friend of yours and then mentions Betty –'

'If you *have* to inquire into my private affairs,' she said, 'Frank is a very close and very dear friend of mine. Betty Turlock was out to get him the minute she met him. I know farmers' daughters are supposed to be fascinating, but I didn't want to see Frank throwing himself away on that sort of girl. *I* wouldn't marry Frank if he were the last man on earth, but he's a friend. There's also a matter of some thirty-five hundred dollars that I have invested in Frank Garwin's career. I put up that money for him to get an education. I paid it out of my allowance. Naturally, I want to see him succeed. He can't do it with a girl like Betty Turlock draped around his neck.'

The confused pound of hurried steps sounded on the stairs from the lower floor of the courthouse.

The Sheriff turned toward the door.

Rush Medford, the District Attorney, pushed open the door. Behind him, Calhoun, Parnell, and another man who was a stranger to the Sheriff grouped themselves into a supporting semicircle.

'Sheriff,' Medford said, 'what's this I hear about you holding a diary of Miss Calhoun's?'

'That's right,' the Sheriff said.

'Give it back to her,' Medford commanded.

'It may be evidence,' the Sheriff said.

'Evidence of what?'

'Well, that's what I'm investigating.'

Medford raised his voice angrily. 'As District Attorney, it's my duty to advise you as to the course of conduct you should follow. I now advise you to give that diary back.'

One of the men behind the District Attorney moved impressively forward. He was, the Sheriff noticed, a well-fed, prosperous man in the forties. the knifelike crease of his trousers, the expensive and unwrinkled appearance of his coat shed an aura of affluence which harmonized with the measured, judicial tones of the man's voice.

'Permit me, Sheriff,' he said. 'I am Oscar Delano, of the firm of Delano, Swift, Madison and Charles. We handle Mr. Calhoun's legal work. I don't want to seem abrupt, but unless we get that diary back, I am instructed by my client to start suit against you at once for the damages caused to my client by your negligence in falsely announcing to him that his daughter had been killed.'

The Sheriff walked across the office, slammed the door of his safe shut, and spun the dial of the combination.

'Start suit,' he said.

'You fool!' Medford exclaimed.

The Sheriff settled back in his creaky swivel chair.

'You haven't got a leg to stand on,' the city lawyer said.

'Well, now,' the Sheriff drawled, 'maybe I haven't. But when you can explain how a mare, wearing a number-ought shoe which measures four and three-sixteenths inches at the widest part can kick a person in the head and leave a mark four and

fifteen-sixteenths inches wide, which means a number-two shoe
– well, then I'll give you the diary.'

'What do you mean?' Calhoun asked.

The Sheriff said, 'However that girl was killed, that mare
didn't do it. I say it was murder. Now then, go start your
lawsuit.'

Next morning the *Rockville Gazette* was on the streets with an
extra.

'MURDER,' SCREAMS THE SHERIFF
'PUBLICITY,' SNAPS D.A.
'POPPYCOCK,' SNORTS CALHOUN

The article which followed showed Edward Lyons, the
publisher and managing editor, at his sarcastic best.

'When the body of an unidentified young woman was found
in the stable of Carl Carver Calhoun, wealthy broker who has
established a country home at Rockville, Sheriff Bill Eldon, with
a nose for publicity at least as sharp as his nose for clues,
promptly announced that the victim was Lorraine Calhoun,
daughter of the broker. The woman had evidently been kicked
by a mare.

'Only after Calhoun and a business associate had driven at
breakneck speed to Rockville, and announced that the victim
was not only no relation to Mr. Calhoun but a perfect stranger,
did the Sheriff reluctantly shift his position. Then, with the aid
of a tape measure and some of his "brilliant" deductive
reasoning, he arrived at the conclusion that he was dealing with
a murder.

'Because of a three-quarter-inch discrepancy between the size
of the shoe on the mare and the imprint of the shoe on the
forehead of the victim, Sheriff Eldon lost no time announcing
his theory of foul play.

'Regardless of the motive which prompted this action on his
part, the result has been all that any publicity-crazed politician
could ask for. When word reached the newsrooms of the city

papers that an unidentified girl had been murdered in the stable of the wealthy broker, reporters and photographers descended upon Rockville in a flood.

'Rush Medford, the District Attorney, brands the Sheriff's charge as "premature to say the least. It is," Medford asserts, "the result of synthetic clues which have been conjured up in the imagination of a man who received some publicity in the metropolitan papers a year or so ago and found the experience pleasant."

'The District Attorney apparently was referring to the murder committed on the old Higbee place last year, a crime in which luck played into Sheriff Eldon's hands, but which netted him some very flattering publicity.

'Doubtless District Attorney Medford is correct in stating that Sheriff Eldon would like to see a repetition of that publicity, just as a kid would like to see Christmas come once a week.

'So far as the death of the young woman is concerned, Rush Medford seems to have kept his head and delivered about the best summary to date.

' "We don't know who this young woman is," Medford said. "We don't know her motive in prowling around the barn of Carl Calhoun. But we do know she had no business being there. She received a kick from a horse which unfortunately proved fatal. Because Sheriff Eldon noted a discrepancy between the imprint of the shoe on the forehead of the victim and the size of shoe worn by the mare, he has inferred foul play. While he has not, as yet, claimed the death as a murder in so many words, he has insinuated as much.

' "He had an opportunity to plant the seeds of sensationalism in ground where he knew they would promptly sprout. The temptation was too strong. I, personally," Medford went on, "abhor using public office as a means of securing publicity. Because of the prominence of Carl Carver Calhoun, who has done Rockville the honor of picking it as the place for his country residence, a duty was placed upon every official of the County to proceed cautiously and do everything possible to see that innocent parties were spared the embarrassment of that blatant publicity which always follows in the wake of sensationalism."

'Carl Carver Calhoun was even more outspoken than the District Attorney. "So far as the Sheriff is concerned," he said, "he is an old man and therefore I suppose I should be charitable. But it is hard to be charitable to a man whose every action seems actuated solely by a desire for personal aggrandizement. I warned him that because of my position and metropolitan connections the news value of anything connected with my name would be greatly magnified. I therefore asked him particularly to be cautious in his actions and not to jump at conclusions.

' "This warning occurred after he had made an erroneous identification of the body in my stable as that of my daughter. Instead of heeding that warning, he went plunging on, confiscating private documents belonging to my daughter, which he doubtless hopes to release to the press at some future date.

"I am pleased to find that your District Attorney, Rush Medford, is a young man of broad mental caliber, the sort of timber from which we should select our Appellate Judges. I only wish the Sheriff had one-half his passion for accuracy, one-tenth of his intrinsic integrity."

'So far, the body has not been identified, but the finding of a Kansas City label on the jacket and the imprint of a Kansas City shoestore in the almost-new shoes worn by the unfortunate victim have given authorities grounds to hope that an identification may soon be made.'

The Sheriff read the *Rockville Gazette* on the early morning bus on his way to see Irma Jessup.

He found her just finishing breakfast in her apartment and getting ready to leave for the Trust Company where she was employed in the Escrow Department.

Irma Jessup listened to the Sheriff, and then elevated delicate arched eyebrows. Her call to Betty Turlock? Just a minor matter. Purely personal. Important enough so far as Betty was concerned but not important to anyone else. Yes, she had called several times. She had told Mr. Turlock that it was quite important. Then she had called another number which Mrs. Turlock had given her.

She laughed when faced with the fact that she had hung up the telephone on being advised that the Sheriff was on the other end of the line.

'Good heavens,' she exclaimed. 'I wondered what I'd stirred up. I just didn't know what to say, and so I hung up.'

'You've read the papers?'

'No, what about them?'

'A young woman was kicked by a horse in Calhoun's barn. Killed her.'

Irma Jessup expressed consternation and sympathy.

'Any idea who she might have been?' Eldon asked.

'No, of course not.'

'Well, now, I don't want to pry into things,' Eldon said, 'but I'm afraid I've got to know what it was you were calling up Betty Turlock about.'

She was ready enough to talk now. 'Betty is a nice wholesome girl. But – well, she isn't exactly Lorraine's type. Frank Garwin had been very much in love with Lorraine. I think Lorraine was in love with him. She put up money to get him through college. He'd had some bad luck. I've known Frank every since we were children. In fact, Frank's folks and my folks were pretty close and there was some sort of business association between them. It was all part of the same transaction when my folks got wiped out. Mr. Calhoun had been in the same company but he was smart enough to pull out before things went bad. I remember he wanted my dad to pull out and I think he wanted Mr. Garwin to. Anyway, that will give you the background.'

The Sheriff merely nodded.

She said, 'I know Frank pretty well. Frank was in love with Lorraine and then – well, he was out of love with her. And I think Lorraine was out of love with him. There had been sort of a drifting apart. Lorraine was in Maine, spending the summer, and – I don't know, Frank thought her letters were a little cool.

He talked to me about it.'

'And he was down at Rockville some of the time visiting the family?'

'That's right.'

'And got to seeing Betty down there?'

'Yes.'

'All right. Now tell me about the telephone call.'

'Frank took the bus and went to Rockville to see Betty. He didn't want anybody to know that he had gone there, but Lorraine found it out.'

'How?'

'I don't know.'

'How do you know that she knew it?'

'She called me and asked if Frank were here. She said she had to see him at once. I knew from the tone of her voice what was in the wind. I felt certain she was going to drive down to Rockville.'

'And you were telephoning to tell Betty that Lorraine was on her way down?'

'That's right.'

The Sheriff quite evidently was disappointed. 'You don't know anything about some young woman from Kansas City about twenty-two years old, weighing about a hundred and twelve pounds, five feet four and a half-inches, neat little figure, dark auburn hair, brown eyes?'

'No.'

'Know of any girl that description that might be a friend of Lorraine's?'

'No.'

The Sheriff took a photograph from his pocket. 'Making allowances for the closed eyes and that wound on the forehead, does she look like anyone you know?'

'Definitely no. I've never seen her in my life – not to remember.'

The Sheriff thanked her and marked his early morning trip on the debit side of the ledger.

*

It was almost noon when the Sheriff climbed the stairs to his office. George Quinlan said, 'Gosh, Bill, I've been trying all over to locate you.'

'What's the trouble?'

'They've identified the body.'

'Who is it?'

'Estelle Nichols of Kansas City. She had a charge account at the store where she bought the shoes and one of the clerks happened to remember her.'

'Any connection with Calhoun?' the Sheriff asked, and couldn't keep the anxiety from his voice.

Quinlan shook his head. 'Looks like we're licked.'

The Sheriff duly noted and appreciated the loyalty of the inclusive pronoun.

'The District Attorney,' Quinlan went on, 'has dug up a witness from somewhere, a girl who says this Estelle Nichols was crossing the country to join her, that she planned on hitchhiking. She'd got a letter from this girl that Medford is giving to the newspapers. It says that she was planning on sleeping in barns as she went through the country.

'She saw the Calhoun place all dark early in the evening. Evidently it was right after Sid Rowan had finished feeding the horses and had started for the movie. And that explains why she would have walked in the door without switching on the lights. She was groping around trying to find the ladder which led up to the hayloft when she ran into this horse.'

'Which horse?' the Sheriff asked.

'Well,' Quinlan said, '– well, a horse.'

'A horse wearing a number-two shoe,' the sheriff said. 'And if she was kicked by a horse wearing a number-two shoe, she didn't fall down where the body was found. Because right there a mare was stabled that was wearing a number-ought shoe.'

Quinlan said, 'The forehead was flattened under the impact. Hawley says that would distort the impression made by the shoe.'

Bill Eldon thought that over. 'Maybe some,' he admitted, 'but not three-quarters of an inch.'

Quinlan's dispirited voice showed how he felt. 'Once they show this girl was a stranger to the Calhouns and went into a dark barn to find a place to sleep – well, we're licked, Bill. That's all there is to it.'

'That letter,' the Sheriff said. 'Who's got it?'

'Rush Medford has the letter, but I took a photograph. Here it is. It's a life-sized copy.'

The Sheriff took the photographic reproduction of the letter which Quinlan handed him. It read:

Dear Mae:

It won't be very long after you receive this letter that you'll see me. I'm going to make it even if I have to hitchhike my way and sleep in stables.

I feel certain that you'll listen to me, even if you have been hypnotized. There are some things I can tell you that will open your eyes.

And, Mae darling, will you see if you can locate the address of that man I was writing you about? I've lost track of him and I'd like to get in touch with him again.

The letter was signed, 'Yours always, Estelle.'

'Who's the girl that got this letter?' the Sheriff asked.

'Someone name of Mae Adrian.'

'And where is she now?'

'Out at Calhoun's.'

'Let's go,' the Sheriff said.

Quinlan's manner showed some embarrassment. 'Rush Medford's out there,' he said, 'and this lawyer of Calhoun's. They've got Ed Lyons out there, and I guess they're – well, I thought perhaps you'd like to wait until later.'

Eldon grinned. 'They're preparing a massacre. Is that right?'

'Well, you can put yourself in Ed Lyons' shoes,' Quinlan said miserably.

Eldon placed his hand on his Deputy's shoulder. 'George,' he said, 'I learned a long time ago that the only way to handle anything that has to be faced sooner or later is to wade right out in the middle and see how deep it is. Come on, let's go.'

They made good time out to Calhoun's country residence. A

half dozen cars were grouped around the stable. The Sheriff found a parking space, nodded to Parnell who was just coming through the gate from the Turlock place, and entered the stable.

He found Oscar Delano, Calhoun's attorney, virtually in charge of proceedings, with Rush Medford, the District Attorney, standing by and giving the benefit of his silent approval. A group of interested spectators was watching the city lawyer. There were, in addition, reporters and photographers from the city papers.

'Well, you can see the situation.' Delano was saying to Ed Lyons, publisher of the *Gazette*. 'This woman was a hitchhiker who, according to her own statement, was sleeping in stables. Someone took that button and sewed a vest on it. However, it's not for me, a rank outsider, to make any criticisms as to the efficiency of one of your County officials.'

'Well,' Medford said, 'I'm the one to criticize. I ... here he is now.'

The Sheriff stepped forward. 'Okay, Medford, I'm here.'

Delano cleared his throat significantly, then became silent.

Ed Lyons said, 'Well, Bill, you got right in the spotlight to fall flat on your face,' and he laughed sarcastically.

Rush Medford said, 'We have now identified this young woman. She was a hitchhiker who made a practice of sleeping in stables.'

'Mae Adrian here?' the Sheriff asked calmly.

A trim young woman with dark hair and large dark eyes stepped forward and said in a thin, somewhat frightened voice, 'I'm Mae Adrian.'

'You knew this dead girl?'

She nodded.

'You've seen the body?'

'Yes,' she said in almost a whisper.

'Positively identified it,' Ed Lyons announced triumphantly.

'And this letter that you received from her, when did you get that?'

'A week ago.'

'And what caused you to come forward?'

'I saw her pictures in the papers. I felt certain it was my friend, Estelle Nichols. So I got in touch with the District Attorney and he showed me the body. I identified it.'

'And you don't know any of these people?' the Sheriff asked.

'No one.'

'What's this in the letter about you being hypnotized?'

She laughed. 'Estelle had had an unfortunate love affair and she thought perhaps I was planning to do something she didn't approve of.'

Oscar Delano said impatiently, 'Well, there you are. The picture is complete. A young woman hitchhiking across the country picks my client's stable as a place to sleep and gets kicked by a horse. Some hick Sheriff sees a chance for notoriety and starts throwing his weight around.'

The photographer for one of the metropolitan newspapers dropped to one knee, focused his camera, and set off a flash, catching Delano standing there in the stable, his attitude that of righteous indignation.

'And which horse do you figure kicked her?' the Sheriff drawled.

Delano whirled to face him. 'Sheriff,' he said, 'I'm going to let you in on a big secret. The horse that kicked her,' and here Delano lowered his voice impressively as though about to impart a very confidential secret, 'was a quadruped that wore iron shoes. I can't tell you the color of his eyes. I leave that to you.'

The roar of laughter that followed furnished inspiration for the news photographer to expose another film, one that showed the old Sheriff standing in the middle of the semicircle of hilarious spectators.

Lew Turlock and his daughter Betty walked across the strip of lawn from the Calhouns' barn, through the gate, and over toward Turlock's garage.

'I think it's a shame,' Betty said. 'All those people laughing at the Sheriff that way.'

'Well, I guess he had his neck stuck out pretty far,' Turlock said, and added, 'It's a darn good thing for you.'

'Why?'

'Well, if it *had* been a murder and the thing had got to the point where they started a detailed investigation, and people found you were supposed to have been with Rose Marie –'

'I know, Dad. Let's skip it, please.'

Turlock stopped abruptly. 'That left rear tire's down,' he said, indicating the family car. 'Got to put some air in it.'

He walked over to the car, took the ignition key from the lock, inserted it into the trunk, and raised the lid. 'You get out the pump, Betty,' he said, 'and I'll –'

He broke off, staring at what he saw lying on the floor of the trunk – a bar with a prong in the form of a huge 'Y'. To this prong had been welded a horseshoe.

Betty said, 'What in the world –'

Her father bent forward to examine the iron bar. The sinister stain on the horseshoe, with some hairs stuck to the reddish brown patches, bore mute evidence of the murderous purpose for which the weapon had been used.

'How in the world did *that* get there?' Betty asked, and reached toward it.

Her father grabbed her wrist. 'Don't touch it! Leave a fingerprint on that and –'

He didn't need to finish the sentence. Betty's hand jerked away from the weapon.

Lew Turlock banged down the lid of the trunk and locked it.

'Betty, how *did* that get in there?'

'Dad, I don't know. I never saw it before.'

'This man you were out with,' Lew said. 'What about him?'

'Frank?'

'Yes.'

'What in the world are you suggesting?'

'Nothing, I'm asking questions.'

'Why, Frank wouldn't hurt a fly!'

'Can you get him on the phone?' Lew Turlock asked, his face grim as granite.

'Why – yes, I suppose so.'

'Come on in,' her father said.

He stood at her side as she placed the long-distance call. When she had Frank Garwin on the line Lew Turlock stepped to the telephone. 'This is Betty's dad. I have a couple of pretty important questions to ask. Did you ever know an Estelle Nichols of Kansas City?'

There was a moment of hesitation. Then Garwin said, 'Yes. I met her a year or so ago. She was working in a bank. Why?'

Turlock said, 'That was the girl that was killed over in Calhoun's barn.'

'Estelle Nichols killed in Calhoun's barn?' Garwin repeated incredulously.

'That's right. Didn't you see her pictures in the morning paper?'

'Yes. But I never thought it could have been – wait a minute. Hold the phone until I get the paper and take another good look.'

Turlock held the phone. A few moments later Garwin's voice came over the wire, a voice that was now filled with apprehension. 'That *could* be Estelle,' he said.

'Come out here,' Turlock ordered, 'and keep quiet until you get here. Make it just as quick as you can. Do you understand?'

'Yes, sir.'

Turlock hung up the telephone, then turned to his daughter. 'They've got that killing tagged as an accident now. If we can keep quiet, the thing will just naturally be hushed up.'

'Father!'

She had never seen quite that expression in her father's face before.

'Blood is thicker than water,' he said and turned away so that his daughter couldn't see his eyes ...

Sheriff Eldon pushed his way through the gate between the Calhoun and Turlock properties and said to Lew Turlock, 'Hope you don't mind if we look around a minute, Lew?'

Turlock, plainly nervous, said too effusively, 'Certainly not. Sure. Go ahead. Help yourself. Anything I can do?'

The Sheriff said, 'I don't know, Lew. Things just don't seem to check out in this case. Now, take that dead girl. Here's a girl hitchhiking across country. She comes into Calhoun's stable wearing a light dress, a skimpy little coat, and shoes with thin soles. And as for luggage – why, she didn't have so much as a toothbrush with her! What I want to know is, if that girl went in the stable and got kicked, what happened to all her stuff?'

'Yes,' Turlock said nervously, 'I see your point.'

'Another thing,' the Sheriff said. 'According to Lorraine's story, she came tearing down here in her automobile and then proceeded to go out and walk for miles and miles along the country roads. Now that don't sound right.'

'Don't seem so,' Turlock admitted.

'You gettin' a soft tire on that car?' the Sheriff said. 'Better pump her up before she goes completely flat.'

Turlock moved away from the automobile. 'I'll get at it. What you want to look around for, Bill?'

'I noticed that Calhoun girl smokes pretty much when she's nervous and I thought maybe she parked her car and kept an eye on your house. Lorraine was jealous of Betty. Of course, she won't admit it.'

'Betty didn't even lift a finger –' Turlock said.

'I know, Lew, but if Lorraine was jealous and had picked a place where she could watch your house and at the same time keep an eye on her car, seein' her car was parked right in front of the stable, it stands to reason she must have seen this Estelle Nichols go into the stable.'

'It was dark,' Turlock pointed out.

'I know, but somebody must have opened the door of Lorraine's car and got into her glove compartment and got out the diary. I don't think you'd do that in the dark unless you knew what you were looking for and this Estelle Nichols apparently didn't know Lorraine Calhoun.'

'Bill,' Turlock blurted, 'don't you think you'd be better off if you quit right now and let this thing just simmer down and run its course?'

'I'm licked now,' Eldon said. 'When that photographer got a

picture of all those folks laughing at me over there, it put me in a spot. I can't get no worse off than I am right now. Come along election time, you can imagine what'll happen. Ed Lyons'll have that picture running in his paper and put under it something like 'How about getting a Sheriff that folks don't laugh at.' Say, that tire's got a leaky valve. You can hear the air hissing out of it if you listen right sharp. Reverse the valve cap and tighten up the valve. What say we save what little air is left in there?'

Turlock started to interpose himself between the Sheriff and the tire, then restrained himself. The Sheriff unscrewed the cap from the valve, reversed the end, and twisted with his thumb and forefinger.

'Shucks,' he said, 'that valve stem is loose in there. Now she's tight. Haven't got a pump in the trunk there, have you, Lew?'

'It's all right. I'll fix it,' Turlock said. 'Don't worry about my car, Bill. You've got lots of things on your mind. Go ahead and look around. Out there back of the pepper tree there's a swing. She might have sat in that.'

'From there she could only see the back of the house,' the Sheriff said. 'Now over here by this hedge would be a good place where a person could ... I think I'll look along there.'

'Come on,' Turlock said anxiously, leading the Sheriff away from the car. 'Let's look.'

They moved along the hedge. 'Look here,' the Sheriff said excitedly. 'There's a newspaper spread out. Someone could have been sitting down there and spread the paper out to keep the grass from staining a dress and – sure enough! There's a dozen cigarette stubs. Now just a minute, Lew. I'd just as soon you didn't get around here. Let's kind of look for tracks – that's right. A person sitting right there and with her back to the hedge could see the front door of your house.'

The Sheriff's voice trailed away into disappointed silence.

'And that's all she could see,' Turlock said. 'She couldn't see anything that happened over at Calhoun's place. Couldn't see the house, couldn't see the entrance to the stable, couldn't even see where the car was parked.'

The Sheriff pursed his lips, then squatted to a sitting

position, cowboy fashion.

'Well,' he said in a voice that was suddenly tired, 'that's the way things go in life, Lew. You get something worked out and think you're doing all right and then something smacks you down. Of course, Lorraine is lying about getting out and walking up and down country roads. She sat down here where she could watch your house, just the way I figured she did. But I guess it ain't exactly a crime to watch your rival's door to see if your boy friend is taking her out. Anyway, that city lawyer over there would sure claim it wasn't.'

The Sheriff started back along the hedge toward the fence and the gate.

Betty Turlock, opening the rear door of the house, stepped out to the porch and saw the Sheriff and her father approaching. Abruptly and self-consciously she jerked back into the house and pulled the door shut.

Lew Turlock said hastily, 'Betty's all upset. Just don't want to talk to anybody.'

'Uh huh, I know how she feels,' Eldon said.

They were approaching the gate when they heard voices.

A group moved through the gate to confront the Sheriff and Lew Turlock.

Parnell included in a gesture Carl Calhoun, Lorraine, Mae Adrian, and Oscar Delano.

'Look here, Eldon. I'm a businessman,' Parnell said. 'Now there's no sense having a lot of friction here. Mr. Calhoun's my friend and associate. He's bought this place here in the country and he's got to live here. I want him to enjoy it.'

'Ain't no reason why he shouldn't,' the Sheriff said.

'Yes, there is. This is a relatively small community. Mr. Calhoun has instructed his attorney to file suit against you on that mistaken identification business. And now that this other thing has been all cleared up, *I* think the whole thing should be dropped.'

The Sheriff said, 'That's up to Mr. Calhoun.'

'We'll just wipe the whole slate clean,' Parnell said. 'We won't file suit. You'll quit trying to —'

'Trying to what?' the Sheriff asked.

Parnell was uncomfortably silent.

It was Calhoun who answered the question. 'Trying to make capital out of an accidental death which unfortunately took place in my stables.'

The Sheriff turned to Lorraine. 'I want to ask Miss Calhoun here if she's absolutely certain after she parked her car she just went out and walked along the country roads the way she told me.'

Lorraine took a deep drag at the cigarette she was smoking, then said, 'Father, isn't there any way you can put a muzzle on this –'

'Because,' the Sheriff went on, 'right over here on the edge of this hedge you can see where she spread out a newspaper to sit on. You can see the tracks of her high-heeled shoes in the soft soil along the edge of the hedge and you can see a dozen or so cigarette stubs of the particular brand she smokes. And if you want any proof on the time and date, why, the edition of the newspaper gives it to you. It's a late edition of the afternoon paper that comes out to bring results of horse races, and she must have picked it up just before she left the city yesterday.'

Lorraine said calmly, 'That's absurd.'

'Well, now, ma'am, maybe it's absurd and maybe it isn't. There's some pretty good footprints there and I notice you wear a distinctive type of shoe.'

'Great heavens,' she said indignantly, 'do I have to account for every step I take? How do I know whether I left a print there or not? I live here and I walk around. If you have any prints made by my shoes, they may be a week old.'

'Nope, they aren't a week old,' the Sheriff said. 'They were made sometime yesterday – sometime after the rain had softened up the ground. And that newspaper shows they were made sometime after five o'clock at night. Now, if you'll be frank and tell me –'

'Come, come,' Delano said in his smooth, suave voice. 'Mr. Parnell was extending an olive branch, Sheriff. Now, if we're going to wipe the slate clean, we'll wipe it clean. After all, my client isn't particularly interested in sticking you for damages, but he has a perfect case. Now, if he's willing to drop it, we'll expect you to meet us halfway.'

'Facts are facts,' the Sheriff said. 'I just want to get them sort of straightened out. And there's one other question I want to ask Miss Adrian here. This dead girl said something in her letter about trying to get an address of some man that she'd met. Who is that man?'

Mae Adrian said, 'A young law student. She'd met him when he was on vacation a year ago.'

'What's the fellow's name?' the Sheriff asked Mae Adrian.

'Good Lord,' Calhoun groaned. 'Don't you ever have enough? Must you always lead with your chin?'

'What's his name?' the Sheriff repeated.

Mae Adrian said, 'No one whom you ever heard of before, Sheriff. He's a law student whose folks lived in Kansas City for a while and were in business there. A young man by the name of Frank Garwin.'

'Frank Garwin!' Lorraine exclaimed. 'Why, I know *him*! He's a very close friend.'

'A friend of the family,' Carl Calhoun hastened to add.

'I've known him for some years myself,' Parnell said. 'What about him?'

Mae Adrian was as nonplussed at the bombshell she had dropped as a sportsman whose 'unloaded' gun roars into an accidental discharge.

'Why I was going to try and find his address for Estelle. I didn't know … Of course, Estelle had just met him there the one time but I guess she had a crush on him. He's a young lawyer, I believe, and Estelle had some legal problem.'

Oscar Delano said authoritatively, 'Now look here, Sheriff, I'll grant you there's an element of coincidence here, but I don't want you trying to torture anything else into it.'

Parnell turned to Lew Turlock. 'Well, I still don't see that it changes the situation any. By the way, Mr. Turlock, I'm in need of a car. Perhaps you'd like to drive us to the city. I'll pay you well. I promised Miss Adrian I'd take her back with me. There'll just be the two of us.'

'Maybe Miss Adrian ain't quite ready to go home yet,' the Sheriff said, 'the way things are shaping up now.'

'Well, she'll be ready in a minute,' Parnell said irritably. 'How about it, Turlock?'

Turlock seemed undecided for a moment, then abruptly caught Bill Eldon's eye and motioned to him. 'Bill,' he said, 'could I talk with you a minute private like?'

'How about taking us to the city?' Parnell asked impatiently.

Turlock said, 'I'll tell you when I get back.'

The Sheriff moved over a few yards from the little group. 'What is it, Lew?'

Turlock said, 'Bill, that wasn't any accident – the woman that got kicked in the barn.'

'I didn't think it was,' the Sheriff said.

'She was hit with a horseshoe put on a club.'

The Sheriff let his eyes bore steadily into those of Turlock. 'All right, Lew,' he said quietly. 'Let's have it.'

Turlock said, 'A few minutes ago I opened up the trunk on my automobile and – well, Bill, there's a club in there.'

'What sort of a club?'

'An iron bar with a prong welded to it and a horseshoe welded to that prong. The thing's about two feet long. And – well, Bill, I guess it's the one that was used in the murder.'

'Did you touch it?' the Sheriff asked. 'That weapon?'

'No.'

'Did Betty?'

'No.'

The Sheriff said, 'Don't say anything to anyone. Tell Parnell he can't use your car because after talking with me you found there's something you have to do uptown. Drive to the back of the courthouse and wait for Quinlan. Don't open up that trunk for anyone until Quinlan can take fingerprints. What does it look like – about a number-two horseshoe?'

'It's about a number-two,' Turlock said, 'and it has some caked blood on it. It's what killed her, all right.'

The Sheriff and Lew Turlock rejoined the little group.

Turlock said, 'I'm sorry, Parnell, I've got to go to town. I guess you'll have to get some other car.'

Parnell said, 'The District Attorney's going into the city and he's taking Miss Adrian in with him. I'll go with him.'

Rush Medford was perfectly willing to amplify that statement. 'I'm going in to interview Frank Garwin,' he said. 'I have just talked with him over the long-distance telephone, using Lew Turlock's phone and a number given me by Miss Calhoun.'

Medford's manner indicated that he had an important announcement to make and he waited until he had the attention of every person there before making it.

'Mr. Garwin has admitted to me over the telephone,' he said, 'that not only was he here yesterday night, but that a *friend* drove him over to San Rodolpho and put him on a bus at that point so he could get back to the city without anyone knowing he was here. The name of that *friend* was Bill Eldon, Sheriff of the County. Under the circumstances, I think an investigation is in order.' He waited another dramatic moment, then turned to the newspaper reporter, 'And you may quote me on that.'

At the Sheriff's office in the courthouse George Quinlan finished dusting the grim murder weapon with a white metallic powder especially prepared to bring out latent fingerprints.

'Find anything?' Eldon asked.

'Not a thing,' Quinlan said. 'It's been wiped and polished with something that's removed every single print that was on it. It might have been a piece of soft leather.'

Bill Eldon fished a cloth tobacco sack from his pocket, held a grooved paper in his left hand, and rolled a cigarette with a few deft motions.

'Well,' he said, 'when you run up against something like that, you just have to read trail, that's all.'

'Only we haven't any trail,' Quinlan said.

'Oh, yes, we have. We've got lots of trail.'

'Such as what?'

'Well, to begin with, we've got the time element.'

'Yes, that's right,' Quinlan said. 'Immediately after Sid Rowan left for the movies.'

Eldon shook his head.

'But it has to be that time, Bill. Rowan had just fed the horses before he left. He put down hay for this mare. The body lying there disturbed her so she couldn't eat. The chute coming down from the loft was chock-full of hay.'

'What kind of hay?' Eldon asked.

'What kind of hay?' Quinlan repeated. 'Why, uh, hay.'

'Barley hay,' the Sheriff said. 'Calhoun's feeding his horses oat hay. He got some barley hay for the cattle, feeds them some alfalfa hay and some barley. The oat hay is for the horses. It's been pretty hard to get.'

Quinlan thought that over.

'What's more,' the Sheriff went on, 'the minute you run across a weapon like this, you know you're figuring on plain, cold-blooded, deliberate murder – murder that was thought out quite some time in advance. The idea was the murder would look like an accident. It'd just be some unfortunate girl that blundered into a stable and got kicked by a horse. Then at the last minute something happened that made the murderer change his plans.'

Quinlan said, 'For my money Garwin is the guilty party. He was getting along all right with Betty Turlock and then this girl that he'd known in Kansas City was coming out. He'd probably left her under circumstances that he didn't want disclosed to the girl he was going to ask to marry him.'

The Sheriff scraped a match into flame and applied it to the end of his hand-rolled cigarette. 'Well, now, George,' he drawled, 'let's look at it from all angles.'

'I am.'

'No, you're not. If Garwin killed her, he must have known she was going to come to that stable,' the Sheriff stated.

'Known she was going to come here!' Quinlan exclaimed. 'He *took* her there. He deliberately manipulated things so she went to the stable. That's why he was late keeping his date with Betty down at the high school grounds.'

'Could be, of course,' the Sheriff said.

'And if it is,' Quinlan said, 'we're worse off than we were before.'

'How come?'

'You took Garwin over to San Rodolpho so he could get a bus and all that.'

'I suppose so,' the Sheriff admitted, 'but somehow I don't size Frank Garwin up for that sort of a boy. He's a pretty nice young chap, sort of shy and sensitive. He wouldn't want to hurt a woman's feelings and would do almost anything to feel he was being a gentleman.'

'That type fools you,' Quinlan pointed out. 'They get in a position from which there seems to be no escape. So then they try to get the obstacles out of the way. You take a two-fisted hard-boiled chap and he'd go to his girl friend and say, "Look, sister, you were a swell babe when I was in Kansas City but there's been a lot of water under the bridge since then and now I have met somebody I like a lot better." '

The Sheriff nodded thoughtfully, his head wrapped in a cloud of cigarette smoke. 'You got something there,' he admitted after a moment, and then added after a few thoughtful seconds, 'I'd like to play this so we could keep Betty out of it as much as possible. Lots of folks would think that Betty was sort of two-timing her folks, saying she was going out to spend the night with Rose Marie Mallard and then meeting this man Garwin.'

'You can't help that,' Quinlan said. 'Every once in a while someone does something like that just when a murder turns on the spotlight.'

'I know,' the Sheriff interrupted, 'but you take a nice kid like Betty Turlock. Sort of seems as though we could protect her a little.'

'We've got our hands full protecting ourselves,' Quinlan said. 'By the time Ed Lyons gets done with a writeup about how there was only one person who knew Estelle Nichols and that person was mysteriously spirited out of town by none other than the Sheriff —'

Bill Eldon nodded. 'Oh, sure,' he said philosophically, 'Ed Lyons is a dirty fighter. You can't expect anything else.'

The Sheriff smoked in silence for a few minutes. Then, as he came to the end of his cigarette, he pinched out the stub with all the care of a man who has spent much time in the frost. Abruptly he said, 'You know, we've got one other clue we're sort of overlooking.'

'What's that?'

'Suppose you wanted to kill someone,' the Sheriff said, 'and get away with it? Would it ever occur to you to take them into a stable at night and hit them over the head with a horseshoe club so it'd look as though a horse had kicked them?'

'No,' Quinlan said.

'Wouldn't to me either,' the Sheriff said.

'But if you were going to kill someone with a horseshoe, you'd naturally want to do it in a stable,' Quinlan pointed out.

'You said it, only you put it backwards.'

'What do you mean?'

The Sheriff grinned, 'If you were going to kill somebody in a stable, you'd maybe get the idea of killing them with a horseshoe. I think *now* we're beginning to get some place.'

The Grand Jury, hastily called in special session by the District Attorney, sat grim-faced. These men were farmers and small businessmen with uncompromising standards of individual integrity. They would be just but stern, and the rumor that the Sheriff had got himself involved by smuggling a witness out of the County was due for a thorough investigation.

Out in the anteroom were the witnesses whom Rush Medford had summoned. And waiting with his lips curled in a smile of anticipatory triumph was Ed Lyons, publisher of the *Rockville Gazette*, ready to drive the final nail in Bill Eldon's political coffin.

The District Attorney briefly outlined his position to the members of the Grand Jury. 'The object of this investigation,' he said, 'is to find out just what's going on here. *I* think you folks are familiar with what's happened. A woman got into the stable of one Carl Carver Calhoun. She was kicked by a horse and died. There are some mysterious circumstances surrounding her death.

'For one thing, the diary of Lorraine Calhoun was found in the manger of the stall in front of which the body was lying. One page had been torn out. It's pretty apparent now that this woman's trip to that stable was not accidental. It was made with some definite purpose and it was probably made with a companion.

'Apparently there is only one person whom this woman knew and who also knew the Calhouns and the setup of the Calhoun stable. That person is Frank Garwin. I want you gentlemen to hear his story. I want you to hear how he left this County. I want you to hear who picked him up and drove him to San Rodolpho.

'I am not going to make any comments as to the motive back of all this. It's the duty of this body to investigate this whole thing. Now then, gentlemen, I want Frank Garwin called as a witness. And I want his testimony taken down in shorthand.'

One or two of the jurors looked over to where Bill Eldon was sitting, tight-lipped. Here and there were glances of sympathy. But the foreman of the Grand Jury voiced the sentiments of all of its members when he said to Medford, 'You're the District Attorney. Go ahead with your witnesses. If there's anything wrong with the way any of the offices in this County are being run, we aim to do something about it.'

Frank Garwin was brought in and interrogated by the District Attorney. He told the same story he had told the Sheriff, admitting, however, that he knew Estelle Nichols, the dead girl, but denying he had known that she was anywhere in the state. He had, he said, lost track of her something over a year ago. They had, he admitted, been friendly, but since then he had had what he referred to as 'other interests.'

Medford passed by the 'other interests' in order to get to the point which was of most interest to him.

'Now, Frank,' he said, 'last night you were here in Rockville?'

'Yes, sir.'

'And where did you go after you left the Calhoun barn?'

'I didn't go to the Calhoun barn.'

'Well, we'll skip that for the moment. Did you see the Sheriff of this County last night?'

'Yes, sir.'

'Where?'

'Well, he picked me up down at the ball park.'

'And what did he do?'

'He – well, he gave me a lift to where I could catch the bus for the city.'

Rush Medford said, 'Now think carefully, young man. Let's not have any misunderstanding about this. Did he take you to where *you* wanted to get the bus, or did he suggest that he should take you to a certain place to get the bus?'

'Well, he suggested it.'

'Why?'

'He thought that it might be just as well if my friends didn't see me around here.'

'I see,' Medford said sarcastically. 'Spirited you out of town, and he did that in a County car, I believe, using the County tires and the County gasoline.'

Garwin was silent.

'Come, come, young man,' the District Attorney said. 'Let's at least answer questions. That's a fact, isn't it?'

'I guess it was the County car. It had a red spotlight on it.'

'That's all,' Medford said.

The foreman of the Grand Jury turned to the Sheriff. 'You want to ask this boy any questions to try and clear this thing up, Bill?' he asked.

The Sheriff merely shook his head.

The Grand Jurymen exchanged glances. There was sympathy in those glances, but there was also a certain underlying significance.

The foreman said to Garwin, 'That's all, young man. You can go back to the room with the other witnesses. You're not supposed to tell them anything about what questions were asked about you and you're not supposed to tell anybody what testimony you gave.'

When Garwin had gone, the foreman said, 'The way I size things up, Bill, the boys sort of think this calls for an explanation of some sort.'

Heads nodded gravely about the Grand Jury room.

'Well,' the Sheriff said, 'the way I look at this case, gentlemen, it was murder. A plain, cold-blooded, deliberate murder.'

Medford said, 'That's fantastic and absurd on the face of it. But the mere fact that you *think* that it's a murder case makes your conduct in spiriting one of the principals in the case out of the County doubly culpable. Now, as I see it, gentlemen, it's pretty clear that this man, Garwin, must have gone to the barn with this young woman. He must have been there when she got kicked, and he must have tried to keep himself from being involved in the subsequent notoriety by simply sneaking out and getting this Turlock girl to give him an alibi.

'Now I propose to call this Turlock girl and prove that she doesn't know where Garwin was *at the time* this woman was killed, that she had an appointment with him and Garwin stood her up and kept her waiting for something like an hour – simply because he was in Calhoun's barn with this Estelle Nichols. May I now call Betty Turlock?'

The Sheriff said, 'I just want to point out that I was makin' an explanation when the District Attorney interrupted me.'

The foreman nodded. 'You go ahead and explain, Bill.'

'When you have a murder case,' the Sheriff said, 'lots of little things become important. But *every* little thing isn't important. The way I see it, there's no use taking a nice girl like Betty Turlock and putting her up here in front of this Grand Jury simply to show the man she's in love with was a little bit late in keeping his appointment.'

'Oh, certainly,' Medford said sarcastically. 'The things that *you* don't want brought out are the unimportant little things. But when you get a half-inch or so discrepancy in the measurement of a horseshoe –'

'Now that will be about all out of you for a minute, Rush Medford,' the Sheriff said. 'I'm making my explanation to the Grand Jury. You can talk afterwards.'

'That's right, Rush,' the foreman said. 'Let's give Bill a chance to explain.'

'Now then,' Bill Eldon went on, 'when I say that was cold-blooded, deliberate murder, I know what I'm talking about. The mare wears a number-ought shoe. The wound was made with a number-two shoe. The mare wouldn't hardly have struck up high enough with a kick to have kicked the girl on the forehead if she'd been standing back of the manger. And you'll notice from the wound, the main force was on the *upper* part of the horseshoe. Now, if the mare had kicked up, she'd be puttin' the power on the *bottom* part of the shoe.'

Medford sneered, 'The trouble with that argument is it proves too much. You're proving that *no* horse could have kicked the girl.'

'That right, Medford,' the Sheriff said. 'You're gradually getting the idea. And if you want to see what killed the girl, here it is.'

The Sheriff nodded to Quinlan. Quinlan brought forward the iron club with the horseshoe welded onto it.

The Grand Jurors left their seats and crowded around the lethal weapon.

'Where did you get this?' Medford asked.

'Never mind,' the Sheriff said. 'I'm making an explanation right now. Now, you gentlemen hadn't better touch this yet because there's some blood and hairs on the horseshoe that we may need for evidence. There aren't any fingerprints on the thing because we've tested it carefully. Someone rubbed it with a piece of chamois skin or something and got all the fingerprints off. Now, if you boys will just go back and sit down, I'll tell you what happened.'

The Grand Jurors resumed their seats. The District Attorney moved over to regard the welded horseshoe in frowning anger.

'To kill a girl with a horseshoe so it would look like an accidental kick by a horse,' the Sheriff went on, 'you'd want to be sure everyone knew she'd gone into the barn. Now, I've got a theory that when this Estelle Nichols wrote her friend that she'd sleep in barns if she had to, she signed her death warrant right there. I think someone who knew about that letter got Estelle Nichols in the barn, and then, when he had her in the right position, clubbed her over the head.

'You see, he had to make just one blow do the job in order to make it look right. He had this diary with him and he needed both hands to swing this club around with the force he needed. He'd torn one page out of the diary, which was the only reason he was after it in the first place. And not having any more use for the diary, he just tossed it into the manger when he swung around to strike that blow.

'The murderer intended to go pick up that diary later on, but he'd figured without the mare. The mare was so nervous that the killer was afraid to go into the stall. As far as he was concerned, there wasn't any particular need to get that diary because he'd already torn out the one page that he'd wanted destroyed.'

'You say this was a man?' the foreman asked the Sheriff.

'Sure it was a man,' the Sheriff said. 'For one thing, look at the welding job. You don't go into some blacksmith shop and ask to have a club welded on a horseshoe when you're intending to go out and murder someone with it. You do the job yourself. Since the war there are some women that know a lot about welding, but to me it looks like a man's job.

'And there are two or three other things that make it look like a man that's been around the country a little bit but not quite enough. A man who doesn't realize there's a difference in the size of shoes on horses. A man who doesn't know the difference between barley and oat hay. Remember what Estelle Nichols wrote this Adrian girl in a letter. You've got a photograph of it there. Somethin' about in spite of the fact she was hypnotized she hoped Mae would listen when Estelle told her the things that you just couldn't put on paper. Figure that out and that means a man.'

Heads nodded in unison around the Grand Jury room.

'Now then,' the Sheriff said, 'if it's a man, it means that Mae Adrian is protecting him, because, according to my theory, the man must have seen that letter from Estelle saying she was going to come out here and sleep in stables if she had to. Right away he made up his mind that he was going to see she was killed in a stable so it would look like an accidental death.

'You can figure it out for yourselves. If this Estelle Nichols really had been sleeping in stables, she wouldn't have slept in one this close to the end of her journey. She could have hitchhiked her way into the city within a couple of hours, joined her friend, and had a bath and a good bed. What's more, no one's ever found anything belonging to this young woman except the clothes she was wearing. Now, if she'd been hitchhiking, she certainly must have had a *few* things with her.

'Therefore, the way I figure it, she had already been in to see Mae Adrian. And the man that killed her picked her up and brought her back to the Calhoun barn. Then he probably went back to Mae Adrian and said to her, "Look, Mae, the most awful thing happened. Estelle and I were in a barn and a horse kicked her. I don't want anybody to know that I was in there with her because it would ruin my business. And seeing it was an accident, you just keep quiet and it will all blow over."

'Remember that this club shows the murder had been deliberately planned. The man who did it hoped he could make an "accident" out of it; but in case he couldn't, he had a second string to his bow. He was going to frame it on Frank Garwin. Why? Because he knew for one thing young Garwin was going to be in Rockville that night. For another, he knew about Estelle asking for Frank's address in that letter.

'That gives us another clue. The man not only knew Mae Adrian real well, but he also knew Frank Garwin, and he also must have known Sid Rowan and his wife were planning to go to a movie. And he also knew Garwin would have an alibi for the last part of the evening. So, if he had to make it murder and pin it on somebody, he wanted the time element mixed up so it would seem the mare hadn't been able to eat her hay because of the body being there.

'So after the killing he put more hay down the feed chute – but he gave himself away by putting in barley hay instead of oat hay. He tried to show the mare wasn't hungry, and in doing that left the best clue of all, because the mare had been hungry and had eaten her hay – the oat hay Sid Rowan had put down for her. But later on the murderer had tried to show the mare wouldn't eat by putting down more hay – and because he couldn't tell the difference between oat hay and barley hay, he proved the fact we were dealing with cold-blooded murder.

'But this murderer was feeling pretty well satisfied with himself. Ninety-nine times out of a hundred, the death would have been considered just an accident and passed off as such. But if something went wrong, he had only to plant the murder weapon in a car which Frank Garwin had been in the night of the killing – *and then be sure the weapon was found at just the right time.* That was the most important thing of all.

'To fix that up, he did a simple thing. He unscrewed the valve in one of the rear tires on Turlock's car just enough to make some of the air leak out. Now if you gentlemen are interested in all this, let's get Mae Adrian in and ask her a couple of questions.'

There was a chorus of quick, eager assents.

Rush Medford started to say something; then, at the expressions he saw on the faces about him, changed his mind and remained silent.

Mae Adrian came in and was sworn.

The foreman said to the Sheriff, 'Suppose you ask her the questions, Bill.'

The Sheriff smiled at the nervous young woman. 'Mae,' he said in his kindly, drawling voice, 'you might as well answer a few questions for us here. We don't like to pry into your private affairs, but we've got to clean this thing up.'

She nodded.

'Now then,' the Sheriff said, 'when you said that you were about to do something Estelle didn't approve of, did that mean you were going to get married?'

'Well, not exactly, I was going with someone, and I was going to let him invest some money I had inherited.'

'Pretty handy with tools, isn't he? Makes you little gadgets out of steel and things?'

Her face lit up. 'Yes, he does. He makes me hammered-brass trays and he welds tubing into ornamental candlesticks and –'

'And what's his name?' the Sheriff asked.

'He doesn't want me to tell who he is and I'm not going to.'

'Did he know Estelle Nichols?'

'I guess so ... Yes.'

'She'd known him pretty well, hadn't she?'

'Well, yes.'

'And you showed this man this letter from Estelle and told him she was coming out, didn't you?'

'Yes.'

The Sheriff said in a kindly voice, 'Now come, Miss Adrian, let's be frank. That man is Henry Parnell, isn't he?'

She clamped her lips together.

'Come, come,' the Sheriff said. 'You might just as well come clean as get in trouble with the Grand Jury for not answering questions. He and Estelle Nichols went to call on Calhoun and a horse kicked Estelle and killed her and then he didn't want Calhoun to know he'd been with this girl in his barn. So you agreed to help him hush it up since it was an accident anyway, and nothing you could do would bring your friend back to life.'

She started to cry.

'And then after it began to look as though things were getting pretty hot, Parnell told you it would be better for you to identify the body and give that letter to the authorities, saying that she intended to sleep in barns, so it would look as though she had gone into Calhoun's barn to sleep. Now that's right, isn't it, Mae?'

She nodded, still sobbing.

'That's a good girl,' the Sheriff said. 'Now you just go in that other room and wait a minute and we'll talk things over later on after you've got to feeling better.'

Once she had left the room, the Sheriff turned to the Grand Jury. 'Well, gentlemen,' he said, 'there we are. I suppose we may as well talk with Parnell. Think we got a pretty good case against him, no matter what he says or doesn't say.'

'What I don't get,' the foreman said, 'is how you knew it **was** Parnell?'

'Well,' the Sheriff said, 'first rattle out of the box, the murderer had tried to make it look like an accident. When he saw he wasn't going to be able to get away with that, he tried to blame the murder on Frank Garwin. Parnell was pretty anxious for me to find that murder weapon there in Lew Turlock's car. The way the air was going out of that tire, the valve hadn't been unscrewed very long.

'I tried to think back, of who left the gathering there in the barn to go over to Turlock's place, and it was Parnell. When I drove up he was coming in through Turlock's gate. He'd gone over and unscrewed the core in the valve stem. And then, of course, when he wanted to rent the car, I knew he *must* be the one, because his idea was to get the car, then call attention to that flat tire, and get Lew to open the trunk where the murder weapon had been planted.

'There are two or three other things. That page missing from the diary showed that the murderer must have had some contact with Lorraine Calhoun back in April. It must have been something that Lorraine wouldn't remember particularly unless she got to reading her diary. Probably when she was in Kansas City her friends had told her something about a slicker named Parnell. She'd put something about this friend in her diary and then forgotten about it.

'But one of Parnell's Kansas City friends knew it was there and must have written him. Made it awkward for Parnell when he was just about to interest Calhoun in a business deal. The thing probably came through Frank Garwin 'cause you remember Parnell blurted out he'd known Frank for years, but he hadn't known Calhoun near that long. So Parnell must have known Frank in Kansas City.

'And that's another thing to remember. Whoever did the thing knew Lorraine's car with her diary in the glove compartment was going to be parked there at the stable, knew Garwin was going to be seeing Betty Turlock secretly, knew Sid

Rowan was going to a movie, knew his way around the Calhoun barn, but didn't know what sort of hay Calhoun was feeding the horses.

'Shucks, it's a cinch, gentlemen – just a plain straight trail pointing to one man and to one man alone, a man who had double-crossed a girl in Kansas City and was now trying to rig another deal here with a friend of hers and getting ready to fleece a rich man. Put that all together and you *know* who it was.'

'Well,' the foreman said, 'let's get Parnell in here and see if we can get anything out of him. Probably we can't, but we can try.'

Parnell came in and took the stand, his manner that of being courteous and helpful.

The Sheriff said, 'Mr. Parnell, you sure you never knew this Estelle Nichols?'

'Absolutely.'

'You know Mae Adrian, don't you?'

'Why, I saw her today, yes.'

'But you knew her before that?'

'I – ah – may I ask what is the object of this questioning?'

'Just tryin' to get at the facts,' the Sheriff said.

'Well, I think I'm entitled to a little something more than that.'

'The question,' the Sheriff said, 'is do you or don't you know Mae Adrian?'

Parnell looked around at the circle of grim, purposeful faces.

'I don't think I care to answer that question.'

'Why not?'

'Frankly, I don't think it's any of your business and I don't like the attitude of the men here.'

The Sheriff abruptly produced the murder weapon.

'I now show you a number-two horseshoe welded to an iron bar. Ever seen that before?'

'No, I suppose that's some sort of a branding iron, but it's a new one on me. I've never seen it before.'

'You will admit, won't you, that you told Mae Adrian you'd gone to the barn with Estelle Nichols and that there'd been an accident? That a horse had kicked her and that you wanted your name kept out of it?'

Parnell wet his lips. 'I refuse to answer that question.'

'On what grounds?' the Sheriff asked.

Parnell took a deep breath, then said desperately. 'On the grounds that the answer might incriminate me.'

'You're darn right it would,' the Sheriff said. 'We don't even *need* an answer. We've got Mae Adrian's testimony and we're going out and take a look at that little hobby workshop of yours and see if we can't find some left-over materials that'll analyze just about the same as the stuff in this murder weapon. And as far as *you're* concerned, Mr. Parnell, you're going to stay right here in the County jail until we've worked up a murder case against you.'

The Sheriff unlocked the front door of his house. It was nearing midnight and he was dog-tired. He'd had a strenuous period of activity and now that the excitement and strain were over, there was a terrific letdown. No use kidding himself, he wasn't as young as he used to be.

Very quietly the Sheriff tiptoed across the hall. His sister-in-law would be demanding all the news if he saw her.

He had almost reached his bedroom when he saw his sister-in-law attired in pajamas and slippers, sitting by a floor lamp in the living room. Across her lap was the evening edition of the *Rockville Gazette* with its big headlines: 'CROWD GIVES SHERIFF THE HORSELAUGH.'

The Sheriff tiptoed over and stood silently looking down at Doris' face. She had removed both upper and lower plates, which gave her face a peculiarly collapsed expression, but even in sleep and with her teeth out there was a sharp, ferret-like expression in the contour of her features. She had carefully drawn her chair to a place where she could command a view of the entrance to the garage through the parlor window and where no one could enter by the front door without her seeing him.

Bill Eldon leaned gently over the sleeping figure, picked up the paper and crossed out the word 'Sheriff' in the headlines, inserting the word 'Publisher' – so that the headlines read:

'CROWD GIVES PUBLISHER THE HORSELAUGH.'

Gently the Sheriff tiptoed into his bedroom.

From the pillow his wife's voice arose sleepily. 'Did you see Doris out there?'

The Sheriff chuckled. 'I saw her,' he said. And then, a few seconds later, as he was slipping out of his outer garments, added 'first.'

John D. MacDonald
No Business for an Amateur

I can probably explain why I got so upset about Howler Browne's troubles if I tell you that in our case it was a little different than the usual relationship between the owner of a roadhouse and the gent who plays his piano. After I was out of the army a year and still not getting anywhere, he took me on out of hunger, and also because twice while we were both working for Uncle Sugar, I pulled details for him so he could sweeten up a dish he had located in Naples.

He hadn't talked much about this club he owns, the Quin Pines, and after he met me on the street in Rochester and I told him my troubles and he took me on and drove me out there, I was agreeably surprised to see a long low building about two hundred feet back from the highway, with five enormous pines along the front of it. It looks like class and a high cover charge. It is. It pulls the landed gentry out of their estates and loads them up with the best food and liquor in the East. And the Howler makes a fine thing out of it.

I guess he got the name of the Howler because of the way he flaps his arms and screams at the ceiling when things don't go just right. He's a big guy, with a fast-growing tummy, a red face, and crisp curling black hair—the kind of a guy who can wear a Homburg and look like the Honorable Senator from West Overshoe, North Dakota. But he has a large heart of twenty carat which probably wouldn't wear well on a politician's sleeve.

I'm Wentley D. C. Morse, the first name and the initials having suffered a contraction to plain Bud. I seem to appeal to the babes with frustrated maternal instincts, probably because I have a nice fresh round face and a well-washed look. I'm not above taking advantage of such inclinations.

I know that when the Howler took me on, he expected me to be a floperoo, a citizen he could stick up at the piano at times when the band happened to be tired. He offered me a room, food, and fifty bucks a week. I snapped at it so quick I nearly bit his hand. I've been slapping a piano around ever since I've been able to climb up onto the stool. I have my own style, whatever that is, and a long string of startling failures at auditions. I have about twenty-nine varieties of rolling bass in my left hand. I like to mess around with improvised discords with the right. I can play the normal corn, just like any other boy with two hands, but I like my own way and sticking to it had kept me in bread crusts until I ran into the Howler.

I did about an hour the first night. I got some surprised expressions from the dowager clique and saw one old party choke on his celery when I stuck some concert counterpoint into the middle of Gershwin. When some kids tried to dance to me, I switched the beat on them until they stumbled off the floor, throwing ocular stilettos over their shoulders. I don't like being danced to. Somehow, it seems silly.

It was nice clean work but I didn't have much chance to talk to the Howler. After a week I began to build up a discriminating clientele. The Howler stopped and listened to the banging of hands after a long number and ordered me a blue spot. In two weeks I was set and beginning to get some small mentions in the trade papers.

Then I began to notice things. The first thing I noticed was that the Howler's cheeks, instead of being nice and round and pink, began to hang like a couple of laundry bags on Tuesday morning. Once I walked out into the kitchen and heard him screaming. He was also flapping his arms. The kitchen help stood around with wide eyes, waiting for him to burst. I stood by to enjoy it.

"Why, oh why," he hollered, "did I ever get into this business? Am I nuts? Am I soft in the head?"

While he was gathering for another burst, I interrupted. "S'matter, Howler? Somebody get a buckshot in the caviar?"

He spun around and said, "Oh! Hello, Bud." He walked out of the kitchen. I shrugged at the pastry chef. He shrugged at the dishwasher, who grinned and shrugged at me. I went back out through the place and up to my room.

The next night we had the fight. It didn't last long, but it hurt business. The cocktail lounge is to the right as you come in the front entrance. The dining room and dance floor is to the left. The joint was packed, as it usually is around eleven. The Howler wasn't around. I was due to play during intermission, so I was in the cocktail lounge waiting for the end of the set.

Two citizens in dark suits started arguing with each other at the end of the bar. One was tall and one was short, but they both had the same greased black hair and the same disgusting neckties. Before anybody could move, the big one backed the little one over to the door and across the hall. At the entrance to the dining room he wound up and pasted the little guy. It was a punch and a half.

The little guy went slamming back into a group of tables occupied by the cash customers. He knocked over two. One of them had four full dinners on it—half eaten. The big one left in a hurry before we could stop him. The little one got up and felt his chin. He clawed the cabbage salad out of his ruffled locks and departed. He refused to leave his name. Then about forty very stuffy citizens departed with cold looks.

I was watching the new hatcheck girl give them their stuff when the Howler came up to me and asked me the trouble.

"Couple of citizens had fisticuffs. A big one fisticuffed a little one right into two lobster dinners, a steak, and an order of roast beef. These people figure you're running an abandoned institution, so they're shoving off."

He spun me around and his face was red. "You dope! Why didn't you hold them?"

"Me? I play the piano. Besides, the big one left in a hurry. And what could you hold the little one for? For standing in front of a big fist?"

He walked off, but I could tell from his back that he was as mad as he could get. I hurried in and started slapping the piano around. I probably didn't play too well, as I was wondering why I had been jumped. After my half hour was over, I dug up the Howler. He was upstairs, and still mad.

I walked up to him and said, "Am I a friend, or just another employee of the Great Browne?"

That jolted him. He grabbed my arm and said, "Okay, so you're a friend. Why?"

"Come on." I didn't say another word until I had led him downstairs and out into the parking lot. I picked a crate that looked comfortable. We climbed into the front seat and I waited until we both had cigarettes going before I continued.

"Look, my boy. I know something is eating on you. You don't act right and you don't look right. Now what is it?"

He waited a while and I could tell that he was wondering whether to tell me. Finally he sighed and sank down into the seat. "Shakedown, Bud. The curse of this business. You get going good and then some smart monkeys figure you got dough to give away just to stay out of trouble."

"How much?"

"A thousand a month."

"Are you paying?"

"Not yet. That's why the little scrap tonight. Just a warning. If I keep holding out, we get a free-for-all and then there's no more customers. Maybe the cops close me up. The county boys are tough."

"Can you afford it?"

"Maybe. It'll be okay for now while the boom's on, but come a slump and I dig into the bank to make payments. You see, I can't deduct the payoff as a business expense. I don't get any receipt. It has to come out of my end after taxes."

"Have you talked to the cops?"

"What's the use? The new group has hit all the joints for miles around. Some of them went to the cops—no help. We got no data on them. They're slick. That's why I wanted one or both of those guys who brawled. Thought I might squeeze something out of them."

"How did they contact you?"

"Phone. Very slick voice. Polite. Told me I needed assurance that my club would run smoothly. Told me he wanted a thousand in tens, twenties, and fifties put in a brown envelope on the first of each month. Then I give it to my daughter Sue and send her walking up the road with it to the state highway in the middle of the afternoon. She's just turned eight. He says if there's any trouble, they give Sue a face she won't want to grow up with."

I cursed steadily for many long minutes.

"That's just what I said," he remarked, "only I said it louder and faster."

"You couldn't take a chance on telling that to the cops and letting them try to get on the trail after the kid's okay?"

"Hell, no. If I pay to these characters, I do it straight. I can't take a chance on the kid. There's not enough dough in the world to mean that much to me."

"Anything I can do?"

"I guess not, Bud. Just beat on the piano the way you've been doing, and we'll jam enough customers in here to make the thousand look like a fly bite. You're doing great, kid. But even if . . ." His voice trailed off and he snapped the butt out onto the gravel.

"But even if what?"

"I'm afraid that if we make more dough, they'll ask for more dough. I can't help but feel that they've got somebody planted on me. The guy on the phone knew a lot about the business. Too much."

"How many new guys do you have?"

"Maybe fourteen in the last two months."

"You've been watching them?"

"They all look okay to me. I can't figure out which one it could be. Maybe I'm wrong. Maybe the guy on the phone was guessing."

"I could help look."

"You could stay out of it. I hired you to give me piano music, not protection from a protection mob."

He climbed out of the car and slammed the door. I heard his footsteps crunching on the gravel as he headed back for the joint. I sat and had another cigarette and did some thinking. A few couples came out and climbed into their cars—but they didn't drive away. The music rolled out across the green lawn and the stars seemed low and bright. It was a good night, but the taste for it had sort of left me. I wanted to help the Howler.

He paid off on the first. I stood with him and watched Sue trudge up the road in her blue dress, the big envelope in her hand. The sun was hot. She went over the hill and out of sight on the other side. We both wanted to run after her but we didn't dare.

In the next twenty minutes I saw the Howler age five years. His face was white and his eyes were strained. He kept snapping cigarettes into his mouth and dragging twice on them before flipping them away.

I grabbed his arm when I saw something coming over the hill. Sue came into sight and the color came back into his face. We shook hands solemnly. When she was twenty feet away, he dropped on one knee in the dust and she ran into his arms, giggling. He held her roughly and slapped her where you slap children with either affection or correction.

He held her at arm's length and said, "Now tell Dad what happened."

"A black car stopped and a man stuck out his hand and said, 'Got that envelope for me, Sue?' and I gave it to him and they drove away."

"How about his voice?"

"He kind of whispered."

"What kind of car was it?"

"I don't know but I think it was an old one. Black, too."

"Did you look at the license like Dad told you?"

"Sure, but it had dirt all over it. I couldn't read any numbers."

"Could you recognize him if you saw him again?"

"Golly no! He held a handkerchief up to his nose like he was going to blow it, but he didn't."

We stood and looked helplessly down into her bland little face. She looked hurt, as though she had failed the Howler somehow. He patted her on the head and told her she had done okay, so she went skipping off to her mother in the bungalow the Howler had built down over the crest of the hill from the Quin Pines. I had met Mrs. Browne, a tall blonde with steady eyes, but I didn't see her often, as the Howler has the excellent rule of keeping his wife away from the joint. More joint owners should try it. I wondered how she was reacting to the ugly choice of having to use Sue as a courier for a shakedown mob.

Even though I wanted to do something—anything—to help the Howler, I couldn't think of a starting place. For the next few weeks he walked around looking as gay as a wreath on the door. And still the customers flocked in. Nothing will ever beat the formula of good food, good liquor, good music, and no clip games. Whenever I asked him how things were going he would shrug and look grim.

It must have been the day before the second payoff day that I burst into the Howler's office without doing any knocking. I had dreamed up the hot idea of getting hold of a midget and dressing it in clothes like Sue wears and sending it down to the highway with a cannon and a chip on its shoulder. I was chewing over the idea and I didn't knock.

The Howler looked up from behind his big desk and he wasn't happy to see me. A man I had seen around the place sat in the visitor's chair. He was a tall slim blond gent with a steel-gray gabardine suit, white buck shoes, a handpainted tie, and a languid manner.

I said, "Excuse me, Howler. I should have knocked," and I turned to go back out.

"Wait a minute, Bud. You probably are going to have to look for a job soon, so you might as well know the score. Meet my lawyer, John Winch. John, this is Bud Morse, my piano player and good friend."

Winch jumped up and grabbed my hand. I liked his warm smile and tight handshake. "I'm glad to meet you, Bud. I've enjoyed your work a lot. I like your *Lady Be Good* best, I think."

I like the way I play that one, too.

I perched on the window sill and the Howler said, "It looks like we're at the end of the line. John can't think of a thing we can do, Bud. The mob, whoever they are, want two grand a month. I can't swing it. I told them I would have to go out of business and the guy on the phone said that was okay with him. I've gone over the books with John and we can't see any way out of it. I'm going to sell out and get out of here."

Winch looked steadily at me and said, "And the trouble with that is that he'll only get the value of the land, building, and fixtures. You can't sell these places on the basis of capitalization of the earning rate. It just isn't done."

I felt sorry for the Howler. His big red face sagged down over his collar. His eyes were as empty as yesterday's lunch box.

"Damn it, why don't you fight?"

He spread his hands. "Nothing to fight with, Bud."

"This doesn't sound like you, boy. Besides, give me another couple of days to poke around. I got a lead."

They both leaned forward. New life came back into the Howler's face. "What is it? Come on, give!"

I opened my mouth to tell him and then decided against it. It was too vague—it would sound silly. Once when I was in college I worked in a shoe store and I learned about shoes. I know good ones when I see them. Even though the Howler had told me just to play the piano, I had done some poking around among the new employees.

I'd noticed that a fellow named Jake Thomson, the new dishwasher, was wearing a pair of beautiful shoes. Looked like a handmade last. Narrow and well stitched. For a guy making twenty-five bucks a week plus two meals a day, they didn't look right. It made me wonder and I had been keeping an eye on him. But you can't tell a guy not to sell out because his dishwasher wears good shoes.

"I'm sorry, gentlemen, but I got to keep it to myself until I develop it a little more." They nagged at me but I kept my mouth shut.

Finally the Howler said, "Okay, John. Forget the sale for a while. I'll pay off the two grand tomorrow and take a chance on Bud."

Winch shrugged and I left before the Howler could change his mind.

The bee was on me. I had to develop the shoes into a big lead in nothing flat. Because I had opened my big mouth, I was costing my boss another $2000. I went up and sat in my room and did a little thinking. I had thought about Thomson enough so that it was easy to visualize him—a slight quiet little man of about forty, with thin lips and oversize hands, receding hairline, and a nose that had been busted a few times. I had already found out that he lived in the Princess Hotel, a fleabag outfit in nearby Casling.

There was something about him that I couldn't put my finger on. Suddenly I remembered what it was. I snapped my fingers and hit myself on the head with the palm of my hand. I realized that without actually noticing it, I had seen him coming out of the kitchen and hanging around the new hatcheck girl.

Then I did some more thinking, I like the looks of the little gal, a round-faced blonde with kind of a Dutch air about her. She looked as though she scrubbed her red cheeks with a big brush. I remembered the lights in her blue eyes and the trim, pert little figure that went with that pretty blonde head. Jerry Bee her name was.

I glanced at my watch. Four thirty. She would be coming back on duty about now. I couldn't take the time to case her carefully. You have to take some people on trust. I decided to enlist her in the Save Howler campaign.

I went downstairs and found her sorting out the tags for the evening business. She smiled up at me with professional cheer and said, "I didn't know you wore a hat, Mr. Morse."

"The name is Bud, and I got to talk to you. Alone. Quick."

"Why . . . ah . . . sure, Bud. Is this a fancy line? You want to try to make a date or something?"

"I would, sometime, but not now. I got other things to talk about. You know where that grapevine thing is? That white wooden thing across the lawn? See you there in two minutes."

I walked off and went through the kitchen. Thomson was fiddling with the controls on the dishwasher. He didn't look up. I went out the back door and walked over the yard to the grapevines. I lit a cigarette and in about a minute she came hurrying across the grass, looking as cute as a bug and very earnest.

I gave it to her quick. "A mob is shaking the boss down. The mob has somebody planted in the joint. I figure it's Jake Thomson, the dishwasher. They're forcing the boss out of business. I've seen Thomson hanging around you. What's he said? What does he act like?"

Her mouth was a round O of amazement. Then when she realized what I wanted, she began to look disappointed. "Gee. He's just acted like any other guy. He all the time wants me to go out with him. I don't want to go out with no dishwasher."

"He hasn't hinted anything about having more dough than a dishwasher should have? He hasn't tried to sound important?"

"No. Nothing like that."

It was discouraging. I sighed and said, "Okay, Jerry. Thanks anyway. Guess I'll have to take it alone from here."

"What you going to do?" she asked, her eyes wide.

"I don't know. Follow him, maybe. Try to get into his room, I guess."

She stepped forward and grabbed a button on the front of my jacket. She twisted it in her finger and said, "Gee, Bud, that sounds so exciting. Do you think maybe I could . . . help?" As she said the last word, she slowly raised her eyes up toward me. I was surprised to notice how long her lashes were. That slow look flattened me.

"Sure. Meet me as soon as the joint closes." I stood and watched her walk back across the yard toward the joint. She was put together in the proper manner. I tried to put my cigarette in my mouth and found that my mouth was still open.

During the long evening I fretted about the job of following Thomson. I knew that having the gal along would make it easier if he noticed us. We could just be having a routine date.

It wouldn't look as fishy as if he found just me on his trail.

The Howler is one of those people who like to have things all cleaned up before the joint is closed. That fit in nicely with my plans. It meant that Thomson would be running stuff through the dishwashing machine long after the last customer had left.

I strolled out into the kitchen a few times between my shows and tried to get a good clean look at him without him noticing me. There was nothing to see. He stood beside the splashing, humming machine and fed in the dishes with quick easy movements. I felt an all-gone feeling in my middle, and hoped that I wasn't wrong—and yet there was the matter of the shoes . . .

I told Hoffer, the statuesque citizen with the South Jersey accent who keeps a fatherly eye on most of the employees, that I was checking to see how many of our people brought their own cars. I didn't want to ask about Thomson by name, so I had to stand and look interested while he rambled through a long list. Finally he said, "And the dishwasher, Thomson, he drives an old heap that I make him park down in the pasture beyond the parking lot." I asked some more questions about matters I didn't give a damn about, then drifted off.

The half moon outlined the square frame of Thomson's car, Hoffer had been right when he called it a heap. It squatted in the tall grass looking like the nucleus for a junk yard. The fenders were frayed and it looked old enough to have a bulb horn.

I stood in the night breeze and listened. The music blatted away in the club a hundred yards behind me. I suddenly realized that if I was right, I could be given a large hole in the head. I shivered slightly and stepped forward to where I could read the license number with a match. Then I hurried back.

Jerry finally scurried out of the barn that the Howler had converted into living quarters for the women. It was twenty to three. The last bunch of noisy customers had driven away. From where I stood I could see the kitchen lights still blazing.

I didn't waste time talking. I grabbed her arm and hustled her over to my coupe. I opened the door and handed her in.

Then I ran around the car and jumped behind the wheel. As I backed out and turned around, I noticed that her perfume smelled good in the closed car.

"What are we going to do now, Bud? Where're we going?"

"Thomson's crate is parked back in the pasture. He'll be through pretty soon. We got to be where we can tail him no matter which way he goes."

She quivered and slid over close to me. "Gee, this is exciting," she said. I drove about two hundred yards down the road and backed into the driveway of our nearest neighbor. His house was dark. I cut my lights and we sat where some high bushes made the gloom thickest.

"We can have a cigarette, but we got to throw out the butts soon as he drives out. If he goes home, he'll go right by us here, out to the main drag."

She agreed and we sat quietly waiting. I found her hand and held it tight. Somehow it was less lonely, having her along—and yet I didn't let myself think of what I might be exposing her to.

Our cigarettes were well down when some dim lights flashed on in the pasture. I heard a roar as an aged motor clattered into life. We ditched the cigarettes, and in a few minutes the old car banged by the driveway.

Jerry gave a little squeak of excitement and I took out after him. I didn't turn my lights on. I stayed well back. I figured that the noise of his motor would cover any sound we might make. I hoped that no eager cop would notice our lights out and decide to get official.

The old car looked anything but ominous swaying along ahead of us. He kept up an average speed of thirty. He stopped at the corner and turned toward Casling. Somehow that was a disappointment. I had wanted him to go off somewhere and report to somebody.

I switched on my lights when we hit the town. He turned into a dark parking lot opposite the Princess Hotel. I drove on by and went around the next corner. I parked and ran back to the corner. I stuck my head around the bricks just in time to see him walk up the steps to the entrance. I gave him plenty of time to get out of the lobby, and then Jerry and I went in.

Once upon a time the Princess was a reputable second-class hotel. I could see from the lobby that it was now running about seventh. It smelled of stale cigars and cheap disinfectant. The sodden furniture and the greasy tile floor held the memories of thousands of traveling salesmen.

There was one light in the deserted lobby. It was over the desk. A young citizen with a bald head, oversized teeth, and a vile necktie gave us a quick glance as we walked up.

"Double room, sir?" he said with a faint leer, spinning the register around.

Jerry frowned at him and I said, "Wrong guess, friend. I got a present for you." I took out a five and creased it lengthwise and set it on the marble counter. It stood up like a little tent.

He reached for it and I tapped him on the back of the hand with my middle finger. They say that concert pianists can bust plate glass with their little finger. I can rap pretty good with my middle one.

He snatched his hand back and rubbed it. "Funny guy, hey?"

"Not at all. I just want to be understood before you fasten onto my dough. I got some curiosity about a guy who lives here. I want to know who comes to see him."

"Maybe I can tell you and maybe I can't. Some of the . . . uh, guests, pay a little extra so they won't be bothered with guys who are curious. Maybe the guy you want to know about has paid us some insurance."

I tried to think quickly. I decided that time was so short it wouldn't hurt to let him know. "Jake Thomson."

"Let me see. Thomson. Thomson." He riffled through a visible file that hung on the side of the cashier's cage. "Room two eleven. No insurance. Now what is it you want to know?"

Just then I heard steps clacking across the tile toward the desk. I winked at the desk clerk and slipped my arms around Jerry's waist. I edged her down the desk into the shadows and murmured in her ear, "Make out like you go for this." She put her hands on my shoulders and I went just a little bit dizzy.

I heard the man behind me say, "Give two eleven a buzz. Tell him Joe is here."

The clerk stepped over to the switchboard. "Mr. Thomson? Desk. Man named Joe wants to come up. Okay?" He yanked out the plug and said, "Okay, go on up. You'll have to use the stairs. Elevator man's across the street getting some coffee."

I felt Jerry stiffen in my arms. When the man had clumped up the stairs, she drew me away from the desk and pulled my head down so she could get her lips close to my ear.

"Hey, I know who that was. Mr. Sellers. He runs the Western Inn. I tried to get a job there just before Mr. Browne hired me."

I turned back to the desk. "You can keep the five. I changed my mind. I'm not curious any more." I tossed it onto the marble counter.

He snatched it up. "Sure, sure, mister, sure. And don't bother telling me to keep my mouth shut. You're a five dollar friend. I don't get so many of those. Maybe I can sell you something sometime."

I walked slowly out with Jerry on my arm. We walked back to the car and sat and had a cigarette. She tried to ask me questions but I shushed her while I did some thinking. It had to be more than a coincidence. Night club managers don't go calling on other night clubs' dishwashers. It fitted in with the shoes.

I could tell by the set of Jerry's shoulders that she was getting annoyed with me. "Hey, Jerry. Wait up. I had to do some thinking. The way I figure it, this guy Sellers is running the shakedown. Jake has to be his plant out at the Howler's place. Now all I got to do is tell the Howler and we'll have the cops give Sellers a going-over. But something may go on here. Do you think you can do something for me? Alone?"

I grabbed her hand again and she softened. "I guess so, Bud."

"You saw that all-night cafeteria across the street and down a ways from the hotel? It's got a big window in the front end. You go on in there and sit where you can see the front of the hotel. Nurse some coffee along and get nasty if they try to charge you rent for the table. I'll be back for you."

She didn't want to be left alone. She said no twice, and finally yes. I let her out and headed on back for the Quin Pines. I was restless and excited. I tried to shove my foot down into the motor.

I skidded into the parking lot in a shower of gravel. The club was dark. I slammed the door and sprinted over the knoll toward the Howler's house. I knew he would be glad to hear the new angle.

After about three minutes of leaning on the bell and banging the door, Mrs. Browne came and opened it a crack. Her hair was in curling gadgets and her eyes looked sleepy.

"Why, hello, Bud. What's the matter? Where's Stephen?"

I had to adjust to that. Finally I remembered that it was the right name for the Howler. "Isn't he in there? Isn't he asleep?"

"He hasn't come back from the club yet."

I stood on one foot and then on the other. I had seen that the club was dark. I didn't know what to say. She looked anxious and less sleepy. Then we both heard it—the thin sharp crack of a shot. Small caliber. From the direction of the club.

I turned without a word or a look and raced back faster than I had come. I had to go over the knoll, across a corner of the parking lot, and across the back yard of the club.

I was making such good time that I skidded and almost fell when I hit the gravel. As I raced onto the dark lawn, a dim shape loomed up in front of me. I swerved and stopped. I must have looked as dark and mysterious to him as he did to me. The fact that he didn't look big enough to be the Howler decided me. I hesitated a fraction of a second and then dove at his knees. It is the last time in my life that I shall ever dive at anyone's knees—even a four-year-old child's.

You leave the ground with your hands spread out. You can't turn in the air. All the opposite party has to do is sling a large fist in between your paws. Automatically it will catch you in the lower half of the face.

The world exploded in a ball of red fire and I lay on my back. The dank grass tickled the back of my neck. I heard footsteps hurrying across the gravel. I didn't want to sit up. I didn't want to move. I wanted to rest in peace.

I found something in my mouth. It turned out to be a small chunk of tooth. I sat up and grabbed the grass to keep from falling off the lawn. In the distance a car roared away. Some late crickets cheeped at me. I got to my feet just as Mrs. Browne came up. Her terry-cloth robe was white against the shadows.

"Mrs. Browne," I said softly and she hurried over to me. "I just got slugged by somebody who was leaving in a hurry." I didn't talk so well with a piece of my front tooth missing. The cold air hurt it. It made me whistle on the letter *s*. My chin was damp and sticky with blood. "Maybe the Howler's around here some place."

She held onto my arm and we circled the joint. We found him half in and half out of the side door. He moaned and I stumbled over him. I lit a match. He was face down, his hand opening and shutting against the concrete. Mrs. Browne moaned and slipped down beside him. I caught her before she hit her head. I slapped her conscious and made her wait while I brought my car over.

We wrestled the Howler into the front seat. She sat and held him up while I drove back across the field to their house. It strained me to get him onto the day bed in the study. While she was phoning the doctor, I pulled his bloodstained shirt out of his pants and took a look. He had a small hole in the center of the plump mound of his tummy. It looked bad.

He stopped moaning and opened his eyes. "Bud!" he exclaimed faintly. "These guys . . . awful rough . . . turned out the last light and started to go home . . . fella backed me into the joint with a gun . . . told me to sell out . . . said the syndicate wanted to take over . . . made me mad . . . wouldn't let me turn on light . . . I tried to grab him and he shot me . . . burning hot . . . legs all numb . . . don't leave me."

I knelt down beside him and said, "Maybe it's all clear now, Howler. I found Sellers, the guy that runs the Western Inn, visiting our dishwasher. Hey! Did you hear me?" He didn't answer. His eyes were shut. He was breathing heavily.

Mrs. Browne came back in, her fingers woven together. "I don't know what to do. I telephoned the doctor. Should I phone the police right away?"

Just then we heard the door buzzer. She hurried to the front door. I heard her say, "Oh!" in a disappointed tone. John C. Winch, bland and tanned, walked into the room.

"Hello, Bud, I just stopped in to see—" he saw the Howler on the day bed and saw the blood. His jaw dropped. "What? When did it happen? Was he shot?"

"Yeah. Shot about twenty minutes ago. The doc should be here. What'd you come over for?"

"I was sleeping and I got a phone call. The man didn't tell me his name. Just said I better convince Browne he ought to sell out or maybe he'd be shot. Told me that I better convince him quick. I dressed and hurried right over."

"Sell out be damned, Winch. That isn't the way to handle this thing. You got to fight."

"Sure, and get what Browne got. You look like you got some of it, too."

I took a look in the mirror. I was a mess. My lips were three times too big and my chin and collar were blood-caked. Mrs. Browne had been standing by listening.

"I want my husband to get out of this, if he doesn't die." She sat in a chair and covered her face with her hands. Her shoulders didn't shake. She just sat there.

"What's the legal opinion about calling in the police?" I asked.

He rubbed his chin and glanced at the Howler. "I guess we can take a chance on waiting to see what the doc says. Maybe we won't have to. It might be best all around if we didn't."

"Leave the cops out of it if you want to, Winch, but I got a lead and I'm going to chase it. I'm beginning to get annoyed at this whole thing."

Before he had a chance to answer, the buzzer whined again and Mrs. Browne let the doctor in. He hurried over and started to push gently at the sides of the wound. I walked out without a word. I was scared, shaken, and mad. I climbed into my car and drove back to the parking lot. I didn't have any idea where to go or what to do.

Just as I reached the lot, a taxi turned in. Jerry got out. I could see her by my headlights. I stopped, walked over, and paid the man off. She stood there until he had spun around and headed out.

She grabbed me by the sleeve. "I watched and finally the man came out with Mr. Sellers. They went off in Mr. Sellers' car. I couldn't find a taxi to follow them. I don't know where they went."

"That's great. That's dandy."

"What's the matter, Bud?" she said, pouting. "Didn't I do it right?"

"Sure, you did fine. Only somebody shot the boss and he's in bad shape. It's probably too late."

"Oh!" She hung her head.

"If he's out, I'm going back and see what I can find in his room. That jerk behind the desk will let me in for a few bucks."

"Can I come?"

"Not this time, honey. You'll just be in the way. You go on to bed and I'll see you in the morning. It's four o'clock already."

She pouted again and walked off toward the barn. I wondered idly why none of the kids had been awakened by the shot. Then I realized that they probably had. In the night club business it turns out most times to be a good idea to stay away from places where you hear shots.

Thinking of shots reminded me that maybe I had better start running around with a gun like everybody else. I hurried up to my room and dug my .32 automatic out of my bureau drawer. I keep it under a green shirt. I seldom use the shirt and I have never used the gun. I won it in a crap game in San Diego, full clip and all.

I ran back out to the car and headed for Casling for the second time. I made good time getting in.

The clerk gave me a gentle sneer and said, "Back again, I see."

"No time for talk, sonny. Do I get a key to two eleven for ten bucks, or do we argue some more?"

He shrugged and turned his back on me. Then he turned around again and slid a key across the counter. I hauled out a ten and gave it to him. He stuck it in his pocket as though it were an old gum wrapper. "Any trouble about this, mister, and I say you snitched it while I was asleep."

I went on upstairs. Two eleven was three doors on the right from the head of the stairs. I listened for a minute outside the door. The room seemed to be dark. No light showed under the door. I slipped the key in and it worked quietly. I shut the door gently behind me and found the wall switch.

It was the world's average cheap hotel room. A scratched wooden bed, one bleary window, pink and white cotton blankets, sagging springs, holes worn in the rug, only one bulb working in the overhead light, dripping faucets in the tiny bathroom, one cane chair, a bureau with a cracked glass top, an ashtray advertising beer, a glass half full of water, and a liverish color scheme of soiled green and dusty maroon.

I tried the bureau first. Cheap clean clothes. Nothing else. I tried the closet. Cheapo dirty clothes. Nothing under the mattress. I stood in the middle of the room and scratched my head. Where do the detectives look?

I was wondering what was under the rug when I heard a stealthy clicking noise at the door. I snatched the gun out of my jacket pocket and stepped into the bathroom. I didn't have time to click the light switch. I felt cold sweat jump out on my forehead. I felt slightly dizzy. I pulled the door shut a little so that I could see through the crack.

The door swung open so violently that it banged back against the wall. No one stepped in. I caught a flash of movement and tried to level the gun at it. A hand and arm reached quickly around the door and flicked toward the light switch. The room became abruptly black. A dim light from the hall silhouetted the door.

Then something moved quickly through the shadows and was in the room with me. I wanted to yell but my mouth was too dry.

Then a husky voice said, "Okay, Morse. Toss your gun on the floor."

The sound of my own name shocked me. I stuffed the gun down into the side of my right shoe and said, "I haven't got a gun. I haven't got anything, Thomson."

There was silence for a few seconds. Then, dryly: "I believe you. That's just the kind of a sucker play you'd make. Where are you standing?"

"In the bathroom."

"Stand outside the door of the bathroom."

I did as I was told. I heard the door shut again and then the lights clicked on. I had been straining my eyes in the dark and the sudden brightness made me blink. John C. Winch stood in front of me, an efficient-looking gun leveled at my middle. He had a smile on his tan face. He stepped forward and slapped my pockets and then stepped back.

"Surprised? Now go on over and sit on the bed."

I walked over. I had to move carefully to keep the gun from dropping out of my shoe. I hoped the pants cuff covered it enough. I tucked my feet back under the hanging spread when I sat down.

"You don't have to tell me, Winch. I can tell you. I've been a dope. You and Sellers and Thomson are behind this thing. You were in a perfect position to know how much the Howler could stand to pay. Now you're greedy and you want his place. You'll buy it through some dummy and start to rake off real profits."

He smiled down at me, but the muzzle of the gun didn't waver. "You're a smart boy, Morse, but not smart enough. You should have figured all this before. Then you could have handed me some real trouble."

"One thing I can't figure. Why let me know you're in on it? You won't be safe now, because you can't scare me."

"Scare you, Bud? Who wants to scare you? I wouldn't think of scaring you."

He stood and grinned down at me. I've never seen a colder pair of eyes. I knew that he wouldn't have to scare me. I wouldn't be able to talk with one of those little lead slugs nestling in my brain. The room seemed to sway around me. I sat on the edge of the bed and let my hands hang down. I could reach the gun in my shoe without stooping over. The mouth of his gun was saying, "Don't move, brother!"

He stopped smiling and nibbled at the edge of his finger. "I wish you'd brought a gun, Morse. You make it tough."

I looked behind him and saw the doorknob move. I've never learned how to keep expressions off my pug face. He probably knew I couldn't swing a gag, and when he saw my eyes widen and where they were looking, he backed off so that he could cover me and the door at the same time.

I watched his eyes and saw them flick over toward the door. I swooped after the gun and brought it up, pressing hard on the trigger at the same time.

"Drop your gun, chump!" I hollered.

I rolled off the bed as I brought the gun up. Nothing happened. I realized with sudden horror that an automatic won't work unless you jack a cartridge up into the chamber first by yanking on the side. I hadn't. His gun snapped and something suddenly picked at my sleeve.

I looked up from the floor and kept pulling on the useless trigger. His cold right eye sighted down the barrel, I could look right into it. I shut my eyes, and another shot blasted in the room. I wondered if I was dead.

I opened my right eye. Winch was still looking at me, but the gun barrel had sagged a little. He was smiling. His eyes didn't look quite so cold. He leaned toward me, farther and farther and then I scrambled aside as he fell over toward me. His head crashed into my left shoulder and he bounded off. He lay on the floor with a neat hole through the top of his left ear. The hole didn't stop there. It went right on inside.

I looked up. The door was open, Thomson stood in the doorway, a gun in his hand. He looked down at me with an expression of infinite disgust. He shoved the gun into his pocket and stepped into the room. He kicked the door shut. He sat down on the wicker chair as I climbed up onto the bed again.

"You better have a cigarette, Morse. Your hand's shaking." He held out a pack and I took one.

"Hand, hell. I'm shaking all over. I'll be shaking just like this on my next birthday. I'm going to keep right on shaking for a couple of years."

"You ought to. So should every other amateur that fools around with stuff like this."

"I'm beginning to think maybe I had you wrong in all this, Thomson."

"You sure did, and I knew you were digging around. I thought I'd let you. Thought it might stir up the big shot here." He reached his foot out and nudged Winch in the ribs. Winch seemed to be flattening out against the floor. "And the name's Burke. Jake Burke. I work for the Associated Restaurant Managers and Owners Group. I'm a trouble shooter. Sellers sent for me and I planted myself in Browne's place. You can figure the rest out. Winch, here, got greedy. He set up a shakedown racket. Then he decided he wanted Browne's place. Made the payments high. Tried to talk Browne into selling. Got Browne in the dark to scare him. Shot him. That was a mistake."

I raised my eyebrows and he said, "Don't look puzzled. I just came from there. Browne'll be okay. Slug went right around him, under the hide, and wedged against his backbone. The doc has it out already. Give him a month and he'll be louder than ever."

"How did you know about me?"

"You! You looked at me like I had shot Lincoln. You followed me about thirty feet behind me. I could see the streetlights reflected on your headlights. I stayed at the top of the stairs and watched you and the gal talk to Jonesy down at the desk. Sellers thought you looked a little queer, too. I told you this is no business for an amateur."

"If you're so smart, why didn't you pick him up quicker?"

"He was too smart, Morse. Used the telephone. Also, I couldn't step in on any of the payoffs. He had kids delivering the dough every time. Couldn't take a chance. Had to wait until he got worried about you catching onto him and about me. I don't think he had me figured, but I guess he was going to try to knock you off with my gun and me off with yours—if you had one."

There was a knock at the door. A gentle knock. Burke shouted, "Come in!"

The door opened and Jerry stepped timidly into the room. She looked down at the body of Winch, and her eyes widened. She circled widely around him and ran into my arms. She was shaking. I put my arms around her. Her hair smelled good. Burke started to laugh.

"This your girl?" he asked. I nodded. He stepped over and grabbed her wrist. He snapped something onto it and yanked her away from me. I started up with the vague idea of swinging on him. He was still laughing. She fumbled in her bag. He slapped the bag down onto the floor and a small automatic bounded out of it and balanced grotesquely between Winch's shoulderblades. She stopped struggling and hung her head.

"I told you you were an amateur. Why don't you think things out, Morse? Winch was in this with this gal. She was the plant in Browne's place. That's why I tried to date her. That's how he got on to me. She told him. And she told him about you wanting her to help follow me. That made him wonder who I could be. How did he know you were here? She waited until he came out of Browne's place and then told him. She saw his car out there. She probably waited in it. How did she get here? She probably came down with him. I figure she probably wore a man's hat and covered her face and helped him collect each month."

He tilted her chin up roughly and looked into her eyes. "I'll even bet she figured out that gag of using kids for the payoff."

She jerked her chin away from his fingers and said, "Suppose I did?"

There was a heavy fist banging at the door and Burke said, "That'll be the cops that I told Jonesy to send for. We'll all have to go down and make out statements and stuff."

He tugged at the steel bracelet on her wrist and whispered, "Come on, honey. Let's go answer the door." Dawn made her face look yellowish.

And suddenly I realized that when I got back to the piano I was going to do a cornball job on *Melancholy Baby*. I was really going to do it up. I'd play it for the Howler.